THE CARESS OF A COMMANDER

LINDA RAE SANDE

Twisted Teacup
PUBLISHING

*To those who served in the armed forces,
then and now—thank you for your service.*

ALSO BY LINDA RAE SANDE

The Daughters of the Aristocracy
The Kiss of a Viscount
The Grace of a Duke
The Seduction of an Earl
The Sons of the Aristocracy
Tuesday Nights
The Widowed Countess
My Fair Groom
The Sisters of the Aristocracy
The Story of a Baron
The Passion of a Marquess
The Desire of a Lady
The Brothers of the Aristocracy
The Love of a Rake
The Caress of a Commander
The Epiphany of an Explorer
The Widows of the Aristocracy
The Gossip of an Earl
The Enigma of a Widow
The Secrets of a Viscount
The Widowers of the Aristocracy
The Dream of a Duchess
The Vision of a Viscountess
The Conundrum of a Clerk

The Charity of a Viscount

The Cousins of the Aristocracy

The Promise of a Gentleman

The Pride of a Gentleman

The Holidays of the Aristocracy

The Christmas of a Countess

The Heirs of the Aristocracy

The Angel of an Astronomer

The Puzzle of a Bastard

The Choice of a Cavalier

The Bargain of a Baroness

Stella of Akrotiri: Origins

Stella of Akrotiri: Deminon

Stella of Aktrotiri: Diana

CHAPTER 1
A GAMBLER CONSIDERS
THE ODDS

*E*arly in 1810

The markers were spread out on the top of a large mahogany desk, spread out so their numbers were more impressive—or depressing—to anyone who dared a glance. "What the hell is going on?" Maxwell Higgins, Earl of Greenley, asked with a hint of menace as he regarded the man who stood before him. Sober for the first time in several days, Greenley felt a dull throbbing in the back of his skull that made it hard for him to concentrate. "Who bought those?" he added, realizing the markers had been held by several different gaming hells scattered around London. Swallowing hard, he realized he might be in some kind of trouble, but for the life of him, he couldn't figure how his gambling markers would have him escorted from Brook's—in the middle of a game of hazard—to Whitehall. He still held the dice in one hand!

Although it was his first visit to the Foreign Office, he never expected to be confronted by evidence of his gambling in one of the offices located therein. Especially the office of Matthew Fitzsimmons, Viscount Chamberlain.

"The Crown," Matthew, replied in answer to the earl's query as to who had purchased the markers. He crossed his arms over his chest. "Does the number surprise you?" he asked, giving the earl his most stern expression.

In all honesty, the markers didn't amount to much. A few hundred pounds, perhaps. It was the amount of money the earl lost on a regular basis in the form of large denomination coins and pound notes that had the viscount concerned.

Greenley sighed before shaking his head. "I suppose not," he replied. "But, why? I could easily pay these off—"

"But you didn't. How much do you suppose you have lost this past year?" Alex Bradley asked, his posture much like the viscount's. "In the form of cash?"

The earl turned to look at the other person in the office, as if noticing him for the first time.

"Who is this?" Greenley asked of Viscount Chamberlain, his tone suggesting he had no patience for the proceedings.

"Alex Bradley," Matthew replied with a hint of impatience. "He's our agent on this operation."

Although Alex was considerably younger than Matthew, he had more experience working in the field, his assignments taking him away from London for months at a time. For this particular assignment, Alex had agreed to take on the persona of a traveling gentleman who enjoyed card games. It was his intention to follow the money once it left English shores and determine where it was going, with whom, and how it was spent.

"Operation?" The earl shook his head, wondering why he had been escorted to the Foreign Office at three in the afternoon on a rather brilliant day. A drink had just been delivered to his table by one of the footmen at exactly the moment Matthew Fitzsimmons appeared and requested a moment of his time. Before he knew it, he was stuffed into a smelly hackney and on his way to Whitehall. He remembered thinking he could have been enjoying a day of sailing, or a trip to his hunting lodge, or a ride in Hyde Park.

Or finishing his game of hazard!

Truth be told, he wouldn't have been doing any of those other things no matter the weather. Ever since the death of his wife shortly after the stillbirth of their fifth child, Maxwell Higgins had taken solace in alcohol and gambling. Although he didn't usually do either to excess, even he had noticed his nights ending later in the morning and his losses mounting. He rarely gambled on credit, making sure to bring banknotes and a few guineas with him to the higher-end gaming hells he preferred.

His opponents had at one time been familiar gentlemen, fellow members of the House of Lords at Parliament. The past few months had featured new opponents, however. Men he had never seen before. They all seemed to be gentlemen— well-dressed and well-spoken—some claiming to have moved to London from more rural locations or visiting the capital on business. Their manner of speech implied they were British. Now that he was in Viscount Chamberlain's office in Whitehall, the Earl of Greenley wondered if there was more to his opponents than he realized.

"British money has gone missing," Matthew stated with an arched eyebrow. "Thousands. Hundreds of pounds every night. Bank notes and coins get spent in the form of lost bets, but they don't end up back in circulation or in accounts at the banks."

Greenley frowned. "So? Maybe people are saving their money in their mattresses," he countered.

"Or maybe it's being taken to the Continent," the viscount replied, his impatience with the earl apparent. "To France. Used to fund spy networks, or buy ammunition, or pay for Napoleon's latest palatial house."

Sighing, Greenley shook his head. "What has this got to do with *me?*" he asked in exasperation.

As if on cue, Alex stepped forward. "You've been identified as an easy mark. You play with guineas and pound notes. You lose far more than you win. You're an easy target for someone looking to leave a gaming hell with a good deal of cash."

The earl swallowed, realizing that Alex Bradley was describing exactly what had been happening lately. Greenley glanced at Viscount Chamberlain, knowing the man had been working in the Foreign Office since before he inherited the Chamberlain viscountcy. "Are you charging me with a crime?"

"No," Matthew replied with a shake of his head. "We are, however, appealing to your sense of patriotism in the hopes you'll assist us with our mission."

Intrigued, Greenley straightened in his chair. "What do I have to do?" he asked carefully, his eyes flitting between the viscount and the agent.

"Gamble. With men you don't recognize, or perhaps with those that you do but don't know well. Lose just as you usually do..." At this, Greenley's frown changed to a scowl. "... And simply provide us with the amount you lost and the name or description or the name of the man who won most of it if you know it. We'll take it from there." He didn't add that there would be other agents watching the gaming—watching and reporting back to him.

His expression appearing dubious, the earl regarded the viscount for a moment. "What's in it for me?" he countered, not especially impressed with their plans for him.

"Money to gamble."

The earl jerked his attention back to Alex. "How much?"

The agent had to suppress the urge to sigh. Even though giving money to a man who was addicted to gambling with the hope he would use it to gamble was a sure bet, his operation still had a budget. "We'll start with fifty pounds a night for three nights a week and see how it goes," Alex replied, trying hard not to wince as he said the words. His annual salary wasn't even as much as what would be spent in a month on this operation!

He studied the earl's reaction as he made the comment, and he wasn't disappointed when he saw Greenley's eyebrow arch in appreciation. "You can supplement your bets with your own funds, of course, but we won't be reimbursing you for any losses you incur," Alex warned. "Nor will we be buying any of your markers."

Greenley nodded his understanding. "If I don't agree?"

Alex traded a glance with Matthew. "The Crown will attempt to collect on these markers, which means you'll have to pay them off," he replied with a nod toward the markers spread out on the mahogany desk. "If you do, you're free to gamble away with the understanding there won't be anyone coming along to bail you out should your losses mount up again."

The earl dared a sideways glance at the viscount. "And if they don't succeed in collecting?" Although his coffers were still rather healthy, they were far lighter than they had been when he inherited the Greenley earldom from his father. Still, he was fairly sure he had the funds necessary to dispatch the markers and still see to his regular expenses. There wouldn't be any funds to use for gambling, however. At least, not until the next harvest. He would be back to having to use markers in the meantime should his losses continue.

Matthew sighed. "Debtor's prison," he stated with a nod.

Greenley frowned, about to accuse the viscount of blackmail. He was an earl, for God's sake! He had to still himself, though. In his rather sober state, his reasoning was far more logical than usual. If the Crown made good on the threat, there would be repercussions. Even if he did agree to the scheme, there was a chance his continued gambling could draw more attention to him and to his heirs. "What about my family?" His sons were nearing their majorities, one daughter had made her come-out, and another would do so in a few years.

"Your sons are free to continue their lives in London or in Staffordshire at your estate there," Matthew replied with a shrug. "I would recommend you send Lady Beatrice to live with a relative. She would do well to have protection since you aren't home much to provide it," he said quietly, referring to the earl's youngest child.

Tamping down the sudden anger he felt at the insult, Greenley had to admit the viscount had a good point. "I will not send Barbara away, though," he stated firmly. "She's... she sees to the household. Pendleton House needs her," he said, referring to his mansion near Grosvenor Square.

Ever since his wife's death, he had avoided spending much time at the house, preferring to stay at his club or in a series of high-end gaming hells during the afternoons and nights. At least he made it to his own bed in the early morning hours, although there were times he wondered how he got there. His drinking had increased with his gambling, he knew. "Besides, Barbara has made her come-out and might land a husband during the upcoming Season," he added with a hint of hope in his voice.

Although the idea of his oldest daughter marrying and moving out of his house held little appeal, it wouldn't be fair to keep her there if she had an opportunity for an advantageous marriage. If he sent her to Staffordshire, he rather doubted she would find a husband worthy of her. He could imagine her arguing with him on the matter, wondering how he would be able to manage without her.

At least, he hoped she might. He hadn't spoken with her much lately.

"Anything else I should know?" Greenley asked, wishing the throbbing in the back of his head would cease.

Alex exchanged glances with Matthew again. "Depending on how much you lose and who pays witness to it, you may become the *on dit* in London," Matthew warned. "The gossips love to remark on those they think might be headed for a fall." He paused a moment. "And you cannot tell a soul you've agreed to do this."

Greenley nodded his understanding. If the Crown was going to fund his gambling from now on, he wouldn't have to touch his coffers. A deal, to be sure. A deal with the devil, perhaps. "I'll do it then," he finally stated. "When do I start?"

Alex allowed a wan smile. "Tonight, if you'd like. Just remember, though, you have a limit," he added with an arched eyebrow.

Sighing, Greenley gave a shrug. "Understood."

When told she would be moving to Staffordshire to live

with her aunt, Lady Beatrice took the news in stride, especially when her father assured her she could return to London when it was time for her come-out in a few years.

Lady Barbara, on the other hand, wasn't as happy to learn she would be staying in London. Although she was fine with seeing to the running of the Pendleton House staff and grounds, she no longer had the support of friends she had met while attending finishing school. Most were young matrons now, married and mistresses of their own households. Some even had children. Others had moved to their family's estates in other parts of England.

Besides the lack of close friends with whom to confide, she found the subtle change in her father's behavior rather alarming. Ever since her mother's death, Greenley seemed to avoid spending time at Pendleton House. His already late nights grew later, his drunkenness more frequent. Rumors of his excessive gambling reached her by way of whispers behind gloved hands. When she asked him about it directly, Greenley told her she had nothing to worry about. "Besides, I am not allowed to tell," he would say. "But rest assured, all is well."

Except all is not well, Barbara thought. She couldn't help but notice the stares of other ladies when she paid calls or visited the local lending library. When she shopped, she was sure clerks were watching her, thinking she would steal their wares since they seemed to doubt she had the funds to pay for them.

When the butler pulled her aside to ask if staff salaries would be paid on time that year, her alarm only increased, although when she spoke with her father on the matter— during one of his rare sober days—he promptly came up with enough money to cover salaries as well as provide modest bonuses for everyone on the staff. He even gave her fifty pounds with instructions she should purchase a new wardrobe. But when she asked how much he planned for her dowry, the earl merely shrugged and said the amount was negotiable.

More concerned than ever, Barbara realized she needed a way out, an escape plan that would allow her to exit Pendleton House and the scandal surrounding her father. With the Season about to start—Easter was mere weeks away —she turned to the only man for whom she had ever felt the least bit of affection. He wasn't an ideal solution. He wasn't a man she had ever imagined marrying. He might be the son of a marquess, but he had plans for a career in the British Navy, plans that would keep him away from England for years at a time.

Given his dedication to duty and figuring he would be leaving London once he received his orders, Barbara knew she had very little time to secure an offer of marriage, very little time to arrange a quick wedding and take her leave of London. Desperate to see her plan come to fruition, Barbara spent the few weeks leading up to Easter seeing to it the gentleman paid calls only on her, that he danced with her at early spring soirées, that he took her and only her on rides in Hyde Park. When an opportunity to spend time in Lord Weatherstone's garden presented itself, she made sure they were there together. And then, on his last night in London, she made sure she spent it with him. The entire night.

When he finally put voice to an offer of marriage during his final night with her, Barbara accepted—despite the fact that her plan had failed.

Failed on every level but one.

There wasn't enough time for a quick wedding—he would be departing London the following day. There wasn't another place she could go to live while he completed his tour of duty.

But she accepted his offer anyway.

For at some point during her seduction of William Slater, Earl of Bellingham and heir to the Devonville marquessate, Barbara Higgins fell in love with the man. Fell in love and then had to say, "good-bye" as she watched him sail away.

Returning to Pendleton House, the massive mansion

occupied by only servants and her father, Barbara resigned herself to a lonely life.

Damn him, she cursed nearly every morning and every night. *Damn him all to hell.*

For the next few months, Maxwell Higgins, Earl of Greenley, enjoyed a rather interesting status as a gambler who consistently lost but always came back for one more game. Everyone in the aristocracy gossiped how long the earl could continue losing at the gaming hells before he would run out of money. Talk of debtor's prison was a frequent subject in Mayfair parlors during afternoon tea. And yet, the man seemed unconcerned, and so talk died down for a time.

That is, until the evening he learned something about Barbara. Something so shocking, his alcohol-addled brain had him reacting in a manner that assured he would never again see his daughter. At least, not if she could help it.

A few weeks later, Alex Bradley bagged his band of money smuggling bandits—a collection of spies tasked with helping France fund their war effort—so the Crown no longer supplied the earl with his gambling allowance. He was forced to use his own funds to feed his habit.

Although his luck was no better when he gambled with his own money, the Earl of Greenley occasionally won a game or two, his winnings sometimes in the form of money or jewelry or the deed to a piece of unentailed property. As he had done in his earlier gambling days, the money would simply end up at the next gaming hell. The jewelry was sometimes pawned or added to his late wife's collection.

The deeds?

Although he considered using them as collateral, he decided they would do him more good if he kept them. He could always sell them if he needed to restock the Greenley coffers.

How fortuitous, then, that he always gave the deeds to his solicitor, Andrew S. Barton, Esquire, for safekeeping.

Fortuitous for someone else as well, for without his

knowledge, one of those properties had become his oldest daughter's home.

Where else could Barbara go? Her father had banished her from Pendleton House, after all. And even if he hadn't, she couldn't stay in London.

Nor did she ever want to go back.

CHAPTER 2

BROTHERS ENJOY A BRANDY
ON THEIR LAST DAY AT SEA

May 1818

"One more day."

William Slater, Earl of Bellingham and commander of the British naval vessel *HMS Greenwich*, looked up from the map he was studying. "The winds favor us," he agreed as he moved to shake hands with the man who stood in the threshold of the captain's quarters. The intruder was not quite a year younger and bore a remarkable resemblance to him. But then, half-brothers usually did.

"I was actually referring to your position, Commander," Stephen said, giving Will a raised eyebrow. The handshake turned into a punch into his upper arm. "Ow!" he added as he moved to rub the spot, rather stunned at Will's assault.

"Don't remind me. I can't decide if I'm looking forward to the life of a gentleman, or if I should request that the War Office deny my request to resign my command."

Stephen regarded his brother for a moment. "After six years, I know I want dry land under my feet," he said with a nod. "Especially given the lack of action on the high seas."

The *Greenwich* hadn't shot more than a single ball from one of its seventy-four cannons in over a year, and that had been done to warn a pirate ship off its pursuit of a civilian vessel on its way past the Straits of Gibraltar.

Will gestured toward the overstuffed chairs at one end of the cabin. "Share a brandy with me? I promise I won't report you to your commander," he teased.

Stephen allowed a wan smile. "I can only stay a few minutes," he said. "I go on duty soon."

Will frowned and pulled out his chronometer, stunned to find the time much later than he thought. "You and me both," he replied. "Christ, I spent far too much time on this last report," he said as he pulled two tumblers and a decanter of brandy from a cupboard. He poured a finger's worth into each glass and offered one to Stephen. "To England," he said, his chin lifting.

"To the Devonshire marquessate," Stephen countered.

Will gave a nod and sighed before taking a drink. Although the brandy had come from France in the form of contraband taken from a pirate ship off the coast of Africa, he rather doubted it was their best these days. Perhaps his father's study would offer a better vintage. Certainly the scotch would be excellent. His uncle, Donald Slater, distilled the best in Northumberland.

"You haven't met him, have you?" Will half-asked, realizing the bastard son of William Slater, Marquess of Devonville, had rarely been to London, at least, not since his mother had moved him to Kent when he was four years old.

Stephen shook his head. "I have not, at least, not as an adult." He took a sip of the brandy, closing his eyes as he felt the liquor burn the back of his throat. "But he owes me nothing."

The commander took another sip of his own brandy before frowning. "He is your father. You were born to his favorite mistress, or so my mother claimed many a time whilst I was growing up."

Stephen winced at the comment. Although he was a bastard, he had been raised in a rather wealthy household, the only son of Marie St. Clair, an apparently celebrated courtesan from France who had escaped before the Revolution and made her way to London about the time William

Slater was in the market for a mistress. Although the man's marchioness was already with child—with Will, in fact—the marquess had sought the services of Marie thinking his wife wouldn't welcome him back into their marriage bed once an heir was born.

He had Marie with child before his first-born was six months old.

"Mother has told me similar tales," Stephen agreed. "But she also said the marquess would only see to my expenses until I reached my majority," he added, finding it odd he hadn't discussed his situation with his half-brother the entire time they had known each other—the two years he had been assigned to the *Greenwich*. Given the differences in their ranks, it seemed safest to simply side-step the issue at first, so neither brought it up before a night of shore leave found them at the same public house in Spain. A few tankards of beer and a number of tapas plates, and the two were fast friends.

One of his brows furrowing, Will shook his head. "I do not think he will turn you away if you deign to visit Devonville House," he claimed. "In fact, I am most certain he will claim you as his son and see to it you're set up with an allowance. Not a generous one, perhaps, but at least enough to allow you to buy a modest townhouse and take a wife."

Having discussed the situation with his mother, Grace Burroughs Slater, when he was about to leave for his first voyage as a naval officer—that had been nearly eight years ago—Will knew his father was sorely mistaken in his beliefs about his mother. At least, by then, the two had returned to life as a married couple, the marquess claiming he had only ever loved her. Too bad Lady Devonville died and left the marquess a widower four years later.

Poor Hannah, he remembered thinking. His only sister missed her come-out that Season, and then again the following Season when their aunt died. Hannah was one-and-twenty before she finally made her appearance at

London's *ton* events, but it was no surprise to him she had been offered marriage the next year.

"Our sister is a countess now," Will announced.

Stephen frowned. "Countess of Gisborn, is she not?" he half-questioned.

Will gave a look that suggested he was impressed by his brother's comment. "She is. Henry Forster isn't your typical aristocrat, though," he said. "Farmer first, inventor second, lands in Oxfordshire," he added. "Or vice-versa."

Stephen grinned then, remembering what he had learned of Oxfordshire and the Cotswold lands therein. "Let me guess. They live in a country manor amongst herds of sheep. She plays Little Bo Peep by day and Countess of Gisborn by night."

Will laughed out loud, a sound that Stephen realized he had never before heard. "Not if Gisborn has anything to say on the matter. Father wrote in one of his letters that he hates sheep." He sobered. "And you really shouldn't say such things of my sister. Hannah is..." He sighed, rather sorry his sister hadn't made a match with a gentleman who preferred London year-round. Or at least for part of the year.

Word from his father had it that Hannah and Henry lived in Oxfordshire year-round and that Henry hadn't yet claimed his seat in Parliament. Apparently the man thought his first priority was to his tenant farmers and the village nearest the Gisborn farms. But at least his earldom hadn't suffered severe famine as had most of England after the Summer of 1816. Apparently the earl had built greenhouses in which to grow fruits and vegetables, and he managed to keep his farmland drained of excess water during the rains that fell most of that summer.

"I hear she rather likes the life of a farmer's wife," Stephen said, his head angling to one side, not adding that he had the word direct from her hand. His half-sister had been sending him letters ever since she learned her brothers were assigned to the same ship. Stephen wondered if Will had been the one to share the news. "I should like to meet her, though," he added hopefully. "Will I be allowed, do you think?"

Will considered the question. He had to give his brother chops for his willingness to jump into the life of a gentleman. "I think she will be very happy to learn she has another brother—"

"You haven't told her?" Stephen interrupted, alarm evident in his features. Well, that confirmed that Will hadn't been the one to inform their sister, which meant that their father had been the one to tell her. "Christ! I had hoped to travel to Oxfordshire to meet her before the snows," he said with frustration.

Will grinned. "I have not. Perhaps Father has mentioned you in his letters, though," he said carefully. After a moment, he added, "I have written her with instructions to be prepared for a surprise. A good surprise." His grin suggested he was teasing his brother.

"You bounder!" Stephen countered, deciding the joke would be on Will when he discovered Hannah had known of Stephen's existence for some time. She seemed most glad of it, which had him hoping she would be as welcoming in person as she was in her writings.

"Watch it! I am still your commander," Will claimed. He lifted his chronometer from his waistcoat pocket. "And we're both supposed to be on duty now," he added with an arched eyebrow.

Stephen was up and out of his chair in an instant. "Permission to report to duty, Commander?"

Will nodded and raised a finger to his forehead. "Permission granted," he replied, giving his brother another punch in the arm.

He watched as his slightly younger brother took his leave of the cabin and rolled his eyes. There were times like right now that he rather wished *he* were the bastard son and that Stephen was the legitimate son. Tomorrow, he would return to London and once again be the Earl of Bellingham, heir to the Devonville marquessate. Although it was merely an honorary title, it was a title none-the-less.

The very last position Will was interested in attaining was that of Marquess of Devonville, but as the oldest—and only legitimate—son, he would one day be the marquess.

From his perch at the bow of the *Greenwich*, Stephen watched the white caps rush past and wondered if he had made the right decision. He could have simply continued serving in the British Navy, perhaps made a career of being a navigator, although he knew he would have to do so on a different vessel with a different crew. The *Greenwich* was due to undergo repairs while docked in Wapping and wouldn't return to service for several months.

Choosing a life in London certainly held more appeal. There was the opportunity to meet more members of the opposite sex, to be sure, but there was also the promise of a life that didn't include sleeping in a hammock every night among a dozen other men and days spent on the deck of a ship bobbing on the ocean, miles of water in every direction.

Having lived a comfortable life with his mother, either because of her profession or in spite of it, Stephen found he missed the comforts of a house. The accoutrements of a well-appointed home. The idea of a wife and children. If what his half-brother had said was true, he might be able to secure such a life.

The thought that he would have to rely on his father to provide the funds for such a life rankled, though. He wasn't a good enough gambler to think he could fund his life at the gaming tables. His skills as a navigator would no doubt be worthless in a city, although his ability to read and write must be of some worth, he thought. He could speak and understand several languages. He could dress himself without the assistance of a valet. He could get along with even the most disagreeable men aboard ship. But as to how he would apply his limited skills to life in London, he had no idea.

Movement off on the port side of the ship had him lifting his spyglass to his right eye. Closing his left, he finally spotted the spray of a whale on the horizon. At least, that's what he thought he was seeing when he realized the arc of water wasn't indicative of a whale. Or any other sea creature.

Land.

Jesus! Stephen glanced at the sails and noted how they were all unfurled and all filled with wind. *Will wasn't joking when he said the winds favored us*, he realized as he lifted his spyglass again and studied the horizon. Even in the growing twilight, he could make out the silhouette of a land mass. Hurrying to the wheelhouse, Stephen entered and rushed to pull down the maps of the coasts of Spain and France. He knew they had been somewhere near the Bay of Biscay the night before. *Could we have already passed by Brest?*

He leaned out of the wheelhouse and took another look at the horizon. *Guernsey*, he realized. *We're in the English Channel!*

Stephen found his brother leaning over the railing on the starboard side, his attention on the moon just then appearing above the western horizon. "We're in the Channel," he said quietly, not wanting to startle his brother.

Will chuckled. "I wondered how long it would take for you to realize where we were," he countered with a grin. "As I said, the winds favor us."

Stephen punched Will in the shoulder. "You must have a favorite ladybird," he accused before moving back to the starboard railing.

Will frowned and turned around to address Stephen's retreating back. "She is not a ladybird, I assure you," he stated firmly. "And you shall stay far away from Lady Barbara Higgins or risk a musket ball in your gut."

Stephen straightened before turning to regard his half-brother.

Barbara?

Well, this was news. "I shall avoid every Barbara at all events, Commander," he responded with a salute.

Will dipped his head, rather surprised by the vehemence in his threat. Even after nearly eight years, it was thoughts of

Barbara Higgins that had him climbing out of his bunk every morning. Thoughts of Barbara that kept him warm at night and wondering as to what might have happened to the love of his life. It wouldn't be long now, he hoped. Wouldn't be long before he found her and pulled her into his arms and made her his wife.

CHAPTER 3
HOMECOMING

he following day in London

Stephen and Will disembarked from the *HMS Greenwich* at the same time, both complaining of sea legs and an inability to walk straight until they were on the pavement and could hire a hackney. They made their way to Devonville House in Mayfair, a Palladian mansion located on the edge of Hyde Park in Park Lane. A magnificent structure lit with gas lamps and surrounded by neatly trimmed bushes and flowering plants, Stephen thought it the most impressive house he had ever seen.

"Come on," his older brother said as he plucked his coat sleeve and led the way to the double-doors at the top of three steps. Topiary bushes trimmed into spirals flanked the doors, and the lion-head knocker seemed to scowl at them as they waited for a butler to answer.

"What about our trunks?" Stephen whispered, jerking on his waistcoat in an effort to straighten it.

Will grinned. "The footmen will see to our luggage," he answered, nodding in the direction of several liveried men who were already making their way to the hackney.

When the door opened, Will didn't wait for the butler to step aside but merely stepped up and into the house. "Good evening, Hatfield. I am home from the wars," Will said lightly.

Stephen was forced to suppress a grin—nay, an out-and-out laugh at the startled expression displayed on the butler's face. *Weren't butlers usually known for their impassive expressions and unflappable manner?*

"Lord Bellingham!" the butler finally said, his gaze dancing back and forth between Will and Stephen, as if he were trying to decide which was really the Earl of Bellingham.

"My brother, Stephen, but I rather think you've already sorted that," Will announced as he made his way to the marble stairs, Stephen tagging along behind and to the side of his half-brother, his gaze taking in the stately vestibule and grand hall leading to the curved marble staircase.

"Should I have a guest room readied?" Hatfield called out from where he still stood in the vestibule.

Will turned around and regarded the butler. "That would be capital. He can take the bedchamber next to mine," he said with a nod.

"Your correspondence is in the study, my lord," Hatfield stated as Will and Stephen moved to make their way up the marble stairs.

Will paused at the bottom step. "Correspondence?" he repeated. "Already?"

The butler arched an eyebrow. "News of your impending arrival has been noted by many, my lord."

"You needn't call me that, Hatfield," Will interrupted, rather surprised to find the butler hadn't changed a bit since Will had last seen him. "But I am a bit curious as to who knows I have returned," he added. He hadn't exactly sent a note to *The Times*. A quick missive to his father, William Slater, outlining his plan to resign his commission in the navy and return to English shores, had been penned only a month ago and sent on a packet the following day. The mail service had obviously improved if others in the *ton* knew of his arrival on English shores.

Or my father has been spreading the news, he considered.

Taking a breath, as if he had to fortify himself, Hatfield canted his head to one side. "The *marchioness* has been most enthusiastic about your return," he said carefully. "I did not mean to eavesdrop on her conversation when she hosted morning tea last week, but I could not help but overhear her comment about your imminent arrival."

Will stiffened. In his absence, his father had married Cherice Dubois, the widow of Baron Winslow, almost exactly a year after the viscount died. Although Will had never met the woman who was now his stepmother, he had heard of her. Even when her husband had been alive, men apparently worshipped at her feet and made sure her dance card was always full at balls. Somehow, the Marquess of Devonville had managed to court and marry her, seemingly within a week of the anniversary of Winslow's death.

Well, his father was a marquess. A handsome man, he supposed. And he was rich.

Although William Slater, Marquess of Devonville, claimed to have loved Will's mother, he certainly hadn't made it clear to her with his early liaisons with a string of mistresses. At least the two had finally spoken of their mutual affection, for the last years of his mother's life had apparently been spent in marital bliss.

William Slater's last missive to Will had included a post scriptum about how much he had loved Will's mother. "I miss her every day, and I so wish we had more time before she passed. As a result, I intend to remain faithful to Cherice for all my days. Please accept her into our family. I have asked your sister to do the same, and she has assured me she will."

The words had been powerful, for Will had loved only one woman his entire life. He could only hope to find she still felt the same way about him—and that she was still available for marriage.

He hadn't heard a word from her in over six years.

"Is Lady Hannah in residence, by chance?" Will asked,

thinking he would like to introduce his sister to their half-brother.

Hatfield blinked and straightened. "Lady Gisborn is in Oxfordshire at Gisborn Hall, Lord Bel... my lord."

Stephen's eyebrows arched. "My lord," he mouthed when Will glanced in his direction.

"I'm an earl, but in title only," Will whispered.

Stephen blinked. "What does that make me?" he asked, *sotto voce.*

"Bastard half-brother of an earl," Will responded in a hoarse whisper, amusement apparent in his response. Raising his voice and turning his attention back to the butler, Will gave the man's response some consideration. Although he knew the Earl of Gisborn disliked London, he still rather hoped the couple visited on occasion. Just because Henry Forster hadn't taken his seat in Parliament didn't mean Will's sister couldn't make an occasional trip to London.

"Gisborn," Stephen whispered, wracking his brain to remember what he had attempted to learn in the past week from an old copy of *Debrett's Peerage and Barontage* Will had given him. "Learn this, and you shall have no trouble at Society events," he had been instructed. Stephen had read the tome every night before blowing out the candle next to his hammock, so his first reaction was to frown and shake his head. "Did she truly marry an old fart of an earl?" he asked in alarm. "I thought you said she was married to a farmer?" he whispered.

Will glanced from his brother back in the butler's direction. "My first thought, as well," he admitted, hoping Hatfield would provide some more information. "But I know his name is Henry, and he's an inventor and a farmer, and the old fart was much older."

The butler angled his head again. "Henry Forster, Earl of Gisborn, inherited his title over two years ago when his uncle died without issue. He has not yet claimed his seat in Parliament, although there is some thought he might do so for the upcoming session."

Stephen straightened, his head angling back as if someone had attempted to take a swing at him. "Henry?" he repeated. "The nephew. So he *is* the farmer and inventor." This last was said with a hint of satisfaction, as if he was proud of having correctly remembered his study of Will's copy of *Debrett's Peerage and Barontage.*

Hatfield nodded. "The very same, Mr..." The butler paused, as if he just then realized he hadn't been introduced to Stephen by any name other than his given name.

"Slater," Will piped up. "Father recognized Stephen as his son when he was born," he added with an arched eyebrow.

Stephen's eyes lit up. Oblivious to the conversation between his brother and the butler, he appeared to have reasoned out something. "Since my half-sister is married to an earl, what does that make me?" he asked, a grin splitting his face when he realized he could claim *two* brothers as earls and a marquess for a father.

"The bastard half-brother of a countess," Will replied, giving Stephen a quelling glance.

"With an uncanny resemblance to you, my lord, if I may be so bold," Hatfield stated, his hands clasping behind his back.

Will and Stephen turned their attention on the butler and then on each other. Dressed as they were, in similar breeches, waistcoats and topcoats, they only appeared different due to their hairstyles and footwear.

"Point taken," Will acknowledged. Realizing they had been loitering too long, Will motioned with his head toward the stairs. "Seems we have correspondence to read," he said with an arched eyebrow.

Stephen nodded and turned to the butler. "Thank you," he said, giving the man a slight bow.

Will rolled his eyes. "There's no need to bow to a servant," he admonished his brother, missing Hatfield's bow in Stephen's direction.

"I know, I know, I grew up with them, too, but that

doesn't mean you shouldn't acknowledge their service," Stephen said.

Nearly pausing on the stairs at his brother's comment, Will angled his head and instead considered the words. He supposed Stephen was right. An occasional nod or 'thank you' couldn't hurt, he supposed.

The two of them had made their way up the steps and to a set of large double doors left slightly ajar. Will opened them and strode into one of the most elegant rooms Stephen had ever been in during his entire life as the bastard son of Lord Devonville. Although his mother's country manor in Kent was beautifully appointed—Marie St. Clair wouldn't have it any other way—this room was richly paneled with dark woods, the coffered ceiling ornate but understated, the draperies made of tapestry, the furniture dark and heavy. A scent of tobacco—probably from a cheroot rather than a pipe—hung in the air. *This is a man's room, no doubt.* He couldn't imagine his mother in here.

"Whose room is this?" he asked as he watched Will open a set of drapes. Light flooded the mahogany-paneled room. A massive desk backed by a leather chair took up the middle. A series of paintings lined the two walls that didn't feature shelves and shelves of leather-clad books. A Grecian couch sat in front of the window that overlooked the side yard.

"Father's study."

Stephen's gaze fell onto a painting of an aristocrat, his visage appearing as if it were an older version of himself. "Our father, I presume?" he half-asked.

"Grandfather," Will corrected him. "He was an admiral when that was painted. Took his seat in Parliament, attended sessions maybe one or twice and never again, so our father made sure to do so," he explained with a wave. "He was ship-board most of his life, but finally agreed to take a desk at Whitehall for his last few years."

Stephen frowned. "What about his other son?" he asked, remembering there was an uncle somewhere in the world.

Will had to suppress a laugh. "You really did study that

book, didn't you?" he teased, giving another glance in the direction of his grandfather. "Uncle Donald lives in Northumberland. Owns a distillery. Makes the best damn scotch in all of the British Isles," he claimed. "With any luck, that's what we'll find in one of these," he added as he lifted a cut crystal decanter from the sideboard. He pulled off the stopper and took an experimental sniff. His eyes closed as he seemed to revel in the scent. "Luck!" he called out before pouring generous dollops into two tumblers. He held out one to his brother.

"Our uncle distills scotch?" Stephen half-asked as he took the tumbler and gave it a sniff. He straightened and closed his eyes. "Oh," he purred. "We never had anything like this," he whispered as he took a cautious sip. "So smooth." He took a large drink and held it in his mouth a moment. After he swallowed, he regarded his brother for a moment. "If our uncle is a distiller, what does that make me?"

Will shook his head. "Bastard nephew of a distiller," he said before taking a drink of his own tumbler. "Jesus, the stuff we took off of those last pirates wasn't even this good," he whispered. He allowed his gaze to span the room before it settled on a silver salver covered in white folded parchments. A closer inspection showed his name written on most of them. "Well, it seems we have some reading to do," he murmured. He tossed a note in Stephen's direction.

His brother caught it easily, one of his eyebrows arching up as he studied the feminine script on one side. "This is for you," he said.

"Read it," Will ordered.

Frowning, Stephen set down his glass and took a seat in a leather chair, a sigh escaping as the padded cushions seemed to swallow him in comfort. He slid a finger beneath the wax seal and unfolded the snowy white parchment. "The honor of your presence is requested at The Lord and Lady Weatherstone's annual ball," he started to read.

"Yes," Will interrupted.

Stephen arched a brow. "Yes?" he repeated.

"Yes. Put that in the 'yes' pile," he instructed. "It's one of the best balls of the year, made more so because Lord Weatherstone lives right across the street. If tradition still holds, then his back gardens will be the choice locale for naughty assignations." He said this last as he waggled his eyebrows and remembered that he and Barbara had shared their first kiss in those gardens.

Another missive flew through the air. Stephen caught it and dutifully opened it. "The Lord and Lady Torrington request the honor of your presence at Worthington House—"

"Yes," Will interrupted, before he straightened and arched an eyebrow. "*Lady* Torrington, did you say?" he asked as he paused in his effort to open an envelope.

"Uh huh," Stephen responded, wondering what had his brother looking so confused.

Will reached out for the invitation Stephen held. His brother gave it to him and he studied the even script. "Did you see pigs flying when we were on our way here?" Will asked then, a smirk appearing on his face.

Stephen gave a snort, understanding his brother's query. "I take it Lord Torrington wasn't expected to marry?"

Will shook his head, thinking to say something like, "Not in my lifetime," but thought better of it. "Well, he's an earl, so he was expected to marry at some point, I suppose. I just didn't expect it would be before me," he responded with a wry grin. "Nor did I expect it would be to my aunt. *Our* aunt," he amended when he noticed how Stephen stared at him.

"On Father's side?" Stephen asked, his eyes unfocused as he struggled to remember the names of the immediate family. "Adele Slater Worthington?" he guessed.

Will gave him a nod indicating he was impressed. "The very same. Can't say I'm surprised she would end up a countess. She was once married to a man who made his fortune in steamships."

Stephen gave this information some consideration. "So what does that make me?" he asked with a quirked lip.

Will had to suppress the urge to laugh out loud. "The bastard nephew of a countess, I suppose," he said before he hurled another missive in his half-brother's direction. "Anyway, an invitation to one of Aunt Adele's *musicales* is the most coveted invitation of the Season since she manages to get the best sopranos and musicians to perform. You have to go."

Catching the folded parchment between his hands, Stephen frowned before returning his attention to the invitation to a *musicale*. "Isn't Lord Torrington your godfather?" he asked, looking up just in time to catch another flying envelope.

"He is," Will acknowledged, impressed his brother would make the connection.

"What does that make him to me?" Stephen asked, ready to say, "A bastard's godfather."

But Will considered the question and shook his head. "Good question," he replied. "It's not as if we *need* a godfather at our age," he added, one brow furrowing.

"He must be ancient," Stephen murmured.

It was Will's turn to frown. "Hardly," he replied. "Forty..." He paused a moment, his gaze directed at one of the paintings. "Three or four, I think."

Stephen nodded, not about to counter his brother's assessment of 'hardly ancient'. "And his character?"

Will looked up from another envelope he was unfolding. "Depends on his mood, I suppose. But he's a good man to have on your side should you find yourself in a scrape."

Stephen wasn't about to tell his brother he had no intention of finding himself in any scrapes. He did have every intention of making the best of any connections he could arrange whilst in London. Just because he was a bastard didn't mean he couldn't find a comely woman to court and marry. The money he had saved over the years would supplement anything his father might bestow on him in the way of an allowance so that he might even have enough to let a townhouse. He knew how to read and write, so he expected there might be opportunities to work as a clerk.

He caught another invitation and opened the corners. Two lines into the script, and he realized it was truly meant for his brother. "Love letter," he announced before handing it over to Will.

One eyebrow furrowing, Will set aside the invitation he had just read to a soirée at the Duke of Huntington's townhouse and quickly took the missive. He read the feminine script, hoping it might be Barbara's. He finally shook his head in bewilderment. "Since I have never met this chit, I hardly think this can be called a *love* letter," he countered, turning over the scented paper to look for a return address.

"Do you know who she is, though?"

Will shook his head. "Miss Comber?" he replied as he checked the signature. "Just a letter of introduction, it seems. Says she is looking forward to meeting me at a ball as she is new to London." He shook his head, wondering if the chit might be a cousin.

"Rather fast of her, isn't it?" Stephen asked, never having heard of a young lady sending a letter to an unmarried man —unless they were betrothed.

"She could be related to us, actually," Will murmured, deciding he would ask his father when he had the chance. "Or maybe she's an Aimsley," he murmured as he struggled to remember who was related to whom. "Who is that one from?" he asked as he noticed Stephen holding up another bright white pasteboard.

Stephen glanced up from the invitation to a *musicale*. "Lord and Lady Morganfield—"

"Put that in the 'yes' pile," Will ordered. "Our father and Morganfield are close. Politically," he added when he noted Stephen's arched eyebrow. He set aside the letter from the unknown chit before reading the names on all the other notes on the salver. "Damn," he whispered. *All this correspondence, and not a single note from Barbara.*

What the hell had happened? He had received letters from her for several months following his departure from London, and then... nothing. His own letters to the daughter of the Earl of Greenley had gone unanswered—and unreturned. Had she met and married someone else? Despite her promise she would remain true to him as he completed his duty to King and Country?

Well, there were ways he could find out without making a damned fool of himself. A visit to her father's house might be the first step, he considered. Or a carefully worded query at Brook's. He winced. He didn't particularly want to be dragged into an evening of gambling that might go on all night. Especially his first night back in London.

"What will he think of me, do you suppose?" Stephen asked, his eyes lifting from a cream parchment invitation to a ball.

Pulled from his reverie, Will glanced in his brother's direction. "He, who?" he asked, shaking his head as if to clear it.

"Our father," Stephen whispered hoarsely.

"I suppose that all depends on your character, young man," a voice tinged with the barest hint of a Scottish accent spoke from the threshold of the study.

Stephen stood up, the pile of notes on his lap fluttering to the Aubusson carpet as he turned to regard and bow to the Marquess of Devonshire.

"Father!" Will said with a broad grin as he moved to embrace the marquess.

But William Slater's attention was bouncing back and forth between the two brothers. "Jesus. I thought it would be easy to tell you two apart, but..." He allowed the sentence to trail off as he wrapped an arm around one of Will's shoulders and indicated Stephen should join him with the other.

Stunned at the welcome, Stephen moved to shake his father's hand. "Stephen Slater, my lord. It's an honor to finally make your acquaintance."

The marquess completed his hug with Will and regarded

his bastard son. "I do believe the honor is mine," William replied with a nod. He stilled himself before taking Stephen's hand and pulling it—and Stephen—into a bear hug. "I once loved your mother, but damn I could have throttled her for keeping you from me," he murmured.

Stephen's eyes widened at this bit of news. Having always been curious as to how he would be accepted—or not—by his real father, he found himself rather surprised the man seemed happy to meet him. Happy to acknowledge his existence.

"Had I known you would be this welcoming, I would have called on you years ago, my lord," Stephen said with a nod.

"They'll be none of that 'my lording'," William countered as he gave Stephen a quick nod and turned his attention back to Will. "Looks like you found the scotch," he added with a wry grin.

Will shrugged. "Uncle makes the best I've ever tasted," he replied. "And trust me, we've tried enough scotches in our time to know. Should I pour you one?"

The marquess regarded his older son for a moment. "Of course," he agreed. He took a look at the invitations and notes scattered about his desk and in the hands of Stephen, who had reached down to pick up the ones that had fallen to the carpet. "Your stepmother has been telling the entire *ton* you were on your way back to London. She wanted to be sure you would have a full schedule, I suppose," he said as he angled his head toward the salver.

"She did an excellent job," Will remarked. "I do hope some of those will include Stephen, though."

His father glanced back and forth at both his sons. "Even if they didn't, no one would know which is which unless you were in the same room, and even then, I rather doubt they could tell you two apart," he stated with a grin. "Rather like Norwick and his brother, although David is no longer with us."

Will frowned. "He wasn't that old, was he?" he countered. "Or did he lose a duel?" he added, remembering the earl had at one time owned a brothel and a gaming hell. Perhaps something from his past had taken away his future.

It was William's turn to frown. "He died in a traffic accident in Oxford Street," he said with a hint of warning. "Broke his neck. His twin brother, Daniel, is the Earl of Norwick now." He accepted the tumbler of scotch Will offered him. "Will you two be at dinner this evening?" he asked.

Will nodded. "Dinner sounds great."

The marquess turned his attention to Stephen. "I do hope you plan to take a room here at Devonville House. At least, until you have a place of your own?" he added.

"Thank you for the offer," Stephen replied. "And, yes, I will take you up on a room. I'm hoping to find employment as a clerk or..."

The marquess grinned at him. "All in good time, my son. I'm sure the War Office could use a man with your knowledge, but in the meantime, there is a Season to be experienced. Let's see if we can't get you two married off, now shall we?"

The brothers stared at one another and then at their father. "Married?" they repeated in unison.

William Slater chuckled. "Nothing like the word, 'marriage' to strike fear in the heart of a young buck, is there now?" he teased.

Exchanging glances again, Will and Stephen nodded. "Nothing like it," they agreed.

Unless you've already found your true love and she's no longer willing to marry you, Will thought with a grimace.

CHAPTER 4

MARRIAGE ON THE MIND

The next morning
"Might I have a word?"

William Slater looked up from his newly ironed copy of *The Times* to find his oldest son peeking into the breakfast parlor. "Aye," the marquess responded as he waved Will into the room. "Come on in. Have some breakfast." When he realized Will wasn't necessarily there to eat, he added, "What is it?"

Will moved into the parlor, glancing about as if he expected to find someone else in the room.

"If you're looking for your stepmother, she's not yet out of bed," the marquess said. He motioned to the sideboard. "Help yourself to breakfast. Take a seat and eat, for goodness' sake. I should hope my cook is better than your ship's cook," he added when he thought Will hesitated too long.

Nodding, Will did as he was told, loading up a cream-colored bone china plate with a rasher of bacon, coddled eggs and toast. "Stephen will be down shortly. My valet is seeing to him," he commented before taking a seat at the round table.

"I can have Hatfield see to hiring another so you two don't have to share Perkins," the marquess offered.

Will shook his head. "That may not be necessary." At his

father's quizzical expression, he added, "I may need to take a trip, depending on what I learn in the next day or so."

The marquess let go of his hold on the newspaper and leaned back in his chair. "Go on."

Taking a deep breath, Will nodded. "I wondered if you knew what might have happened to Lady Barbara? Barbara Higgins?"

William blinked and shook his head at the query. "Now there's a name I haven't heard in a long time," he murmured. "Not since just after you left London," he added. "What's this about?"

His shoulders slumping, Will thought about how much to admit to his father. How much he should tell him about Barbara. And if he should tell his father about his last night in London.

His last night with Barbara.

"I... I proposed marriage to her just before I left London," he said in a quiet voice.

The marquess straightened, one eyebrow arching in surprise. "Indeed? I had no idea you were courting her! Or anyone else, for that matter. Did Lady Barbara... did she *accept* your offer?"

Will nodded. "She did. Promised she would wait for me. I received a few letters from her the first year after I left, and then... nothing. None of my letters to her found their way back to me, so I assumed she was receiving them—"

"Never assume correspondence has been delivered as expected," his father interrupted. At Will's look of surprise, the marquess added, "Letters to and from a naval officer are frequently intercepted," he explained, his words curt. "Just ask Chamberlain. He deals with it all the time at Whitehall."

Matthew Fitzsimmons, Viscount Chamberlain, had been working at Whitehall for most of his life. Despite his rank as a peer of the realm, the man had devoted the time he wasn't in chambers to the politics of war in the Foreign Office. Now that Napoleon had finally been defeated, William rather hoped the viscount could enjoy a more sedate life, especially now that his viscountess had just given birth to their first child in late January. *Better late than never,* he supposed.

"Still, I would have expected to hear *something* from her. Is she... did she marry someone else?" Will asked, almost prepared to hear the worst.

The marquess shook his head. "Not that I'm aware. I'm quite sure I would have heard if she had. Greenley attends all the sessions of Parliament, at least, he used to, but ..." He paused a moment. "Come to think of it, I haven't seen Lady Barbara for... years," he murmured. "Pretty gel, that one. I wasn't aware you had a tendré for her."

Coloring at his father's words, Will nodded. "More than a tendré, I should think. I am quite in love with her, and now that I'm home, I was hoping we could arrange our wedding."

William sobered and considered his son's words. "It's been a long time, son," he whispered in concern.

"Almost eight years," Will agreed. "Is her father in town, do you suppose? I think I should start there. Ask his permission and all."

His father frowned. "Truth be told, I haven't seen Greenley at any of the early Season events. Heard some rumors suggesting he's been gambling too much, enough to land him in debtor's prison if you believe everything you hear, but..." He allowed the sentence to trail off before he brightened. "His house is probably staffed, though. I should think the butler at Pendleton House might be of some help."

At that moment, the breakfast parlor door opened and Stephen leaned in. "Here you are," he said, his face splitting with his grin when he spotted Will. The grin lessened when he realized his brother and father were in what appeared to be a rather serious discussion.

"Ah, Stephen. Come join us," his father said as he indicated a place at the table. "My bride isn't yet up and about for the day, so you'll have to settle for me and your brother for company," he added.

Stephen glanced between the two men. "I apologize. I think I may have interrupted—"

"Nonsense. We were just discussing lost loves," William said with a nod to Will.

The younger brother stilled himself before giving a nod of disappointment on Will's behalf. "So, she's married then?" he half-questioned.

William's brows arched up. "Not that we know for certain," he replied, rather surprised Stephen would know about Will's choice for a wife, although, after giving it some thought, he realized the two probably had discussed it at length. What else would two brothers talk about whilst on a ship if not their futures?

"Well, that's something, I suppose," Stephen said with a nod to his brother. He helped himself to a plate at the sideboard and began piling the various foods onto it, trying to ignore the sense he was being watched.

"Coffee, my lord? Or tea, perhaps?"

Stephen stilled his movements when he realized he was being addressed by a footman.

My lord.

He rather liked the sound of the words, even if they didn't apply to him. Much simpler than *lieutenant.*

"Coffee, thank you," he responded with a nod. He took the seat his father indicated and tucked into his breakfast, oblivious to the stares of his father. When he glanced up at his brother, he regarded him for a moment. "So, where are we off to today?"

Will suppressed the urge to laugh. "*I'm* off to Pendleton House. You're welcome to join me, but—"

"I would like to tag along, if that's all right. I need to learn my way 'round London, and I've a letter to send off to my mother."

Will gave a shrug. "Hatfield will see to your correspondence," he replied. He gave his father a quick glance just as Cherice Dubois Slater, Marchioness of Devonville, breezed into the room. The men all stood up in haste and bowed in her direction.

"Here you all are!" she said with a happy smile and a

quick curtsy. "I suppose I should have guessed that growing boys could be found where the food is," she added as she moved first to allow her husband to place a peck on her cheek and then to her place at the table. "I want to hear all about your plans for the day," she went on as she allowed a footman to hold a chair for her. "Please, sit down. Eat!" she encouraged. A footman quickly saw to her breakfast, placing a slice of toast and a single egg on her plate. "Tea," she said before the footman could offer.

"Good morning, my lady," Stephen offered with a nod, rather stunned at how the woman changed the atmosphere of the breakfast parlor from that of a quiet, somber retreat to a whirlwind of activity. Even the servants seemed to move about more quickly.

"Now, sweeting, they're hardly boys," William said before holding out his cup so a footman could refill it.

"No, they aren't, are they?" Cherice agreed with an arched eyebrow. "By the end of tonight's soirée, I rather think one of you will be in love, and the other will be betrothed. Am I right? Oh, do say I'm right."

Stephen glanced over at his brother, finding Will displaying a look of shock. "Or one of us will be both," he offered when he realized Will was too tongue-tied to respond to the woman's demand.

"Oh! I *do* like how you think!" Cherice replied with a wink. "Now, have you clothes appropriate for a soirée? For a ball? Or do I need to join you in a trip to the tailor's shop?"

At Stephen's sudden look of doubt, Will said, "I'm quite sure I have something he can wear, my lady."

When Cherice's expression went from joy to disappointment, Stephen realized she was hoping for an excuse to go shopping. "I rather think I should at least look for an appropriate waist coat," he said carefully. "Although, I was just telling my brother here that I don't yet know my way 'round London."

The joy returned to the marchioness' face. "I'll accompany you," she said brightly. She turned her attention on her husband. "It is all right for me to be escorted by your son, is it not?" she asked, acting as if she required her husband's blessing for a shopping trip.

"Of course, my sweeting, but do be sure to introduce him as your *stepson*. I shouldn't want you to be the *on dit* in next week's *Tattler*," William warned with an arched eye brow.

Her eyes wide, Cherice looked as if she was trying to decide if she should be offended by her husband's remark or glad for it. "Of course, I will," she finally replied, turning to give Stephen a quick grin. "I can be ready to leave in a half-hour. That is, if I'm able to secure some pin money from your father. I don't want to put *everything* I buy on credit," she claimed as she gave her husband a suggestive grin.

"Dear heart, I'll give you enough so that you needn't put anything on credit," the marquess said, lifting up the copy of *The Times* and turning his attention to it.

Stephen boggled at his father's words, wondering how much his stepmother intended to buy. "I shall be waiting in the vestibule, my lady." When he noticed Will motioning with his fingers, drawing what appeared to be some kind of conveyance in the air, he added, "And I'll see to the... equipage to get us there," he added, giving his brother a look of confusion.

When Cherice had finished her bit of breakfast and taken her leave of the table and the men had retaken their seats, Stephen leaned over the table. "What was...?" He motioned in the air with his fingers, much like Will had done. "That?"

His attention was diverted to his father when he heard the man chuckle from behind his newspaper. "*That* was a town coach, my son. Had he done this," he stopped to place the tips of his forefinger and middle finger on the table so he could walk them a few steps. "He would have meant a horse. But Cherice will only ride during the fashionable hour, and since you're going shopping, she'll insist on being taken to Bond Street in the town coach."

Will had to suppress a smile. "If she's anything like my

mother, you'll be glad for it, as I expect you'll be the one carrying all her purchases."

Stephen nodded his understanding. "She sounds just like my mother," he replied with a grin.

Although my mother always had her own funds for shopping.

CHAPTER 5

IN SEARCH OF A MISSING WOMAN

*L*ater that day in Mayfair

Although not located in the more fashionable Park Lane, Pendleton House had the distinction of being closer to Grosvenor Square, and of being the only house on the street adjacent to it. Will knew its bright white Portland stone exterior was meant to intimidate. At least, that's what he thought it was designed to do as he dismounted one of his father's horses, Thunderbolt, and regarded the front doors of the mansion. Although no one seemed to be home, a stableboy soon took his horse and the front door opened to reveal an older butler.

"Good morning, sir," the portly man said as he regarded Will. "May I be of assistance?"

Will gave the man a calling card. Although old—he'd had them printed when he returned from Portsmouth and the Royal Naval Academy but before he had received his orders to report to the *HMS Drake* for his first assignment, the information on the card was still correct. "I am in search of Lady Barbara. Is she in residence?"

The butler's reaction had Will realizing that not all butlers kept an impassive expression on their faces when in the presence of visitors. "She is not, my lord," the butler replied with a shake of his head. His eyes took on a look of worry, though. "I have not seen her ladyship for… many years now."

"Why ever not?" Will asked, his own expression displaying his sudden concern. He had expected the man to tell him where he might find the chit, not act as if she might be dead.

The butler seemed to consider his response before daring a glance outside. He stepped aside. "Perhaps you would be more comfortable discussing this inside, my lord?" he offered.

Will nodded and made his way into the vestibule. Unlike most entryways into the newer Palladian mansions along Park Lane, this vestibule was dark, its ceiling low and free of embellishment. The walls were also unadorned. No paintings or embroideries graced the surfaces, no gas-lit torches illuminated the space. Even the marble beneath their feet seemed darker than most.

He was prepared to stand in the vestibule to hear the butler's comment, but the man continued on his way into the house. At the first door on the left, he paused and indicated Will should precede him into the room.

"I take it Lord Greenley is not in residence today," Will said carefully.

Shaking his head, the butler waved to an overstuffed chair. "He is not. And, in fact, there is some thought that he will not be returning to London for the Season. My master is… not well."

Will blinked. Maxwell Higgins, Earl of Greenley, always seemed younger than his years. Although he gambled and imbibed as much as any of his fellow lords, he did so knowing his limits. And his purse's limit. At least, he used to. From what his father had said that morning over breakfast, Will now wondered if maybe that had changed.

"Since when?"

The butler allowed a shrug. "If I may be blunt, my lord—?"

"Be blunt," Will demanded.

"Ever since he banished Lady Barbara from this house."

Will stared at the servant. *Banished?*

"What happened to cause him to do such a thing?" Will asked as he leaned forward, a fierce expression on his face.

"I do not know. I do not think anyone but he and her ladyship know the reason, my lord," the butler said with a shrug. He appeared uncertain as to what he would say next until Will noticed.

"And?"

"I am of the opinion she sought refuge, perhaps in Oxfordshire, my lord."

Oxfordshire?

The Greenley earldom seat was somewhere in Staffordshire. Why would Barbara be in Oxfordshire?

"Refuge?" Will repeated. The word implied Barbara had run away. That she'd had nowhere else to go. "With whom?"

The butler shook his head. "I only know this because I overheard his lordship... yelling... at his solicitor one afternoon. About seven years ago now," he explained. "He was incensed about something he had learned, and he insisted she be sent away from London, never to return."

Jesus! What had Barbara done to elicit an order of banishment from Pendleton House? "What did she do?"

Shrugging, the butler finally took the seat opposite of Will's. "My lord, that is the question that was on the entire household's mind the night she took her leave of Pendleton House. She had but one trunk. Not even her lady's maid accompanied her—"

"Where? Where did she go?" Will interrupted, alarmed at the information. "Did she...?" At this, he had to close his eyes and prepare himself for news he did not wish to hear. "Marry someone beneath her station?"

The servant shook his head. "No, my lord, nothing like that," he said quickly. "Although, I cannot help but think a marriage would have helped her situation."

His brows furrowing, Will regarded the butler for a moment. "Why?"

The butler sighed. "There was some talk above stairs that her ladyship might have been... *compromised*, my lord. And that her father somehow found out, and rather than call out the man responsible, he simply banished her." He paused a moment and lowered his voice. "Actually, I don't believe his lordship even knows where she is."

Suddenly light-headed, Will was forced to close his eyes. *I compromised her,* he thought then. *Ruined her. Ruined her so that she would be forced to marry me and only me upon my return to England.*

Jesus! What have I done?

He hadn't expected to be away nearly eight years. He had thought to serve for four or five years and then sell his commission. Use the earnings to buy a fashionable town-house so that they might live comfortably in London until he was forced by his father's death to become the Marquess of Devonville.

But who had Barbara told? He hadn't said a word to anyone. He hadn't disclosed their secret.

Not even to his father.

"Who started the talk?" Will asked finally, noting the butler seemed willing to share whatever information he could with him. So much for discretion when it came to the servants of Pendleton House!

"I cannot say. Her lady's maid was left without employ-ment, of course, seeing as how there wasn't another lady in the house once Lady Barbara took her leave."

Not another lady. Well, Barbara's mother had died in childbirth when Barbara was only thirteen, Will remem-bered. And if there wasn't another lady in the house, then what had happened to Barbara's sister, Beatrice? Perhaps she had married. Perhaps Greenley had never remarried.

The maid, Will decided. She might have been left embit-tered by having lost her position. Might have spread gossip. Might have made claims that were simply untrue.

Might have spread the truth.

"Did she gain another position soon after? In another

household, perhaps?" Will asked. Would the maid know where Barbara had gone off to?

"I cannot say, my lord. I honestly do not know."

So, the lady's maid was a dead end.

"Do you know where Barbara went when she left here?" Will asked in a voice far more calm than he felt. He had decided patience would gain him more information than the sudden demands he wanted to make of the butler. He wanted to yell and make accusations and stomp his feet in frustration. Wanted to make threats he had no hope of seeing through to their bitter end.

"I believe her ladyship was sent somewhere west of Lord Ellsworth's summer home," the servant said. "North of the Isis River." He paused a moment. "Truth be told, my lord, I am quite sure Lord Greenley doesn't know where she is. He had his man of business see to the arrangements. I think because..." He did not finish the sentence, as if the thoughts of a servant were not to be considered.

"He did not wish his conscious to force him to go there?"

The butler nodded. "Something like that," he agreed, his eyes downcast. "I honestly thought he would have her brought back. That he would change his mind and decide he had reacted badly to mere gossip," he whispered. "But he only became more and more embittered with each passing year. I've seen him burning correspondence on more than one occasion, as if he thinks she is dead."

Will nodded his understanding, realizing why his letters may not have reached Barbara. But his mind was already considering the butler's earlier words. *Ellsworth?* That would be the Earl of Ellsworth, he remembered. He had no idea where the earl's summer estate was located, but someone else would know such a thing.

Will sighed as he scraped his fingers through his hair. "And his man of business? Where might I find him?" Will asked as he straightened in his chair.

The butler sighed. "It was Andrew Barton, my lord. I

have not seen him in many years, but last I knew, he had an office in Oxford Street."

Will nodded, hoping he had enough to go on. "Anything else I should know?" he asked, hoping the man might provide a tidbit of information that could lead him directly to Barbara. Even if the woman was married, he wanted to be sure she was safe. Be sure she had protection.

Wherever she was.

The butler regarded him for a long moment. "May I ask as to your intentions, my lord? I ask only because I have known Lady Barbara since her birth. Not a day goes by I don't wonder what's become of the poor girl."

His shoulders slumping, Will considered how to respond. *The truth*, he decided. What could it hurt?

"I intend to make her my wife," he said with a good deal of authority. "Make her my countess, and then my marchioness when the time comes."

The butler's face brightened for the first time since he had opened the door of Pendleton House that morning. "Very good, my lord," he responded with a nod. "Very good."

CHAPTER 6

A SHOPPING TRIP YIELDS
CLOTHES AND CURIOSITY

eanwhile, back at Devonville House

"I rather wish I'd had the opportunity to meet your mother," Cherice said after Stephen handed her into the Devonville town coach.

"She lived in France until she was twenty and then in Westminster for a few years," Stephen countered, thinking they wouldn't have had many opportunities to meet. "Until we moved out to Kent when I was... four or five."

Cherice angled her head to one side. "I'm afraid I wouldn't have been allowed to be seen in the same company as Miss St. Clair," she said in a quiet voice. "Propriety and all."

Stephen blinked and then shook his head, color suffusing his neck and face. "I apologize. I sometimes forget she had a... profession." After a slight pause, his eyes widened. "You don't have to worry about her and my father, though. They haven't been—"

"Oh, I know Devonville isn't about to take up a mistress again," Cherice said with a shake of her head. "He's made that quite clear. Several times." She allowed a wan smile. "Some men can be so proud, though." At Stephen's frown and look of confusion, she sighed. "I'm sure your mother has explained why it is the aristocrats favor mistresses rather than their own wives, hasn't she?"

Stephen blinked and continued to display a rather red face. "My lady, I don't believe she ever discussed the topic," he replied, remembering only how his mother spoke of the marquess as if he was the love of her life.

Despite knowing William Slater would never be allowed to marry her, Marie St. Clair had agreed to end a contract with an earl to be exclusive to the marquess. She knew she wasn't William's first mistress, but she was definitely his last. Bearing his son ensured the two would be tied to one another for the rest of their lives, even if she was no longer a part of his. They'd had several happy years together, though.

Cherice settled into the squabs and angled her head, a small smile lighting her features. She wasn't a young woman —perhaps forty, Stephen guessed—but she obviously did what other aristocratic women did to look their best. Despite the clouds overhead, she kept a parasol with her at all times and never allowed a ray of sun to strike her face. Her maid was quite good at styling her hair, and her modiste created gowns that enhanced her every attribute.

"Every aristocrat has to marry and sire an heir," she stated evenly, as if she was imparting a school lesson to the young man who sat across from her in the town coach. "If there isn't a direct heir, their younger brother or some nephew or cousin inherits their title."

Nodding, Stephen said, "I'm quite aware of the inheritance rules, my lady."

Cherice went on as if he hadn't said a word. "Sometimes, and this used to be more common than it is now, they had to marry someone to whom they had been betrothed through an arrangement, usually by their parents."

"But, that's no longer the case," Stephen started to say.

"Officially, that's true," Cherice hedged. "But we all know of marriages that are more arrangements than unions of affection. Now, when a man has been forced to marry out of duty, and he doesn't feel any affection toward his wife, he takes a mistress, usually a woman he claims to love, so that he can have his own life away from the life he is duty-bound to live."

Stephen stared at Cherice, rather surprised at how matter-of-fact she seemed with her recitation. He leaned forward, his face taking on a look of disbelief when he realized why Lady Devonville might be telling him about mistresses. "Lord Winslow had a mistress?" he whispered, wondering why the baron would have looked elsewhere for affection when Cherice Dubois was his wife. The woman seemed agreeable. She was beautiful. Why would a man seek a mistress when he could have her in his bed?

Her eyes widening with Stephen's query, Cherice sighed. "He did. Several of them, in fact," she said quietly. "Oh, I think he tried to have me believe he didn't *employ* them, but he rarely came home before dawn, and let's just say that was the reason his young brother inherited. *I* certainly didn't bear him an heir."

Not sure how to respond, Stephen merely nodded. He frowned, thinking he understood her line of conversation. "Are you... *offended* that I've come to stay at Devonville House? Because, if you are, I can certainly leave..."

Cherice inhaled sharply, realizing the young man had gleaned more from her talk than she expected. "No. Actually, I am not. I suppose I should be, but... I find I rather like you. And your brother, of course." She allowed a wan smile. "Your father is very free with his affections toward me—he pursued me, you see—so I don't believe a mistress is in his future—"

"He wouldn't dare take a mistress," Stephen interrupted. At her look of astonishment, he added, "My mother made me promise to challenge him to a duel should he do such a thing. I thought she was teasing at the time, but... now I think she was concerned for your welfare."

Blinking, as if she might be fighting back tears, Cherice regarded Stephen for a long time. Even if Marie St. Clair didn't reside in London, she would have known about Lord Winslow's mistresses. Probably knew one or two of them personally. "Oh," she finally breathed. "Now I really do wish I had met your mother. I believe we would have been the best of friends." This last was said just as the coach jerked to a halt. "Well, shall we then?" she asked as she nodded toward the door, any evidence of her tears gone.

Stephen stepped down from the Devonville town coach and glanced up and down the busy shop-lined district known as Bond Street. Ladies milled about, some escorted by companions while others were trailed by maids and foot-men. Pasteboard boxes in various colors hung from hands or were stacked in the arms of servants. He had a brief thought to climb back into the coach and hide but had to give up on the idea when Lady Devonville appeared and took his hand.

"The best tailor is Jeffrey Garth, but since we don't have an appointment, I'll have to see what I can do to convince the man to see you," Cherice said as she stepped down from the coach. "Huntington's soirée is this evening, and I rather think it will have all the shops rather busy. This way," she said as she directed Stephen to the walkway.

"You really needn't trouble yourself, my lady," Stephen countered, feeling a bit out of his element. Although he had shopped in a variety of coastal towns throughout Europe and the Mediterranean, he found he was rather intimidated by the sight of the brightly colored storefronts and shingles that lined both sides of Bond Street.

"Oh, it's no trouble at all," Cherice replied happily. "I have my final fitting for the gown I'm to wear to Lord Weatherstone's ball..." She pointed in the direction of a shop with swaths of fabric on display in the window. "And then I'll see to a pair of slippers and some gloves."

She led them into the tailor's shop, a small but elegantly decorated space. Lined with wood paneling and deep carpeting that swallowed up their footsteps and the sounds from the street, it smelled of wool and lemon and men's cologne.

"Good afternoon," a young man said as he hurried in

their direction, his eyes quickly determining the quality of their clothing before they even came to rest on theirs.

"Is it already?" Cherice replied brightly, a hint of disappointment showing despite her words. "Is Mr. Garth available, perhaps? I'd like to pick up my husband's order. That is, if it hasn't already been sent by courier to Devonville House. Oh, and Mr. Slater is in need of a suit of clothes for Lord Huntington's soirée this evening," she added as she indicated the young man who stood next to her.

"Just a waistcoat, is all," Stephen interjected.

The man's eyes widened at hearing the Devonville name. "The order hasn't yet been dispatched, my lady," he said with a nod. "I'll let Mr. Garth know you're here." He hurried off and disappeared through a curtained doorway while Cherice moved to a display of topcoats.

"I do think you'll want a topcoat of your own for balls," she murmured, fingering the lapel of a black swallowtail coat. "By now, your brother's are no doubt horribly out of fashion," she added as she regarded a cutaway coat. She glanced in his direction and back at the coat. "I do think this will be perfect," she murmured just as an older gentleman appeared from behind the curtain.

"Lady Devonville, so good of you to pay a call," Jeffrey Garth said as he hurried up and bowed.

Cherice curtsied and allowed the tailor to brush a kiss over the back of her gloved hand. "Jeffrey, you are a sweeting to see me when I don't even have an appointment," she enthused. "How is Rebecca? I haven't seen her in an *age*," she added with a shake of her head.

Stephen stiffened, trying to determine who Cherice meant with her comment. He wondered if he should introduce himself or if Cherice would do so when the tailor replied, "She grows more beautiful with every passing day, and not just because I have completed a new gown for her," he said with an arched brow.

Cherice turned to Stephen. "Stephen Slater, this is Jeffrey Garth. The very best tailor in London and probably the best modiste as well, but the damned man won't make clothes for any other woman but his wife."

Stephen did his best to hide his shock at hearing Cherice's curse. "It's very good to make your acquaintance, sir," he said as he held out his right hand. "You must have a very happy wife."

Rather surprised at the offer of a handshake and at the comment about his wife, the tailor took Stephen's hand and shook it, his gaze passing from him to Cherice and back again. "And you, my lord," he replied. "And I do my best to see to my Rebecca's every desire." This last was said with a slight arch of an eyebrow, as if he was hinting at something Stephen should find important. "Am I to understand you're in need of a bespoke suit for tonight's soirée?"

Glancing in Cherice's direction, Stephen gave a hesitant nod. "At least a waistcoat, and a topcoat, I suppose. It's seems my father's marchioness has found the perfect coat," he said with a nod to the cutaway coat she had just been fingering. He wondered at the man's query, and thought to ask Cherice about it later.

The tailor eyed the coat critically and then turned his attention back on Stephen. Before he said anything, he turned to Cherice. "My lady, I will require at least an hour with Lord Stephen. Do you wish to go shopping, perhaps? Or may I see to a glass of champagne whilst you wait?" He waved toward a Grecian couch with a low table in front.

Cherice angled her head and considered her options. "I am tempted, Jeffrey, but I do believe I'll go to Madame Suzanne's for my fitting." She turned her attention onto Stephen. "Come for me there when you're done here, darling," she said with a wave and then took her leave of the tailor's shop.

Stephen bowed and watched her go, secretly relieved she wouldn't be watching while he was being fitted.

"I adore her," Jeffrey said, plucking the cutaway coat from its mount. "If you'll remove your coat, we'll see to this one."

Removing his topcoat, Stephen slipped into the one the tailor held for him. "You have known her a long time?" he asked carefully, wondering at their casual manner.

Jeffrey nodded. "She has been one of my wife's friends since... since before our marriage," he said, sounding hesitant with his response.

Frowning, Stephen wondered at the man's words. "You said that as if your wife didn't have many friends," he commented, pulling the coat onto his shoulders until it settled into place. The sleeves, a bit long, were barely large enough to encompass his muscled upper arms.

Studying the fit of the coat with a critical eye, Jeffrey shook his head. "She does not, my lord. She married me, you see, despite my warning of what would happen when she did."

Stephen regarded the tailor a moment. "I don't understand," he said with a shake of his head.

Plucking a piece of lint from the sleeve and shaking his head as he regarded the coat for another moment, Jeffrey sighed. "I am a tailor," he said simply, as if that was reason enough. At Stephen's continued look of confusion, Jeffrey sighed again. "My wife is Lady Rebecca Grandby. Oldest cousin of Lord Torrington and Michael, William, and Gregory Grandby, among others," he said quietly. "And she is nine years older than me."

Finally taking the man's meaning, Stephen nodded. "I see," he murmured before removing the coat. "However, if you knew her station in Society would be so adversely affected by marriage to you, why, pray tell, would you ask for her hand?" he asked, realizing almost immediately his query was far too personal. "Forgive me, I—"

"I didn't," Jeffrey replied with a crooked grin. "I did, however, finally agree to *her* marriage proposal." At Stephen's look of surprise, he added, "I believe it was her fourth or fifth. I lost track, you see, given the number of times she asked, and I declined for obvious reasons. Who could abide an earl's daughter married to a tailor? But she was so insistent, I finally realized I had better do her bidding or lose her forever. Something *I* couldn't abide, as it turns out."

His face coloring up, Stephen finally allowed a grin. "You *dog!*" he whispered hoarsely, realizing there had to be some reason the woman wanted the man so much.

The tailor allowed a grin, apparently feeling more at ease with Stephen. "Happy wife, happy life," he said lightly. "Try this one," he urged as he held another topcoat open for Stephen.

"Even though she doesn't have many friends?" Stephen queried.

Jeffrey angled his head. "Or perhaps because of it. She does not put on airs, nor does she pretend a status she cannot attain given our marriage, so her friends are true friends and not just acquaintances."

Stephen nodded his understanding, pulling the coat onto his shoulders. The fit was far better than the first, and the sleeves did not extend beyond his wrist. "My wife may have the same challenges," he murmured, realizing that a daughter of the aristocracy wouldn't marry a bastard unless she truly felt affection for him. He always figured he would end up with a commoner when he had given any thought to marriage, but how would he meet one if he was attending balls and soirées where only members of the aristocracy were in attendance?

"Pardon?" the tailor replied, his brows furrowed.

Sighing, Stephen thought he may as well admit his relationship to the Marquess of Devonville. "I am Devonville's bastard."

The tailor shrugged. "But he has acknowledged you as his son?" he half-questioned, knowing the answer since Lady Devonville had been on his arm when he walked in.

"He has," Stephen agreed.

"Society will accept you then," Jeffrey said with some authority. He turned his attention to the topcoat. "This is a good fit, but would you like to try another?"

Stephen shook his head. "I'll take this one," he said. "And

a rather... decorative waistcoat, should you have one that's already finished?" he asked hopefully. "But not... flamboyant. I shouldn't want to look like a molly."

Jeffrey Garth regarded Stephen with a quirked eyebrow. "That's the spirit," he said as he led them to another area of the shop. He opened a drawer to reveal an elaborately embroidered waistcoat, the satin fabric shimmering in the dim light. Pulling it off the tissue on which it rested, he carefully unbuttoned the fabric-covered fastenings and opened it for Stephen. "Lady Devonville will be ever so pleased with your choice."

Although he didn't much care if he did impress his stepmother, Stephen hoped perhaps other women at the soirée would be. Pulling on the waistcoat, he had a glimpse of himself in a cheval mirror on the other side of the room and decided right then and there he would buy the waistcoat. "Indeed, Mr. Garth. I do believe she will be. Now let's hope some other young ladies are as well."

The tailor gave him a nod. "They will be, I assure you, my lord."

CHAPTER 7

A MAN OF BUSINESS MINDS
HIS OWN

Later that afternoon in London

Finding Lord Greenley's man of business wasn't difficult. Will had been told his office, located in Oxford Street, was right next door to one of London's busiest charities. "Lady E's," the Pendleton House butler had said as Will took his leave. "I'm told broken, unemployed men go in, and they come out all dressed up with a position awaiting them. Several have been hired into service in Park Lane, in fact."

Will rather doubted the charity worked that quickly, but he could certainly applaud any endeavor that helped men who had fought for King and Country and were left with the scars to prove it. He wondered if any of his own injured men had availed themselves of the charity when they returned to London.

Sure the charity didn't exist when he was last in this particular neighborhood, Will studied the shingle above the door. *Lady E's 'Finding Work for the Wounded', est. 1815.* Even before he could wonder as to the identity of Lady E, a trio of bedraggled men, two limping and one whose face sported a scar along his temple, made their way into the office. One held the door as a young woman stepped out, her attention on the men who had just entered.

"Mr. Overby will be with you shortly," she called out over her shoulder, nearly colliding with Will when she resumed her exit from the office. "Oh, I do beg your pardon," she said, turning her aquamarine eyes onto the tall man who was staring through the glass of the charity's front door.

Will tore his attention from the men who had just entered the charity and stared at the woman who appeared in the later stages of breeding. "Lady Elizabeth?" he murmured, his brows furrowed in doubtful recognition.

Elizabeth Carlington Bennett-Jones, Viscountess Bostwick, returned the stare, finally blinking when she realized the identity of the rather handsome man who stood before her. Darkly tanned and sporting long hair pulled back into a queue, he looked entirely out of place in Oxford Street. "Bellingham?" she cried as she extended a gloved hand. "Oh, my, I almost didn't recognize you," the viscountess said as she openly examined the man who stood before her.

"Nor I you," the earl countered, his face splitting into a huge grin. "You look..." Will stopped, his gaze sweeping over her fashionable pelisse and hat, stopping for a moment on the protrusion that had her pelisse opening just below the buttons on the bodice.

"Fat, I know," Elizabeth said with a roll of her eyes. "By this time next month, I won't be, though," she added with a happy grin. "When did you return? I've heard nothing!"

"Just a couple of days ago, in fact. Is this charity yours, by any chance?" he asked waving to the shingle above Elizabeth's head.

She gave a nod and seemed to grow several inches taller. "It is, indeed. The result of a rather odd situation I found myself in because of a rather uncharitable old biddy," she added, implying there was a story behind the charity's beginnings. "There are times I think I must have been *mad*, but the rewards have been well worth it."

Will grinned at how much Elizabeth Carlington had changed since he last saw her. She hadn't yet had her comeout back then, but she was ever-present at her parents' annual soirées and the garden parties offered by other aristocrats during the early summer months.

"I cannot help but wonder if any of the men under my command might have made their way to your endeavor," he said with a furrowed brow. "Although the *Greenwich* didn't have to fire her canons very often, nor did we take fire as others who were not so lucky, I still had some injured crewmen."

Elizabeth shook her head. "I don't recall anyone mentioning having served on that particular ship," she replied. "But then, I no longer have the opportunity to read every application that comes in."

The comment had Will realizing there were probably hundreds of wounded soldiers seeking assistance. "I rather imagine there are far more than you are able to help," Will suggested sadly.

Elizabeth gave the comment some consideration. "True, but we do our best. Not everyone is employable, either, but we help those we can." She paused, wondering why the marquess' son was outside her charity's office. "Were *you* about to go in?" she asked, concern apparent on her face.

Will allowed a chuckle when he realized she might have thought he was wounded. "Next door," he replied as he motioned to the office of Andrew S. Barton, Esquire. At Elizabeth's suddenly arched brow, he added, "I'm in search of some information I think he may know." He paused a moment when a thought struck him. "Did you... were you an acquaintance of Lady Barbara Higgins, by any chance?"

The viscountess angled her head, wondering at the earl's query. "She was a few years ahead of me at Warwick's," she replied, referring to the grammar and finishing school some of the daughters of the aristocracy attended in London. "But now that you mention it, I have not seen Lady Barbara in... *years*," she said, her voice nearly a whisper. "Nor her father, come to think of it."

"Brothers?" Will prodded, realizing either one of them might still be in London.

Elizabeth shook her head. "Somewhere in Staffordshire, I imagine," she replied with a shrug. "Some families haven't yet returned to London for the Season."

Will nodded, realizing the entire family may have taken their leave of London and moved to the seat of the Greenley earldom. If the butler's news was true, they were no doubt dodging the bill collectors. "I've taken entirely too much of your time, my lady," he said as he reached for her gloved hand and brushed his lips over the back of it.

"Nonsense. And now that I know you've returned, I'll be sure to have George make your acquaintance."

Will blinked. "George?" he said with a frown.

Elizabeth grinned as a hand moved to rest on the evidence of her impending motherhood. "George Bennett-Jones, Viscount Bostwick," she said proudly. "The best thing I've done in my entire life was propose to him," she said before her eyes widened, as if she had just then realized to what she had admitted. "And if I hear that bit of gossip from anyone else, Will Slater, I shall know who to scold at the next ball," she warned with an arched brow.

His eyes widening at the surprising news, Will shook his head and assured her he would tell no one. "And if you see someone at a ball who looks exactly like me but isn't me, be assured your eyesight is fine. I've brought my brother with me to London."

It was Elizabeth's turn to blink. "But, you haven't *got* a brother. Have you?" she responded, her own eyes suddenly widening.

"Yes, as a matter of fact, I do. He was born on the wrong side of the blanket, but bastard or not, he's the best brother a man could hope to have," he claimed in a low voice. "Perhaps you can rescue him at a ball if he seems a bit lost at sea," he hinted.

Elizabeth beamed. "I shall look forward to it. Now, I really must go, or George will send out an army of footmen in search of me," she said as she angled her head. She dropped a decent curtsy, despite her belly.

Will bowed and watched as the viscountess hurried to a waiting town coach, the Bostwick crest painted in bright gold on the door. *Damn, she looks happy,* he thought as he watched the coach merge into traffic and disappear down Oxford Street. Taking a deep breath, he turned back to face the door to the solicitor's office and let himself in.

"If you're here about the leak in the roof..." The solicitor looked up from a stack of papers on his desk and regarded Will for a moment, his gaze taking in the earl's expensive top coat and polished boots. "Pardon. I've been expecting a repairman most of the morning."

Will took note of a pair of crutches leaning against the end of the man's desk. "Please, don't get up on my account. I've just come for some information you may know."

Andrew Barton regarded the young man who stood before him and realized two things: The man had served in either the army or the navy, and he was probably in search of a woman.

What *was* it with the men who visited his office these days? Why, just the week before, he had spoken with Randall Roderick, Marquess of Reading, as to the particulars of one Constance Fitzwilliam, who was in London to discover the whereabouts of her inheritance. Apparently the marquess had been successful in his quest to find and marry the gel—the notice of their marriage had been in *The Times* only the day before. The marriage had saved Barton from having to send out an investigator in search of a supposedly stolen inheritance. Thank the gods Lord Norwick, her cousin, had stepped in and provided her the supposedly missing funds.

Barton had far more important matters to see to than chasing down wayward bank accounts and women.

He had half a mind to open a locator service so that men might more easily find the women they had somehow lost along the way. He could name it *Find Her, Keep Her,* he thought with a grin, deciding if a man was stupid enough to lose a woman after finding her, then *lose her, weep for her* would be their lot in life.

He wasn't about to repeat the process.

"What's her name?" Barton asked as he motioned for the young man to take the chair in front of his desk. Not, "What's *your* name?" which would be of no help if he didn't know the identity of the chit in question.

Will couldn't help the flush of color he felt on his neck and cheeks. At least his cravat would cover the worst of it. "Lady Barbara Higgins. The Earl of Greenley's daughter," Will stated evenly.

Barton kept an impassive expression on his face as he considered the name. "And when was the last time you saw her?" he asked, rather more curious than he expected to be. He hadn't heard Barbara Higgins' name mentioned in...

"Eight years, sir. The night before I reported for duty on the *HMS Drake*." He didn't add that he had asked after her when he had returned to town for his mother's funeral a few years ago. His leave had been far too short to attempt contact, especially when someone mentioned that her family was at their country estate.

Navy, then. Definitely an officer from the looks of his clothes, Barton figured.

"Letters?"

Will blinked. "A few. And then... nothing. I've been told mine might have been burned before they could reach her ladyship. The butler at Pendleton House recommended I call on you, by the way."

Barton resisted the urge to groan. The servant was probably the only other man in town who knew he *had* been the Earl of Greenley's man of business. At least, he had been until the earl's sudden decline in wealth left him unable to pay Barton—and the gambling debts that might one day force the Crown to take back the earldom.

"The last I knew, she was occupying a cottage near a village in Oxfordshire. Broadwell. It's very near to Ellsworth's summer home, although I do not believe he still holds title to that property."

Will's first thought was of sheep and a barony somewhere

near there. And then he realized Ellsworth's summer home must be adjacent to the Earl of Gisborn's lands. "How far from Gisborn, do you suppose? From Bampton?" he asked. "I only ask because Gisborn is my brother by marriage."

Andrew Barton straightened in his chair, blinking as he considered the identity of the young man who sat before him. "Devonville?" he said with some alarm.

Will shook his head. "Not yet, and hopefully not in my lifetime. Bellingham." At the solicitor's look of confusion, he added, "My father has married a younger woman who seems to have youthened him," he whispered with an arched eyebrow. "Good thing, too, since I'm not looking to inherit a marquessate anytime soon."

The solicitor nodded, not sure how to respond. But the thought that he was interested enough in Lady Barbara's fate to pay a call not only at Pendleton House but to follow up with him had Barton deciding he wished to help the earl.

"I have not been in contact with Lady Barbara for over a year. I used to..." At this, he paused, realizing that if he said more, he would be divulging that he had been secretly sending funds to Barbara—funds he had skimmed from the Greenley earldom.

"Please know that any information you provide will be kept in the strictest confidence, Mr. Barton."

The solicitor angled his head, suddenly suspicious of the young man's motives. Perhaps he was looking for Lady Barbara in an attempt to use her to collect a debt owed by her father. "What are your intentions toward the lady?" he asked then, a hint of anger coloring his words.

Despite the change in the solicitor, Will allowed a lopsided grin. "I intend to marry her, of course," he claimed happily. He sobered, though. "But first, I have to find her."

Andrew Barton let out the breath he didn't know he had been holding. "Well, then, I suppose I had better draw you a map," he murmured, pushing aside the pile of papers in front of him to place a sheet of blank parchment onto his blotter.

"Just give me the directions, if you would," Will said.

"I've been a commander of a British naval vessel for the past six years. I do believe I'm capable of following verbal directions."

The solicitor regarded him for a moment, sketching a simple map. "You may be able to navigate, my lord, but I cannot unless I have the particulars before me," Barton said with a smirk. He continued to draw a crude map showing the position of a cottage, the village of Broadwell and the road leading to it from a bridge over the River Isis. "That's Tadpole Bridge," Barton said as he pointed to the drawing. Will nodded his understanding. He could use the same map to find his sister's home.

When Will Slater took his leave of the solicitor's office, he knew exactly where he could find the cottage in which Lady Barbara had been sequestered since she had left London.

Now he had to hope she could still be found there.

CHAPTER 8

A STEPMOTHER EXPLAINS A FEW THINGS

M *eanwhile, in Bond Street*

"Mr. Garth mentioned his wife is a Grandby," Stephen said as a way of introducing what he hoped would be a simple conversation with Lady Devonville about marriages involving members of the *ton* and those on the fringes of Society.

Cherice's eyes widened as she tore her attention away from the town coach window and put it squarely on Stephen. "Did he now?" she replied, straightening in the squabs. After an hour of standing on a box at Madame Suzanne's surrounded by three seamstresses, she winced at the pain she felt at the sudden movement.

"Are you ill, my lady?" Stephen asked in alarm as he leaned forward to take one of her gloved hands. Although he had expected they would visit several shops besides the modiste's where he had found her dressed in an elaborate ballgown, Cherice claimed she was finished with her shopping and wished to go home. Rather relieved he wouldn't be expected to spend the entire afternoon shopping with the marchioness, Stephen had simply nodded and taken a seat in a comfortable chair obviously provided for the benefit of men such as he—those who acted as escorts for ladies intent on shopping until they dropped.

Lady Devonville had definitely dropped.

"I'll be fine. I had forgotten how difficult it is to stand still for so long in dance slippers," she said as she indicated the pasteboard box positioned next to her on the squabs.

"Did Madame Suzanne finish your ball gown?" he asked, realizing just then he hadn't been asked to carry more than the box of slippers. His own boxes from the tailor's shop were larger and heavier than hers.

Cherice shook her head. "The hem will take a day, perhaps two," she replied. "But she claims it will be done and delivered in time for Lord Weatherstone's ball."

Stephen nodded, wondering how he could steer the conversation back to the tailor and his wife. "Mrs. Garth probably never has to leave her home to be fitted for a gown," he hedged, pretending to be interested in the shops they passed.

"Just what is it you wish to know about Rebecca Garth?" Cherice asked then, her manner perhaps more sober than usual given her discomfort. *Goodness!* If she was this sore after just one hour of standing on a box, how would she feel at the end of tonight's soirée? She couldn't spend the entire evening in the ladies' retiring room!

Angling his head to one side, Stephen realized he wasn't as comfortable discussing his situation as he had been with the tailor. "How is it she came to love a tailor? Enough to... want to marry him given her station in life?"

Cherice suppressed the gasp she nearly allowed, stunned by Stephen's forthright question. "Well," she replied, readjusting her position in the squabs. "Mr. Garth was certainly chattier than usual, it seems."

Stephen shook his head. "I may have encouraged him to speak more than he would have," he said in the man's defense. "It's just..." He paused and took a breath. "We are similar in our positions with respect to Society—"

"Hardly," Cherice interrupted, her head shaking from side to side. "Your father has recognized you as his own. You're free to move about in polite Society as you wish. Mr.

Garth..." Here, Cherice paused before shaking her head. "Mr. Garth is a *tailor*. Even a marriage to an earl's daughter cannot elevate him."

"But it's certainly affected *her*," Stephen countered.

His stepmother turned her attention to the window again, her lips pursed as if she had bit into a lemon. "Yes, it has. But Rebecca Grandby was never going to be a proper lady," she murmured.

"Why ever not?"

Cherice finally turned her attention back to Stephen, realizing the young man would begin asking others about her friend if she didn't tell him what he wanted to know. The last thing she wanted was for Rebecca to suffer from renewed gossip about her proclivities. "She was never a demure, proper young lady, that Rebecca," she said with a shake of her head. "Which is why some of us liked her so much and others found her behavior... intolerable." When Stephen still regarded her with an arched eyebrow, Cherice lowered her voice. "She enjoyed certain *activities* she shouldn't have had any knowledge of before she was married. Or even after, probably. With... men who were willing to be..." Here she stopped and swallowed. "Mr. Garth was the first man to... meet her demands and make his own. He sees to it she is *happy*. He worships her as much or more as she does him. And he makes her beautiful clothes, some she can even wear in public."

Stephen blinked, trying to imagine the tailor with a strong-willed woman, a domineering woman, a woman intent on causing as much pleasure as she did pain. He wondered if Jeffrey Garth had seen something in the woman no one else had—a tigress looking to be tamed, a tigress he knew he would have to occasionally allow out of her cage to scratch and claw. A tigress he would have to recapture in his net so that he might remind her of the power he held over her.

Although he had heard tales of women who wielded

riding crops in their bedchambers, Stephen had never shared a bed with one, nor did he wish to now. "I shall be sure to look to marry a young lady who is demure," he murmured.

Cherice allowed a huff as she regarded him with a shake of her head. "If you wish to be happy in your marriage, you may want to seek a woman who is not so very demure," she replied with an arched eyebrow. "Else you may find yourself a frequent visitor at Mrs. Gibbons' establishment."

Stephen frowned at his stepmother's comment, not exactly sure who Mrs. Gibbons was but pretty sure he understood the nature of her establishment. "Do you have a recommendation?" he asked, thinking perhaps Lady Devonville had someone in mind to be his wife.

Shaking her head, Cherice sighed. "You must choose. But do so only after you've courted her enough to know her character. And her mother's. To know if you two will suit."

His eyes darting to one side, Stephen wondered if she meant he should suit the daughter or if she meant the mother.

"Both," she said in a hoarse whisper, as if she could read his mind. "There's nothing worse than an overbearing mother to cast a poor light on a daughter of marriageable age."

Nodding, Stephen thought perhaps Cherice Dubois' mother had been just such a mother. He doubted his own would behave that way if she'd had a daughter. "Anything else I should consider? Anything else I should do?" he asked, figuring he may as well hear everything Lady Devonville had to offer.

Cherice arched an eyebrow as she considered his question. "For God's sake, be sure to kiss her at least twice before you ask for her hand." At Stephen's suddenly widened eyes—Cherice was quite sure she had shocked the poor man—she added, "There are those who claim it is the most intimate act you can do with a woman, but at least you will know if you'll be welcome in her bed."

Nodding, Stephen considered her words. "I'll remember,"

he replied, rather glad when he realized they had just pulled into the half-circle drive in front of Devonville House. Another minute in Cherice Dubois Slater's company, and he would be forced to pay a call at Mrs. Gibbons' establishment that very afternoon.

CHAPTER 9

THE FIRST SOIRÉE

*L*ater that night at the Duke of Huntington's townhouse Will Slater, Earl of Bellingham, stood on the landing at the top of the stairs leading down to the ballroom in Lord Huntington's impressive townhouse, his heart racing. It wasn't as if he had never attended a soirée before, but for some reason, he suddenly felt entirely out of his element. Entirely foreign to the festivities that had apparently already begun below. Entirely ill at ease.

"Are you all right?" Stephen asked from where he stood a few feet away on the landing. "You look as if you're about to be sick." Even during the worst storms at sea, Stephen had never seen his brother looks so green around the gills.

Will glanced over at his half-brother, startled to find him looking more confident and far more excited about that evening's soirée than any bastard son had any right to. "You look as if you're *happy* to be here," he accused, tugging on his topcoat for at least the tenth time that night. Everything felt smaller, tighter, more oppressive than his naval uniform. At least he was wearing a scarlet waistcoat, although now that he could see what the other men in attendance were wearing, he realized he should have chosen a more embellished option featuring more embroidery, or more metallic threads, or more... *more.*

Or he could have simply worn his uniform. He was allowed, of course, although since he had already resigned from the British Navy, he didn't think it appropriate to wear the uniform.

Now he wished he had.

He glanced over at Stephen's ensemble, frowning when he realized the man was wearing the very waistcoat he should have been wearing. One with a good deal of embroidery worked with metallic thread. One that fit him as if it were made by Weston. Even his dance shoes were more appropriate. Black, with silver buckles.

Will was about to suggest they trade waistcoats when the butler announced them from where he stood off to the side. "William Slater the Third, Earl of Bellingham, and Mister Stephen Slater."

Too late, he realized. Will nodded to the room below, as did Stephen, and they began their descent. He was aware of a number of *lorgnettes* being lifted to noses, of the slight pause in conversation, of eyes rising to regard them as they made their way down the stairs.

"Trade with me."

The words were out of this mouth before Will could think of the repercussions.

"What did you say?" Stephen replied, his eyes occasionally darting to the steps below his feet. *Goodness! How many were there?*

"Be the Earl of Bellingham," Will replied quickly, his face kept impassive as he continued his descent.

Stephen blinked and resisted the urge to halt his descent. "And who will *you* be?" Stephen countered, daring a quick glance at his brother.

"You," Will answered. They reached the ballroom floor in another three steps. Realizing Stephen was staring in his direction, Will responded to a comment made to him by David Carlington, Marquess of Morganfield, before waving a hand in Stephen's direction. He made his first introduction to the Carlingtons. "Lady Morganfield. Lord Morganfield. So very good meet you. I am Stephen Slater," Will said as he bowed before the Marquess and Marchioness of Morganfield.

Stephen stared at his brother in horror. *What the hell?* His brother hadn't been joking when he made the suggestion they trade places! He turned to find a bevy of young ladies rushing up with their mothers to meet him, and suddenly, all he could think about was how easy it was to say he was 'Bellingham.'

Too easy.

He dared another quick glance in his brother's direction along with an arched eyebrow. "You owe me," he said in a hoarse whisper when Will was close enough to hear him.

"By the end of the night, you may feel otherwise, my lord."

Stephen blinked and regarded his brother with a hesitant grin before moving to the next woman in line to meet him.

CHAPTER 10

A FATHER AND SON DISCUSS
A WOMAN

The next day
The Marquess of Devonville regarded his oldest son as Will stood in front of the desk in the study, his hands clasped behind his back and looking as if he were the newest member of a ship's crew. "You look as if you're the bearer of very bad news," William stated with a hint of worry. He turned in his leather chair and pulled a bottle of scotch and two tumblers onto the desktop. He nodded toward the chair facing the desk. "Take a seat before you fall down, son," he said as he poured the liquor.

Will did as he was told, his hands moving to rest on his knees, then his thighs, then back to his knees. When his father placed the tumbler of scotch at the edge of the desk, he resisted the urge to simply down the entire contents in a single gulp. "I find I am in need of some advice," Will finally said, lifting the glass to match his father's move.

William Slater arched a graying eyebrow, trying but failing to hide a hint of amusement. "Is this about Lady Barbara, perchance?"

Nodding, Will sighed. "Yes, of course."

The marquess blinked and leaned forward in his chair, his forearms settling onto the blotter. "You still haven't found

Greenley's daughter?" he asked, his expression giving away his concern.

"No. I... I wondered if you might have asked any of your associates where she is living these days? During the soirée," Will half-asked, hoping his father would have some insights as to why Barbara had left London.

William shook his head. "Truth be told, I haven't spoken with anyone about Lady Barbara. I wasn't sure you wanted me to," he amended. "Do I need to make some inquiries? If I do—"

His son shook his head. "The night before I left, we made promises to one another. We exchanged letters for a time, and then.... I heard *nothing* from her. After a visit with the butler at Pendleton House yesterday, I have reason to believe my letters were never forwarded to her ladyship."

William frowned. "And why not?" he prodded.

Will shook his head. "The butler could only say that Lady Barbara and her father were estranged, that she had moved out of Pendleton House years ago. If you know anything, anything at all about what happened, pray tell me now," Will begged.

Straightening in his chair, the marquess regarded Will for a time before shaking his head. "As I said, I've heard nothing. I can't imagine she just left London unless she married or..." At the sight of Will's wince, his father paused. "Did you... *ruin* her?"

His eyes on the carpet beneath his boots, Will nodded. "I did. That last night before I left London—"

"Will," the marquess whispered. "How could you?" he asked hoarsely.

"She came to me. To my apartments. Wanted to ensure she was the last thing I thought of as I left, I suppose. I often wondered if she thought to change my mind about serving on a ship."

"You could have been assigned at Whitehall," William interrupted. "As an heir, it would have been the more responsible thing to do," he added with a huff.

"You and I both know I wasn't going to do my duty behind a desk," Will retorted, ducking his head when he realized arguing now was pointless. He had already served far longer than he originally intended—he had thought to be gone no longer than five years—and he had already proven himself to those at the War Office who might have thought it wrong for the heir to a marquessate to serve in the military. But without a younger brother—a spare heir—Will figured it fell on him to do his duty to King and Country by serving in the Navy. Had the yearning to marry and start a family not come upon him during his last year on the *Greenwich*, he might have followed in his grandfather's footsteps and stayed in the Navy far longer. He might have one day been an admiral like his grandfather.

But thoughts of Barbara had haunted his dreams. Thoughts of Barbara carrying his child had consumed his waking hours. Thoughts of their children playing on the back lawns of Devonville House had him yearning for a life in London, a life with his family in the country during the summer months.

The marquess stayed silent while he watched his son ruminate on whatever had him seeking his advice. He had heard the rumors of Greenley's insolvency. Heard the earl might end up in debtor's prison as a result of excessive gambling debts. The man had already lost his countess—she had died after childbirth, although some claimed she died of a broken heart when the baby was stillborn. "You mentioned you paid a call at Pendleton House?" he asked in a quiet voice.

Will nodded. "Yesterday. After we spoke. The butler suggested I see the solicitor, Mr. Barton in Oxford Street, which I did. He... His news was not good," Will said quietly.

"Is she married?" his father asked, deciding learning Barbara was married would be the worst news. That she had died would be the absolute worst.

"Not that anyone knows," Will replied with a shake of

his head. "Mr. Barton suggested she was living in a cottage in Oxfordshire."

At this, the marquess raised his head and angled it to one side. "Oxfordshire. Where abouts? Perhaps your brother-in-law knows something," he murmured. "Not that he knows everything that happens in Oxfordshire, of course, but it's worth a letter. Or perhaps a trip, I should think," he added when he noticed Will's anxious expression.

At the suggestion of a trip, Will straightened in his chair. "I hoped you might agree. I have the basic directions on how to reach the cottage in which she was last known to reside," he said quickly. "With your permission, I'll take a horse and ride there..."

The marquess nodded his head. "Of course. But what of your brother? Do you intend to take him along? You two seemed to have formed quite a bond—"

"I need him to remain here. To act in my stead—"

"To pretend he is you?" William interrupted, one eyebrow arching nearly into his hairline.

Will's shoulders slumped. "You know about that?" he questioned sheepishly.

His father chuckled. "Wouldn't be the first time two brothers who looked alike tried to pull the wool over the eyes of the *ton*," he replied with a quirked lip.

His eyes showing a glimmer of humor, Will shook his head. "But you and Uncle Donald look nothing alike," he countered.

William blinked. "Oh, I wasn't referring to *me* when I made the comment," he said. "The Fitzwilliam twins come to mind, however," he added, referring to the late Earl of Norwick and the current earl, Daniel. He paused a moment. "Just be careful. Stephen thinks he is supposed to be finding you a wife, but it sounds as if you have already decided on a woman to fill that role."

Suppressing a grin, Will nodded. "I figure whoever he finds will make a fine wife for him, don't you suppose?"

William Slater gave a slight shake of his head. "Only if

he's inclined to take a wife. I do not believe he has yet decided on such a fate for himself."

Will considered his father's words. "I suppose not. But I have to admit, I rather like him doing my duty when it comes to attending Society events."

The marquess rolled his eyes. "Just be careful," he warned. "I shouldn't want you to end up betrothed to two women at the same time."

The oldest son blinked. And blinked again before a smile split his face. "Or him," he said with a chuckle.

The marquess sobered. "Or him," he agreed.

CHAPTER 11

TRADING PLACES

*L*ater that night

"You have got to be kidding me," Stephen said as he regarded his brother from the other side of the billiards table. He had just taken a shot that should have resulted in at least two balls falling into their pockets, but Will's comment had him nearly tearing the felt with his cue.

"Of course. And I apologize. I didn't mean for you to miss your shot," Will said when he realized his words had discombobulated Stephen more than he thought they might.

Ignoring the apology, Stephen frowned and moved to join Will, the game of billiards forgotten. "Just like that? You're leaving London, and you expect me to be *you?*" He had to admit, it had been rather fun to play his brother when those at the Duke of Huntington's soirée all thought he was the earl. He had been the happy subject of a series of congratulatory comments about his service to King and Country, about how handsome he had become, how he must be in the market for a wife now that he was back in London.

Well, that last comment had been a bit disconcerting, since he wasn't really in the market for a wife just yet, but he supposed it gave some of the mothers some hope.

But to have to pretend to be Will Slater for…"How long?" he asked, his brows furrowing. At some point, he had thought to ride to Kent to visit his mother. He had sent her a letter the day he arrived in London, but he hadn't seen her in an age.

"Just until I can find Barbara and get back here to London," Will replied with a shrug. "A week. Maybe two if I spend some time with our sister."

Stephen sighed, thinking of the events they had agreed to attend over the next week or so. "That means I go as you to the Weatherstone ball and the Torrington's *musicale* and the Morganfield soirée," he clarified.

"And a few others. I expect there will be more invitations for the week after next," Will said matter-of-factly.

Stephen shook his head. "What if... what if someone you know approaches me expecting me to know them?" he countered, not wanting to look like a fool should he be expected to know that someone.

"I've been gone for... well, I was back briefly for my mother's funeral, but I didn't stay long, and that was four years ago," Will replied as he gave his brother's query some consideration. "It stands to reason I wouldn't recognize some of my old friends. Just act... act like you finally recognize them when they introduce themselves, and you'll be fine."

Not entirely convinced, Stephen finally gave his brother a nod. "What about Father?"

Will angled his head. "He's a bit dubious about the plan, but he didn't forbid me from doing it," he replied. "I think he's more concerned about the number of broken hearts you'll leave in your wake," he teased.

Stephen rolled his eyes. "Me? *You'll* be the one doing that," he warned, deciding anything done in his brother's name would be Will's responsibility. When he realized his protests weren't having their desired effect, though, he finally sighed. "All right. But you owe me," he said in warning.

Grinning, Will leaned over the billiards table and set up his shot. "When you have every eligible debutante in London lining up for an introduction at Weatherstone's ball, you'll be thanking me," he said. He pulled back on the cue and took his shot, allowing a shout of satisfaction as two balls landed in pockets.

The two balls Stephen had intended to sink.

"Bastard," Stephen murmured. His eyes widened. "And since we're trading places, then you really are the bastard," he proclaimed with a huge grin.

Will straightened from the table and regarded his brother for a moment. "I suppose I am," he agreed.

CHAPTER 12

AN EARL HEADS TO OXFORDSHIRE

The following day

The ride to Hurley, the halfway point for his trip to Oxfordshire, didn't take as long as Will figured when he set out early in the morning. He had spent the night before at Brook's, arguing with himself as to the practicality of making a trip that might end poorly even while he made small talk with a few of the other gentlemen who weren't playing cards or who weren't already engaged in conversation with others. Very few recognized him, which boded well for Stephen, but Will felt lost when he recognized only a few, and those three had attended school with him at Eton.

A glass of brandy and a cheroot later, he took his leave and headed back to Devonville House to join Stephen for a game of billiards.

As for the trip, he had decided it would probably end poorly. If he kept his expectations low, at least he wouldn't be too disappointed if he couldn't find Barbara or if he found her already married to someone else. At least there was the promise of seeing his younger sister and meeting her husband for the first time.

And my nephew, he remembered, a grin forming as he packed some clothing into a saddlebag. He decided to plan to stay at least a week, making sure he had dress clothes appropriate for dinners at Gisborn Hall as well as those for his ride.

The word he had from Greenley's former solicitor suggested he would find what—or rather whom—he was looking for just outside of the hamlet of Broadwell. When Will asked Mr. Barton what might have happened to the letters he had sent to Barbara, the balding clerk sent his eyes skyward and then allowed a shrug. "I am sure I cannot say for certain," he replied. "But either her father burned them along with everything else with her name on it, or she has perished."

The words had Will wincing, but he knew they were said instead of others that would prove harder to hear.

Perhaps she accepted someone else's offer of marriage.

That would be harder to hear, he realized, his heart clenching at the thought of Barbara with another man.

Perhaps she had simply moved away and not left word as to her new location. What else could explain her lack of response to letters sent every month for nearly eight years?

Well, there had been a few at the start, Will remembered. Beautifully scripted missives written in her perfect penmanship, not a drop of errant ink to be found on the elegant parchment. The last one, still folded and stuffed into his waistcoat pocket, had been on courser paper, though, the ink showing signs of having bled into the grain and ruining her otherwise flawless lettering. It was still readable, though, and included words he lived for years hoping to experience first-hand.

I love you, Will Slater. Come back to England. Come back to me.

Well, if she was still living in the cottage Mr. Barton claimed was her residence, then Will would find her. With any luck, he would find her before nightfall the next day.

Although he hoped to make it farther on his first day, he spent the night at the *Olde Bell* in Hurley, the inn a halfway point between London and Oxford. Once he had seen to Thunderbolt's care, he enjoyed a filling supper. If Thunderbolt was as happy to run the following day as much as he had that day, then Will figured they would make it to Broad-well the following afternoon.

Saddle sore and anxious, he finally fell asleep when exhaustion proved too much, his last thoughts of Barbara.

CHAPTER 13

LADY JANE MEETS AN EARL ...
OR DOES SHE?

*M*eanwhile, at Lord Weatherstone's ball
"Oh, do stand up straight," Lady Pettigrew admonished her youngest niece.

At five-foot and nothing, Jane Browning regarded her aunt with a quelling glance. "Any straighter and I shall fall over backwards," she claimed *sotto voce*. Couldn't her aunt see that she had her shoulders pulled back as far as they would go? The sleeves of her ball gown would allow nothing else. It was as if they had been sewn on backwards, forcing her elbows into her sides and her shoulders in a direction they weren't supposed to go.

The viscountess sighed. With only one more niece to see married off this Season, she found herself hoping for a fall wedding for Jane. Should a willing suitor for her youngest niece present himself, she was tempted to offer him a good deal of money in addition to Jane's dowry if he agreed to a spring wedding. Anything to divest herself of her last unmarried niece!

So it was a rather pleasant surprise when the man she thought she recognized as the Earl of Bellingham appeared before Jane and asked if he could claim the next dance on her card! The earl might have been an earl in name only—she was sure he was the son of William Slater, Marquess of

Devonville—but at some point, he would inherit the marquessate.

A future marquess! The idea of Jane as a marchioness had her imagining a coronet atop her niece's coiffure, a town coach at her beck and call, credit at the very best shops, and not just one modiste, but several to make all the gowns that would be required for such a position.

Lady Eugenia Pettigrew watched Jane as the young woman angled her head to one side, the motion displaying her long neck and blonde ringlets to their best advantage.

At least the chit didn't remember the older woman's instruction about requiring an introduction before accepting the offer of a dance. Titled gentlemen were exempt from the rule as far as Lady Pettigrew was concerned. At this point, *all* gentlemen were exempt, she decided.

"Y ou can have your choice of several, my lord," Jane replied with a curtsy, holding out her wrist and a charcoal pencil in the direction of the apparent Earl of Bellingham.

Stephen regarded the lines on the dance card, finding most of them empty. *Goodness! This won't do*, he thought as he noticed the look of anticipation on the pretty girl's face. Although nervous, she seemed the typical aristocrat's daughter—blonde, blue-eyed, and put on display by a sponsor anxious to be rid of her in the Marriage Mart.

"This one, then," Stephen said as he waved away the charcoal and offered her his arm. He ignored the look of alarm that suddenly appeared on the viscountess' face in favor of noticing the young lady's blue eyes as they widened, the stunned expression indicating he had either made a huge mistake or that she was truly surprised by his offer of a dance.

Without a backward glance in her aunt's direction, Jane placed her hand on the handsome man's arm and allowed him to lead her to where the other couples were lining up for the next dance.

"I did not notice which dance this is," Stephen said as he glanced about. He watched as a man placed a hand at his partner's waist while he raised his other hand in midair. A second later, the woman had placed one of her gloved hands against the man's hand.

"The waltz, my lord," Jane replied with a curtsy.

Stephen stilled. "Until just a few days ago, I have been at sea for... eight years, my lady," he managed to get out, remembering to add two years to his own length of service since that's how many years Will had served in the British Navy. "And I have only seen the waltz performed whilst I was in Italy." *Or was that Austria?* When someone insisted he visit Vienna while on his leave from the *Greenwich?*

After so many years away from England and so many port cities around the Continent and Africa and along the South China Sea, he couldn't keep track of what city was where. "But I shall give it my all and try very hard not to step on your beautiful slippers," he added with a wink.

Jane grinned despite her nervousness, rather liking the man's playful manner. "It's a three-count dance, my lord," she said in delight. "And one I'm not usually allowed to dance." This last was said with such happiness, Stephen wondered why she wouldn't be allowed. Did the chit have any idea of how her face lit up with her comment? Of how truly happy she seemed at flaunting convention to dance a dance she was apparently not allowed to dance?

And who in the world had made such a ridiculous rule?

"Do you know how to do it?" he asked, a hint of panic making him think he may have made a mistake in choosing this particular dance to learn more about the pretty chit he had spied in the line up along the far wall of Lord Weatherstone's ballroom.

Given every young woman along that wall stood with a sour-faced chaperone, Stephen figured they were all wallflowers. And unmarried. Jane seemed to stand out from the others, however, her gown a beautiful ivory rather than the stark white most of the other young ladies wore. The color matched her pale blonde hair and seemed to make her blue eyes especially blue.

"Of course, my lord," Jane replied with a hint of mischief.

"Then let us show them their mistake, my lady," he countered, giving her his winningest smile. "I expect you to lead until I catch on." He was about to say her name and then realized they hadn't been introduced. "What shall I call you?"

Jane's eyes widened again before she smiled in return, a beautiful pink flush covering her features as she angled her head again. "Jane," she answered simply, deciding she didn't want to provide her full name just then. Since the young man was apparently newly returned to English shores, he wouldn't know of her older sisters' quests for husbands nor of her aunt's desperate attempts to marry them all off in two Seasons.

Or less.

And he didn't need to know. Her aunt may have wanted her married, but Jane had no intention of accepting any offers this year or next or maybe even never. Unlike most her age, she aspired to be a spinster. Unmarried ladies could do almost anything they wanted to—travel, attend social functions and even take lovers—without repercussions from Society. A far more suitable life than being married, Jane thought.

"And you?" she asked, hoping her waltz lessons with the French dance master, Monsieur Girard, would come back to her when the music started. At the moment, she didn't know if she would be able to tell her left foot from her right foot.

Stephen leaned toward her. "Stephen," he said in a low voice. "And it shall be our little secret," he added with a wink as the orchestra began playing.

Jane's eyes widened at hearing the name. She expected him to say "Bellingham" or maybe "William" given she had provided only her given name. But Stephen? *Must be one of his middle names*, she reasoned as she lifted one hand to his and placed the other on his shoulder.

Stephen wasn't really sure of what he was doing at first, but in studying how the other couples on the dance floor made their moves and by following Jane's initial strong lead —she had obviously taken his comment to heart—he was able to quickly copy the moves and was soon leading his enthusiastic partner in a dance that was most exhilarating.

"How is it I haven't seen you about in London?" Jane asked, not giving a whit that she didn't have a voucher to dance the waltz. If anyone admonished her, she would simply claim the Earl of Bellingham had requested the dance. What could they do to her? She rather doubted she would ever again attend an event at Almack's, and not just because the lemonade was tepid, or the lobster cakes were dry, or the ratafia tasted as if it were made with too much orgeat. She just wasn't going back there.

Ever.

Stephen allowed a quick glance at his dance partner, rather surprised she had enough confidence to address him. She seemed rather withdrawn when he had come across her as she stood with her chaperone near the wall of similar young ladies. "I just retired from the British Navy," he replied, deciding the truth would work in this situation. "I haven't been in London in an age." Which was true. And it wasn't necessary for her to know that he hadn't been raised as an aristocrat's son, even if it had been as close as one could get without actually being one.

Marie St. Claire might have been a courtesan, but by the time Stephen was out of short pants, she was married to a member of the gentry in Kent. Since he wasn't particularly wealthy—he died while Stephen was at Eton—and his mother hadn't taken a lover after his father and her ended their liaison, Stephen figured she had been left with a generous endowment. Remembering her frequent correspondence with Gregory Grandby, a man who apparently made the wealthy wealthier with his recommendations of how to invest their funds, Stephen realized his mother must have followed his advice.

Jane allowed a wan smile. "Such a shame, my lord. Your presence would have been most welcome earlier this spring. Probably any spring, for that matter." Hell, the man would have been worshipped at any ball had he simply stood on the dance floor and looked eligible.

Jane had to suppress the urge to grimace. Had she really just said what she thought she said? And out loud?

Stephen grinned, rather liking the bold comment of his dance partner. "Well, I was at Lord Huntington's soirée," he hedged, realizing she must not have been in attendance. He would have noticed her, even if she had hidden behind a potted palm.

Her eyes seemed to dim. "I rather wish I had been there as well," Jane replied. "But my aunt was not available to chaperone me."

Stephen gave a nod as he noticed an impending collision. "Is this your first year out?" he asked, managing to avoid Lord Sinclair and his partner as the man seemed to step on the poor lady's satin slipper.

Jane's face fell. She had hoped it wasn't obvious. "It is, my lord, but having three older sisters meant I simply had to wait my turn."

Three older sisters? Poor thing! Stephen felt relief when he realized she wasn't as young as she might have been. "Are you entertaining suitors then?" he asked, more because he was curious as to how she would respond than because he had any intention of joining them. This was a reconnaissance mission, after all. He was merely collecting the names to give to Will when he returned from his trip to Oxfordshire.

He still couldn't believe Will's comment that he intended to simply pick one and marry her based on his half-brother's recommendations—if Barbara Higgins couldn't be found.

How could a woman who had pledged herself to Will

simply disappear from London? Until she could be found, Stephen had to at least appear as if he were in the market for a wife on behalf of his brother. Although the two men were similar in many ways—not the least of which was appearance —they didn't share the same tastes in women.

At least, they hadn't in the past.

*J*ane nearly stumbled at the question. But, of course she was entertaining suitors! Isn't that what chits did when they were nineteen years old? It didn't mean she had to accept any offers, however. "I might," she said with a nod, her face coloring up even more than it already was due to the exertions required by the dance.

Despite his claim of not knowing how to waltz, the earl had taken over leading them in the dance and was proving to be a quick study. "Or will rather, should any make their intentions known," she corrected herself, once again secretly mortified she could say such a thing out loud when the earl deftly pulled her onto a slightly different path to avoid a collision with a another couple.

Goodness!

They had managed to avoid being trampled by Lord Sinclair, sideswiped by Lord and Lady Tuttle, and completely taken out of the dance by the left feet of Lord Brougham.

"Fair enough," Stephen replied, deftly avoiding another run-in with Lord Sinclair. Did the man have no sense of rhythm? No sense of direction? His poor partner's slippers would be ruined before the end of the dance!

Jane allowed a smile. "And you? How long have you been in England, my lord?"

*S*tephen rather liked the way her question sounded with its honorific attached.

My lord.

I could get used to this, he decided, wondering how far his brother had made it on that day's travel. "Not even a week, my lady," he answered, once again maneuvering them around a couple apparently intent on causing a collision. "Although we docked in Wapping, I had... responsibilities that required I stay on board until a few nights ago."

The strains of the music faded and Stephen slowed his movements until Jane stood before him, one gloved hand still gripped in his. He remembered to bow and watched as she curtsied. Not an awkward, jerky curtsy he had seen some women attempt to perform in the port cities in which the *Greenwich* had docked over the years, but one that displayed Jane's grace and poise. If William decided on her, Stephen thought she would make an acceptable marchioness. Her bold manner might even be a requirement for the position.

Aware he was warm—too warm given the superfine topcoat and embroidered waistcoat he wore—he kept her hand and moved her toward the already open doors that led out to a dimly lit garden.

The cool air and sudden quiet was such a relief, Stephen sighed audibly. "I apologize. I fear I am not yet comfortable in a crowded ballroom," he said quietly. "Nor am I used to the odors of colognes and perfumes." The odors aboard ship were certainly nothing pleasant, but those in the ballroom were positively cloying.

Jane glanced up at her escort, rather excited he would simply take her out of the ballroom without first checking with her aunt to make sure it was acceptable to do so. It wasn't, of course, but Jane didn't think her aunt would mind too much. The old woman seemed determined to rid herself of the responsibility of sponsoring Jane—the sooner, the better.

"Because it is such a large room?" Jane commented, thinking the rooms on a ship would be small. "Or because it's such a crush?"

Stephen angled his head, deciding she was perceptive. "Claustrophobic, in fact. That, and because it's rather crowded," Stephen replied with a nod. "And warm, and..." He paused, realizing too late the setting in which he found himself alone with a young lady unaccustomed to what he usually did with women in such a situation.

Just walk, he told himself, thinking there must be a garden path that would take them away from the house but circle back after a time. "Will you be missed?" he asked, hoping she wouldn't be scolded when she returned to her chaperone's side.

Jane had to suppress a snort. "I rather doubt it. My aunt is probably thrilled at the moment. She's no doubt imagining you kissing me and proposing marriage, and she probably already has the entire wedding planned..." She ceased speaking, her eyes clamping shut as she suddenly stopped walking.

Stephen stopped in his tracks and turned to regard the young woman on his arm. He allowed a chuckle as he noticed her other hand lift to her forehead. "Oh, my mother would be doing the same thing if she were here," he said with a lifted brow.

Jane opened one eye and regarded Stephen for a moment. "I apologize for my boldness, my lord," she managed to get out as she shook her head.

Stephen grinned. "No need to apologize, my lady," he countered. "But given the circumstances, would you be adverse to a kiss?" he asked, thinking she would deny him what he found he really wanted that very moment. *Goodness!* The chit was downright adorable! How could he resist at least asking for a kiss?

Jane blinked. And then she blinked again as she lifted her eyes to meet his. "Truly?" she replied, as if she were in awe.

Stephen stilled himself, realizing that not only would she allow a kiss should he bestow one on her, but she would welcome it! He glanced about in search of other couples. If he did kiss her, he didn't want anyone else to pay witness to it.

He didn't want to be accused of ruining the chit.

"Have you been kissed before?" he asked as he led them

to the other side of a hedgerow that provided a screen from the French doors of the ballroom.

Jane was stunned by the man's question. "Of course not," she replied with a shake of her head. "But should you be so inclined, I would not deny you," she said in a breathy whisper.

Stephen blinked. And then blinked again. *Christ!* Jane was suggesting that she was willing to have his kiss be her *first* kiss!

There was that moment when he thought to simply wrap an arm about her shoulders and pull her hard against his body, to capture her lips in a kiss that would leave her breathless and boneless and gasping in surprise. But he forced himself to consider all the options.

He didn't want her angry with him. He didn't want her claiming he had ruined her. He didn't want her fainting to the flagstones beneath their feet. "Really?" he responded, nearly kicking himself when he heard his lame reply. "Pardon me, I just..." He took a deep breath. "I am not accustomed to..." *Kissing.*

Well, it wasn't as if this would be *his* first kiss. It wouldn't be, of course, but it wasn't as if he had a good deal of experience in kissing young women, either. He had only ever kissed the daughter of a countess in Italy (and only because she had initiated it) and his mother, of course, but that had always been a peck on her cheek, and so it didn't really count.

"Young ladies claiming they would welcome your kiss?" Jane offered in a voice that suggested she was disappointed by her comment.

"Kissing in general," Stephen corrected. At Jane's widening eyes, he added, "Perhaps we could... learn together?" he suggested, completely forgetting he was vetting the young lady for his brother.

The poor girl might end up as his sister-in-law!

For the rest of their days, they would both know that they had stood in the Weatherstone gardens and practiced kissing under a quarter moon and a paper lantern.

Jane didn't give him an answer. At least, not verbally. She was suddenly pressed up against the front of his body, her head angled up just below his, her lips slightly parted and her eyes nearly closed. Stephen accepted the invitation, lowering his lips to hers until they locked into place.

He reveled in the feel of her pillow soft lips, in the light scent of lilac and lavender that reached his nose, in the barely audible moan he heard from her—*or is that me?* Although he didn't dare push his tongue between her lips, he was tempted to do so. He could not deny it. And he thought she would accept the assault.

Despite his attempt to prevent himself from doing so, he wrapped an arm around her waist and pulled her harder against the front of his body.

He expected she might protest, that she might put up her hands against his shoulders and push him away, but she did no such thing. She merely returned the kiss, angling her head so that she might better fit her lips to his.

Although he had never kissed like this—even the kiss with the count's daughter had ended quickly—Stephen realized he had better end this one. He could feel his loins tightening, and at any moment, his arousal would be quite evident behind the placket of his satin breeches.

Before he could end the kiss, though, Jane suddenly did at the sound of her name being called from behind the hedgerow.

"Thank you, my lord," she whispered before stepping back, giving him a curtsy, and then hurrying off.

Unsteady on his feet, Stephen stilled himself and struggled to breathe. He was tempted to hurry off after the chit, to ask for more information about where he might find her. She hadn't provided her family name, after all. Having such an enthusiastic partner in kissing, especially one so young, had him about to go after her. But he forced himself to remain where he was when he heard the voice of an older woman. "There you are. Have you been out here alone all this time?"

Stephen held his breath, wondering how Jane would

respond. Would she admit to having spent a few moments alone in the gardens with him? Would she claim she had been ruined by the Earl of Bellingham? Would she admit to having allowed a kiss behind the hedgerow?

Allow? he countered to himself. *She* had been the one to initiate the kiss, to press her petite body against his, her curves filling his voids as she lifted herself on tiptoes and kissed him senseless.

"I just needed some fresh air, Aunt Eugenia," he heard her respond, her voice light and sounding ever so happy. "The ball is such a crush, and it's a simply wonderful night, don't you agree?"

Well, at least his brother wouldn't be forced to offer for her hand, Stephen reasoned when he realized she wasn't going to tell her aunt about the kiss. But that thought had disappointment settling over him. If a wife were as agreeable as Jane, how could a marriage be so awful? *Would a wife such as her allow me such delectable kisses every day?* he wondered. *Allow such intimacy?*

He thought of Cherice Dubois' comments about kissing, rather glad she had encouraged him in that direction.

Stephen sighed and straightened his coats as he contemplated his return to the ballroom, deciding he would start his list of potential wives for Will with Lady Jane's name at the very top.

CHAPTER 14

LADY LUCIDA IS SAVED
FROM AN AMOROUS
POTTED PALM

*M*eanwhile...

Lady Lucida Fletcher watched as Lady Jane danced the waltz with the young man she had heard was the son of the Marquess of Devonville. *Home from the Navy*, someone had said. *Ever so charming*, another had said. *Not the least bit proud*, still another whispered. Which made her wonder how it could be the man was dancing the waltz with a chit who hadn't yet been granted a voucher to do so!

Lucida did her best to tamp down her jealousy. Why, if the Earl of Bellingham wanted to dance with her when the orchestra played the second waltz of the night—the last dance before the supper was to be served at midnight, she supposed—who was she to turn him down? If Lady Jersey should admonish her, so be it. Should the patronesses of Almack's decide she was no longer welcome at the dance hall on Wednesday nights, then she would simply accept another's invitation.

Her mother, Lady Margaret Fletcher, had arranged for the Almack's season subscription without having consulted her, after all. Had she done so, Lucida was quite sure she would have declined the offer. Although the dancing was quite invigorating and the gentlemen were rather good sports about dancing all night—what else could they do given there wasn't a card room?—the lemonade was tepid and the lobster cakes were, well, made of lobster, and hadn't she had quite enough of it in her lifetime?

Glancing about, she wondered as to the whereabouts of the Earl of Bellingham. Not only was he missing from the ballroom—so was Lady Jane!

Well. She allowed another sigh of disappointment. Lady Jane was no doubt enjoying a tryst with the randy earl in the gardens at that very moment!

But could she blame the poor girl?

Of course not!

Had the earl invited her for a turn about the gardens, she would have gladly joined him. Had he paused by the fountain and offered a kiss, she certainly wouldn't turn down the opportunity. It was past time she experience her first kiss.

Perhaps the earl would enjoy it enough to offer a second!

Oh, she could only hope.

Lucida rolled her eyes, rather doubting she would experience her second, let alone first kiss, at any time during the evening's entertainments. But, oh to be strolling with the earl in the gardens! Far better to be outside enjoying the greenery and the attentions of the earl than to be keeping company with the potted palm that seemed to have moved another step closer to her shoulder since the waltz began.

Lucida took a step to the left to avoid a palm frond that seemed determined to rest on her shoulder. Frowning, she wondered how long it had hovered there, ready to reach down and latch onto the tulle and satin sleeve of her white ball gown. Once it had attached itself, it would be nearly impossible to free her sleeve from its grip, the rough edges entwining themselves into the tulle so she might be forced to take a leaf home with her. Even as she regarded the tip of the frond, it seemed to sway in her direction as if it sensed she had moved away.

"It appears as if this palm tree has decided to claim the next dance with you. Perhaps you'll grant me the one after that?"

Lucida's eyes widened when she looked up to find the Earl of Bellingham looking down on her, mischief apparent in his hazel eyes.

For a moment, Lucida was left speechless. Obviously, the earl had paid witness to the palm moving in her direction just as she suspected it had done! Perhaps he had even seen its frond fondling her shoulder!

And now he had come to rescue her!

Would he challenge the potted plant to a duel, she wondered? For having impugned her honor by caressing her bare shoulder without her permission to do so? For nearly grabbing onto her sleeve so she would be forced to fight with the devilish frond until she would have to tear it from its leaf in order to escape? But, no, she realized as she remembered the rest of what he had said about accepting its offer of a dance.

Did he honestly think she would accept the offer of a dance from a potted palm? Why, she would be left doing all the work of leading the dance given the palm was quite secure in its Chinese pot!

And then she realized the earl was teasing her, his lips slowly spreading into a grin that made him appear far more handsome then he did when she had watched him dance the waltz with Lady Jane.

Her own lips soon matched his before she dipped a curtsy. "I actually gave the palm my apologies only a moment ago," she replied with a roll of her eyes. "He was being rather too friendly given we've never been properly introduced," she explained as she angled her head. "And now I fear he didn't take it well," she added, moving a few inches farther away from the insistent frond.

Stephen took the hint. "Stephen Slater," he said as he bowed over her extended hand and brushed a kiss over the back of her tight-fitting satin glove.

"Lady Lucida," she replied, realizing she had never introduced herself to a gentleman before. She usually had the company of her mother or another relative who took on the task of seeing to it she was properly introduced. "It's very good to make your acquaintance, my lord."

Stephen arched an eyebrow, noting the chit didn't provide more of a name to help him figure out who she was with respect to the others in attendance. Still in a mischievous mood, he held out a hand in the direction of the potted palm. "This is Fred, by the way. He's frightfully dull, I'm afraid, although I was of a mind to challenge him to a duel when I realized he was about to take liberties."

Lucida blinked. She could have kissed the earl right then and there.

"Pistols at dawn, do you suppose?" she asked as she gazed at the rather handsome man. No wonder he was the evening's most popular lord! She almost dared a glance beyond his shoulder to determine how many chits had their attentions directed to her, their faces green with envy. The longer she kept the man's attention, the greener their faces would become, she thought in delight. She rather wished he could dispatch the palm, though. She was sure the damned frond was once again inching closer to her sleeve!

"I rather doubt he could hold up a dueling pistol, let alone aim it," Stephen countered doubtfully, his attention on the offending palm tree.

Oh, my stars, Lucida thought in surprise. *He's flirting with me!* "Swords, then?" she suggested, one eyebrow arching up as she tried hard to suppress her growing amusement. *Hopefully one with a dull blade.* The palm deserved nothing less than to be badly shredded. To be separated from its stalk and its fronds split apart into dozens of frondlets.

Frondlets? Was there such a word?

Stephen shook his head. "I cannot believe that would be a very fair fight, my lady. Fred would end up in shreds all over the marble floor, and then some poor servant would be left cleaning up the mess." He paused before giving her a shake of his head. "No, I think I shall give him the cut direct and remove you from his influence." His bent arm appeared before Lucida. She blinked before she wound a gloved hand around it, rather surprised he wasn't seeing to the dismemberment of the offending plant. Didn't he know Fred would simply turn his attentions on another unsuspecting chit? *Well, it won't be me,* she thought with a sigh. She would never again stand anywhere near a potted palm in her entire life!

"Thank you for saving me from Fred, my lord. Had he accomplished his sinister plan, I would find myself ruined. Why, I would never be able to trust another potted plant for as long as I lived." *And I shan't. Fred is a such a rake, they must all be,* she thought.

*S*tephen allowed a chuckle, rather happy to know there was another chit at the ball who had a sense of humor and wasn't afraid to use it. "So glad I could be of assistance." He dared a glance in the direction of the dance floor to find a longways dance had commenced some time ago. It would be awkward to insert themselves into the proceedings now. "Perhaps we can take a turn about the gardens," he suggested. "Until the next dance," he added when he realized he would be no better than Fred in her estimation should they find themselves a dark alcove in which to engage in a bit of kissing. Probably beneath the fronds of some randy palm tree.

"Only if you keep the errant palm fronds at bay, my lord," Lucida replied happily as they made their way to the double-doors leading to the flagstone terrace.

About to assure her he would, Stephen noticed Lady Jane dancing with a man not much older than he was.

"What is it?" Lucida asked, pausing to follow Stephen's line of sight and feeling disappointed to find his attention on Lady Jane.

"Who is that man dancing with Lady Jane?"

The wave of jealousy was hard to tamp down, but Lucida did her best to keep her voice light. "My cousin, George," she replied matter-of-factly. When she realized the earl probably wouldn't be familiar with the viscount—the man had only held his title for two years—she added, "George Bennett-Jones. He is Viscount Bostwick now."

Stephen gave a nod, his brows furrowed. "He was rather free with his affections toward that auburn-haired woman next to the punch bowl," he remarked, having paid witness to the man kissing the woman on her cheek earlier that evening. Later, he had seen the man kiss her on the nape of her neck when he joined her for a conversation with Lord and Lady Morganfield.

Lucida relaxed, realizing his attention wasn't on Lady Jane at all. "That woman would be *Lady* Bostwick. She is Morganfield's daughter. You would remember her as—"

"Lady Elizabeth Carlington," he interrupted with a nod, recalling a conversation he'd had at the soirée. Some of what he had read in Will's copy of *Debrett's Peerage and Barontage* was beginning to make sense, although the edition he had worked so hard to learn was obviously out of date.

He resumed leading them out of the double-doors onto the terrace, his brows still furrowed. "Does she mind, do you suppose?" he asked after a time.

"Mind?" Lucida repeated, not sure of the earl's meaning.

"Being the subject of so much affection? In public, I mean," he clarified, his expression suggesting he was still bothered by what he had witnessed by the punch bowl.

Lucida allowed a grin then. "Lady Bostwick welcomes it, I am sure. I have never seen her admonish my cousin for displaying his affections, even if it's not acceptable for him to do so."

Stephen continued frowning. "Would you? Admonish your husband, I mean?" he asked. "Should he kiss you in public so that anyone might see?"

*R*ather startled by the question, Lucida took a moment to consider her answer. "I suppose it depends on how much affection I felt for him," she finally replied, still rather surprised by the topic of their conversation. "And how much he felt for me, of course." They walked along in silence for a moment, Stephen still rather deep in thought.

When he didn't reply, Lucida thought she might have said something he found disagreeable. "May I ask as to why you're wondering, my lord?" Lucida queried gently, finding the topic easier to speak about than the weather or the latest French fashions. Besides, the man seemed genuinely curious about her opinion, something she had never experienced with the other men she'd had occasion to speak with at Society events. She was rarely in London, after all, preferring the family's country estate in Sussex.

Stephen took in a deep breath, rather surprised at how fresh the air seemed despite the lack of rain for the past few days. "I admit to a bit of... curiosity... about the members of your sex. Especially when it comes to matters of affection."

Lucida was suddenly glad they were out-of-doors so her blush couldn't be easily seen under the paper lanterns that bobbed in the slight breeze. "The affection itself, or how it is displayed?" she countered carefully.

Pausing a moment, Stephen considered her query. "Would a woman dare display her affections? Like your cousin does?" When he noticed Lucida's look of puzzlement, he shook his head. "In public, I meant, of course," he amended.

"Well, probably not for just anyone to see," she replied quickly. "I rather think everyone would think her fast if she did." She paused a moment. "Although if someone noticed how she held her fan in a certain gentleman's direction, I suppose they would be able to discern her... affections."

S tephen blinked. *Held her fan?* He struggled to recall if his mother had ever mentioned fans whilst she explained the arts of seduction. "I do believe I have been away at sea far too long, my lady, for I do not know of what you speak."

Lucida felt a glimmer of hope at hearing the earl's admission. How much should she tell him? What could she demonstrate without making a fool of herself? Or him?

She lifted the closed fan that dangled from her wrist and held it up between them. "The way a lady holds her fan can inform a gentleman as to her situation. As to her... intentions," she said softly as she opened the fan.

Stephen angled his head, his brows furrowing as he regarded the fan. Even in the dim light, he could make out the painting that decorated the thin fabric covering the body of the fan. Several men and women in evening dress were standing about in what appeared to be a well-appointed parlor. "Perhaps you can demonstrate?" he suggested, silently cursing his mother for not having told him about ladies' fans.

Although she appeared shocked by his request, Lucida gave a nod. "If I am fanning myself slowly..." She opened the fan wider and held it beneath her face, flicking her wrist so the fan barely moved. "It means I am married."

"Are you?" Stephen asked, his eyes widening.

Lucida shook her head. "No, my lord. If I were, I assure you, I would not be wearing this hideous white ball gown."

Stephen frowned. "But your ball gown is quite beautiful."

Blinking, Lucida suddenly decided she would wear the very same gown at every ball for the rest of the Season. "Thank you, my lord. Now, if I fan myself very quickly, like this..." She flicked her wrist so the fan swept up a breeze that even Stephen could feel from where he stood. "It means I am betrothed."

Taking a step backward, Stephen's eyes widened. "You could have said something earlier, my lady," he said with a hint of disgust. "I would rather not be challenged to pistols at dawn, even if it is with a palm tree," he said with not the least bit of humor.

Lucida's mouth dropped open for only a moment before she realized he was teasing. "I assure you, I am not betrothed, my lord. And I was quite clear when I gave my answer to the potted palm."

Stephen shook his head. "Fred is probably all droopy with disappointment now," he murmured, moving so he stood closer to her.

"I rather doubt it," she countered. "He's probably already turned his affections on Lady Jane." The words were out of her mouth before she could censor them. Seeing the earl's sudden arched eyebrow, she lowered her fan to her side and glanced away.

"Are you angry with Fred?" Stephen asked, his manner rather sober. "Jealous, perhaps?"

"Of course not!" Lucida responded, her own manner suggesting she was irked by his comment.

"You're not jealous of Lady Jane, are you?"

The fan suddenly snapped shut. "No. Why would I be?"

Stephen moved another step closer. "She stole a palm tree from you," he whispered, one eyebrow arching up. "Fred, who spent a good deal of time in your company," he added, his manner still most serious.

"She cannot steal what was never mine," Lucida replied curtly. She half-opened the fan and pressed it to her lips, her sigh audible.

Stephen knew the signal for a kiss even if he had never learned fan-speak. He lifted a finger to her wrist and pulled it away, so her hand and the fan it held dropped to her waist. Stephen leaned over and pressed her lips with his until the pillows of her lips completely touched his. He knew immediately she had never been kissed before. She held her breath as if breathing would break the spell he had cast over her.

Gently suckling her lower lip, he placed one hand on her bare upper arm and did the same with his other. The palms of his hands gently tugged her closer to his body as his lips captured more of hers.

She tasted of champagne and strawberries and smelled like honeysuckle. Or perhaps they were merely standing near a honeysuckle bush. Stephen didn't know, nor did he care. He simply continued the kiss as if he were freely allowed the impropriety of kissing a debutante.

When Stephen finally pulled away, he didn't do so because Lucida pushed his shoulder, or because she made some sound of protest, or even because he needed to take a deep breath. He did so because he heard her name being called from somewhere far away.

Lucida stared at him, her eyes suddenly blinking as if she'd been awakened from a deep sleep. "What is it?" she whispered when she could finally figure out how to use her lips for something other than kissing.

Stephen had half a mind to tell her Fred was looking for her, but he gave her a quick grin. "I heard your name."

Faith! Lucida stilled herself. She'd had no idea kissing could be so... *pleasant.* So invigorating. So breathtaking and so very...

"Lucida!"

The sound of her mother calling her name suddenly had her gasping. "Forgive me," she managed to get out before giving Stephen a curtsy and hurrying off toward the ball-room, her fan dangling from her wrist as her hands scooped up the sides of her gown lest she trip on the skirts as she hurried away.

*S*tephen caught sight of a stockinged ankle as she made her way around the hedgerow and had to tamp down the reignited desire he felt for the young woman.

Forgive me?

He should be the one asking for forgiveness! *Faith!* He had been the one to pull her into that kiss. He had been the one to press his lips against hers and gently force them open with his own. The one to angle his head ever so slightly so his lips fit against hers. To suckle gently and then let go, only to recapture her lips again and again. And then he had been the one to make the kiss last far longer than any kiss should last.

He rather doubted he had ever kissed a woman for that length of time in his entire life! Why, his lips still tingled from their touch on hers!

He should be ashamed, he supposed, although he certainly didn't feel particularly ashamed. Even though he had been tempted to use his tongue to explore her teeth and mouth, he had resisted the urge in favor of simply tasting her lips. Of reveling in her light scent of honeysuckle and those from the greenery surrounding them. Of gently holding her steady within the circle of his arms.

Had Lady Lucida wanted to stop him from kissing her, she need only push him away or put voice to some kind of protest. Instead, she had simply moved closer so the fronts of their bodies touched, so she could lean against him as he continued to taste her. She had even hummed her apparent approval!

Taking a deep breath, Stephen considered how long he should stay behind the hedgerow. *A minute or more?* It might take that long for his arousal to subside, although if he continued to think about the damned kiss, he would be sporting the bulge in his breeches for the rest of the night!

Stephen turned around intending to find a stone bench on which he might sit while he waited when a figure suddenly appeared from beyond the end of the hedgerow.

"Good evening."

Stephen took a step back. "Good evening," he answered, uncertain as to whom he addressed as he couldn't make out the identity of the man in the dim light.

"I'm George."

"Stephen. Slater," he managed to get out, his voice far calmer than he felt. He extended his right hand and the man reached out and shook it.

"Nice evening for a walk. Or a secret assignation, perhaps?" George hinted.

Stephen nodded, wondering at the man's comment. "It is," he finally answered. Was this George the same George that Lucida had mentioned? Did the man think Stephen had taken liberties with his cousin? *Am I about to be challenged?* "I thought to get some air. The ballroom is a crush, and the palm trees seem intent on misbehaving," he managed to get out before he realized someone else was about to join them.

"Oh, George, I thought I would never be able to take my leave of Mother..."

The two gentleman turned their attention to the woman who suddenly appeared from around the end of the hedgerow, but George was quick to wrap an arm around her waist to ensure she didn't collide with Stephen. "Careful, my sweeting. We're not yet alone," George said in a lowered voice, his amusement apparent.

"Bellingham! Oh! I beg your pardon!"

Stephen recognized Elizabeth Carlington Bennett-Jones and realized this George was, indeed, George Bennett-Jones. He bowed and reached for Lady Bostwick's hand. "You needn't, my lady. I was just about to return to the house," he managed to get out. He gave George a nod. "Enjoy your secret assignation. I promise, I won't tell anyone you're out here," he added with a quirked brow.

George angled his head and allowed a grin. "Do take care with Lady Lucida, won't you? She is my favorite cousin, and although she favors the country, I shouldn't want to hear she's been ruined this evening."

Stephen stopped in his tracks and turned to regard the viscount with a wry smile. "If your cousin was ruined this evening, it was at the hands, or the fronds, rather, of a rather large, amorous potted palm named Fred. Good night."

George and Elizabeth both frowned as they watched the young man depart the hedgerow and head in the direction of the house. "Oh, and I was so hoping Lucida was out here being kissed by him," Elizabeth said with a sigh. "He is Devonville's son, although I'm not quite sure which one," she murmured. "I cannot tell the two apart."

George rolled his eyes, positive his cousin was being kissed by the son of a marquess.

But not the earl, William Slater.

Stephen Slater was the bastard.

When Elizabeth reached up and kissed him on the side of his neck, all thoughts of his cousin and the Slaters took their leave, and George concentrated on kissing his wife.

*R*eturning to the ballroom, Stephen slowly made his way to the opposite side of the room, intent on finding the refreshment table. He didn't really want to dance with anyone else—and rather doubting he would be allowed to dance again with Jane or to spend another moment with Lucida—Stephen decided to merely watch the proceedings as he pondered what to tell his brother. Jane was probably too young, and the viscount had said Lucida preferred the country.

And then it dawned on him.

What could he say to his brother? He didn't even know their last names!

Stephen had just decided he wouldn't mention them at all when he caught sight of a young woman entering the ballroom from the hallway. At first hidden behind a footman carrying a tray of champagne glasses, the chit deftly helped herself to one before stepping sideways. Her gaze seemed to take in the painted ceiling, the walls—everything but the people in the room. That is, until she spotted him.

Stephen gulped. Pale blonde hair, silver-gray eyes and a pink gown had him thinking he was seeing a rather young version of his mother. *She's gorgeous*, he thought, reminding himself to close his mouth.

Perhaps I will stay at the ball a bit longer, he decided as he helped himself to a glass of champagne and made his way toward the chit.

CHAPTER 15

WELCOME TO OXFORDSHIRE

The next morning
Awake when the first rays of light pierced his room, Will was the first to eat breakfast and take his leave of the inn at Hurley.

The thought of seeing Barbara Higgins again had his pulse increasing, his Hessian-clad heels digging deeper into the ribs of his mount. Although not a large horse—the warm blood wasn't a Thoroughbred but rather a pure-blooded Arabian from North Africa—Thunderbolt was fast. And he loved to run. Too bad the roads out of London had been too crowded for him to do so.

Now that Will could see the bell tower of Saints Peters and Paul church, its octagonal spire a testament to its Norman origins, he knew they were closer to their destination. Thunderbolt was enjoying a run down a country lane that, according to the last road sign Will had studied when they first crossed the River Isis, would lead them to the hamlet of Broadwell.

And her.

His heart raced faster, partly due to the exhilarating ride and partly because he was nervous. Whatever he discovered, he promised himself he wouldn't show anger or disappointment or sadness. He had been practicing his very best impassive expression the entire day, finding it was not so very different from the one he wore most days aboard ship.

Slowing his mount as he reached the village's only public house, William studied the shingle. *The Five Bells* was no doubt named for the bells that could be seen in the church's bell tower, although he hadn't heard any of them ring as he made his way to the town.

"Good afternoon," Will heard as he glanced around. His attention fell on a short man who had just come out of the public house.

"Afternoon," Will acknowledged with a nod, wincing as he dismounted. Although he had occasionally ridden a horse during his eight years in the Navy, he had never done so for two days straight. Thirsty and in need of information, he decided a few moments spent at *The Five Bells* could only help his disposition. "Is there a stable where I might find someone to tend to my horse?"

The man merely pointed farther down the road. A young boy was running toward him. "I can take him, mister!" the boy called out, managing a bow before he reached for the reins.

Will hesitated giving up his hold on Thunderbolt, thinking the horse would easily break free from such a young boy should he be spooked. But Will relaxed when he noticed how the boy had already fished a carrot from his pocket and allowed Thunderbolt to pluck the snack from his hand.

Reaching into his purse, Will tossed the boy a penny. "Where will you take him?" he asked, not seeing a stables along the dirt road.

"There," the boy pointed in the direction of an open building, more a barn than a stables.

"I'll be along shortly," Will said with a nod, deciding to watch to be sure Thunderbolt didn't try to escape the boy's lead. But he realized the boy must have had more treats hidden in his pockets, for Thunderbolt continued walking alongside the boy until they disappeared into the barn.

"He'll water him and brush him good," the short man

said as he regarded Will, his gaze taking in the quality cut of his clothes and his boots.

"Thank you," Will said as he turned to enter the public house. "Are you the proprietor?" he asked as he stepped up to the door.

"Just a customer," the man offered. "Miss Susan will see to an ale for you," he added as he set off toward a cluster of buildings.

The interior of *The Five Bells* reminded Will of many such taverns he had visited over his six-and-twenty years. Dark, until his eyes could adjust, it smelled of sour ale and baking bread and the sweat of working men. An older woman stood behind the bar in the taproom, her mobcap failing to keep her curly fuzz of hair covered.

"You look as if you could use an ale," she remarked as she pulled a glass mug from a shelf. "Something to eat?"

Will nodded. "Anything hot?" he asked as she set the mug of ale on the countertop.

"Meat pies. Just took some bread out of the oven, too," she replied. "Just passing through?"

The question reminded Will he didn't know exactly where he could find Barbara. "I'm in search of a woman—"

"Aren't ya' all?" Susan countered with an arched brow, her grin nearly toothless.

Will allowed a grin of his own. "Name's Barbara. Does she live somewhere near here?"

Susan angled her head to one side, as if she was trying to decide whether or not she would give him the information he sought. "Are you here to give her trouble? Poor girl doesn't need any more, if ya' are."

A look of alarm crossed Will's face. The woman must have recognized his concern, for she soon changed her manner. "She lives in a cottage just down the road past town. Right side. She just planted a garden, so don't be tramplin' through it. And she don't do tumbles, so don't be thinkin' ya' can bed her. She's got a gun, and she knows how to use it."

William blinked. And blinked again before he shook his

head. "I assure you, my lady, I have no intention of doing anything that would result in my getting shot," he said, wondering if they were discussing *his* Barbara.

She has a gun? And knows how to use it?

"Thinkin' of going there now?"

Will gave a shrug. "I hoped to," he acknowledged.

"Then you would be wise to bring some supper with you. God knows she could use some meat on them bones. The boy, too." She assembled several meat pies into a linen cloth and folded it.

Draining his ale, William regarded the wrapped meal and offered her a sovereign. "Anything else I should know?"

Susan gave the coin an appreciative look. "If you are lookin' for a tumble, Grace will be workin' later this evenin'," she replied, one brow arching up suggestively.

William didn't bother to suppress another grin. "Thanks." Gathering the linen-wrapped meal into the crook of one arm, he took his leave of *The Five Bells* and set out to retrieve his horse.

CHAPTER 16

A COMMONER CRASHES
A BALL

Back to the night before...
Victoria Comber's gaze followed the retreating back of the man she had just kissed, his unhurried steps taking him toward the rear entrance of Lord Weatherstone's garden. She was tempted to follow him, just to determine if he was actually leaving the ball for good or if he intended to circle around and re-enter the house through the front door.

Despite their earlier dance and conversation and their time in the gardens—or perhaps because of it—she found herself rather intrigued by the son of a marquess.

Lord Bellingham—she was quite sure he was the son of the Marquess of Devonville and held the courtesy title 'Earl of Bellingham'—had been a rather pleasant dance partner and an interesting person with whom to converse.

Entertaining, certainly not too serious, his introduction had been rather odd. Why had he referred to himself as 'Stephen Slater' as opposed to 'William Slater' or 'Will Slater' or simply 'Bellingham'? She would have expected him to say 'Bellingham' once she realized who he was.

She decided 'Stephen' was probably a middle name he preferred. At some point, she would have to consult her aunt's copy of *Debrett's Peerage and Barontage* to confirm her suspicion.

Now, if Stephen Slater had given any thought to her unexpected presence at the ball, he certainly didn't show it in his expression nor in his conversation. For the entire length of the English Country Dance, she was sure someone would recognize her, or at least realize that they *didn't* recognize her and call her out.

After all, she was there without an invitation.

And without a title.

She was the niece of an earl. That's as close a relation as she was to any member of the *ton*.

Having arrived after the receiving line dispersed, she was able to divest herself of her mantle and make her way to the ballroom without speaking a word to anyone. She simply merged into the thinning crowd of latecomers so her lack of a chaperone went unnoticed. Her satin and tulle gown, a soft pink that accentuated her pale blonde hair and porcelain skin, was daring in that it was a color other than white. She was unmarried, after all, and wearing a colored gown suggested she was a young matron.

She felt like it at times. *I'm almost three-and-twenty*, she thought with a sigh. *Some come-out.*

First ball since her arrival in London. No invitation. No chaperone.

What's the worst that could happen?

I could stumble down the stairs after being announced.

Well, she ensured *that* didn't happen by not going down the stairs. Which meant she wasn't announced.

Entering the ballroom without needing to be announced was her first true challenge.

If the Weatherstone mansion was like any other, there would be more than one way to get into the cavernous space. If she hadn't been wearing a mantle, she could have just entered through one of the French doors from the garden, but surely someone would have noticed her sneaking down the alley whilst dressed for a ball. And she wasn't sure if she would be able to keep her slippers from becoming soiled should she accidentally step into a puddle. Or some excrement from a horse. Leaving footprints on a gleaming ball-room floor wasn't her idea of making a grand entrance. There was also a servants' entrance, but getting to it would have proved as difficult to navigate as the alley.

Instead, she had simply arrived late and acted as if she belonged there, holding her head high and allowing a footman to assist her in removing her mantle. She had given him a nod and hurried along as if she knew exactly what she was doing.

Which she did not.

She had never crashed a *ton* ball before.

But, oh, how exhilarating this was to simply pretend she belonged there! If anyone asked her who she was, she decided she would simply tell them the truth. "Miss Comber," she would say. If they paused and looked the least bit confused, as if they were trying to determine to what family she might belong, she would add, "Aimsley is my uncle."

Which was true.

Her mother had married the youngest brother of Mark Comber, Earl of Aimsley. The youngest brother, who was also the black sheep of the family. The one who eschewed the aristocratic life he had been born to and removed himself entirely from it by relocating to Hertfordshire.

To take up farming.

But those at the ball didn't need to know that.

She shivered, wondering why anyone would give up a life that included such elegance, such decadence, such obvious wealth and privilege. But her father claimed he couldn't abide the lifestyle and simply had to give it up.

At least her mother was the daughter of gentry, although Victoria never understood why Alexandra Regan would give up her life in a comfortable manor house in Middlesex to marry a farmer.

"Surrounding yourself with beautiful things just makes you want more beautiful things," her mother tried to explain one afternoon. "But to what end? A house full of *things* isn't a home."

Victoria was pretty sure she could make a house full of things a home if she was given half a chance. Even a house half-full of things when she gave it some more thought.

At least her parents employed several servants to see to their household and some of the farming duties. And Alexandra had an excellent modiste in Madame Herbert, a flamboyant woman whose salon was filled with artfully arranged fabrics and notions. An entire afternoon could be spent just looking through her pattern books, another afternoon spent choosing the fabric and trims, and yet another spent being fitted for ensembles.

The pink gown Victoria now wore was one of Madame Herbert's creations, a rather pretty frock decorated with a ruffled tulle bodice and cap sleeves that angled off her bare shoulders. The deep ruffle at the bottom barely skimmed the floor. Paired with elbow-length white satin gloves and some earrings her Aunt Mildred had loaned her, the dinner gown was transformed into an acceptable ball gown. Victoria silently thanked Madam Herbert when she realized she didn't look as if she had just arrived from the country.

Which she had.

On the mail coach. Three days before.

Her brother had been her escort, seeing to it she was safely delivered to the residence of their aunt and uncle, Mildred and Anthony Regan, before Rufus headed to a men's club for an evening of gambling. He went on to Brighton the day after, claiming a need for surf and sand.

Although Victoria had never before met her much older Aunt Mildred, she was surprised to find the woman would have been a dead ringer for her mother, except that her hair was nearly completely gray. "Goodness, I do hope you have some entertainments in mind that don't require a chaperone," Mildred had said when she led Victoria to her bedchamber, a small but beautifully decorated corner room on the second story of their townhouse. "I gave up on the social niceties years ago. Still go to the theatre now and again with your uncle, although I go to actually *watch* the play."

Having never been to the theatre, Victoria wasn't sure what her aunt meant by the comment, but she figured she would find out. She intended to go the following evening with her aunt in tow. Since her uncle had left for Sussex the day before and would be gone for a fortnight, he wasn't available as an escort. But not having a chaperone for other events meant Victoria would have to be creative about how she arrived at events. About how she got there.

Given the traffic in Park Lane due to the Weatherstone's ball, the hackney that delivered her tonight had to stop nearly a street away. Undaunted, Victoria had stepped down from the equipage and simply hurried along until she caught up to a group of other similarly garbed ball goers and acted if she belonged with them.

Once she had divested herself of her mantle, she merely followed the others, most of whom turned into the ballroom where a butler announced their arrival. When she realized the man was actually calling out names and titles, she continued down the hall, passing several couples who appeared to be loitering near the door to the library.

When she noticed a footman carrying a tray of champagne glasses, she followed him as he passed through a door farther down the hall, and *voila!* Victoria was in the ballroom holding a glass of champagne and trying ever so hard to keep her mouth closed.

She didn't think she had ever been in a room with more lit candles. Or perhaps the house had been piped for natural gas—she had heard some in London were entirely gas-lit.

The chandeliers, and there were at least three of them, looked as if each could hold more than fifty candles. The sconces along the walls were all lit, as were the candle lamps decorating the refreshment table.

Once she had taken in all the lighting, her attention went back up to the moldings that decorated the circumference of the elaborately painted ceiling. Her gaze was drawn to the opposite corners of the room, where columns flanked the line of windows and French doors. The walls, papered in a pale mint, were probably meant to make the room seem larger, but at the moment, it was so crowded, Victoria thought it rather claustrophobic.

"A rather impressive ballroom, is it not?"

Victoria had to suppress the urge to gasp when she realized the question was directed to her. "It is," she agreed with a nod, her attention suddenly on the rather handsome young man who stood before her. "It's my first time," she blurted out, almost immediately regretting the comment.

"Mine, too."

Blinking, Victoria regarded the teasing visage and allowed a grin. "Do you honestly expect me to believe that?" she asked as she took in the young man's topcoat and elaborately embroidered waistcoat. His hair was cut short and framed a tanned face featuring a pair of hazel eyes that positively twinkled with mischief. The grin that displayed his perfectly pillowed lips only added to his amused expression.

Perfectly pillowed lips?

Victoria inhaled sharply at the thought, wondering how she could have thought such a thing. She didn't even know the identity of the bounder, and she was already sizing up his lips for...

Kissing!

Blinking, she regarded the man and then swallowed. *Is it my turn to speak?* Or was she waiting for him to respond to some nicety she had said?

Then she remembered her query.

Do you honestly expect me to believe that?

Well, it wasn't her best come-back, but then she hadn't but a moment to consider anything else. The man looked as if he attended *ton* events on a nightly basis—his casual manner and expensive clothing were a testament to it.

And now he was laughing. Chuckling, rather, obviously amused by her question.

Well, at least he wasn't an uptight bounder.

"I do, actually. I've been away from London for many

years," he replied with a nod before he gave her a bow and reached for her hand.

Not used to having the back of her hand kissed, Victoria watched in wonder as his perfectly pillowed lips brushed over the satin of her glove. For that brief instant, she rather wished she wasn't wearing gloves, or that her lips were where the back of her hand was located, for she could only think the kiss was wasted on the fabric.

I'll never wash that glove again!

"Stephen Slater," he said as he straightened. He suddenly glanced around. "I apologize. I probably should have waited for someone to introduce us, but—"

"No apology necessary... Mr. Slater," Victoria replied, her hesitancy due to his name. He didn't mention a title, although he looked as if he should have been at least a baron. *Slater. William Slater. Marquess of Devonville. Too young to be the marquess, which means he's the heir or the spare.* "Miss Victoria Comber," she added as she curtsied, wincing when she realized she hadn't practiced the move wearing the rather tight dance slippers she had borrowed for the night. "It's very good to meet you."

"*A*nd you," Stephen replied. "Comber, did you say? As in... the Earl of Aimsley?" he asked, racking his brain to remember the names of the sons and daughters of Mark Comber. *Andrew, Alistair...* For the life of him, he couldn't remember having seen the name 'Victoria' among the earl's progeny.

Victoria's eyes widened at hearing how quickly the young man associated her with her uncle. "Niece," she replied quickly, hoping he wouldn't determine she was a nobody when it came to the others in attendance.

"Ah," he replied, looking rather relieved. He glanced down at the hand he had just released the moment before. "Aren't you dancing this evening?" he asked, one hand indicating her lack of a card tied about her wrist.

Victoria lifted her hand, as if it had been slapped, and then noticed how a card dangled from the wrist of a young woman who stood near them. "I... I didn't receive a card," she replied with a shrug. "But I'll certainly grant you a dance should you want one." She held her breath when she realized he hadn't actually *asked* if she wanted to dance. "That is, if you wish to dance. With me," she added, suddenly more nervous than she had been when she entered the vestibule of the house.

Faith! She had come to the ball just to see what happened at such events, to look at the pretty gowns and admire the handsome men, and watch the dancing. She hadn't intended to be one of the ones actually doing the dancing!

When she dared a glance back up at Stephen, he was displaying that mischievous grin again as he lifted a hand. "You've made this ever so easy, Miss Comber," he said, waiting for Victoria to place a hand in his so that he could lead them to where lines of men and women were forming up for the fourth dance of the evening.

"I shouldn't wish it to be difficult," she countered, glancing to her left and right in an effort to determine what she should do next. She didn't even know which dance was scheduled!

Had she dared to enter the ballroom through the main doors, she supposed she would have been given a card, but she would have no doubt had to display an invitation and then been announced by the butler. When they discovered she didn't have an invitation, she was sure she would have been escorted back to the vestibule and asked to leave the premises, sans her mantle!

The possibility of such an embarrassing scenario had her suddenly wondering why she would dare try to attend the ball in the first place.

Curiosity, of course.

She remembered it now that she found herself in line with at least a dozen other young ladies facing a line of men who regarded them with varying degrees of interest. Another glance had her realizing she was the only one not wearing a white gown.

Criminy!

She wondered if Mr. Slater... *the son of the Marquess of Devonville* would have the courtesy title of 'Earl of Belling-ham'. *Bellingham!*

She wondered if Bellingham thought she was married. Or, God forbid, an old maid! Or, perhaps if what he said was true and this *was* his first ball, he wouldn't know the rule about debutantes wearing white.

She could only hope. Especially as she looked rather pink compared to the other young ladies flanking her.

In the meantime, the orchestra's tuning had ceased and they were suddenly playing "The Comical Fellow". Victoria wasn't quite sure what happened next, but she found herself performing the dance by rote, as if she was disconnected from her legs and arms, and they were off dancing without the rest of her. She was forced to follow, of course, but she was also able to watch her partner, who after a stutter-step start, seemed quite able to perform the contradance quite well.

His first ball, indeed.

Victoria found herself having a bit of fun, not caring a whit if her ankles went on display for a moment as she made the turns and twirls required of the dance.

"They're playing my song," Stephen said when he met her in the middle, just before they rotated around one another.

Victoria blinked and nearly lost her place in the dance. "Your song?" she repeated, forced to figure out if she knew the name of whatever it was the orchestra was playing at the moment.

"I am having a bit of fun is all," Stephen said when they met again. "I am actually a rather comical fellow."

Victoria could have kicked herself—and nearly did when

she realized she had taken a wrong turn and had to recover her place in the line—when she realized the name of the music being played. "Do not disappoint me now, my lord," she replied as she made her turn around him and then went off to the man on his left.

Stephen did his turn with the next young lady, rather amused by Victoria's comment. When he rejoined her in the middle, he said, "You don't think of me as a jester?"

Victoria grinned and rolled her eyes as she made her way to the next man. When she was once again moving around Stephen, she said, "Either that, or you are very adept at fibbing."

*S*tephen nearly stopped in his tracks.
Fibbing?
Did Miss Comber really think him more serious than a comical fellow? Truly, he wasn't a jester, although he knew he could entertain a crew of water-weary enlistees when required. He wasn't a joker, but he could trade barbs and jokes with the funniest of those who populated port city taverns. If any music suited him to a tee, then it was this music, he decided. "You wound me."

*V*ictoria nearly lost her place in the music as she comprehended his comment.
Wound him? She rather doubted her rebuke could wound a man. Unless he had developed a tendré for her, which she suddenly found a rather interesting turn of events. And one she rather hoped was the case.

Hadn't she been hoping she might be kissed by his perfect pillowed lips at some point during the evening's proceedings?

"If I have, I suppose I shall have to kiss it and make it better," she replied in a voice that suddenly sounded loud in her ears, especially since the music had just ended rather suddenly.

All the dancers stopped, the ones nearest her turning to stare in her direction when her words could be heard over the waning notes of the music.

Victoria felt the warmth of a blush rise up her throat and cover her face. She was quite sure she was as pink as the gown she wore.

Stephen stared at her a moment, his expression not indicating if he took the comment as a dare or if he was offended by her remark. But he realized immediately that her comment had been overheard and that he would be seeking restitution in the form of a kiss.

She had suggested it, after all. And who was he to turn down the opportunity to be kissed by a rather daring young woman dressed in pink but not otherwise looking as if she was anything like the other young matrons in attendance?

Stephen bowed to her curtsy and immediately moved to offer her his arm.

Her eyes wide, as if she realized his intentions and was suddenly having second thoughts, Victoria placed her hand on his arm and found herself being led toward the wide open French doors she had been admiring only moments before. Although the tight dance shoes pinched her feet, she managed to keep an impassive expression on her face in the event anyone turned to take notice of their sudden departure.

The cool air was as bracing as it was a relief when they were suddenly beyond the confines of the claustrophobic ballroom.

"Oh," she gasped as Stephen hurried her along the flagstone path that led to the garden lit with paper lanterns. He slowed his pace when they were beyond the lights of the ballroom.

"I apologize. I had to get you out of there," Stephen said as he turned to regard her. "I thought it best for your reputation that it look as if..." He paused, realizing his reason for removing her from the ballroom was as necessary as it was an excuse to discover if she was serious about kissing him. "We were... married," he finally managed to get out.

Victoria blinked, realizing the man had a point. How many people had heard her make that final comment? She must have sounded like a wanton!

"Thank you," she said quietly. "I truly didn't intend to offend you in any way," she added with a shake of her head.

Stephen regarded the pretty young chit, thinking it was too bad she wasn't Aimsley's daughter. *Will could do with a wife like her.* Cheeky and brave and ever so daring in a way that had him wondering if she were a virgin or would welcome a tumble later that evening. "I wasn't that offended," he admitted, "Although I suppose I should request a kiss to make it all better," he added with a grin.

Victoria stilled herself, her eyes finding their way to those perfectly pillowed lips. "And if I have no experience at providing such a balm?" she queried quietly, the air escaping her lungs in a rush.

Allowing a slight smile, Stephen leaned over and touched his nose to her forehead, brushing it across the soft skin until his lips took purchase and left a kiss where spirals of her blonde hair fell from her temple.

Victoria allowed a quiet gasp and lifted her face to regard him. "Who *are* you?" she whispered, feeling as if he had cast some sort of spell over her.

Stephen allowed a wan smile. "A comical fellow, I suppose, who seeks a maiden's kiss as payment for her doubt."

*S*taring into his hazel eyes, which at the moment appeared far darker and not the least bit comical, Victoria found herself leaning toward him, her face upturned and her lips slightly apart.

Stephen's lips met hers, just barely touching for a brief

instant. Victoria was sure the hairs on the back of her neck lifted in response, the electricity between them charging the air. She moved closer to him, her lips pressing against his so they locked into place. The charged air between them was suddenly in her, causing her body to feel as if it was weightless and boneless. His arm was suddenly behind her waist, pulling her hard against the front of his body so that she at least felt as if she wouldn't float away.

The lips she had imagined kissing earlier that evening proved far more adept than they had any right to—they suckled and supped hers as they worked to remove any hesitation she might have had at kissing—and there was a moment when she realized just how it was some young chits found themselves ruined.

For, at that moment, she wanted nothing more than to *be* ruined.

How bad could it be, after all? Perfectly pillowed lips had her entire body coming out of some sort of deep sleep, coming awake to discover just how pleasant and pleasurable it was to be kissed.

To kiss.

A nervous giggle escaped Victoria's lips just then, briefly breaking off the kiss. She was quick to recapture Stephen's lips, though, hungry to resume the sensations.

When they finally ended the kiss—a mutual ending, as if they both needed to gasp for air—the two stared into each other's eyes.

"Damn," Stephen breathed.

"Oh, aye," Victoria agreed with a quick nod, her forehead ending up pressed against his shoulder.

*S*tephen wrapped his arms around her shoulders and held her against the front of his body, not sure what else to do. It would take a moment for his arousal to subside, and despite the layers of fabric that separated their skin, he was quite sure he could feel her hardened nipples pressed into his chest.

"I should apologize—"

"Don't you dare!"

Stephen stilled himself, his lips moving down to kiss the side of her head, a quiet chuckle following the gesture. "If you tell me you are married, so help me—"

"I am not," Victoria replied, her head lifting so she could stare into his hazel eyes. She thought his expression fierce, as if he might be capable of committing some dark, awful deed just then. She could feel his body relax against hers, feel his exhalation of breath, feel her own body molding to fit against his.

His body suddenly stiffened. "Where is your chaperone?" he whispered, as if he thought someone might suddenly appear and challenge him to a duel at Wimbledon Common.

"I have none," she replied in a whisper. When she glanced up at him, she noticed his look of disbelief. "I crashed the ball."

Stephen pulled away to regard her, as if he didn't believe her claim. "Crashed?" he repeated.

Victoria nodded, rather liking the way he still held her against his body, as if he needed her frame for support. Which he did, when she thought about it. "I didn't have an invitation," she added with a small shake of her head.

"Neither did I," Stephen admitted, remembering that none of the invitations addressed to his brother included his name.

"But I hear men are always welcomed at these events," Victoria countered, her brows furrowed.

Stephen's own brows arched up. "Oh?" he replied.

Victoria nodded. "Oh, yes. There are never enough men at these balls. Or so my mother used to claim," she added quickly, realizing she didn't know first-hand if that were the case or not. She had barely made it into the ballroom before Stephen had made his introduction. And then they were dancing and kissing...

She felt Stephen's hold lessen so that her feet reclaimed their hold on the ground. She allowed a small sound of protest, wanting him to know that he could continue to hold onto her as long as he needed. She wasn't about to complain.

"What ball will you crash next?" Stephen asked in a whisper, his manner ever so serious.

Victoria blinked. She hadn't given it any thought. She had only heard about Lord Weatherstone's ball. About the assignations that took place in the library and out in the gardens.

She remembered the cluster of couples outside what must have been the library and realized they were probably queuing up to use the room. Perhaps Bellingham would like to continue whatever he intended to do next in that room. She was about to suggest they move there when she realized how truly wanton she would sound should she make that suggestion.

"I hadn't given it any thought, my lord," she replied with a shake of her head.

Stephen's eyes widened, realizing she spoke the truth. "When will I see you again?"

Victoria gave the question a good deal of consideration. "I have absolutely no idea."

Stephen's lips were suddenly on hers again, as if the answer would lie there instead of in her words. When he finally pulled away to rest his forehead against hers, he allowed a sigh. "I am not who everyone thinks I am," he whispered urgently.

Her eyes widening, Victoria listened and then lifted her head so she could see his eyes. "If not Stephen Slater, then who are you?"

Stephen blinked, realizing he had given his own name when introducing himself to her. "I am Stephen Slater, son of Devonville," he admitted. "But I am not who *they* think I am," he indicated with a nod toward the ballroom.

Victoria allowed a glance toward the ballroom before

returning her attention to Stephen. "A comical fellow?" she asked in a hoarse whisper.

Will shook his head before letting go his hold on Victoria. "I am, actually. But they do not think so," he whispered before giving her a deep bow and then hurrying off into the gardens.

*V*ictoria watched him go, wondering at his words. If he truly was the son of Devonville, then he was the heir to a marquessate. But she was quite sure there was only one son in that family, and his name was William, which had her wondering about Stephen's claim.

Who are you, Stephen Slater? she wondered before she turned and headed back to the ballroom. *And when will I see you again?*

CHAPTER 17

A MAN FINDS A WOMAN

The following afternoon
"Donald!"

The sound of a feminine voice calling out his uncle's name had Will pulling back hard on the reins. Thunderbolt, not happy about his gallop being interrupted, threatened to rear back, but Will quickly exerted control and managed to slow the horse to a trot just as he heard the word, "supper" appended to the call of the name.

Redirecting Thunderbolt, Will allowed the Arabian to regain his speed. He was forced to slow him down again, though, when they cleared a hedgerow and a small cottage appeared silhouetted against the setting sun.

At first glance, Will thought the cottage appeared rather charming. The light gray-colored stones were nearly covered with ivy, the thatched roof golden in the late afternoon light. Just as Susan from *The Five Bells* had described, a square of newly-turned earth lay off to one side of the building.

A second glance had him frowning, however. Some of the stones had obviously shifted, forcing one of the windows to appear crooked. The shutters, once green but now missing most of their paint, hung crooked. And the obvious hole in the roof had Will wondering how many buckets were lined up beneath it to collect the water that no doubt made its way into the hovel every time it rained.

By the time Thunderbolt picked his way up the rocky drive to the cottage, there were no signs of the woman whose voice had called out to Donald. Glancing around the yard—there was a bit of lawn and a few early spring flowers scattered about—Will quickly realized there weren't any outbuildings other than a privy. Nor was there a dog to guard the premises.

Will dismounted and quickly hobbled Thunderbolt, the Arabian obviously unhappy about being left just beyond the reach of the flowers. Digging into a saddlebag, Will pulled out an apple and offered it to his mount. Placated, Thunderbolt took the apple and made short work of eating it as Will made his way to the front door. About to knock, he paused a moment, noticing the rusty hinges that barely held it in place. He feared if he knocked too hard, the door would crash to the ground.

Allowing a tentative knock, he stepped back and forced himself to breathe. There was no guarantee that the Barbara the proprietor of *The Five Bells* had mentioned was the same Barbara he sought. No guarantee his Barbara would even *be* here. No reason to suppose she would still be living in Oxfordshire. Except that this cottage did match the map that Mr. Barton had drawn for him.

For a brief moment, he rather hoped he wouldn't find her here, for it meant something awful must have happened to change her circumstances—or those with whom she lived.

The door slowly opened a crack, and given how dark it was so close to the cottage, Will couldn't make out anything about the person who opened the door except that she had hands with long fingers—and given their rough appearance—fingers that performed work.

"Pardon the interruption, miss," Will said with a bow. "I come in search of a woman I understand might live here. Your mistress, perhaps? Lady Barbara?"

There was a pause before the door slowly opened

more, the woman's face finally revealed by the light from a candle lamp she held in her other hand. In her left hand. A tiny gold band encircled the base of her fourth finger.

Will blinked. And blinked again when he realized it was Barbara who stood before him. Although her face appeared blank at first, her eyes widened and her mouth formed an 'o' when she recognized him.

"Barbara?" he murmured, his head angling as his eyes did a quick sweep down and back up. She wore a serviceable day gown in a drab brown that had obviously seen better days, the threadbare fabric faded and patched near the hem. A mobcap covered most of her hair, but blonde tendrils spilled out near her temples.

Another second, and she had the cap pulled from her head, revealing a messy bun. She held the cap to her middle, acting as if she had been punched in the stomach. Her eyes dropped from his to his riding coat, to his buckskin breeches, and finally to his dusty boots. "I am," she finally admitted, her head bobbing. She lifted her eyes back to his and allowed a sigh.

Something wasn't right. Will knew it even before he spoke another word.

Barbara was the daughter of the Earl of Greenley, the granddaughter of another earl on her mother's side. What awful circumstance had her living in a ramshackle cottage? Looking as if she were a common servant?

And already married!

The questions could wait, though, for at the moment, he merely wanted to hold her. To hold her meant she would be real and not just a figment of his travel-weary imagination. He stepped up and wrapped his arms around her slight shoulders. "Barbara," he breathed, the palms of his hands sliding over a body too lean and too thin. He could feel the sharp bones of her shoulder blades beneath the thin fabric of her gown.

"Bellingham?" she whispered, her words nearly lost in the

wool of his topcoat. Although she didn't fight his hold on her, she remained rigidly upright.

"Aye," he answered, finally giving up his hold on her to study her more closely. "God, I've missed you."

Barbara raised her eyes to his, the dark circles beneath them giving her a haunted look. Her high cheekbones, at one time making her appear every bit the aristocrat's daughter she was, now only accentuated her sunken cheeks. Lush lips weren't the berry color he remembered, but their shape hadn't changed. Nor had her eyes.

Striking, piercing eyes of silver gray, although they lacked the sparkle they had at one time displayed.

And the mischief.

"Why have you come?" she asked, her head angling to one side.

Will blinked. "I... I'm home. I finished my service to the Navy, and I've returned to England," he answered quickly, careful not to display the dismay at hearing her question. This wasn't exactly the welcome he expected, but then, he had imagined worse.

Far worse. She could have been dead.

The gray eyes regarded him, nearly lifeless, before they turned to look at something behind her.

Pushing the door so it opened wider, Will was about to step into the house when he was forced to pause.

A dueling pistol was aimed in his direction.

A dueling pistol in the rather steady hand of a very young boy. "One more step, sir, and I shall shoot you," came the warning.

Well, this is definitely unexpected.

Will stood on the threshold, his attention flitting back and forth between Barbara and the boy.

Her steely gaze still on Will, Barbara turned her head to the side. "Put down the gun, Donald," she said, her voice as calm as if she were telling him to sit down and eat his supper.

The gun remained level, its stock held up by the boy's other hand. "He hasn't introduced himself, Mum. And it's not right proper for him to be pawing you like that," the tow-headed blonde boy replied in defiance.

Mum?

A quick perusal of the boy showed his clothes were in worse shape than Barbara's, the breeches missing their knees and the socks displaying small holes. His arms weren't as thin as his mother's though, suggesting he probably ate better than she did.

"Nevertheless," Barbara replied in a tired voice, "You don't want to be shooting your father."

CHAPTER 18

A FATHER AND SON DISCUSS LOVE

*M*eanwhile, back in Devonville House

Stephen regarded the door to his father's study for several seconds before deciding to knock. His closed fist was just about to make contact when he heard Lord Devonville's baritone voice call out, "Come!"

Momentarily stunned, Stephen finally reached down and pushed the handle. He ducked his head around the door.

"You needn't skulk, son," William said, his manner rather serious. "I'm not going to bite."

Blinking, Stephen stepped all the way into the study. Not having spent his life living under the same roof with his father, Stephen found himself wondering just where he stood in the household. And with his father. Although nothing had been done or said to make him feel unwelcome, he couldn't help but think his status as a bastard made it awkward for the staff—and his father.

"I beg your pardon. I didn't wish to interrupt—"

"Nonsense," William responded, tossing his quill onto his blotter. "Anything to save me from having to finish this blasted letter," the marquess added as he waved to the chair in front of the desk. "I take it you're missing your brother, aye?"

Stephen nodded. "A bit, I suppose. I was hoping I would

have more time with him. To learn the ropes around here, so to speak." Knowing those on a ship certainly did him no good in polite society.

The marquess pulled the bottle of scotch from the credenza behind his desk and poured them both a finger's worth. "London, do you mean? Or here at the house?" He passed a crystal tumbler to Stephen and lifted his own in salute.

Stephen followed suit but didn't take a drink just then. "A little of both, I suppose. I can't help but think you weren't expecting me—I only came because Will insisted I do so—and that I'm imposing—"

"Nonsense," the marquess repeated, his brows furrowing. "In fact, I'm rather glad you're here. Especially since my eldest has decided to depart for Oxfordshire. By now, I expect he's either found his prey or has given up and is spending some time at Gisborn's place."

Leaning forward, Stephen regarded his father for a moment. "Do you... do you believe he will find her?" Will had never mentioned if his father supported his search for Lady Barbara or if the marquess thought it a wild goose chase.

"Truth be told, I don't know what—or whom—he'll find. I only wish he'd made mention of her *before* he reported for duty. Then I could have at least made overtures with her father. Paid a call, or had my wife do so—she was still alive back then," he added with a troubled expression.

"If you *had* known... and it turned out Lady Barbara found herself... with child...?" He paused when he noticed William's expression of surprise.

"Is that what this is about?" William interrupted, straightening in his chair.

Stephen shook his head. "Well, I don't know for sure, but according to what my mother used to say, a lady of the *ton* doesn't go missing from London unless she's sent away. Or runs away. Usually because she's done something."

"Or had something done to her," the marquess said *sotto*

voce. He sighed, remembering his conversation with William. "Your brother admitted to having ruined her the night before his departure. At her request, supposedly, but I didn't raise him to run away at the first sign of trouble. *I* certainly didn't."

Frowning, Stephen found he was holding his breath. "Excuse me?" he whispered hoarsely.

William angled his head and leaned over the desk, his voice low as he said, "When I got a child on your mother. You, as it turns out." He sighed again. "I loved your mother. More than I did my own wife back then. She was my salvation from duty, you see. I knew I was about to inherit. I knew everything that would be expected of me for the rest of my life. Just because my father had made it all very clear to me didn't mean I had to look *forward* to it. I was determined to have a life of my own choosing, if only for a few nights a week. Although I didn't intend to father a bastard, I remember feeling rather... *honored* that Marie would deign to have my babe. She told me she hadn't given birth to any others. Had things been different..." He allowed the sentence to trail off, his head shaking slightly.

Stephen stared at his father, his brows furrowed. "You mean, if she hadn't been a courtesan and if you weren't about to inherit a marquessate, and you weren't already married, you might have married her instead?" his whispered in disbelief, realizing too late that he had said a few too many 'if's.

Allowing a wan smile, William finished off his scotch and set the tumbler down on the desk. "First off, I do not think your mother would have given me any consideration if I wasn't about to inherit a marquessate. She was particular in that regard." When he noticed one of Stephen's eyebrows arch up much like one of his own might do at the very same unexpected comment, he added, "Your mother was a celebrated woman. She had been born at Versailles and raised at the palace, trained by your grandmother to follow in her footsteps. By coming to England when she did, she barely avoided the Revolution and managed to keep her head. A rather calculated move on her part, I came to find out."

"What are you talking about?" Stephen interrupted.

"Your mother is a smart woman. Just because she lived at court and was insulated from what was happening in the countryside, she knew the peasants were getting restless. She knew it was time she take her leave of France when she did. So she packed her things, begged her mother to join her on a trip over the Channel—something your grandmother refused to do, I might add—and left a few weeks before the hoards descended. She even had a signed contract with an earl before she set foot on these shores."

"*What?*" Stephen asked in surprise, straightening in his chair. His mother had never mentioned anything about having to escape France, or of having had a contract with an earl.

"I paid him off to walk away. I was at the dock when he went to meet her for the first time, you see, and so help me God, I was in love with your mother before she managed to make her first curtsy."

Attempting to suppress a grin at hearing how his mother had affected his father, Stephen lifted his tumbler and finished off his scotch. "She tells the same tale about meeting you," he remarked finally.

William nodded, wondering just then if Marie St. Clair would have returned to London had he sent for her after his wife's death. Had too much time passed, though? Or would they have been able to recapture the magic that had been their time together for the first few years after he had inherited?

Probably not, he decided. By then, Marie had been married and widowed and was apparently enjoying life in the Kent countryside, away from prying eyes and gossipers and apparently retired from her days as a courtesan.

"I wish to settle an allowance on you," William announced suddenly. "Not too much, for I don't want you tempted to lose it all at the faro tables—"

"I'm not much of a gambler these days," Stephen interrupted with a shake of his head.

"But enough so that you can afford a townhouse, a horse or two, and a wife," his father continued, ignoring his son's claim.

Stephen frowned. "In that order?"

William straightened and then frowned himself. "Well, I should think that once you've decided to take a wife, you'll need a house in which to live, then a horse to ride whilst you're making your way about London—and you'll need one or two to pull a carriage so that you can go courting—and then the wife, so... yes, I suppose in that order. Anything over that, and you'll have to earn it yourself."

Allowing a broad smile, Stephen felt a wave of relief settle over him. With the most expensive items covered by his father, he would be able to support a wife on a clerk's earnings in fine style. "Very good, sir. Thank you."

The marquess gave him a nod. "Don't thank me yet. I may have gotten you into a bit of a scrape," he warned.

Stephen squirmed. "Oh?"

His father bobbed his head back and forth, as if he was trying to determine how best to give his son some bad news. "Chamberlain could use you in the Foreign Office. I told him you might be interested. I don't know if the pay is any good, but—"

"I'll take it," Stephen replied quickly. At his father's look of surprise, he added, "Well, now that Will has gone, I find myself with too much time on my hands. About time I found a position and reported to work."

William Slater regarded his son with a sense of pride. Although he hadn't had as much influence on raising the boy as he would have liked, he realized Marie had done an admiral job on her own. Perhaps her husband had helped, as well. "I'll make the introductions. Perhaps at the theatre tomorrow night. You will join the marchioness and me in our box, I hope?"

Stephen nodded, realizing he had another form of

London entertainment at which to meet potential wives for his brother. He was beginning to think Will would be ready to marry when his search for Lady Barbara proved fruitless. Then he could start a search for his own wife.

My own wife?

He gave a slight shake of his head. *Now where the hell had thought come from?*

CHAPTER 19

A SECRET REVEALED

*M*eanwhile, in Oxfordshire
Barbara's words had Will doing a double-take.

Father?

He had half a mind to look behind him, thinking perhaps another man stood there in the doorway. Barbara was wearing a wedding band, after all. But a split-second later, he realized her comment was made about him.

About me.

William straightened to his full six-foot, one-inch height and regarded the boy for several seconds. Slight of build—or perhaps the urchin seemed small because he looked as if he could use a good meal or two—he was blonde and had eyes that could have been blue or gray. It was hard to tell in the dim light inside the cottage.

Frowning at both the circumstances and the words Barbara had just spoken, Will turned his attention back to her. She appeared weary and frail, and William wondered if the dark circles were due to lack of sleep or lack of food—or both.

Cooking odors suddenly assaulted his nostrils. His attention went to the stove, where steam escaped from beneath a lid over a pot.

Barbara's gaze followed his, and she was suddenly in motion, hurrying to lift the lid before the liquid inside bubbled over. Somehow, she captured some of her skirts into her hand before she did so; otherwise, William was sure she would have burned herself.

"Donald. Put down that gun and wash up for supper," Barbara ordered, her voice making it sound as if she had given him the order earlier. Ladling the boiling broth into wooden bowls, she glanced over her shoulder to find her visitor still regarding her with furrowed brows. "You're welcome to stay for supper. We don't have much, but..."

Will shook his head. "Pardon the interruption, my lady," he said finally. "Is your..." He nearly choked when he finally got the word out. "Husband here? I wish to have a word with him."

Barbara placed the bowls of soup on the table and angled her head. "I've no husband, but you'll be keeping that to yourself," she stated firmly.

The sense of relief that settled over Will was palpable. Still, if she wasn't married, why did she wear a ring? "I have provisions aplenty. I'll be but a moment," he said as he gave a bow and took his leave of the cottage, squeezing his eyes shut when the late afternoon sun hit his face.

Jesus, what the hell has happened to Barbara? She was an earl's daughter, but from her appearance, she was apparently living no better than the poorest tenant farmer. Worse, even.

He glanced around, wondering if anyone lived nearby. Given the woodlands and a slight hillock off to the east, he realized this cottage was all by itself. Even the bell tower and spire of Saints Peter and Paul wasn't visible from where he stood.

He took another look at the shabby cottage and shook his head. *What the hell had happened?* The place was barely habitable.

Thunderbolt nudged him as he removed the saddlebags from him. About to dig for another apple, Will thought better of it and instead offered the horse a handful of grain from another saddlebag. "Someone needs these apples more than you do," he murmured as he loosened the reins and led Thunderbolt to an area that offered some greenery on which he could snack.

When he had first arrived, Will thought a stableboy would appear from behind the cottage and see to the horse, but from the looks of everything—and the boy named Donald—Will wondered if the boy had ever handled a horse. There wasn't even a lean-to or a barn on the property in which to shelter one, although from where he stood he could see a pile of old lumber that might have at one time been a loafing shed.

Helping himself to a rusty bucket, he found the water pump and filled it, wincing when he realized he had some rinsing to do before the water was clear enough for the horse to drink.

Once he was satisfied Thunderbolt could be left where he was, Will threw the saddlebags over his shoulders and made his way back to the front door of the cottage. He didn't bother knocking, but rather opened the barely-there door and made his way inside.

From where she sat at a makeshift settle, Barbara seemed surprised to see him. "I didn't expect you to return," she said, reaching out a hand so it rested on Donald's shoulder. Apparently the boy had made to get up from the table at the sound of the door opening, probably so he could get the gun and level it at their intruder.

Not sure how to respond to her comment, Will lowered the saddlebags onto a low table in front of a settee, the only piece of furniture in the place that looked decent. Opening one of the bags, he pulled out the cloth-wrapped meat pies he had purchased at *The Five Bells* along with a wedge of cheese and the apples he had brought for the horse.

Donald's eyes widened at the sight of the food as Will placed it on the settle in front of him. "Is that for us?" the boy asked, obviously incredulous.

"Donald!" Barbara admonished the boy. "You do not speak until you're spoken to," she hissed.

"It is," Will acknowledged with a nod, rather surprised to be addressed by the youth, although Barbara's words suggested she had been trying to teach him proper manners. He pulled a knife from his boot, wiped it on the only kitchen linen he could find, and cut the apples in half. Then he went to work on the cheese, slicing it into smaller wedges. Taking the only other chair at the settle, he lifted his eyes to meet Barbara's. He was sure he saw tears, but she blinked twice as he gave her a nod and they were gone. "How long have you lived here?" he asked as he pushed the fruit toward his hosts.

"My whole life," Donald replied, a bit of broth dribbling down his chin.

"Donald. You're not to speak until you're spoken to," Barbara admonished him again.

"But I thought he *was* speaking to me," the boy replied, his voice nearly a whisper. He turned his attention back to Will. "I apologize, Mister...?"

"Slater. Commander Will Slater." He reached out his right hand to shake the boy's hand. "Late of his Majesty's navy," he added when he noticed how wide the boy's eyes had opened with his introduction. His handshake was firm, however, and not the least bit hesitant.

"You were the master and commander of a *ship?*"

Will had to suppress the huge grin he nearly displayed at how awed the boy seemed by his introduction. "I was. *HMS Greenwich* these past few years." Although Donald seemed genuinely impressed, he couldn't help but notice that Barbara merely stared into her soup.

"How long have you been here, Barbara?"

She sighed and angled her head. "As I said before, over seven years," she answered, her gaze turning to one of the meat pies.

Will shoved it onto her plate. *Seven years?* That was almost as long as he had been away! "Why here?" he countered, one hand waving to indicate the cottage.

Barbara regarded him with the wariness of a caged animal. "The choices were here or with my aunt in Staffordshire." She didn't elaborate, leaving Will to understand that life with her aunt would have been far worse, although, at the moment, he couldn't begin to reason how.

"Do you... *own* this cottage?" he asked then, not sure he wanted to know the answer. He was sure he heard her attempt to stifle a snort.

"It is my understanding the property is unentailed. It is part of the Greenley earldom," she explained as she sliced the meat pie. "Since everything around and south of here belongs to a barony, I have often wondered if Greenley won it in a card game."

The 'Greenley earldom'. Not 'my father's earldom'.

"Does your father's current man of business know that it's in dire need of repairs?"

Barbara sighed. "I'm quite sure it's the reason it was offered to me," she replied before taking a bite of the pie. From the way she seemed to savor the filling, Will realized she probably hadn't eaten anything so substantial in a very long time.

"I'll see what I can do in the morning," Will said before he tucked into his own meat pie and tried the soup. Although there wasn't much more than a few pieces of onion and the slight flavor of chicken, it was hot and rather satisfying just then. "Perhaps we can talk later?" he half-asked, giving a slight nod in Donald's direction when Barbara displayed a look of surprise.

"I suppose," she agreed, returning her attention to her meal. "When did you get back to London?"

William took heart at the query, thinking perhaps a good meal would restore her to the woman she had been when he left her. That had been just after Easter in 1810, he remembered. George III was still the king, although it had become apparent he wouldn't be for long. They had been in the gardens behind Lord Weatherstone's mansion in Park Lane, kissing one another by the fountain and saying the words they would say again the following night, the night he had professed his love for her and she had given him her virtue.

His eyes widening, Will glanced over at Donald. *Is he my son?* he wondered, remembering her earlier comment. But why hadn't she written to tell him? "Just a few days ago," he finally answered.

Barbara blinked. And blinked again. "Not long, then," she replied, obviously surprised by the news.

He shook his head. "No, but it took a couple of days to figure out where to look for you. When I confirmed with the Pendleton House butler that you were no longer in London, I consulted with your father's former solicitor. He gave me this address." He paused a moment. "My letters to you... I sent them all to Pendleton House."

Barbara's eyes widened at his simple statement. She had received a few of them, but then she had been forced to leave her father's house. Her correspondence couldn't have been forwarded if no one at Pendleton House knew where to send it. Shaking her head, Barbara's shoulders slumped. "I didn't get them," she said simply. "I rather imagine my father burned them and any others that might have come for me."

Will frowned, realizing just then that the Earl of Greenley and his daughter were definitely estranged. What else could explain why he would send her to this God forsaken hovel? His correspondence hadn't been forwarded. And although he had received a few letters from her during his first year at sea—a delightful surprise when his ship pulled into port cities, even if some of the letters were more than a month old—no others found their way to him.

"Jesus," he breathed, his attention returning to the young boy whose eyelids were growing heavy given his suddenly full belly. *Had the earl disowned his own daughter because she...?*

He didn't have a chance to finish the thought when Barbara noticed his attention on Donald.

"Off to bed with you," she said, giving the boy's arm a shake. "We've work to do tomorrow, and your lessons, too."

Donald's eyes popped open, and he nodded. "May I be excused?" he whispered sleepily.

"Yes, of course. I'll be there in a few minutes to tuck you in," she said, pulling his plate and utensils towards her and stacking them with the others on the table.

The boy took his leave of the settle and disappeared into a room off the kitchen.

Will watched the boy as he took his leave, surprised at how familiar his gait seemed, at how his features mirrored his own at that age. "Did your father disown you? Because of... because of him?" Will finally asked in a whisper as he stood up and joined her at the makeshift sink. A pot of water was steaming on the back of the stove, and Barbara slid the dishes into it before turning to regard Will.

"He did," she said with a nod.

Will's arms were around her in an instant, pulling her hard against him. "Jesus, Barbara," he whispered. "If only I'd known..."

"What?" she responded curtly. "What would you have done?" She spat out the question, obviously annoyed with him.

The question had Will loosening his hold on her.

What would I have done?

Realizing she was testing him, he answered quickly. "I would have written to my father, of course. Requested he make arrangements for you to live in one of the Devonshire properties. With servants. Arranged for an allowance, a nurse for the boy, a tutor..."

Barbara's eyes widened in surprise at how quickly he responded, but they soon narrowed. "You would have sent me away to live in the country, just as my father did, to avoid the shame," she accused.

Will winced, his head jerking back as if he had been slapped. "Barbara, no," he whispered. After a pause, he added, "He *is* my son, isn't he?" It wasn't a question so much as an affirmation of what she had said earlier. He knew if he asked it, she would take offense. But at that moment, he needed to know she hadn't been with another man. Hadn't shared her body with another suitor.

What had Susan said back at *The Five Bells?*

She don't do tumbles, so don't be thinkin' ya' can bed her.

Christ! The last thing he wanted to do was make her feel any worse than her father had managed to do by sending her to live in a ramshackle cottage.

"He looks like I did when my first tutor arrived," Will said then. He felt her stiffen before she finally relaxed and allowed him to pull her hard against his body. After a moment, he moved them to the threadbare settee, lowering her to the cushions before he took a seat next to her and once again wrapped an arm about one of her shoulders. "Tell me what happened, I beg you," he whispered.

Barbara sighed. How many times had she imagined this conversation? How many times had she imagined the telling? Imagined the possible reactions? Did Will truly believe her claim that Donald was, indeed, his son? "I didn't know I was with child until you had been gone for nearly four months," she finally whispered. "I know it sounds naive of me, but I didn't—"

"What finally gave it away?" he asked, remembering his crewmen describing their wives' pregnancies. One complained about how his wife ate too much and at all times of the day and night but seemed to give off an ethereal glow while another claimed his wife knew she was with child within a month of their marriage because she craved foods she had never liked before.

Barbara gave him a quelling glance. "I developed a..." she pulled away and used a hand to sweep over her abdomen. "A bump," she finished. "And my maid told me she had known for some time I was *enceinte*, but she figured she had best not say anything lest she lose her position."

Since there weren't any servants in the cottage, Will realized the maid probably hadn't left with Barbara when she was sent away, so she had lost her position at Pendleton House.

"How old is he?" he asked, deciding the dishes could wait

until later. Or the morning. He would no doubt wake up before her and see to them. It wouldn't be the first time he did something domestic. Being a ship's commander required he be able to perform any of the duties required to keep the thing afloat.

"A bit over seven years, I suppose," she replied, one brow furrowed as she considered his question. "Truth be told, I don't keep track of the time."

Seven years?

"So, your father sent you away just as soon as he found out?" Will asked, his angry expression displaying his opinion of the Earl of Greenley.

Barbara nodded. "We were all at Pendleton House for Christmas. I had hidden my condition from everyone but my lady's maid, but my aunt noticed at dinner one night. She was so shocked, she couldn't keep it a secret. She told my father right after dinner." She ignored Will's wince at the comment and added, "I was on my way here two days later."

Will gave a start. "Your father didn't speak with mine?" he asked in surprise.

She frowned at his question and then shook her head. "I didn't tell anyone about us," she replied, her manner almost defensive. "Despite his threats of death and dismemberment and to... to *disown* me, I figured it was my secret to keep," she explained. "So, he disowned me."

Will shook his head. "Jesus, Barb," he whispered. "They had to have known it was me... right?"

Barbara gave a one-shoulder shrug. "How would they? I told no one about us."

Will frowned. *How could they not?* Didn't everyone know he intended to ask her for her hand in marriage when he returned from his service in the British Navy?

Apparently not.

He hadn't exactly made his intentions known. And apparently, she hadn't either.

Perhaps what was so obvious to him wasn't to others. He and Barbara had been discreet at balls and soirées—they'd had to be—and he had only called on her when he was in the company of others. At balls, they never danced more than twice together. And the only time they left a ballroom together was that night at Lord Weatherstone's ball, two nights before he was due to report to duty. The night when he had declared his undying love and had kissed her by the fountain and promised a life with her.

They had done much more than that the following night, though. When she had shown up at the back door of his Bruton Street townhouse wearing a mantle that hid her from nosy neighbors. When she told him she intended to spend his last night in London with him.

His plans to spend the night carousing—he thought to go to White's and perhaps visit a brothel—were suddenly all about her. All about seeing to making her his own.

After her declaration of love, they hadn't said another word. He had merely led her to his room, undressed her while she did her best to undress him, and fallen onto his bed.

Had she ever protested what he was doing—had she ever hesitated—he would have stopped in an instant, for he had spent that entire night expecting her to come to her senses and tell him to stop.

Once he had her stripped of clothing—he hadn't even allowed her to keep her stockings on her legs—he had gone about pleasuring her in every way he knew from his time with one particular courtesan at Lord Norwick's brothel, *The Elegant Courtesan.*

Marlena, he remembered.

Although the prostitute wasn't particularly beautiful, she was knowledgeable. Enthusiastic. And quite free with her favors, instructing him on how his pleasure might be more enhanced if he did certain things to her first.

Of course, he followed her instructions, marveling at how erotic a woman in ecstasy could look beneath him. Marveling at how much more excited he could be when he knew she welcomed his hardened cock within her honeyed folds. How exciting and satisfying giving pleasure could be, even if he did not always take it in return. How intense pleasure could be if he denied himself once or twice during an intimate encounter.

Just thinking of those nights with Marlena had served him well when Barbara showed up for his final night in London.

Despite finally taking her virtue—she had begged him to do so—he knew she felt no pain when he did so. For when he finally buried himself in her warm, wet cocoon of comfort, she was in the throes of the ecstasy he had set off with his tongue and lips.

A moment after her soft cries of his name penetrated the dark, he had taken his release and marveled at the sensations he felt at her expense. Never had he experienced such satisfaction with Marlena. Never had he felt so replete, so complete in his life.

He had ruined Barbara, completely and thoroughly. There would be no advantageous marriage for her unless she married him. He had seen to that.

Deliberately.

"Marry me," Will whispered as he buried his nose in her messy bun. She no longer smelled of honeysuckle and lemon soap, but it mattered not. She would again once they returned to London.

When Barbara didn't respond right away, it felt as if his heart had suddenly stopped. Another moment, and he was forced to pull her body away from his, his intention to grill her as to why she wouldn't immediately agree to his marriage proposal. She had to know it was coming. He had promised her as much that last night they had been together.

It was then he realized she was sound asleep.

Although he had given some thought to pleasuring her before she slept that night, he found he couldn't be too disappointed.

He had found her, after all. Found her unmarried. Found her still willing to be held in his arms.

And found her with his son.

My son.

Before the thought faded, he stood and lifted her into his arms. He carried her to the only empty room behind the kitchen. Guided by the dim light from a single candle, he managed to pull down the worn counterpane and bed linens before standing her next the small bed.

Having unfastened the buttons of her gown down her back, he made quick work of removing her gown and petticoats, both garments so threadbare he worried they might tear as he pulled them down. Despite her apparent state of exhaustion, Barbara helped in divesting her body of her corset, a task made easier when Will completely unlaced the ties. She wore no stockings, which had Will wondering if she even owned a pair. The soles of her slippers were nearly worn through.

Will thought to merely leave her there and find a place to sleep somewhere else in the cottage. But the thought of leaving her was one he found he couldn't abide. He considered the floor, but the desire to stay close to Barbara had him deciding to simply wrap himself around her once he had her placed on the bed.

"What do you think you're doing?" Barbara whispered, suddenly struggling against Will's hold.

"Shh. I'm trying to help you undress for bed."

When Barbara elbowed him in the ribs, Will hissed and took a step back, essentially removing the support he had been providing in keeping her erect. Barbara fell backwards, and might have fallen to the floor, but Will was quick to capture her against the front of his body. "Be still," he whispered, his hands grasping her waist. He winced as he felt how thin she was. The last time he had held her, she'd had more meat on her bones. In fact, he couldn't remember feeling—or seeing—any bones behind her pale skin back then.

When the fight seemed to leave her body, Will moved a hand up her arm and leaned his head over her shoulder.

"What is it, my lady?" he asked in a hoarse whisper. Will felt her body seem to slump, as if all the fight had gone from her.

"How did you find me?" she asked, her head turning slightly so he could hear her quiet voice.

Will sighed. "I paid a visit to Pendleton House and then to Mr. Barton," he replied, realizing she had already forgotten what he had told her earlier.

Barbara suddenly turned in his arms, a look of shock on her face. "Did you speak with Father?"

Although the single candle barely lit her face, Will could swear he saw fear in her eyes when she asked the question. "No," he said with a shake of his head. "I only spoke with the butler," he added when she didn't respond. "He mentioned the solicitor. Jesus, Barbara, why didn't you write to tell me what was happening with your father? My father claims he might be in debtor's prison..."

Barbara pushed herself away from his body and stared at Will. "So, it's true then? He's gambled away *everything?*"

Will straightened, wondering how she already knew. "My father isn't one to listen to gossips, so he only guessed it," he answered quickly. He watched as Barbara's gaze seemed focused on something not there. "What have you heard?"

The woman finally returned her attention to Will. "There's a public house in the village—"

"*The Five Bells.*"

Barbara gave a start. "Were you there?"

Will frowned, sure he had mentioned it when he arrived. "I was. It's how I learned which cottage was yours," he replied quietly, hoping the boy in the adjoining room was still asleep. "It's where I bought the meat pies."

"So Susan knows you're here?" she countered, shock apparent on her features.

Shaking his head, Will said, "She was quite clear that you wouldn't be providing a tumble, if that's what you're worried about," he countered quickly, hoping she didn't think him capable of taking her against her will.

Barbara relaxed. "She's made overtures—"

"I can imagine," Will replied with an arched eyebrow.

Closing her eyes, Barbara shook her head. "I assure you, I have been with no other man but you. And I have no intention of allowing any man into my bed, such as it is. You included," she added with a finger pointed into his chest.

Will felt the tip of her fingernail as it left a half-moon indentation in his skin. "Barbara," he whispered in reply, disappointment evident in his voice.

"I mean it, Bellingham. I..." She stilled and turned to face the small bed. "Take your leave of me and never return," she whispered. "Please."

A sense of dread filled Will at that moment. How could she simply send him away? Deny him the opportunity to renew their acquaintance? Deny him the opportunity to ask for her hand in marriage? She was obviously as poor in coin as she was in spirit. She needed his protection. She needed his funds.

She needed his love.

Couldn't she see that?

"Why are you turning me away?" he asked in a whisper, his voice catching on the last word. He could tell by how her shoulders shook that she was weeping. One of her hands had already lifted to her face, probably to wipe away her tears. "You came to me. You pledged your love to me. You said you would wait..." Will allowed the words to trail off as he considered what to do. He couldn't leave her. A few more weeks and she and the boy would probably die of starvation if illness didn't take them first.

He leaned over and placed a kiss on her back of her shoulder. "Please, don't do this," he murmured before raising his head. When she didn't reply, Will took his leave of the room and shut the door.

Barbara stared at the closed door for nearly a minute before she sighed, her body shaking with a sob.

What have I done?

What I had to do, she reasoned. For ever since Will Slater had left her nearly eight years ago, she had learned to despise him for having left her, for his broken promises, his lack of communication.

Oh, there had been a few letters at first. Letters proclaiming his undying love and devotion. His assurances that he would see her again soon. His words of how he envisioned their future in London.

And then... *nothing*.

No more letters arrived at Pendleton House. No letters were forwarded to her in Oxfordshire.

Nothing.

It was as if he had fallen off the face of the earth.

And maybe he had. Perhaps his ship had been shot full of cannon balls from a French frigate, or set afire by vengeful pirates, or he had contracted some awful disease and perished at sea. Barbara had no idea what could have happened. And wasn't that the problem with loving someone who had gone to sea intending to serve King and Country?

Damn him.

Damn him and the British Navy. Damn Whitehall. Damn Napoleon and Admiral Nelson and anyone else who had kept Will Slater from returning to London. From staying with her when she needed him most.

From being with her when she bore his son, screaming and in more pain than she ever thought possible.

Thank goodness Susan had come to call, come because she wanted the company of another woman that afternoon. The older woman helped deliver the squalling infant who had caused her banishment from her life in London.

She owed Susan. And she hated owing someone when there was nothing she could afford to offer in return.

Barbara nearly fell onto her bed, exhaustion sending her into a restless slumber. Although she thought she heard the sounds of dishes being washed just outside her door, she allowed sleep to take her completely.

CHAPTER 20

TAKING STOCK OF A POOR SITUATION

*W*ill sighed as he regarded the interior of the ramshackle cottage. *How can anyone live in such a poor excuse for a home?* he wondered as he moved to see to the dinner dishes. He turned down the flame on the stove, hoping there was enough wood to keep it alight the rest of the night. A quick perusal of the hole in the roof indicated it was repairable, as long as he could find a few solid boards to replace those that had rotted.

When he had done what he could inside, he went outside and took a deep breath. He needed to get a note off to his father to let him know he had found Barbara. *The Five Bells* was no doubt a mail coach stop, or perhaps he could find a courier there. Mounting Thunderbolt, he set off to return to the public house and make the necessary arrangements.

A young man who was about to set off for London and assured Will he would see to the delivery of his note in exchange for the money Will offered.

"You ride at night?" Will asked in surprise, thinking the man would be set on by highwaymen or that his horse might step in a hole and come up lame.

"I do," the courier replied. "The roads are decent enough,

and there's a full moon," he claimed. "I change horses, of course, so I should be there by late afternoon tomorrow."

The man finished saddling his horse while Will penned his note, assuring him it would be delivered to Devonville House on the morrow. Then he was off.

After an ale, Will returned to the cottage. He removed the saddle and hobbled Thunderbolt so the horse would remain in the yard for the night.

Under the light of the full moon just above the horizon, he surveyed the wood available in the backyard, deciding that with a bit of clever design, he could add onto the partially collapsed shed and create a loafing shed for Thunderbolt as well as repair the roof of the cottage.

Satisfied he had done as much as he could given the deepening twilight, Will let himself back into the cottage. He regarded the settee, deciding it was far too small for him to use for sleeping. The floor didn't hold any appeal after his extended ride on his horse. That left the bed in which Barbara slept. Although small, he was sure he could fit as long as he held Barbara close to his body as they slept. Despite his sudden weariness, the thought had his cock responding.

He opened the door to Barbara's room and sighed with relief when he found her sound asleep. He regarded her a moment, her translucent chemise casting her body in a golden glow from the candlelight. She was thin, but her breasts were still round and her hips flared out from the tiny waist he remembered from their only night together.

His last night in London.

He shook his head and gave a thought to his own state of dress. Considering the young boy in the next room, he decided he didn't want to be discovered sleeping next to Barbara should Donald wake up and come into the room. But given the circumstances—she had claimed the boy was his son—he figured it was time the youngster learned that his parents would be sharing a bed.

Will shed his waistcoat, linen shirt and stockings, secretly wishing he had brought more than a just few changes of clothing appropriate for what he would need to be doing the next few days. Depending on the weather, he thought he might see to getting them on their way to London in three or four days. He would have to find a gig to let, or arrange for their transport on a mail coach.

The thought of returning to London had him remembering his sister, though. *She lives in Oxfordshire now. Somewhere near Bampton*, he recalled from his father's comment. Well, from the map the solicitor had drawn for him, he was fairly sure Bampton was nearby. He would see about paying Hannah a visit. See about meeting his brother-in-law. Meeting his nephew. *And seeing Harold*, he thought with a wry grin as he remembered his sister's Alpenmastiff.

Settling onto the mattress, Will frowned when he realized the bed in his quarters aboard ship was of a better quality than this one. He sighed and wrapped an arm around Barbara's waist, pulling her so she lay tucked up against him, her head finally resting in the crook of his other arm. Kissing the top of her head, he fought sleep for a moment before he finally allowed it to take him.

CHAPTER 21

CONFLICTED THOUGHTS

*H*er senses on alert when she was aware of someone entering her room, Barbara forced herself to remain still as she considered what to do.

Scream?

Run from the room?

And then what?

She remembered Will had been with her in the room, his strong arms wrapped around her middle as she stood pressed against him. Oh, to have him with her always! But she knew that wasn't possible. Will was committed to his duty. Committed to a life that couldn't include her. Couldn't include her son.

Their son.

He would leave again, she was sure. He would return to London.

So when she felt the weight of his body settle into the mattress behind her, she nearly let out a yelp. She stilled herself, though, especially when one of his large arms settled over her waist. She felt Will's kiss as if she were in a dream, the gentle pressure atop her head much like when her mother had kissed her there.

Mother!

Oh, how she wished she could confide in her. Seek out

her counsel and learn what she should do. What she should have done all those years ago.

The woman's death had been hard on the entire family, on her father probably more than any of the children. Seeing her lifeless eyes as she held the last babe—stillborn and some said the reason for her untimely death—Barbara remembered knowing life would never be the same in the Greenley household. Maxwell Higgins grew more bitter, his nights spent drinking and gambling at Brook's. Her brothers, off at school and somewhat insulated from the worsening situation at home, knew to behave or suffer the wrath and public humiliation of their father. Beatrice, her younger sister, was soon sent away to live with an aunt in Staffordshire, which left Barbara to run the household.

And she had.

For three years, she consulted with the servants, met with vendors and did what she had to do to keep Pendleton House in good repair. Her efforts didn't go unnoticed, at least not by others. Will even spoke of how proud her mother would be of her efforts. "You would make a fine wife for any aristocrat," he had said one night in the gardens. "But I hope one day you'll be my fine wife."

Bless his heart.

The Earl of Greenley was never satisfied, however, his quick criticism and angry manner forcing Barbara to seek solace in William's arms. Learning he would soon be leaving London on a naval vessel, his intent to eventually have his own ship, Barbara realized she would lose her one champion, the one man to whom she was gradually giving her heart, and that last night he was in London, her body.

Seven months later, on that awful Christmas night after dinner, her father had flown into a rage, banishing her from the household with little more than the clothes on her back and a trunk stuffed with whatever she could grab from her bedchamber.

Although she had been able to stay with a friend in London for a day until she could meet with her father's man of business—in private—she knew word of her condition would spread through the parlors of Mayfair. She needed to take her leave of London right away.

Ruined and with no prospects, she agreed to Mr. Barton's suggestion that she settle in the cottage in Broadwell in Oxfordshire. "It's unentailed, and I rather doubt the earl even remembers he owns it. But there will be no servants," he warned. "And I can only supply you with funds when I'm able to hide their disbursement from your father."

She had agreed to the arrangement, of course. What else could she do? Living with her aunt when Beatrice was apparently already a hardship on the older woman wasn't an option.

"You'll want to wear a gold band."

The words had her frowning. "I beg your pardon?"

Mr. Barton allowed a sigh. "You'll have an easier time of it if everyone thinks you're a widow. War widows are quite common these days," he explained with an arched brow. "Make something up. Say your husband died at sea."

The words had Barbara giving a start. It was possible, after all, that Will Slater would die at sea. But she decided to heed the man's advice. She acquired a simple gold band in Ludgate Hill and set off on the mail coach for Oxfordshire.

For six years, she and her son—William Slater the Third's son—lived somewhat comfortably in the small cottage, a horse making it possible to ride to the nearby village for supplies. She learned how to garden. A nearby farmer sold her hay and grain for the horse and milk and eggs for their breakfasts. She collected apples from a tree on the property. She raised a few chicks so she would only have to buy their feed to have eggs and an occasional roasted chicken. She learned how to make preserves from the vicar's wife in Broadwell, the older woman obviously curious as to how Barbara ended up in the small village but never enough to come right out and ask. Barbara wasn't about to offer the information. Better everyone think she was a war widow.

During the first year, she wrote letters to Will in care of

the British Navy, wondering if they would ever find him, but after only the few letters she had received at Pendleton House, she never heard from Will again.

Then, just last year, after the horrible Summer of 1816 and the following winter, the funds suddenly ceased to arrive every month. A discreet query addressed to Mr. Barton requesting funds for repairs to the cottage was returned, unopened.

With no money and no other means to make money, Barbara sold the horse. Another month passed before a curt note arrived from her father's man of business.

My employment with Maxwell Higgins, Earl of Greenley, has ended. Badly. I should hope by now that you have married and are under a husband's protection. I can no longer send funds, nor do I think my replacement will be able to do so as the gambling debts have amassed beyond the earldom's ability to pay. Your father may end up in debtor's prison should all the notes be called in. Your siblings have been notified of the same. Yours in service, Andrew S. Barton, Esq.

Stunned by the news of her father's debts, Barbara felt more despair for her brothers than she did for herself. Both would have reached their majorities by now. She could only hope they had their own means to make their living, for without funds from the earldom, they would be unable to court young ladies, unable to live respectable lives in town. Upon his death, her father's debts would become theirs.

Meanwhile, the funds from the sale of the Cleveland Bay were soon spent, the larder emptied, the last chicken slaughtered.

That had been a week ago.

For Will Slater to suddenly make an appearance after eight years seemed as much a lifesaver as it did a curse. She was quite sure he intended to take her and Donald back to London, but Barbara knew she could never go back there again, nor could she take her son.

She had been shunned by her father, given the cut direct, and sent packing eight years ago. Now that her father was apparently in debtors' prison, her entire family was no doubt disgraced, a ripe topic for Mayfair parlor gossip mongers and their like.

She wasn't about to go back to London. *Ever.*

CHAPTER 22

CURIOSITY OVER A CHIT

hat same night in London
Stephen made his way into the Devonville House library, rather stunned to find the room filled with far more books than his stepfather's study contained. An over-stuffed sofa covered in a floral print was flanked by lamps at one end and positioned in front of a Palladian window. A small table topped by an arrangement of hot-house flowers was situated on the opposite end. In between, the two long walls were made up entirely of shelves from floor to ceiling.

He had always thought the library in his mother's house in Kent was impressive, but at half the size of this one, he realized it was probably more the standard of home libraries. He realized he was gawking in amazement and forced his mouth to close. The odors of vellum, vanilla and freshly polished wood only added to the heady experience.

Not sure where to start, he simply perused the titles on the first shelf directly across from the door.

"Were you looking for a particular book?"

Stephen whirled around to find Cherice regarding him from the open door. "My lady," he replied, bowing out of habit.

"I didn't mean to startle you," Cherice said with a grin. "You just looked so lost."

The bastard son of her husband angled his head to one side. "I didn't realized there was the equivalent of a lending library in the house," he replied with a quirked lip. "I am in search of a copy of *Debrett's Peerage and Barontage*."

Intrigued and rather surprised by his response, Cherice moved to a shelf very near to the one Stephen stood in front of and pulled out a leather-clad volume with a foil-stamped spine. "Here's the newest edition," she said as she handed over the book. "Are you looking for someone in particular?"

Taking the tome from his stepmother, Stephen realized the cover had never been opened. "Not really," he lied, his intention to discover where Victoria Comber fell in the mix of aristocratic children. "Will had a copy aboard ship. Made me learn it, but it was rather out-of-date, and after last night's ball, I realize I need a refresher," he commented with a shrug.

"Well, whatever you do, don't die of boredom," Cherice said as she made her way to the door. "We're going to the theatre tomorrow night, and I expect you'll want to attend."

Stephen nodded. "Father already invited me," he replied. "Of course, I plan to join you." He didn't add that he was going because there was the possibility of meeting Viscount Chamberlain about a position in the Foreign Office.

Cherice beamed as she curtsied and took her leave of the library, leaving Stephen to wonder at his stepmother's curiosity. Returning his attention to the book, he made his way to the sofa and took a seat, thumbing the edges of the pages until he found a particular earldom name.

Aimsley.

CHAPTER 23

A MORNING CHANGES
EVERYTHING

The next day in Oxfordshire
Barbara awoke slowly to the distant sound of pounding. She remained in her small bed, listening intently to determine what might be making the thumping noise. Certainly no one at the door. This wasn't a quick succession of knocks, but rather steady, deliberate pounding. Closing her eyes, she tried to recapture the dream that had escaped when she awakened.

Will.

What a vivid dream!

The memory of him holding her against his hard body had her sighing. How many times had she crawled into bed and hoped she would relive the experience of her one night of bliss with Will Slater? How many times had she since cursed that night? Cursed herself? Cursed Will? Cursed him, and then in the next breath, thanked him for giving her a son? If only the other circumstances of her life weren't so desperate!

There were no more balls and powder for the dueling pistol, and without a bow and arrow or the skills to use them, she had no hope of shooting any game for meat. It would be a month or more before the first vegetables would be ready in her meager garden. The few pence she had left from selling the horse might buy some eggs and enough provisions for a week, but then what?

Although her sewing skills were adequate, there were far better seamstresses to be found in Broadwell and nearby Langford. No one required a laundress or a maid in these parts. Even the public house had enough employees to service the small clientele.

"Unless you want to be spreadin' your legs for the unmarried menfolk, I've got no work for you," Susan had said when she last paid a call on the proprietor of *The Five Bells.*

Barbara Higgins refused politely and thanked the woman for her time. As the daughter of an earl, she had no intention of turning to prostitution to make her way in life. She would starve first, she decided.

Hunger pangs finally had Barbara sitting up in bed, which is when she noticed her state of dress.

Or rather, undress.

She was stunned to find she wore only her chemise. Her other garments had been carefully folded and placed on the chair under the window. A moment later, her face was in her hands as she remembered why her dream of Will had been so vivid.

He was here.

She glanced about the room again, turned on the bed to look for evidence he had lain with her. But the linens were only slightly mussed, and the counterpane was neatly folded at the bottom of the bed.

Barbara moved to the chair and began dressing, startled when she found her corset laced up. Hadn't Will undone all the laces the night before? Or had she dreamed that? She buttoned up her gown as far as she could, intending to ask Donald to finish the job as she usually did.

Stepping out of her room, she peeked into her son's room to find him still asleep despite the return of the pounding sound. The smell of coffee filled the front room of the cottage, an odor so unexpected she actually stopped in her tracks to inhale deeply. A quick glance into the pot on the stove found it nearly full. Another pot contained at least two servings of porridge.

Breakfast!

She quickly pulled down a wooden bowl from the shelf and paused as she realized the pot of warm water for doing dishes had been emptied and refilled with clean water. The plates from the night's dinner had been washed and replaced on the shelf. Even the settle had been wiped clean of crumbs from the night before.

Filling the bowl with porridge, she was about to sit down to eat when the door opened. Startled at first, she moved to stand up and then simply stared at the man who was regarding her with a grin.

"I apologize for making so much noise," Will said as he moved toward her.

Barbara continued to stare at him. "Where did you find the porridge? I... I thought it was all gone."

Will hesitated before giving her a nod. "It was. I brought some with me." He shook his head. "Actually, I was *forced* to bring along some food by the cook at Devonville House. She was quite insistent that there wouldn't be anything to eat in all of Oxfordshire," he explained as he joined her at the settle.

"You'll have to tell her she was right when you go back," Barbara replied with a wan smile.

Will leaned over and kissed her on the temple. "I'll take you to town later today. We'll need to get enough food to last until we head for London."

Barbara straightened and regarded him blankly. "I'm not going to London," she stated with a shake of her head.

Taken aback by her response, Will stilled himself. "Well, not today, of course. Probably not for a week or so. I still have to arrange transportation—"

"I'm not going back to London," Barbara repeated, and then returned to eating her porridge.

Will considered her words and decided it would do good to argue the point so early in the morning. "When may I take you shopping then?" he asked. "If you're not going to London, you'll certainly need to fill your pantry."

He had her there, she knew. "We have to take Donald, too," she murmured. "I cannot leave him alone."

"Of course," Will agreed. "I couldn't find a gig in the back. And where's the horse? I can tell there was one—"

"I sold him. We needed the money for food," she interrupted. "Horses are expensive. And we never had a gig. I just... walk when I need to go to the village."

Slumping at her words, Will frowned. "Barb," he sighed, disappointment evident in his voice. He took a deep breath and let it out.

"What were you building?" she asked, realizing their conversation was as frustrating for him as it was for her. Better to change the subject and hope he didn't bring up London again.

"Rebuilding, actually. The shed for the horse," he replied as he stood up. "And the roof on this place when I get to it later today. I don't know how long the repair will hold, but you shouldn't have need of more than one bucket during the next rain." He filled a mug with coffee. "Would you like some?" he asked as he held out the steaming cup in her direction.

Barbara angled her head. "Yes. I've no sugar or milk, though," she said with a shake of her head.

"I didn't make it too strong," Will said as he gave her the mug. "We usually didn't have sugar or milk on the ship, either."

Barbara frowned. "You had to make your own coffee on your ship?" she asked in surprise. "Did you have to make the repairs, as well?" she teased. The grin on her face was the first hint of humor she had shown since Will's arrival.

"Sometimes. Usually the cook would make coffee, but he tended to forget there was no sugar or milk," he explained with an expression of amusement on his face. He sobered. "I'm nearly finished out back. I just came in for coffee," he said as he stood up. "Come join me? It's a beautiful morning."

Finished with her porridge, Barbara considered the invitation. "I suppose, but..." She turned so her back was to him. "Can you do up the last few buttons?"

Setting his mug on the table, Will grinned. "You'll make a lady's maid out of me yet," he murmured as he moved to fasten the buttons. When he finished, he lowered his head so he could kiss the nape of her neck.

Closing her eyes, Barbara allowed a small sigh. Is this how mornings could be if Will was in them? She was reminded of her dream from the night before.

A dream?

Or had he really held her in his arms as she slept?

"I do hope I didn't crowd you too badly in the bed last night," he whispered, his lips nipping her earlobe.

Barbara whirled around in his arms, her eyes wide. "So... you *were* there?"

Will glanced off to one side. "There really wasn't anywhere else to sleep, and I just wanted to—"

"Did you...?" She stopped and tried to calm herself, realizing he couldn't have done anything untoward.

"I just held you. I... promise, I did nothing more," he murmured. He paused a moment. "Well, I might have..." He reached out with a hand and pantomimed holding one of her breasts. "And I think I kissed you a few times. But I promise, I did nothing more," he claimed. When he saw her look of shock, he added, "I admit, I wanted to do more, but I was afraid I might end up being shot if I did."

Barbara blinked, feeling the indignation fall away as she allowed a wan smile to show. "Donald couldn't have shot you if he *wanted* to. There aren't any more bullets," she whispered.

Will lowered his head so their foreheads touched. "Well, that's a relief," he replied. "I do not think I could abide being shot by my own son."

Taking her by the hand, Will led her out the door and

around to the back of the cottage. The timbers of the old shed and been erected to form a loafing shed in which Thunderbolt stood helping himself to a pile of old hay. His saddle and tack hung from a couple of nails. "I'll work on the cottage door next," Will said as he finished his cup of coffee.

"Donald and I were going to do that today before his lessons," Barbara said, a look of relief crossing her face. "But I have a feeling your repair will last longer."

Will gave her a nod. "By the way, how far away is Bampton?"

Barbara allowed a shrug. "Four, maybe five miles," she replied, pointing east.

Not as far as I thought it might be, Will thought with some relief. "And the Gisborn lands?"

At the mention of Gisborn, Barbara regarded Will with suspicion. "A bit closer," she replied carefully. "Why do you ask?"

The earl gave her a wry grin. "I am thinking it's time we paid a call on my sister is all," he responded.

"Lady Hannah?" Barbara guessed, frowning as she said the name. At Will's nod, Barbara continued frowning. "Why would your sister be anywhere near that old fart of an earl?" she asked, not apologizing for her language.

Will seemed surprised by the question, wondering if perhaps his father's assessment of Lord Gisborn's age might have been a bit off in the telling. "She's actually Lady Gisborn now, which means she's married to that old fart of an earl," he replied lightly. His frown suddenly matched Barbara. "Wait. Just how *old* is the Earl of Gisborn?"

Barbara finally allowed a shrug, realizing her assessment of the earl's age was merely due to the comments she had heard about the man whilst she was in Broadwell. "I've no idea, really," she replied. "I've heard reports that he is a miser and a..." She paused, her face taking on more color than Will had seen on it since his arrival. "Well, he's not a very well-liked man."

Will angled his head, thinking perhaps Barbara had the

current earl confused with the late earl. That man's reputation had been rather unflattering, but he didn't know how much of it was shared by Hannah's husband.

"Hannah seems rather enamored of the man," he commented. "But I am thinking we should probably find out for ourselves."

Barbara blinked, wondering what Will had in mind. "Do you mean to pay a call on Gisborn Hall? Today?" she asked, thinking he would take his leave and be gone from her life for good. The thought had her feeling relief. Now that he had seen what a cake she had made of her life, seen that she had an illegitimate child and no means to support herself, he would simply excuse himself and ride off. But a feeling of loss settled over her just as quickly.

Should Will Slater leave her, never to return, she knew she would have nothing to look forward to for the rest of her life. Nothing on which to hold any hope. She might have cursed him for what she had done all those years ago, but she didn't hate him for it. She had Donald because of what she had done.

"Well, tomorrow, actually," Will replied with a nod. "I still have some work to do on the roof, and you said something about Donald's lessons."

Barbara considered his words, finally allowing a shrug.

"If it's only four miles, we can be there in less than an hour..." Will explained. At her widened eyes and remembering Donald might not be able to walk as fast as the adults could, he quickly amended his estimate. "Under two hours."

Barbara shook her head. "We?" she repeated.

Will blinked, looking as if he'd been slapped across the face. "Yes," he hedged. "I'm not about to leave you. I just *found* you," he said as he leaned over and gave her a kiss on her forehead. "Besides, I want to meet my brother-in-law, and I want to introduce you to my sister."

It was Barbara's turn to blink when she heard Will's words. "How do you intend to introduce me?" she asked in alarm.

Will shrugged. "As my betrothed, of course," he replied, as if eight years hadn't passed since the last time they spoke of marriage and a life together.

"Are you.... are you sure this is a good idea?" she asked, her brows furrowed with worry. How would he explain Donald?

Will considered her words and gave a shrug. "I guess we'll find out tomorrow."

CHAPTER 24

AN AUNT AND AN UNCLE
WONDER ABOUT A NIECE

ack in London...
Mildred Regan watched from the front window of the townhouse as her niece, Victoria, stepped up and into a hackney. She knew she really should have joined the young woman for the performance at Drury Lane Theatre, but she had seen *The Merchant of Venice* too many times, and the thought of attending without her husband was a bit frightening. The theatre held over three-thousand people! Even in the company of her niece, Mildred knew she would feel panicked in the midst of so many.

Besides, Victoria was old enough, Mildred thought. She looked even older given the gowns her mother's modiste had created for her before Victoria made her way to London. The fabrics, luxurious silks, fine lawn, satin and tulle, had been made into designs from the latest *La Belle Assemblée*, the stitching exquisite. Not a single gown was white, which given Victoria's pale blonde hair and silver-gray eyes, was a blessing. The poor girl would have looked entirely washed out in virginal white.

Mildred's husband, Anthony Regan, was off on one his trips to the village of Kirdford in Sussex, spending a few weeks with his brother, William, to help the medical doctor set up a new clinic. Joshua Wainwright, Duke of Chichester, had provided the funds for the new building as well as the equipment and supplies Anthony was delivering, claiming he wanted his dukedom to have the very best medical facility. Mildred was fairly sure it was only because the Duchess of Chichester was expecting another baby that had the duke spending so much on the venture.

Although Anthony could have sent one of his many clerks to accompany the shipment of equipment, Mildred didn't begrudge her husband the trip—encouraged him to take it, in fact. "I rather doubt you're going to relish another woman in the house, especially one on the hunt for a husband."

The man allowed a shrug. "Why ever not? She's got a good head on her shoulders. Hopefully some young buck will take notice and make an offer for her hand. She's not getting any younger." This last was said with an arched eyebrow, an admonishment, perhaps, that Mildred's sister, Alexandra, had waited far too long to send Victoria to London in search of a husband.

Victoria would be three-and-twenty in a few days, after all.

Mildred crossed her arms and gave her husband a quelling glance. "Have you forgotten already?" she countered with an arched eyebrow.

Her husband gave her a frown before realization dawned. Their own daughter, now married and living in Kent with a law clerk, had endured two Seasons of heartbreak, tears, and temper tantrums before accepting an offer of marriage. "Oh, how could have I forgotten?" the physician whispered in mock despair. "You don't suppose Vicky will have as much trouble?" he hedged, thinking Victoria wasn't a typical country chit.

"I have no idea," Mildred responded with a shake of her head.

Sensing his wife's unease at what was to come, Anthony arranged for an additional footman for the household and a lady's maid for Victoria. By the time he took his leave two days after the girl's arrival, Anthony thought Victoria seemed well-read, rather sharp in her reasoning ability, and clever. She was also reasonably attractive, if one could get past those silver-gray eyes. There were times he thought them rather angelic and at other times, demonic, depending on Victoria's mood at the time.

"She'll do fine," Anthony said as he gave his wife a peck on the cheek and took off for Sussex.

Mildred merely gave him a nod, deciding not to share her sister's opinion just then. Alexandra had sent a letter ahead of Victoria's arrival with the warning that her daughter had developed *an independent streak that bodes well for her in life but foretells of trouble for any man who should wish for a compliant wife.*

Well, it was a good thing she had the independent streak, Mildred decided, for the poor girl would be attending some events on her own.

Like tonight's play.

As for how it would look for a chit to attend the theatre without a chaperone, Mildred figured the sheer numbers in attendance would help Victoria to simply blend into the crowd, probably much as she had done the night before at the ball she gone off to in a rush. She claimed to have received a last-minute invitation, but Mildred thought perhaps she had learned of the fête and thought to simply to show up as if she belonged there.

There was much to be said for an independent streak in a young woman.

CHAPTER 25

AN EVENING AT THE
THEATRE, PART ONE

*L*ater that night in Mayfair

Stephen tugged on his waistcoat, wondering if wearing the same one he had worn to the soirée and ball earlier in the week was appropriate. He walked into his brother's dressing room, stunned at the line up of topcoats and waistcoats that hung from pegs along one wall. Most were conservative, one-color coats with no embellishment, although there were a couple of embroidered waistcoats. He tried one on, it's deep green-on-green stitches appearing as satin against the matte-finished fabric. Would the embroidery be considered too flamboyant by Lord Chamberlain, the man for whom he might become a clerk at Whitehall?

A red waistcoat caught his attention, and Stephen pulled it off its peg. Featuring brass buttons and a slight pattern in the tapestry fabric, Stephen thought it a better choice for the evening. He finished buttoning it and moved to take his leave of Will's bedchamber when he realized he was being watched.

"The green one would have been my first choice," Cherice said from where she leaned against the doorframe. "But Devonville tells me you're after a position at the Foreign Office, so I suppose the red will have to do."

Stephen nodded. "My thoughts, exactly, my lady," he

said, moving to pull on his topcoat. Cherice was already moving to open the coat for him, though. "Thank you," he murmured after he pushed his arms through the sleeves.

"I'll see to it the butler arranges a valet for you on Perkins' days off," Cherice said as she watched him do up the buttons.

"Oh, that won't be necessary, my lady. I've been dressing myself since I was in short pants," he replied as he turned his attention to threading cuff links through the holes at the bottom of his sleeves.

"I suppose you didn't have servants aboard ship," she said, realizing he wouldn't be used to a servant seeing to his clothes.

"None, my lady," he agreed. "What will we be seeing at the theatre tonight?"

Cherice gave a shrug. "*The Merchant of Venice*, I believe. Which means Edmund will be playing Shylock."

Edmund? Perhaps she meant Edmund Kean, Stephen figured. Although his mother had frequently attended the theatre during her days as a courtesan, Marie St. Clair hadn't done so as much after her marriage. Not having been brought up going to the theatre as an entertainment, Stephen only knew of the actors from what he had been reading in *The Times* since his return to London. Their personal lives seemed far more entertaining than the plays they headlined!

"Ah, there you are," his father said as he appeared just outside Will's bedchamber.

"Stephen is borrowing one of Will's waistcoats. He's worn his new one too many times this week," Cherice said as she joined her husband and gave him a peck on the cheek.

"I rather doubt anyone we meet tonight will even notice," William stated. "But if we don't take our leave right now, we'll be tardy and *everyone* will notice," he added with an arched eyebrow.

Stephen nodded and followed William and Cherice down the stairs and out the front door of Devonville House. The town coach waited at the curb. "When do you suppose I will meet Lord Chamberlain?" Stephen asked after he had taken his seat in the coach. William and Cherice were seated side-by-side and riding in the direction of travel.

"I rather imagine just before the play starts," his father replied. "We have a box at the Drury Lane Theatre. Lord and Lady Chamberlain will be our guests this evening."

Stephen blinked. "Oh, that is convenient," he remarked, suddenly nervous. He had expected an introduction and an opportunity to say a few words in the hopes of landing a position. Instead, he would be spending hours in the man's company.

"I rather doubt Caro will wish to stay for the second half of the play, though," Cherice commented lightly. At Stephen's upraised brow, she added, "She gave Chamberlain an heir not even six months ago, and she doesn't like to be away from him very long."

"Neither does Chamberlain," William chimed in. "The man is my age and just became a grandfather, too!"

Stephen's attention bounced between his father and Lady Devonville until he remembered Caro was Caroline Fitzsimmons, Viscountess Chamberlain, and Lord Chamberlain was Matthew Fitzsimmons, Viscount Chamberlain. He quietly thanked his brother for having loaned him a copy of *Debrett's* on the ship, although he really wished it had been a newer edition. Although he had spent over an hour reading the one in the Devonville House library that afternoon, he had only studied the pages on the Aimsley earldom.

Cherice sighed. "Now we've gone and thoroughly confused you," she said with a shake of her head. "Caroline and Matthew Fitzsimmons have been married for... oh, dear, far longer than I can remember."

"At least twenty years," William finished for her when she threw up her gloved hands in resignation.

"Caro's niece—"

"Daughter," William interrupted, wincing when he realized he knew more about Lady Samantha's parentage than Cherice and shouldn't have said anything. "May as well be," he amended with a wave of his gloved hand, hoping she would ignore his correction.

Cherice's brow furrowed before she simply shook her head. "Your father gets a little confused sometimes," she said *sotto voce*, leaning forward so her comment could only be heard by Stephen. "Lady Samantha wed Lord Plymouth last year and just had a boy of her own."

Stephen couldn't help but notice his father rolling his eyes, so he figured the man had overheard Cherice's comment. *But who was Lord Plymouth?* Stephen screwed up his face in concentration. "Yorkshire?" he guessed. "A marquess?"

"Very good," William said with an approving nod. "And not a marquessate I would want," he added with a shake of his head. "I'll take a comfortable home in Mayfair over a drafty castle on the moors and troublesome coal mines any day."

Stephen allowed a grin, wondering if there was an estate home somewhere in Northumberland where the Devonville marquessate was based. He now knew his uncle, Donald, helped oversee the lands with the help of an estate manager when he wasn't distilling the best scotch in the northern counties.

The town coach slowed and came to a halt in front of the theatre. Stephen was the last to step out, his eyes lifting until he realized the theatre wasn't the one he remembered from his youth. "Is this... is this the right theatre?" he asked aloud, rather impressed at how grand the new white building appeared.

"Oh, that's right. You're probably remembering the one that burned down," William said as they made their way up the steps to the faux-columned entrance. "Awful fire, that one, and that building wasn't that old," he added as they made their way amongst the masses of theatre goers making their way into the building. "Although this one isn't quite as large, they can still seat more than three-thousand people," he commented. Then he pointed across the expanse of seats on the main floor. "See all those chandeliers?"

Stephen followed his father's finger and realized there were three levels of chandeliers hung at regular intervals around the entire semi-circular theatre, each one illuminating a level of boxes. Some boxes were already filled with patrons. "The number of candles must be—"

"It's all gas-lit," William stated proudly. "I do like our box in this one better, too. The view of the stage is far grander."

Stephen nodded his understanding, his gaze flitting about in the hopes of seeing someone he might know—perhaps one of the chits he had danced with at the Weatherstone ball. But as the Slaters made their way up several sets of stairs, he realized the crush of people made it impossible to make out the faces of the patrons. It wasn't until they were on the same level as the Devonville box that the crowds thinned and he could make out distinct people in the crush.

"Ah, here we are," William said as he paused outside the door to the theatre box. He stepped aside to allow Cherice to enter just as the Fitzsimmons appeared at the top of the stairs.

"I apologize for our late arrival," Matthew said as he gave Cherice a bow and took her hand. "My son was just demonstrating his ability to crawl on his hands and knees as we were about to leave the house," he said, a bit breathless from the climb.

"So good of you to invite us this evening," Caroline said as she afforded them a curtsy. She turned her attention to Stephen. "Bellingham?" she said with a hint of uncertainty.

Stephen bowed over her hand. "Stephen Slater, actually. It's an honor to make your acquaintance, my lady," he said before bestowing a kiss on the back of her satin-gloved hand.

Matthew stepped forward, holding out his right hand. "I am Chamberlain," he said, giving the young man an assessing glance.

Stephen shook it as he gave the man a nod. "Stephen

Slater, formerly of the *HMS Greenwich*," he said by way of introduction.

"I understand you may be interested in a position at Whitehall," Matthew said as they moved to enter the theatre box.

"Indeed, I am," Stephen replied, his attention drawn to a young woman who stood at the end of the hall. Dressed in a beautifully tailored gown of coral velvet, her pale blonde hair done up in a riot of curls and braids, she seemed to be rather interested in their party. She made no move to join them, however. In fact, when she realized she had been spotted, she suddenly turned around and disappeared down an adjacent hallway. Frowning, Stephen was about to enter the box when he realized he did know her.

Lady Jane? No, she had been far shorter and not nearly as blonde. And besides, there was no prune-faced chaperone standing behind her.

Lady Lucida? No, she wasn't blonde, and besides, where was Fred? Why, there wasn't a potted palm anywhere in the vicinity. Nor had he seen Lady Fletcher or Lord and Lady Bostwick. *Yet.* It seemed as if the entire populace of Mayfair was in the theatre.

Victoria! The one wearing the pink gown that perfectly complemented her creamy complexion and set off her elaborate coiffure to good effect. The one who couldn't be a debutante if she tried, for she was far too bold and self-assured. The one whose kiss had left him discombobulated. Or was it her second kiss that had done that?

The one who claimed to have crashed the ball!

Stephen wondered if she had done the same to get into the theatre or if she had a ticket to be there.

"See someone you know?" his father asked when he noticed Stephen's hesitance at entering the box. The marquess followed Stephen's line of sight to where the woman had been standing.

Shaking his head, Stephen turned his attention on his father. "I'm not sure. I thought I saw..." He blinked, realizing

Victoria had reappeared at the end of the hall, her rather fetching coiffure different from the one she had worn at the ball. Her gown, a coral the color of the inside of a conch shell, had Stephen imagining her on a sandy beach, beckoning him to follow her as she made her way to some secret place where they could kiss without being interrupted. Without being seen.

What the hell? Where had that thought come from? Stephen wondered as he realized he needed to be thinking about something other than how her gorgeous gown fit her perfect body, of how the snug bodice set off her rising moons and clung to her long legs when she walked. Of how the fabric draped over her bottom and swayed as she walked.

Christ! She wasn't even walking! How could he even know what she looked like when she swayed?

Walked, rather.

Stephen shook his head in an attempt to clear it.

Victoria was glancing about as if she was looking for someone, her nervousness apparent when she crossed her arms over her chest, a small reticule dangling from her wrist. Unfortunately, the move only enhanced her already delectable cleavage and Stephen was quite sure he gulped.

He hoped his father hadn't heard him.

A chime sounded from somewhere down below.

"We need to take our seats," William said *sotto voce*, his gaze following Stephen's until he spotted the young woman. She was now the only person left standing in the hallway as the others who had been mingling outside of their box had moved into them to take their seats.

"Miss Comber. I danced with her at Lord Weatherstone's ball," Stephen whispered.

William regarded the woman for only a moment before turning his attention back to Stephen, a knowing look crossing his face.

He had been young once—twice, actually—his head easily turned by beautiful chits with pale blonde hair and dressed in watered silk and velvets that enhanced their slim bodies to best effect. They had even been more impressive without their gowns on, he remembered, their delectable kisses and supple bodies welcoming his for nights of passion so intense, he had been left breathless and replete, happy and content. Hell, he had married one and bedded the other for several years and rather wished it were possible to have two wives, especially when they both gave him a son.

William almost felt sorry for his bastard son, except he couldn't quite bring himself to it. Stephen would have to learn first-hand what it was like to be overcome by a woman. To be forced to think of her day and night until he either found another or decided she was the one.

"Well, it appears she's been separated from her party," the marquess said, giving his son an arched eyebrow. When Stephen gave him a blank look, William leaned in and whispered, "Well, don't just leave her standing in the hall, son. Invite her to join us. She can look for her friends or family during the intermission."

His eyes widening in surprise, Stephen gave his father a nod and hurried down the hall. Giving the chit a quick bow to her rather solemn curtsy, he moved to take her gloved hand. "Are you lost?" he asked in a whisper, kissing the back of the white fabric. He couldn't help but notice it wasn't the same satin glove he had kissed the night before.

"No more so than you," Victoria said with a hint of mischief as she placed her arm on his.

"There's no need to be cheeky," he countered, thinking he might be making a big mistake in inviting her to join them in his father's box. He was being considered for a position as a clerk at the Foreign Office, after all. "You're welcome to join me in my father's box."

At first thinking he was going to have her removed from this level of the theatre, Victoria gave him a look of surprise. "Truly?" she whispered. "You would save me from certain societal suicide?"

Stephen blinked before giving her a quelling glance. He nearly blinked again when he again noticed the color of her eyes, a sort of silver-gray he had seen nearly every day of his life before he left England on a naval vessel. They were the same color as his mother's. And he would have continued to stare into them except he noticed her expression. He angled his head. "Having to wait in the lobby for the intermission isn't necessarily societal suicide," he replied, knowing she would have to wait before being allowed to take any of the seats on the main floor. "You would no doubt have a number of fellow stragglers and latecomers with whom to wait for the intermission."

"I wouldn't though," she whispered with a shake of her head. "I would simply take my leave altogether. I wish to see the entire play, after all."

Stephen led them back to his father's box. "How should I introduce you?"

Victoria nearly stopped in her tracks, not having thought that far ahead when she decided to see if she could gain entrance to someone's box instead of having to sit in the cheap seats down below. "Miss Comber, of course," she replied, her grin as teasing as her earlier manner. "Or had you forgotten?"

As if I could forget, he nearly replied, remembering all too well what her kiss had done to him. And how he would now be forced to sit with her for hours!

Quirking his lip, Stephen waved her through the door to the box, ducking in behind her just as the curtain lifted to reveal the stage. In the dim light, Stephen had to wait a moment for his eyes to adjust before seeing her to a seat behind Lady Chamberlain. He took the chair next to hers, settling into it as he noticed the viscount giving him a glance. He nodded to the man, disappointed that they would have to wait until the intermission before discussing the position at the Foreign Office.

Unfamiliar with the story of *The Merchant of Venice*, Stephen was soon caught up in the tale of an aristocrat in need of a loan so that he might court a woman named Portia. Since he certainly had no intention of borrowing a large sum of money when it came time to pursue a wife, Stephen couldn't understand why a man like Bassanio would expect his best friend, Antonio, to loan him the money, especially since Antonio had apparently had to bail out the nobleman many times before. Either Antonio was a very good friend or he was entirely too trusting, Stephen decided. The shipping magnate didn't even *have* the money to give to his friend, and so had to borrow it from Shylock, a Jewish moneylender, with a promise to pay it back by a certain time.

Given how poorly Antonio had treated Shylock in the past, Stephen could certainly understand why, if the loan couldn't be repaid on time, Shylock demanded a pound of flesh from the merchant. When it was time for the intermission, Stephen was almost hoping Shylock would be able to take his pound of flesh.

When it came to the test to gain Portia's hand—her father had devised a plan to have her suitors choose between three caskets—Stephen found himself imagining Victoria's father doing something similar. As for which casket he would choose in pursuit of Portia, Stephen could certainly understand why the other suitors would choose the one of gold or the one of silver instead of the one filled with lead—although he rather doubted he would choose any of them. They would all weigh far too much to transport! Besides, he rather doubted Victoria would simply accept whatever man chose some random casket, no matter what was inside. He thought her far too independent.

She would probably be offended by the whole ordeal! Yes, better he not choose any of the caskets.

When the curtain lowered for the intermission, the general noise level in the theatre increased as people stood up from their seats and began conversing. Stephen was aware of people in the hall behind their box and was reminded that Victoria probably wished to look for whoever she had come with to the theatre.

"Oh, Stephen, do introduce us," Cherice said when she turned around from her front-row seat and pretended to discover Victoria sitting next to him for the first time. Stephen was quite sure she was aware of the young lady's arrival just as the play started.

Victoria was quick to get to her feet and perform a perfect curtsy. Stephen gave Cherice a nod. "Lady Devonville, Lady Chamberlain, may I present Miss Victoria Comber? I hope it was acceptable that I asked her to join us. She was separated from the rest of her party when the chime sounded."

Victoria kept a smile pasted on her face as Stephen made the introductions. He was secretly glad when all three women were suddenly engaged in conversation, although he had to feel sorry for Victoria when he realized neither Cherice nor Lady Chamberlain knew the girl and were asking as to her family when he approached the viscount.

He wasn't surprised to overhear her mention the Aimsley name. From what he had read that afternoon in the latest edition of *Debrett's Peerage and Barontage*, her father was the youngest brother of the Earl of Aimsley. She was the grand-daughter of an earl. She had as much right to a place in Society as anyone else, he supposed. *More than me,* he realized, feeling rather blessed that his father hadn't given him the cut direct when Will insisted he join him in London rather than go onto his mother's house in Kent when they finished their service in the Navy.

"My lord, I apologize for not being able to continue our conversation earlier," Stephen said, his hands clasping behind his back in order to hide his nervousness.

"Ah, but saving a damsel in distress takes precedent, does it not?" the viscount replied with a grin.

Stephen allowed a slight smile, deciding not to mention that he rather doubted Victoria Comber had ever been in distress and certainly didn't need saving. Except from him should he get the opportunity to kiss her again.

What the hell? He was supposed to be discussing a job opportunity, not thinking of kisses!

"I am in need of a Navy man in my office at Whitehall. Are you interested?"

Stephen tried hard to keep an impassive expression, but found he could not when Lord Chamberlain was so quick to get to the point. "Yes, of course, my lord."

"Can you read and write?"

Stunned the man had to ask, Stephen nodded. "Yes. Eton, of course, and then the Royal Naval Academy," he added, wanting the viscount to know he wasn't trying to gain a position based on being the son of a marquess.

"How many years on board a ship?"

"Six."

One of Matthew's eyebrows arched up. "And how many served with your brother?"

Stephen sighed. "Two, my lord." He wondered why the viscount would ask him about the time he served under his brother, but soon learned with Lord Chamberlain's next question.

The viscount allowed a grin. "Come close to killing him a time or two?"

Blinking, Stephen shook his head. "No," he replied carefully. "We get along rather well, actually."

This bit of information seemed to intrigue the viscount. "I cannot tell you much about the position here," he said, waving a hand to indicate the theatre. "However, if you could come to my offices at Whitehall tomorrow, I should like to cover the responsibilities in more detail, and introduce you to one of my operatives."

Operatives? Stephen had to suppress the urge to cock an eyebrow at the comment. "What time shall I be there?"

Lord Chamberlain gave a shrug. "I'm usually in my office by nine o' clock," he replied, watching Stephen closely to determine if the early hour would have him wincing.

"Since I am usually up with the sun, I shall have no trouble being there at nine," Stephen said with a nod. "Thank you, my lord."

Matthew Fitzsimmons angled his head. "Don't thank me

yet. You may not like the position. Or let's hope you decide it's work you've always wanted to do." He turned his attention to the ladies, who were still engaged in chit-chat. "Caro, I do believe we should be taking our leave," he said in a quiet voice. "I wish to check on my son before he's too sound at sleep."

Caroline Fitzsimmons gave her husband a look of surprise and then covered her mouth with a gloved hand. "Oh, goodness. I apologize, but I must take my leave," she said to the other two woman. "Chamberlain insists on being home when little Matthew is put to bed," she murmured, her happy expression at odds with her words.

The Fitzsimmons took their leave of the box, and Stephen found himself once again standing next to Victoria. "Did you wish to join your party now?" he asked, secretly wondering if she had come to the theatre alone. "I'm not sure how much longer the intermission will last," he added, his manner suggesting she should decline the offer of assistance.

Cherice was quick to intervene on Victoria's behalf. "Oh, come now. You really must join me in the front row. If your friends are to find you, you must be *visible*," she insisted.

Giving Stephen a surreptitious wink, Victoria accepted the marchioness' invitation and took the seat that had been occupied by Lady Chamberlain.

For the rest of the play, Stephen wondered if Victoria would be mentioning what happened in Lord Weatherstone's garden while she spoke in quiet whispers with Cherice.

CHAPTER 26

AN EVENING AT THE THEATRE, PART TWO

Stephen leaned over toward his father. "Thank you for arranging the introduction to Lord Chamberlain," he whispered.

William regarded his son a moment. "That's what fathers are for," he murmured. "And when we get back to the house, I expect you'll be required to explain how you know this young lady," he warned with a hint of amusement.

Giving his father a nod, Stephen resettled himself in his seat behind Victoria and tried to concentrate on the play. He found it was no surprise Antonio couldn't pay back the loan, but found Shylock's reaction rather barbaric. Just because his daughter had married a Christian and taken most of the moneylender's money, and probably because Antonio had been rather rash with his antisemitism, Shylock was determined to get his pound of flesh. Stephen figured that since Bassanio and Portia had married and were off to Venice to repay the loan, Shylock would be more than satisfied with twice the loan amount. Stunned that Shylock insisted on taking Antonio to court to claim his pound of flesh, Stephen rolled his eyes. Shylock had obviously never been to war, had never seen a mortal wound, or he wouldn't be so quick to demand the pound of flesh.

Stephen's mind wandered. He wondered if Will had

found Barbara and then wondered if Victoria had come to the theatre with a chaperone. If she hadn't, he would have to insist on seeing her home, although he had no idea where that might be. After what she had said at the ball, it was possible she was staying in Cheapside. Or the Seven Dials!

Damnable woman!

First she crashes a ball and then gets me in the garden for a round of kissing... He had to shake his head in an attempt to clear the memory, for his body had already reacted to his thoughts of her kisses, of how her body had been pressed against the front of his, of how her fingers clutched his shoulders as his arms held her upright. She had tasted of champagne and smelled like lemon and honeysuckle. Or maybe they had merely been standing near a honeysuckle bush. He didn't know nor did he care just then. The entire episode had been so intense, he had barely been able to stand up for the duration of it let alone keep his wits about him.

Perhaps it would be better if he *didn't* offer her an escort to wherever she was staying, he decided. What if she wished to renew what they had started in the gardens? He would deflect her advances, of course. Insist she keep her hands off of him. Deny they had shared anything more than chaste conversation during the ball. None of that had been his fault, he reasoned. Victoria had been rather fast when he gave it some more thought. A wanton. Why, he shouldn't even be seen in her company!

When his attention was once again back on the play, he listened closely as a doctor of the law espoused the importance of mercy. "Mercy is twice blest: It blesseth him that gives and him that takes," he heard, realizing almost immediately that the man wasn't a man at all, but rather Portia, attempting to talk Shylock out of taking his pound of flesh.

Although Shylock refused any compensation, insisting on his pound of flesh, Stephen considered Portia's words. Perhaps Victoria wasn't entirely responsible for what had happened in the gardens the night before. Of course, he would see to her safety once the play was over. Offering her a ride and an escort to her wherever she was staying was the least he should do. He would feel awful should something happen to the chit.

The rest of the play seemed mired in legalities, the tale similar to one his mother had made him read when he was between semesters at Eton. Once again bored, Stephen grew curious. Did Victoria had any suitors? She had assured him she wasn't married despite the pink gown she wore. He wondered how old she was. Wondered when the damned play would end so he could offer her his arm and escort her to the Devonville coach...

The roar of applause had Stephen jerking in his seat. Pulled from his reverie, it took a moment for Stephen to determine Antonio's wealth had been restored to him and he wasn't missing any of his flesh. Everyone in the play seemed to have made amends.

A happy ending.

Rising slowly to his feet, he found his gaze settling on Victoria. Cherice was already engaging her in conversation, something about the next time they might meet.

"In the event Miss Comber is without an escort home, would it acceptable for me to offer her a ride in the coach with us?" Stephen asked of his father.

William arched an eyebrow. "I would expect you to do nothing less," he replied with a nod. "Since you've asked about it, I'm made to wonder if you already know she's without an escort. Is that the case?"

Stephen gave a shrug. "I cannot yet answer that," he said with a sigh, almost hoping there was an escort somewhere in the building. For if there was not, then Victoria Comber was a truly improper young lady. She had come to the theatre by herself. Probably in a hackney.

Stephen was saved from having to ask, for when the ladies stood up and turned to regard the gentlemen, Cherice angled her head and said, "We'll be giving Miss Comber a ride home this evening. I do hope it's not inconvenient?"

William and Stephen exchanged knowing glances and shook their heads. "Not at all."

By the time the Devonville town coach finally made it to the head of the queue of carriages waiting out in front of the Drury Lane Theatre, a light rain had begun to fall. Since the theatre didn't feature a portico in front, the Devonville party waited until the driver had the coach door open before making their way down the steps and to the equipage.

Having brought along a shawl, Cherice merely raised it over her elaborate coiffure and grasped her skirts in front of her so they were somewhat protected from the rain. Victoria, however, had nothing in the way of a shawl or mantle, her long-sleeved gown's velvet of a weight suitable for cooler weather. Realizing she would be drenched before they made it to the coach, Stephen removed his topcoat and draped it over Victoria's shoulders.

Rather surprised by his show of chivalry, Victoria regarded him for a moment before giving him a nod. "Thank you, my lord," she murmured before following on Cherice's heels and allowing the driver to assist her up the step and into the coach. Ensuring she was facing against the direction of travel—she didn't think it appropriate to take the seat next to the marchioness—Victoria allowed a giggle as she settled herself.

The warmth of Stephen's topcoat enveloped her in comfort, the scent of amber a subtle reminder of how close he had been to her in the theatre box. How close he had been the night before when they had kissed in the Weatherstone gardens. She barely had a second to take in the luxurious interior of the coach—the red leather squabs more comfortable than any hackney could boast, the lanterns next to each window bathing the maple veneer in a golden light—before the marquess entered and seemed to pause before taking the seat next to his wife. Stephen followed, his expression indicating his surprise at finding he would be sitting next to Victoria as opposed to the marquess.

The driver's head ducked into the coach. "Where to, my lord?"

William Slater gave Stephen an arched eyebrow. "Devonville House. I'd like to get my marchioness home before she catches a chill. Then you can see to getting our guest to her home," he added, his attention on Stephen.

"I truly appreciate the offer of a ride, my lord. I could have easily taken a hackney," Victoria said.

"Not without an escort, Miss Comber," he replied sternly. "Especially this time of night. Aimsley would not be pleased to learn his niece was traveling by herself."

The hint of warning in his voice was unmistakable, making Victoria realize she had erred in thinking she could attend the theatre alone when her aunt backed out of chaperoning at the last moment. It wasn't as if she had walked to the theatre, or thought she could walk home. She merely thought taking a hackney was the answer.

Goodness! There was so much to learn about being a proper young lady!

"Are you warm enough?" Stephen murmured, rather glad the close quarters afforded a warmer ride than if there had just been the two of them.

"Oh, quite," Victoria replied, feeling ever so embarrassed so that her cheeks were red. "In fact, would you like your coat? I don't really need it," she said in a quiet voice, not wanting to disturb the marquess and marchioness. They both seemed lost in thought as they sat holding hands in the dim light.

Although she didn't mean to stare, she couldn't help but notice how the two seemed so comfortable with each other. Almost as much as her own mother and father, who any number of times could be found holding hands or sneaking kisses after dinner. She hadn't expected it of their ilk, though. Didn't aristocrats marry out of duty rather than because they felt affection for one another?

"Did you like the play?" Cherice asked, her attention back on Victoria.

The young woman straightened in the squabs. "Oh, very much. I thought Mr. Kean was magnificent," she replied. "If I didn't know any better, I would have thought Shakespeare had written the part of Shylock specifically for him to play."

Cherice gave her a grin. "It is his role," she agreed. "And what did you think, Stephen? Did you have a favorite?"

Having spent most of the second half of the play daydreaming, he was about to say, "Not particularly," when he remembered Portia. Or her thoughts on mercy, rather. "I was rather impressed by Portia's speech about mercy," he said thoughtfully. "Shylock would have proved himself a better man had he taken her advice, but then the play would have been shorter."

Stephen was aware of Victoria's gaze on him, of how her brow furrowed before she seemed to slump into the squabs. Before Cherice could respond, the town coach halted. From the slight jerk behind him, Stephen knew the driver had stepped down from his box. A quick look out his window and he realized they were already at Devonville House.

"Well, it was very good to meet you, Miss Comber. I'm sure we'll see you again soon," Cherice said before she allowed her husband to help her from the carriage. She turned her attention to Stephen, giving him an arched eyebrow before she stepped out of the coach.

"Would you like to sit in the direction of travel?" Stephen asked, curious if Cherice thought he should depart the coach and allow Victoria to ride alone or if she wanted him to accompany their guest.

"I'm quite fine right here," she insisted. "Unless..." At Stephen's quick glance in her direction, she added, "You would prefer me to sit across from you?"

Stephen allowed a wan smile. "You're fine where you are."

The trap door in the top of the coach opened. "Where to, my lord?"

Giving Victoria a nod, Stephen waited for her to reply.

"King Street. Where it meets Foubert's Place," she said as she gave Stephen a nervous glance. "Carnaby."

Well, that address wasn't quite what he expected. "Who lives there?" he asked lightly, hoping she wouldn't think him too nosey.

Victoria allowed a sigh. "My aunt. My mother's older sister, Mildred Regan," she finally said. "She agreed to be my sponsor for the Season, but, unfortunately, she doesn't go to many events."

"Not even the theatre?" Stephen asked with a quirked lip.

Giving him a quelling glance, Victoria huffed. "She was supposed to be there. She promised. And then…"

Stephen frowned. "What happened?" he asked, worried about the health of Mildred Regan.

"She claimed she overdid it whilst we were paying calls this afternoon, and she begged off after her maid had already done my hair and dressed me." A tear appeared in the corner of her eye. "Please, I beg you, do not tell the marchioness."

Turning his body so he could reach for her shoulder, Stephen stared at Victoria. Was she truly about to cry? Or was she merely putting on a show for his benefit? "I won't tell her," he agreed, "But you must tell me something. And you must be truthful."

A quizzical expression replaced the one of sorrow. "Of course," she agreed, turning so she faced him on the shallow seat, one shoulder sinking into the squabs.

"How many men have you kissed?"

Victoria blinked. And blinked again as she straightened on the seat. "I do not see how that is any of your concern, sir," she replied, rather indignant just then.

Stephen narrowed his own eyes at her. "I am one. How many others are there?" Try as he might, he couldn't get the hint of anger out of his voice. He didn't even know why it was there, or even why he wanted to know how often she kissed other men. But for some reason, at that moment, he wanted to know. He *needed* to know.

Victoria's resolve to ignore his question melted away after a moment. "One. My second cousin," she finally admitted. "We were five at the time."

Furrowing his brows, Stephen considered her answer for a moment. "Did he put his tongue in your mouth?"

Victoria allowed a rather loud gasp. "Of course not!" she replied, now really indignant. "He was *five!*"

"Did you put your tongue into his?"

Stephen realized after the fact that he really should have been more aware of the fact that her right arm was entirely unencumbered, even by his topcoat resting over her shoulders, for when she leaned back and swung at him, he felt the full force of her open hand as it impacted his left cheek.

"Ow!" he exclaimed, his eyes squeezed shut against the sting of the blow. Had his eyes been open, he would have seen her wince and the surreptitious shaking of her right hand, probably because it felt as if all the bones were broken.

"You *rake!*" she exclaimed, her anger most evident. "My first kiss—at a ball, no less—and you have to go *ruin* it with... innuendo and rude questions!"

Stephen sighed, realizing he had angered the girl. Offended her with his assumption that she had kissed other men besides him. Been kissed by other men besides him. But, dammit, her kiss—or series of kisses, rather—had been so delicious. So passionate. So perfect.

How could he be her first?

I am her first!

The thought had him feeling rather proud just then, so it wasn't a surprise his ego would follow suit.

Before he quite knew what he was doing, Stephen had his arms wrapped around her shoulders and his mouth pressed against hers, a move made easier in that she was still so startled by his earlier implied accusation that her mouth was open and perfectly placed to accept his.

He thought at first she was going to fight him off. And he wouldn't have blamed her one bit. He couldn't quite believe what he was doing, but then he was lost just then, lost in the sensation of her soft lips against his, in the sensation of a slight buzz which he realized was due to the fact that he was pressing far too hard. Bruising her lips, no doubt. He couldn't even imagine what his looked like.

Softening the kiss, he gently nipped her lower lip and took her mouth again, this time using his tongue as he had the night before, teasing her tongue to join his, tasting her teeth and tongue and once again nipping her lower lip, kissing her jawline, her neck, the line of her collarbone to the hollow at the base of her throat.

He felt more than heard her soft moans, felt more than heard her staccato heartbeats where her bosom was pressed into his waistcoat. And he would have continued his assault of soft kisses along the tops of her breasts except that he was suddenly aware that the coach had come to a bumpy halt. The telltale jerk of the driver dismounting from his box had Stephen straightening, although he still had his arms around Victoria's shoulders.

He dropped his forehead to hers while he attempted to catch his breath. "I'll walk you to your door," he managed to get out.

Victoria shook her head against his. "I would rather you didn't," she whispered.

The coach door opened at the same time Stephen pulled his arms from around her shoulders, one of his hands clutching his topcoat as Victoria stood up and took her leave of the town coach. She managed to look rather steady as she did so, a feat Stephen found he admired in the chit.

He rather doubted he could stand up just then.

"Good night, my lord. Thank you for the ride."

"Good night, Miss Comber," Stephen said, his voice sounding far more normal than he expected. "I look forward to seeing you again at another event."

He listened intently, hoping to hear her say something similar, but a quick look out the carriage window, and he realized she had already reached the door to No. 31 King Street.

The driver leaned into the coach just as Stephen finished

pulling on his topcoat, the scent of Victoria's lemon and honeysuckle hair filling his nostrils. "Where to, Mr. Slater?"

A combination of frustration and angst nearly had him mentioning Covent Gardens—a visit to a brothel seemed in order—but he remembered he would be meeting with Lord Chamberlain in the morning and thought better of it. Besides, what kind of prostitute would allow the kissing he had just experienced with Victoria Comber?

What kind of *woman* would allow that kind of kissing?

Well, there was one, he decided. Their paths would cross again, he was sure. And if they didn't, he at least knew where he could find her.

Realizing the driver was still waiting for a response, Stephen finally sighed. "Devonville House," he murmured.

"Very good, sir."

CHAPTER 27

A MARCHIONESS SEDUCES
HER HUSBAND

ater that night

Cherice pressed her ear against the connecting dressing room door to William's bedchamber, listening for evidence he was still awake. Sounds of his incessant pacing had her sighing. She wondered how long he had been at it. She rather expected he would pay a call to her bedchamber that evening—he had given her clues he would do so—but after more than an hour, he still hadn't made an appearance.

She dared a glance in the cheval mirror at the other end of the dressing room, rather liking how her translucent pink dressing gown appeared in the dim light. With only a single fastening between her breasts, the robe did little to cover anything, its edges flaring open in the front to display her bare belly and the dark hair at the apex of her thighs. Beneath it, her feet were adorned with tiny heeled slippers topped with pink feathers.

Whatever had her husband troubled could probably be alleviated with a tumble, she decided. A tumble and quiet conversation.

Cherice knocked twice before opening the door. She gave William a teasing grin before slipping entirely into the room.

"Have your feet worn a hole in the carpet?" she asked as she reached up to give him a kiss.

The marquess wrapped his arms around her shoulders and pulled her against the front of his body. "Not yet," he murmured. "And I see you've come to save me from doing so," he added as he pulled away to give her an appreciative glance at what little she was wearing. "Is this new? You do know that little button won't be attached for very long," he warned with an arched brow.

"My maid can sew it back on in the morning," she replied, her own arched brow matching his in height. She had worn the negligée several times before, but usually with a satin nightgown beneath. Some nights required more to pull off a seduction. "But before you see to ruining yet another negligée, you really must tell me what has you so vexed." Even as she said the words, her hands were spreading open the edges of his dressing gown so her palms could slide over his bare chest, her fingers tangling in the crisp, graying curls.

William allowed a sigh before he answered. "I wish to see my sons settled. Married. To women they adore," he answered with a sigh. He paused a moment. "I don't want them wasting precious time on the wrong choice, or worse, no choice at all."

Cherice stilled her hands. "Is there some reason to suspect that will happen?"

The marquess sighed again before reaching up with both hands to remove the pins from Cherice's hair, a wan smile appearing as locks of her hair tumbled down past her shoulders. "Will has to have found his Barbara by now, so perhaps they will marry soon," he replied as he took out a few more pins. "Good grief! How many of these damned things does your maid put in here?" he groused, his fingers combing through her hair to find even more of the U-shaped hairpins.

"Two dozen, at least," Cherice replied in a whisper. "And a few more for good measure. You never know when your husband will decide to make mischief." She paused in her teasing and sobered. "Tell me something, though," she said, remembering her conservation with Stephen about why Barbara might have left London. "Did Barbara leave London because she was sent away?" she asked with an arched eyebrow.

William stilled his hands, his fingers dropping to her shoulders. "Sent away?" he repeated.

Cherice nodded. "Yes. Was she ruined? Expecting a child, perhaps?"

Her husband simply stared at Cherice for a moment. "Did you hear something back then? Gossip, perhaps?"

Cherice shook her head. "No, of course not. But there are only two reasons young ladies are sent away from London—"

"What's the other?" William interrupted.

"For a trip to the Continent," she replied with a shrug, as if he should have known.

Sighing, William finally gave her a nod. "Will admitted to ruining the chit," he whispered. "The night before he left to meet his ship." He sighed again. "So, you think she was with child?"

Angling her head to one side, Cherice sighed. "I wish I could say I don't, but I didn't know Lady Barbara, so I suppose I do." She dared a glance up at him. "Are you disappointed I would think the worst of your son? Because I don't. He seemed intent on finding her. On making her his wife. He's held a candle for her all these years."

The marquess shook his head. "As usual, you're a perceptive woman," he murmured. He had been stunned when he read the note from Will. A courier had delivered it just before they left for the theatre. "When he found his Barbara, he also found her with a seven-year-old boy." He carefully watched his wife, expecting some kind of reaction, and was surprised when she merely arched an eyebrow. "Which means you're a grandfather! When will he bring his family home?" she asked, anticipation evident in her voice.

William allowed a wan smile, rather happy to hear she wasn't scandalized by the thought of a bastard grandchild. "Patience, my love. They haven't seen each other in a very long time," he warned, remembering how cautious Will's words seemed in the missive that had arrived that afternoon. "He has some courting to do to convince her ladyship she should marry him," he added.

Rather surprised by this bit of news, Cherice's disappointment was evident. "He's not coming back in a few days, is he?" she whispered with a frown.

"I rather doubt he will return in a fortnight," her husband countered, pulling her so she was pressed against the front of his body. "Which means it was probably fortuitous that he left his brother to act in his stead. I just wish he was looking for a wife for himself and not for Will," he added before kissing Cherice on the forehead.

His wife brightened. "Oh, I wouldn't worry about Stephen. I do believe he's being chased by a chit, but he hasn't yet figured out he has to catch her," she said with a teasing grin.

William furrowed his brow, as if trying to figure out what she had just said. "Come again?"

"I would love to, but you'll have to make love to me. I do believe you intimated you would," she replied with a pout, her hands sliding down the front of his body until her fingers deftly stroked his hardening manhood and then cupped his sac.

Gasping at her bold move, William had his hands cupping the globes of her bottom and lifting her up and onto the bed before she could let out a sound of protest. She did let out a sigh of disappointment, though, when his teeth clamped onto the tiny button enclosure of her negligée and bit through the thread. He proudly held the button between his teeth for a moment before blowing it onto the carpeted floor. Returning his attention to Cherice, he allowed a sound of appreciation. "*Mon cherie*, you do know how to take a man's mind off his troubles," he whispered, before lowering his lips to her breasts and belly.

Cherice raked her fingers through his thinning gray hair and giggled. "*Oui, monsieur,*" she replied before inhaling sharply when he impaled her. "*Oui!*"

CHAPTER 28

A POSITION WITH A PIRATE?

he next morning

Stephen opened the brown paper surrounding his Navy uniform, admiring how carefully the blue frock coat with its white lapels was folded, how precise the sleeves of his shirt were ironed. The breeches looked nearly new. The laundress had done an admiral job in restoring it to wearable condition. He had a meeting with Lord Chamberlain at nine that morning, and he had every intention of looking as presentable as possible.

Once he was dressed and had his boots shined to a high gloss, Stephen made his way down to the main level of the house, intending to head for the stables. "Would you like me to summon the carriage, Lord Stephen?" Hatfield asked when he realized Stephen was about to take his leave of the household.

"I thought to ride a horse." At the butler's look of disapproval, Stephen realized he should think again. "Is there something smaller than the town coach I could take?"

Hatfield smiled.

Fifteen minutes later, Stephen was happily driving his father's sporty red phaeton toward St. James Park and the Foreign Office.

Despite having served in the British Navy for six years,

Stephen was unprepared for the size of the military complex that housed Horse Guards and the Foreign Office. After seeing to it his equipage and the Cleveland Bay that pulled it would be looked after by a stablehand, Stephen headed for the building in which Lord Chamberlain had his offices. He realized from a clock on the desk of a clerk that he had timed his arrival about right. A few minutes more, and he would have been late for his appointment. "Lieutenant Slater to see Lord Chamberlain," he said when the clerk looked up from a stack of papers on his desk.

"Ah, the naval position," the man said as he regarded Stephen before struggling to stand up. Once he was headed toward a door on the far wall, Stephen realized the man walked with a limp.

"War wound?" he guessed as they made their way.

"Aye. Waterloo. Hard to believe it's been three years already." The clerk knocked on the paneled door and paused before opening it.

From where he stood, Stephen could see the viscount behind a huge desk. From the way the man was regarding something directly in front of him, Stephen realized there was someone else in the office with him.

Lord Chamberlain waved a hand. "Come in. We don't stand on ceremony around here," he said.

Stephen entered the office, giving the clerk a nod as he passed him. "Lord Chamberlain," Stephen said as he gave the man a bow. He turned to the other man and was startled to see a familiar face regarding him. Blinking, he realized he recognized the man—Stephen was quite sure it was Captain Jack Crawley, a pirate of some renown—but the man was dressed in clothes suitable for a gentleman.

What the hell was a pirate doing in the Foreign Office? "Crawley?" Stephen guessed, his expression fierce and his reflexes on alert.

"I get that all the time. Alex Bradley, actually," the man replied with a sly grin, his right hand extended.

Stephen shook it, although he hesitated before doing so.

"Forgive me. It's just that… you look *exactly* like someone else I've come across."

Matthew Fitzsimmons gave a snort and stood up. "Look who's calling the kettle black," he teased as he moved to shake Stephen's hand. He turned his attention to Alex. "Commander Will Slater is his brother. I doubt I could tell them apart side-by-side unless they were in uniform," he claimed.

A hint of recognition crossed Alex's face. "Ah, yes. I remember now. You were on the *HMS Greenwich*. Boarded my ship when we were docked at Havre. Not that you had any jurisdiction there," he added with a hint of derision.

His brows furrowing, Stephen realized he did recognize the man. And he *was* the pirate! "Captain Jack Crawley," he breathed.

"I am," Alex agreed. "Or *was*, rather, for a couple of years. I'm back at my desk for the time being," the operative explained with a nod. "Crawley was my cover while we were searching for smugglers," he added when he noticed Stephen looking to Matthew for confirmation. "Mostly liquor, but occasionally we'd intercept something more interesting."

The viscount rolled his eyes as he gave a chuckle. "I think he's referring to my niece, Lady Samantha. He found her and Lord Plymouth stranded on an island off Spain last year. She's Plymouth's marchioness now, thanks to Alex here, and has a baby boy of her own." he said proudly. He frowned. "But not because of Bradley," he added.

Alex cleared his throat, uncomfortable at hearing the viscount's comment. "I was looking for a ring of smugglers doing business in Yorkshire. They were operating on the coast—on Plymouth's land—using some caves to hide their wares. Once the ring was caught, Chamberlain let me come back here to work," Alex explained. "*Comment est votre français?*"

Stephen had to suppress the urge to wince at the operative's poor accent. Having grown up speaking the French language—his mother rarely spoke English if she could avoid it—Stephen arched an eyebrow. "*Meilleure que la votré,*" he replied.

Alex frowned before indicating he understood. *Better than yours.* "I suppose your mother taught you," he said with a shrug. "She worked for us during the Peninsular Wars, you know."

It was Stephen's turn to frown before he realized the two would have looked into his background before considering him for a position. "She did," he agreed, wondering what his mother had done for them. He remembered her spending hours at her escritoire transcribing documents, but he never asked why.

"Education?" Alex asked, his hands clasped behind his back.

Stephen nodded. "Eton and the Royal Naval Academy," he replied. Although he figured the viscount might know what he had been required to learn at the academy in Portsmouth, he wasn't sure if Alex Bradley did. Every student was required to learn about the construction and architecture of ships, navigation, mapping, how to the handle sails, gunnery, and rope work. On top of that, there were fencing and dancing lessons, courses on politics and diplomacy, and French and mathematics classes. "My specialty at the academy was navigation," Stephen added, hoping he might qualify for whatever the men had in mind for him.

"Well, we're actually in need of a translator to help with intercepted messages. Analysis. The paperwork," Alex remarked, one eyebrow arching up.

Stephen nodded, deciding he rather liked being considered for something more than a clerk's position. "Understood. So... when do I start?"

Alex and Matthew exchanged glances of amusement. "How about right now?"

Stephen regarded the two men and gave a nod. "I'm ready."

CHAPTER 29

A BROTHER VISITS A SISTER

Meanwhile, in Oxfordshire

Henry Forster, Earl of Gisborn regarded the team of four horses pulling his latest invention and finally glanced over at his wife. "Is it how you imagined it would be?" he asked, his hand seeking hers so that he could intertwine his fingers with her slender ones. He smiled as she angled her head against his shoulder.

"It's a bit larger than I imagined, in fact," Hannah Slater Forster, Countess of Gisborn, replied as she watched the groom complete his work to harness the draft horses to the wide plow. Besides the axle that sported a series of discs, each mounted at an angle, there was a set of wheels at either end. Above the axle, a framework arced up to a central bench from which a person could drive the team of horses. "And rather high for the driver." She absently drew the fingers of her right hand through the hair atop her dog's head, the two-year-old Alpenmastiff dutifully stationed next to where she stood.

Harold was hopelessly devoted to his mistress. He followed her slipper-clad heels wherever she went.

Well, except for the earl's bedchamber. He wasn't allowed in there, but instead spent his nights in her bedchamber or in the dressing room that connected the two rooms.

The earl nodded. "Heavy, as well, but it couldn't be helped," he said as his attention was drawn to a man leading a horse along the lane in front of Gisborn Hall. There was a woman and a young boy perched on the small horse. "Now, who might this be?" he murmured, not recognizing the couple nor the child.

Harold's eyes lifted before he turned and regarded the intruders. He let out a 'woof ' before he bounded in their direction, his tail wagging in circles.

Hannah turned to follow his gaze and Harold's direction of travel, her brows furrowing at the odd sight.

"Harold! Heel!" she called out, afraid the large dog might do harm to the people on the lane. Her eyes widened, though, and she gasped. She took off running in the direction of the visitors, her skirts bunched up into her fists so her ankles were on display as she made her way down the slight hillock to the road below.

"Hannah!" Henry called out, stunned by her sudden departure but rather glad Harold was far ahead of her. However, once Harold reached the man, his tail wagged furiously, as if he recognized their visitors.

Frowning, Henry followed Hannah down the incline to the road, but did so at a steady walk. He had only gone a few steps when he witnessed Hannah throwing her arms around the man, who swung her about so her feet were off the ground for almost an entire revolution. Jealousy had him quickening his pace so that he was nearly running when he reached his wife. The sound of her soft laughter had him even more incensed. Who the hell would dare lift his wife from the ground and twirl her around in such an indecorous manner? And why was Hannah allowing it?

Welcoming it, even?

Even Harold bounced about, as if he knew the man.

But how could that be? Harold only knew the men who worked in the fields nearest Gisborn Hall. And he knew Thomas Cavanaugh, the man from whom Henry had purchased the Alpenmastiff after Tom's dog, Maggie, had given birth to a litter two years ago.

Henry was about to scold the interloper and bodily remove his wife from the man's hold when the visitor suddenly let go of his hold on Hannah and sobered, apparently realizing his life might be in danger.

"Good day, my lord," Will Slater said with a nod, a bit breathless. "'Bout time I met my brother. I am Bellingham. Hannah's brother," he added, thinking the man with the rather fierce expression needed additional information as to how he was related to Hannah. "I apologize. I haven't seen her in nearly four years."

The anger flowed out of Henry in an instant, his face brightening as he heard the words. "Oh, well, that's a relief. I thought I was going to have to meet you with pistols at dawn," he replied before he leaned forward, his outstretched right hand clasping Will's. "Henry Forster," he added. After a quick perusal of Will, Henry wondered why he hadn't met the man whilst at school. He appeared to be about the same age as Henry. "Oxford or Cambridge?" he asked, expecting the man to say, "Cambridge." Henry had attended Oxford, of course.

Will shook his head. "Royal Naval Academy," he responded as he made his way to the other side of the horse. Harold followed on his heels, his tail wagging furiously. "Just resigned my commission and returned to London a few days ago," he added. He lifted his arms so that he could grasp Barbara's waist and lower her from the horse.

From the look in her eyes, he knew she didn't want to be introduced to his family. Given the poor state of her gown, and the worn out clothes her son wore, she was probably feeling embarrassed.

"No need to be nervous," Will whispered so that only she could hear. "He's a farmer. And this is..." He glanced down at the dog. "Harold, I think, although he looks a bit too young to be the Harold I remember."

"He's an *earl*," Barbara countered, attempting to tamp

down the panic she felt. What if the man had been in London when she was forced to flee? What if he knew why she had left London all those years ago? *What if he knows about my father?*

"And this is my betrothed, Lady Barbara Higgins," Will said as he led her to stand before his sister and Henry.

Barbara struggled to bob a curtsy after having spent the last two miles on the horse, gratified when she realized the earl and countess had their eyes downcast as they formally curtsied and bowed in response.

Hannah could barely contain her excitement. "A sister!" she cried out, moving to take Barbara into her arms. "Oh, Will Slater, you are in so much trouble," she said before she released the rather startled Barbara from her grasp. "You've no doubt been engaged since before you left London," she accused, her attention going to the young boy who stood staring at all of them. Harold was sniffing him from head to toe, his tail wagging the entire time. She winked in his direction, wondering if he was merely a very young stable hand or a relative of Barbara's.

Will took a deep breath before nodding, noting Barbara's stunned glance in his direction. "Something like that," he said lamely. He turned when he realized Donald was still standing next to the horse, his hands gripped around Thunderbolt's lead as Harold sat next to him. "And this..." He paused, not sure how to introduce Donald.

"This is Donald," Barbara said with a nod, clasping a hand around the young boy's bony shoulders and pulling him close. Harold repositioned himself so as to sit next to the boy, his tongue hanging out one side of this mouth.

Hannah was quick to crouch down so that she was eye-level with the boy. "It's very good to meet you, Master Donald. I am Lady Gisborn..." She paused to gesture to her husband. "And this is my husband, Lord Gisborn."

Donald's glance darted between Hannah and Henry before he gave a formal bow. "It's an honor to make your acquaintance, my lady, my lord," he said, his delivery as practiced as if he lived at court.

But Hannah wasn't paying as much attention to his bow as she was to his face. His eyes. His hair. The shape of his chin. For the young boy looked just like her brother did in the miniature of him as a boy that decorated her mother's bedchamber.

She glanced at Harold, rather surprised her dog was so accepting of their visitors. He should have been on alert. Should have acted to protect her. Should have at least barked! Instead, he had welcomed their visitors. Acted as if he knew them.

But, how could that be?

From what Will had said in his introduction, her brother wasn't yet married to Barbara. So where was her chaperone? Or a companion? Daring another glance at Barbara, she noted the worn gown she wore, hints of recent repairs to the hem and sleeves, the slippers that looked as if they should have been given to a dog to use as a chew toy long ago.

Pasting a smile on her face, Hannah stood up and turned her attention back to Barbara and her brother. "Do come in for tea," she insisted, her gaze going back to the horse. Although a saddlebag hung from behind the saddle, there was no evidence of a valise or any other luggage indicating they intended to stay.

So from where had they come?

"Will, it's past time you met your nephew. Are your trunks coming in a coach?" she asked, her gaze directed back along the road on which they had traveled, the little-used lane that made its way along the north edge of the former Ellsworth Park property.

Will stutter-stepped before he shook his head. "Truth be told, we weren't sure we would find you, sister," he replied quickly. "Father's directions weren't very exact, I'm afraid, which makes me think he hasn't yet paid a visit here. I'm an uncle, did you say?"

Hannah's eyes widened. "You've seen father, then? Since you returned from duty?"

"Oh, aye," Will replied, offering his arm to Barbara as they turned to climb the slight incline and make their way toward Gisborn Hall, Thunderbolt dutifully following Donald. "I even managed to attend a soirée in London before I headed for Broadwell," he added, silently cursing himself for not having told Barbara about his one social engagement prior to his heading out to look for her. He couldn't exactly expect his brother to replace him in all the social activities without first showing him the ropes, however. "Does my nephew have a name?" he asked, his query directed to anyone who might answer him.

"Randolph, although it wasn't my first choice for him," the earl replied with an arched eyebrow. He allowed his wife to drop back so that she could walk alongside Barbara, her arm interlocking with the woman as the young boy moved to join them, his hands clutching the horse's reins.

"Did you even recognize anyone at the ball?" Henry asked then, noting how Harold seemed to accept their visitors as if he had known them his entire life.

"Hardly," Will acknowledged, wondering at the earl's comment about his son's name. There hadn't been any Randolphs in the Devonville line, but perhaps the Gisborn line was full of them. "My father's associates, of course. Like Morganfield and Lord Torrington. He's married to my aunt Adele, which in itself was quite a surprise," Will added. "But..." He paused, giving the earl a shake of his head. "I was a bit out of my element."

Gisborn nodded. "You have your land legs back, though," he replied, the comment not a question. The lawn beneath them merged into a crushed granite path that curved and led to the front door of Gisborn Hall.

Will allowed a chuckle. "I do. And I can still ride a horse, which I did not realize how much I missed doing until I was on my way to Broadwell." At Gisborn's sudden frown, Will dared a glance at Barbara, whose attention was on Hannah as his sister happily chatted with her. He supposed in an area this remote, Hannah rarely had callers. The two had just stepped onto the path a few yards ahead of them. Will hoped Barbara's slippers would hold up long enough to get her to the front door. He was sure her soles were nearly worn through.

"I wondered when we might meet," Henry said as he watched his wife and Barbara walk toward the house, Donald following along with the horse and Harold at his side. Henry allowed them to move ahead of him and Will so they couldn't overhear their conversation.

Will nodded. "As did I. I admit, I was concerned when I heard my little sister was married to the Earl of Gisborn—"

"Because you were afraid she had married my uncle, no doubt," Henry interrupted, a wry smile crossing his face.

"Only for a moment," Will agreed, his own face splitting into a grin. "I never thought she would have to leave London, though," he added, sobering.

Henry gave a shrug. "She has been a godsend for this place," he said as he waved a hand toward Gisborn Hall. "For me." After a pause, he added, "She has never complained about how far we are from London, I think because her friends are all married and busy with families of their own."

Will angled his head, realizing Hannah had already been away from London for two years. This was her home now. "And you? Have you always lived here?"

"Indeed." He frowned as he glanced back toward the house. "I was beginning to think I was going to have to admonish my staff," he said under his breath. "We don't get many visitors."

Will followed his line of sight to find a stableboy running in their direction. Breathless, the young man bowed and took the reins from Donald. "I apologize for the wait, sir," he said before he hurried off with Thunderbolt, his manner with the Arabian suggesting he had dealt with high-strung horses in the past.

"Where did you say you walked from?" Henry asked as

he nodded back toward the road.

"Broadwell. About four miles from here, I think."

"Why Broadwell?" the other earl asked, his face screwed up with curiosity.

Will allowed a grin. "Not a 'what' so much as a 'who'," he replied with an nod toward his betrothed. At least, he hoped she was still his betrothed. In all that had happened in the last day and a half, he had only proposed the one time, and apparently Barbara hadn't been awake for it. After her comments about London, he hadn't again brought up their future as a married couple. "Lady Barbara."

Henry frowned. "Were you staying at *The Five Bells?*" he asked, a look of concern still on his face. "I know of the inn, of course, but I've never had reason to patronize the place."

Will took a breath and held it a moment. "No, actually. Barbara lives in a poor excuse for a cottage just outside of the village. I arrived the day before yesterday and am left wondering how she's managed to make a living there for the past seven years. Rotting roof, no servants, no financial support—"

"Christ," Henry breathed. "Who is she?" he asked in a low voice, as if he were afraid he might be overheard.

"Lady Barbara Higgins. Greenley's daughter," Will responded when Henry didn't indicate he recognized the name.

Henry paused mid-step. "The Earl of Greenley's daughter?" he repeated, a hint of surprise on his face. He had never heard of a member of the aristocracy having taken up residency in the small village to the west. "Are you sure she wasn't just... visiting there?" he asked, his brows furrowed. No member of the peerage occupied the village—the land surrounding it was independent of the Crown. Perhaps Barbara was a merely friend of the baron who owned most of the properties in that area and was staying there temporarily.

Will took a deep breath. "She has lived there for almost the entire time I was away at sea," he whispered. "If you could call it living. Pray tell, what have you heard about her?

I want to know everything. No matter how awful, no matter how scandalous—"

"There's not much to tell," Henry interrupted, realizing the younger earl had imagined something far worse than the reality. "If she is indeed the one I'm thinking she is, I've only ever heard of a widow living with her young son in a run-down cottage. Won't entertain callers—men or women—nor accept help from Miss Susan, the woman who runs *The Five Bells*," he explained, one eyebrow arching up. "Truth be told, I intended to pay a call in the next month or so, once the seeding was done," he said. At Will's sudden glance, he added, "Broadwell isn't exactly part of my earldom, but it isn't under the baron's realm either, and the Crown hasn't exactly paid it any mind. Last I spoke with Miss Susan, she was of the opinion the two would starve to death if I didn't do something. I was thinking if the situation was as dire as Miss Susan described, I would simply move them to the dowager cottage over there," he said as he nodded toward a neat stone cottage just outside the front drive to Gisborn Hall. "There's a good garden and an opportunity to earn a living as a seamstress or laundress."

Will glanced back toward the cottage, impressed at how well kept it looked. "Did you know she's an earl's daughter?" he asked then, suspicious as to the earl's motives.

Henry shook his head. "I did not," he replied. "Which means Miss Susan doesn't know she is, either," he added with an arched eyebrow. "No one has said anything to that effect. I just thought if she were willing to move, it would be good to have another woman in the area. I think it's hard for Hannah not to have friends close by. Ever since Nathan's mother married and moved to the far side of Bampton, Hannah's been a bit... lonely."

Will relaxed, heartened to know his brother-in-law didn't have plans for the woman Will intended to make his *wife*. But word that his sister didn't have other young matrons with whom to take tea and go shopping had him frowning. "Do you suppose you will ever move to London?" he asked finally.

Henry shook his head. "If we ever go to London, it will only be so I can attend sessions of Parliament, and so we can participate in the Season's entertainments. I don't think we'll ever live there year-round."

Relieved to hear that Henry was at least planning to take Hannah back to London for a visit, Will nodded. "Are you afraid she won't want to come back here?" Will asked slowing his approach so they wouldn't get too close to the women who still walked ahead of them.

Henry paused and shook his head. "I hadn't given it any thought. Perhaps you'll have to ask her," he said with a hint of reluctance. The last thing he wanted was for his wife to want to live in London year-round. "What of your Lady Barbara? Does she wish to go back?"

Will shook his head. "She said she will never go back there." At Henry's look of confusion, he added, "I believe she is of the opinion that everyone in London knows something that would preclude her from ever being able to show her face there again," he explained with an arched eyebrow, his manner indicating he couldn't guess what offense might warrant such a thought. "I've spoken with the butler of Pendleton House, and he didn't mention any scandal surrounding her. Just said she left the household. Figured she had gone to live in the country for a time."

At Henry's frown, Will shook his head. "Later," he whispered, glad Hannah was doing such a good job of keeping Barbara's attention on her with her gentle queries.

Will's attention went to the dog. He watched as Harold merely walked alongside Hannah as he had done for his entire life. A quick calculation had Will realizing this Harold couldn't be the same Harold his father had brought home all those years ago, though. "How old is Harold?" he asked as he nodded toward the Alpenmastiff.

Henry swallowed, realizing Will would have known the original Harold from when he was about the age this Harold was now. "Just a bit over two years old," he replied.

Will sighed. "I take it the original Harold died?" he murmured, daring another glance at Hannah's back.

Henry nodded, remembering the cold, snowy night he had come home to discover his wife missing from Gisborn Hall. He had found her nearly frozen as she wept over Harold. The poor dog had died after saving Henry's son, Nathaniel, from the river. "My son is alive because of that dog," he said in a quiet voice.

"Nathan?" Will asked, remembering the boy's name from a letter he had received from Hannah. At Henry's look of surprise, Will gave a shrug. "Hannah wrote about him in one of her letters. She's rather fond of him," he said with a nod. "Where is he, by the way?" he asked.

Henry's gaze fell on the back of his wife, his eyes glued to the gentle sway of her hips beneath her day gown. "Abdington," Henry replied. "For school," he added, realizing Will might not be familiar with the prep school.

Will nodded his understanding. "I'm surprised you didn't hire a tutor and keep him here," he commented.

Henry considered the man's words. "He had a tutor in the village for several years, and I was tempted to keep him here," he admitted. "But I was educated at Abdington and thought I owed him that. And a few years at Oxford."

Will chuckled. "Like father, like son?" he teased.

"Indeed," Henry replied.

Parkerhouse, the ancient butler who had worked at Gisborn Hall since before Henry's birth, opened the front doors and stepped aside to allow the party to enter.

"Could you see to tea and a luncheon and biscuits in the parlor, please?" Hannah said as she led everyone through the vestibule. "Cakes, too, if the cook has any made." Before she had made it to the stairs, she paused. "Oh, and Parkerhouse, please do have a guest bedchamber prepared for the Earl of Bellingham and his wife. And their son can stay in Nathan's room. And be sure to let Cook know there will be five for dinner and that we'll have guests for several days," Hannah added before she led the entourage up the marble stairs to the second floor.

The butler bowed and made his way toward the kitchens as Hannah continued up the stairs to a newly refurbished parlor.

When Will caught Barbara's look of alarm in his direction, he gave her a nod of understanding. "I don't think that will be necessary, sister," he started to argue, rather shocked to hear Barbara referred to as his wife. He rather doubted Barbara would be willing to share a bedchamber. As for their son, well, his sister did have that detail correct.

Was it that obvious? Or had Barbara said something to her?

Or was Hannah merely covering for him?

Hannah turned on the landing and regarded her brother with wide eyes. "You cannot walk all the way back to Broadwell tonight," she countered. "Why, it's..." She turned to Henry, figuring he would know exactly how far it was to the village.

"Four miles," he said under his breath, one of his eyebrows arching in amusement.

"Four miles," Hannah repeated, as if her brother didn't already know the distance, and four miles may as well have been four hundred miles.

Will allowed a chuckle. "I know how far it is, Hannah," he replied with a grin. "Which is why we don't need to be availing ourselves of your hospitality tonight."

"Nonsense. What else are you going to do?" Henry argued as he continued through a set of double-doors into what appeared to be a newly refurbished parlor.

When Will noted his sister's crestfallen face, he sighed. "We can discuss it later," he murmured, realizing the earl had a point. They may as well stay. Perhaps he could convince Barbara to return to London with him. Agree to marry him. Move into a townhouse in Park Lane. Live the life he had imagined them living all those years ago.

Hannah's smile returned, as if she had won an argument.

CHAPTER 30

A MARQUESS CONFRONTS A VISCOUNT

*B*ack in London...

William Slater took a deep breath before making his presence known to Matthew Fitzsimmons, Viscount Chamberlain. The slightly younger viscount had just finished a hand of cards when he noticed William giving him a nod.

"I'm done for the evening, gentleman," he said as he pushed away from the card table in White's. A few groaned their displeasure at losing the fourth man in their game before another stepped up to take his place.

Matthew joined William, taking the glass of brandy a footman held for him.

"Devonville," he said with a nod. "Should I be concerned?" he asked as he indicated the brandy balloon, giving the glass a quick swirl before lifting it to his nose.

William shook his head. "Depends, I suppose. I'm in search of information about Greenley and have reason to believe you may know what's become of him."

Matthew hesitated before taking a sip of the brandy, wondering why the marquess would think to come to him with questions about the Earl of Greenley. Had someone said something?

He pointed toward a pair of upholstered chairs in front

of the fireplace. The other marquess moved to take a seat and noticed how a nearby butler quickly took his leave of the room. A nearby footman also disappeared. Well, at least their conversation wouldn't be overheard by any of the staff at White's, he considered.

Once he was settled in one of the chairs, Viscount Chamberlain regarded William for a long moment. "He owes money to nearly every gaming hell on the east side," he whispered. "He's mortgaged to the hilt. His unentailed properties have all been sold in attempt to pay off what he owes, but he simply owes too much. He's about to land in debtors' prison."

William hissed, the news surprising him. Why hadn't he heard the man was about to go to prison? "What the hell happened?" he asked in a quiet voice. "He never used to gamble—"

"He never used to drink to excess or miss entire sessions of Parliament, either," Matthew interrupted, his manner suggesting he wasn't comfortable speaking about Maxwell Higgins, Earl of Greenley. The two had been friends at one point, before their political positions forced them onto the opposite sides of issues. And before the issue with the missing British pounds had the Foreign Office deciding to use the earl as bait.

The Marquess of Devonville sighed. "So, what happened?"

Matthew allowed a sigh, his brandy forgotten. "His wife died shortly after his fifth child was born and died. He sent his youngest daughter to live with a relative and a few years later, he sent the oldest away."

The other marquess couldn't help but notice Lady Barbara's name wasn't mentioned specifically, nor was she said to have been banished. "But, why?" William asked, his head shaking in confusion.

Matthew shrugged, tempted to tell William the truth. He knew the marquess would keep the information quiet.

Instead, he gave him the line he'd rehearsed for moments such as this. "Broken heart. Broken spirit. I know you've probably heard he beat his wife, but he swears he never did such a thing to her or the girls," he explained. "While he was in mourning, he started drinking too much, and pretty soon he was losing at the tables. He was too proud to get his daughters back, too proud to admit there was a problem. That is, until someone started buying up his markers. Even then, he didn't tell anyone he owed more than his worth in debt."

William hissed at hearing the words. "Who owns the markers?"

Matthew blinked. *Damn!* He could claim he didn't know, but at that moment, he decided he had better give the Marquess of Devonville some of the truth. "The Crown," he replied simply.

William blinked. And blinked again before setting his brandy balloon onto a side table and leaning forward. "How long have we known each other, Chamberlain?" he asked in a low voice.

Matthew Fitzsimmons sighed before rolling his eyes. "If you so much as breathe a word of this to anyone, I can have you brought up on charges of treason," he whispered.

Ah, now we're getting somewhere, William thought with a bit of satisfaction. "Not a word," he agreed with a shake of his head.

Leaning forward so he could whisper and still be heard, Matthew said, "What I said about his drinking and gambling was true. And the Crown does own a few markers from gaming hells," he added with an arched eyebrow. "But Greenley is working for me right now. Has been, off and on, for almost eight years."

William allowed a nod. "But not because he wanted to," he guessed, a graying eyebrow arched in query.

The viscount shook his head. "It took some persuasion, it's true, but the man did owe money. We just made it possible for him to continue to gamble in a effort to determine where his losses were going after they left the gaming tables."

The marquess considered this bit of information and finally nodded. "For eight years?"

Matthew sighed before settling back into his chair. "As I said, off and on. Some investigations take longer. This one... this one is about to wrap up. The guilty party—a foreign party, I might add—will be apprehended within the month, and justice shall finally be served." He paused a moment. "The first one only took a few months. Others... a year or more."

Eight years? William was beginning to see a connection. "And once this justice is served, what will become of Lord Greenley?" he asked, steepling his fingers beneath his chin.

Frowning, Matthew shook his head. "Well, he won't be going to debtor's prison, if that's what you're asking," he replied.

"His family?"

The viscount gave a shrug. "His sons will be informed they have their inheritances, and his daughters..." Here, he stopped and frowned. "The youngest has been living with an aunt in Staffordshire. She's still of an age to make an advantageous marriage."

William waited, wondering if the viscount would admit to knowing the whereabouts of Barbara. When Matthew didn't say anything more, he sighed. "And Lady Barbara?" he prompted.

Closing his eyes a moment, Matthew shook his head. "If Greenley's damnable solicitor wasn't so honorable, we would know where he sent her," he complained. "Barton arranged for her to live somewhere. We know he was secretly sending her funds, but we could never figure out to where they were being sent," he explained. "Even after Greenley fired him, he still wouldn't tell the earl where he had sent Lady Barbara. We thought cutting off her funds would drive her back to London—"

"*What?*" William interrupted, stunned at the viscount's

information. "You had a solicitor send an unmarried woman away from London without... without *protection?* Without *money?*" he questioned, his voice rising above the whisper the two had been using to converse.

The viscount held out a hand and glanced around, his nervousness apparent. "We truly thought Barton would divulge her location, but the man—"

"Oxfordshire," William said before glaring at the viscount for several seconds. When he noted Matthew's look of surprise, he added, "My son just found her in Oxfordshire."

"Jesus," Matthew whispered. "Is she...?"

William shook his head. "He said he found her, and she's unmarried. I've no idea if she's well or sick or working as a prostitute or—"

"Christ," the viscount whispered, his head shaking from side to side. He arched an eyebrow. "Your son, did you say? Why was he looking for her? And who told him where he could find her?" He paused a moment and furrowed his brows. *Barton, no doubt. Bastard!*

"Bellingham, yes," William replied. "He... loves her. Has since before he left London. Wants to make her his wife."

A profound sense of relief settled over the viscount just then. "She left London in a bit of a hurry," he said in a low voice. "And not because we encouraged it, or because Greenley did, as far as we know. We could have provided protection had she stayed. She was the one seeing to Pendleton House. Seeing to providing Greenley a bit of a normal life given everything we had him involved in," he added.

The news rankled William. "She's been gone from London for over seven years," he stated with a hint of anger. "No protection, no funds. Had she been *my* daughter—"

"I know, I know," Matthew replied, one hand held up as if he could shield himself from the marquess' scolding. "My niece was missing for a time. I remember the sense of hopelessness. The sense of dread."

William allowed his anger to dissipate. His oldest son was somewhat to blame for Barbara's quick departure from London. But to withhold funds in an effort to force a stubborn woman to return to London? A woman who probably thought the worst of her father and everyone else in the *ton*, for that matter? Desperate women could—and would—do desperate things. He had to hope Barbara was all right.

Well, he would know more just as soon as the mail coach arrived in the morning. Hannah would send word if William and Barbara had made their way to Gisborn Hall. She would let him know the situation.

"My son's future wife had better be all right," William said firmly. "And whatever you have Greenley doing on behalf of the Foreign Office had better be finished soon," he warned.

Matthew Fitzsimmons, Viscount Chamberlain, allowed a nod. "Understood," he replied.

CHAPTER 31
TEA TIME

*M*eanwhile, back in Oxfordshire

Although Donald tried his hardest to keep his eyes open, the long day of travel and several biscuits had him nodding off in the chair nearest where Harold had plopped down to watch over everyone.

"Poor thing," Hannah murmured as she glanced over at the boy. He may have only been a few years younger than her stepson, Nathaniel Forster, but he was so much smaller. Frail, almost. At Barbara's look of alarm, Hannah was quick to add, "He's had a rather busy day for one so young."

Barbara relaxed. "He has," she agreed with a nod.

"I know you've already traveled too much today, but would you like to take a turn with me in the garden?" Hannah asked, noticing how the men were already engaged in their own conversation.

The older woman dared a glance in Will's direction. She couldn't help but see how comfortable he seemed in the upholstered chair, one booted ankle resting on the opposite knee while he spoke of his time at sea. Despite his having walked the entire distance from Broadwell, his boots were still reasonably polished, the dust having been wiped off whilst they were in the vestibule. "I would like that," Barbara agreed, setting her cup and saucer on the low table in front of the settee on which she sat. A quick glance at the other furnishings in the parlor had her realizing that although the room looked newly refurbished—fresh paint lightened the walls and new drapes framed the mullioned windows—the furniture was old and a bit shabby.

Hannah stood from her place on an adjacent settee, which had the men suddenly standing. "We'll be in the garden." She lifted her chin in Donald's direction. "If you could just let him know when he wakes up. I shouldn't want him to wonder where his mother is," she added.

Henry moved to take Hannah's hand. He lifted it to his lips. "I'll let the nurse know if she brings Randolph down," he murmured before kissing her knuckles.

Hannah grinned. "I should think his uncle will want to spend some time with him," she replied, giving Will a teasing grin.

Will smiled. "I must be the only uncle in England who hasn't seen his nephew," he murmured. He pointed to Donald. "And Randolph is Donald's cousin," he added, meaning to ask Barbara if any of her brothers had children of their own yet.

Hannah and Henry both turned to regard Will. "Two times over, if you count Nathan," Hannah said proudly. "But Randolph should be in the nursery napping for another hour. You can meet him when he wakes up."

Nodding, Will and Henry remained standing as the two women took their leave of the parlor and headed for the garden. Once they were out of earshot, Henry turned to regard Will with an arched eyebrow. "Something tells me we have a lot in common."

Will angled his head to one side before he realized what Henry might have meant with his comment. "If you mean we're both the fathers of bastard boys, then, yes, we have that in common," Will admitted with a nod. He just then realized he was part of a large contingent of aristocrats who had fathered bastard children. At least he intended to be a father to his son, though. The boy already had his name. Even if he could never inherit the marquessate, at least he could be raised as a Slater.

Henry shook his head. "There is that, I suppose," he agreed, his brow furrowed. "I was thinking more about our women, though. They're far more... *industrious* than typical chits of the *ton*, wouldn't you say?"

Will blinked before giving his brother-in-law a nod. *Industrious? Stubborn* was probably a more appropriate term, but he wasn't about to counter the earl's claim.

A STEPMOTHER WARNS OF TROUBLE AHEAD

*B*ack in London...

Stephen reread the invitation for Lady Torrington's musicale, remembering his brother's edict that he attend. *An invitation to one of Aunt Adele's musicales is the most coveted invitation of the Season since she manages to get the best sopranos and musicians to perform. You have to go.*

Well, he would definitely be attending—he had promised Will he would attend as many *ton* events as he could while the commander was off in Oxfordshire with his Lady Barbara. From what his father had said at breakfast that morning, he and Cherice would be at the *musicale*, as well. "I can't very well miss my own sister's soirée," William had said with an arched eyebrow when Stephen asked if he would be attending. "Besides, it's high time you met her."

Not having met Milton Grandby, Earl of Torrington, and his countess, Adele Slater Worthington Grandby at Lord Huntington's soirée—his first *ton* event—Stephen now found himself wondering why he wasn't introduced.

Had Will had second thoughts and worried that Adele might shun him? He was a bastard, after all. There wasn't any requirement that she recognize him as her nephew, or that the earl acknowledge him at all. Or perhaps the earl and countess hadn't even been at the soirée.

Well, they would certainly be at their own *musicale*. He wondered if they would make the connection when he was introduced, although the reaction he had been noticing from others reinforced what he and Will had discovered aboard ship—they were nearly identical in appearance. Perhaps he would have an opportunity to say a few words to the woman in an attempt to gauge her thoughts on the matter.

"There you are," Cherice said as she breezed into the study.

Stephen looked up from the Torrington invitation and gave a quick glance at the silver salver. He could hardly believe how popular his brother was! Every day saw the silver salver replenished with invitations to every sort of soirée, party, ball, lecture—he understood why some in the *ton* had social secretaries.

"My lady," he said as he dropped the missive he was reading and gave her a bow. "I thought you would be out paying calls on this fine morning," he said, noticing she wasn't wearing a morning gown. Despite the rain the night before, or perhaps because of it, the morning was clear and sunny. He would be leaving for the Foreign Office in a few minutes, Alex Bradley having requested him to attend a meeting at ten o' clock.

Cherice bobbed a curtsy despite having a flat, paper-wrapped package under one of her arms. "I will be this after-noon," she replied. "This came for you," she said as she handed him the package.

"Me?" he repeated, rather surprised she would be delivering something the butler would normally see to doing. He undid the tie that held the paper and unwrapped a sapphire blue waistcoat embroidered with an array of birds and flowers. Far more elaborate than the one he had purchased from the tailor, this one also looked far more expensive. He glanced up in time to see Cherice's reaction to his look of surprise.

"Do you like it? I saw it at Schweitzer and Davidson and

decided it would be perfect for the *musicale* this evening," she gushed. "I do hope it fits."

Stephen's eyes widened. "You bought it for me?" he countered, wondering if it was even proper for her to do so. She wasn't *really* his stepmother.

"Oh, your father paid for it, of course. I merely picked it out. You will wear it, I hope?"

His gaze taking in the artistry of the embroidery, Stephen nodded. "I will. Thank you," he replied. Having seen how audacious some of the waistcoats had been at Lord Weatherstone's ball, Stephen realized the one he held was almost conservative.

Cherice smiled, angling her head to one side. "I am glad you're staying with us. I was so looking forward to Will being here, and then he went off to who-knows-where, and, well..." She sighed. "It's a large house."

"It is," Stephen agreed, although the one he had grown up in wasn't much smaller. "I appreciate your welcoming me. I couldn't help but think I was an unexpected guest when Will insisted I stay here."

Taking a seat in a nearby leather chair, Cherice shook her head. "Not at all. Although, I have to wonder if you will be staying for very long given how popular you are at all these social engagements."

Frowning, Stephen took the chair opposite. "I don't know what you mean," he hedged. How could his popularity —or his brother's, actually—have an effect on his living at Devonville House?

Cherice gave him an impish grin. "Oh, please, Stephen. You're the *on dit* in all the parlors I've been to these past few days. Why, I've heard reports from Lady Pettigrew that you danced a waltz with her youngest niece, who didn't even have a voucher to do so."

Stephen blinked, aware of the sound of a scold in her voice. "In my defense, my lady, I was unaware a gel couldn't dance a waltz without a voucher," he replied apologetically. "Who makes such ridiculous rules? And I did warn Lady

Jane that I didn't even know how to waltz, so I'm not sure it really counts. Does it?"

Suppressing the urge to giggle, Cherice sighed. "You have been excused this one time since you were away from England for so many years," she replied carefully. "However, it cannot happen again without you being attached to scandal," she warned.

Sobering, Stephen nodded. "I understand, my lady. I shall not dance a waltz again."

Rolling her eyes, Cherice shook her head. "Of course you will waltz again. I'll merely be sure you do so with someone who is allowed." She straightened in her chair. "Now, I understand you've also been rather chivalrous."

Stephen realized just then the power of the gossip mongers in Mayfair's parlors. When Cherice had said he was the *on dit*, she wasn't exaggerating. "And how might I have been chivalrous?" he dared asked.

"Why, Lady Fletcher claims you saved her daughter from a rather amorous potted palm. *Her* words."

Stephen blinked. And blinked again. Had Lady Lucida actually told her *mother* about the potted palm? About its rather fast frond? And if so, had she also discussed their conversation about what he might *do* to said palm? About what he did to *her* in the gardens?

"Why, Stephen Slater, I do believe you're blushing like a girl fresh out of the schoolroom!" Cherice exclaimed, a huge smile on her face.

He knew he was. He had felt the heat of it even before it reached his throat, before it reached his cheeks. "My lady, I... I was tempted, I admit, but I assure you, I did *not* dispatch that potted palm. Nor did I challenge it to a duel at Wimbledon Commons," he claimed evenly. "However, if you had seen what it was trying to do to Lady Lucida's sleeve— why, it was behaving in a most scandalous fashion—you would understand why it was I was forced to intervene and remove her from its presence."

It was Cherice's turn to blink. And blink again as she

considered his words. "I knew they could be troublesome plants, but I never thought... oh, dear," Cherice replied, apparently undecided as to whether she should laugh or be frightened at the prospect of spending time in the presence of a plant.

Stephen couldn't quite figure out if she were being melodramatic or if she was teasing him or if she was truly frightened by the thought of the plants and what they could do to ballgown sleeves.

"I always thought them a rather helpful decorative accessory behind which one could steal a kiss or two," Cherice hedged. "Not that I have ever had to participate in such an assignation, mind you," she added with a shake of her head, which had the ringlets at her temples bouncing about her lightly rouged cheeks.

Stephen had to resist the urge to imagine Lady Devonville meeting his father behind such vegetation in order to enjoy an assignation, deciding that she probably had, indeed, enjoyed such an encounter.

How would she know to ever speak of it otherwise?

The saucy minx.

"Who has the best palms for coverage?" he asked, deciding the information might be helpful should he ever require the coverage.

"Oh, the Morganfields, of course, but then some of us require the extra foliage as we're rather prone to sudden fits of passion..." She stopped and allowed a sigh, realizing she had been caught. Her rosy cheeks grew even more rosy before she allowed a grin of embarrassment. "Why is it, do you suppose, that the most enjoyable things in life are so... *forbidden?*" she asked in a wistful voice.

"Like waltzes, do you mean?" he replied with an arched eyebrow. "I do not know, my lady, but it is a shame sometimes."

Cherice regarded him for a moment. "On that note, I suppose I should ask you about Miss Comber," she said, one eyebrow arching up.

The humor seemed to leave Stephen all at once. "What do you wish to know?" he asked, trying to sound as innocent as possible when he knew he was failing.

"She told me she's rather taken with you."

"She did?" Stephen couldn't help but sound surprised by the comment, just then remembering that Cherice and Victoria had been huddled together in quiet conversation during the intermission at the theatre. And they had spoken before Victoria had slapped him in the face.

Cherice sighed. "Stephen! Are you really as thick as the other men in the *ton?* I had hoped you were a bit more... *perceptive* of what was going on around you."

"I am!" he countered, tempted to tell her he'd been hired by Lord Chamberlain to act as an analyst in the Foreign Office because the man thought him capable. "I was. But, I have to admit to a bit of confusion about Victoria... Miss Comber," he corrected himself.

Stifling her grin, Cherice waited patiently.

"What are they saying about her in the Mayfair parlors?" he asked, thinking the *haute ton* probably thought the daughter of a man who had eschewed the aristocracy to be prime gossip material now that she had shown herself at a ball.

Shaking her head, Cherice regarded Stephen for a moment. "Nothing, actually. I mean, Lady Chamberlain may ask after her when I go to Lady Norwick's for afternoon tea, but I've heard nothing about the girl from anyone else." She allowed a sigh. "Although, after tonight's *musicale*, there may be a bit more discussion about the chit."

Stephen stilled himself. "And why might that be?"

Cherice gave a shrug. "I may have encouraged your aunt to invite her to tonight's fête, although I wasn't sure where to tell her to send the invitation," she hinted.

He wasn't quite sure why he felt a combination of relief and dread at hearing Cherice's words, but Stephen breathed a sigh. "Number thirty-one King Street," Stephen replied before realizing he said too much too soon. "That's where she is staying with an aunt," he added.

Cherice considered his comment before allowing a sigh. "Do you *want* her to be at tonight's *musicale?* I mean, what do *you* think of her?" she asked carefully.

Stephen thought to claim it was time he leave for White-hall, but noticed the time on the mantel clock still showed only a bit after nine. "Honestly, my lady, I'm not quite sure what to think of her. She's... bold. She's rather free-thinking. She's certainly not fresh out of the schoolroom," he added with an arched eyebrow.

Cherice considered his response for a moment. "However did you meet her? And do not try to claim that last night was the first time you laid eyes on her. You knew her from some-where else, I'm quite sure of it."

Nodding, Stephen replied, "I ran into her—literally—at Lord Weatherstone's ball. She claimed she had never been at a ball before and that she didn't have an invitation."

Cherice's eyes widened at the same time her mouth opened into an 'o'. "She *crashed* Lord Weatherstone's ball?" There was a hint of awe in Cherice's question before her face suddenly fell. "With no chaperone, either, I suppose," she added with an arched eyebrow.

Stephen realized just then that Cherice was probably imagining Victoria Comber to be a... a courtesan or worse— a prostitute. "True," he agreed. "However, as the niece of Lord Aimsley, I cannot believe she is... bad *ton*," he ventured.

"Aimsley?" Cherice repeated, rather surprised at this bit of news. Now she understood why her husband had mentioned him in the coach the night before.

"Aye, her father is the Earl of Aimsley's youngest broth-er," he explained, having discovered the information in the copy of *Debrett's* he had been reading in the library. "She's staying with her aunt for the Season."

Cherice gave the comment some thought before offering, "Cheapside?" There were so many King Streets in London.

Stephen had almost imagined her suggesting 'Wapping'.

"Carnaby. Just north of Golden Square," Stephen replied, wanting her to know it wasn't as bad as she was imagining.

"Oh," she managed to get out. "Well, that's a bit of a relief. I shouldn't want you marrying someone who isn't worthy of you."

Stephen blinked. "Marrying?" he repeated. *Worthy?* He was a bastard! "I'm not looking to marry, my lady. At least, not yet. My only reason for meeting these girls was to determine which one would make a suitable wife for Will if he was unable to find Lady Barbara."

Cherice angled her head to one side. "Oh, Stephen. You doth protest too much," she replied happily. "Lady Jane is far too young for your brother and for you, Lady Lucida would be better suited to someone who wants to live in the country, and Miss Comber is, well, far more suited to *you*, don't you suppose?"

Blinking as fast as his head was spinning, Stephen furrowed his brows and stared at his stepmother.

Victoria Comber as a *wife?*

"Besides, your father received word that Will found his Lady Barbara. Apparently she's still unmarried, although your father didn't say anything else." She decided to remain mum on the topic of Will's son.

Stephen nodded his understanding, resisting the urge to ask if she was found with Will's child. He did feel some relief on his brother's behalf, but he had to wonder why an earl's daughter would leave London, apparently intending never to return, unless she found herself pregnant. Stephen had already shared his thoughts with his father, but he didn't want to think the worst of his brother's woman, either. Or his brother. "Well, that's good news," he said, realizing he no longer had to vet chits on his brother's behalf.

"Yes, since it means you can concentrate on finding your own wife," Cherice said as she dropped a curtsy. "Do have a good day at your... work," she added before she took her leave of the study.

She was gone before Stephen could offer a bow or his complaint of, "I'm not looking for a wife!"

With a sigh, he made his way to the phaeton parked out front for the ride to Whitehall.

CHAPTER 33

BROTHERS SPEAK OF
BASTARDS

eanwhile, back in Oxfordshire
Will followed Henry's lead as the earl returned to his seat in the parlor, noting how the man's gaze had followed Hannah until she was completely out of sight. He slowly lowered himself into the upholstered chair and gave his host an arched brow. "I take it you married her for love," he half-questioned.

In the middle of reaching for another cake from the tea tray, Henry paused and considered Will's words. "Truth be told..." He paused, wondering if he dare admit what had really happened to make him choose Hannah as his wife. "We agreed to marry because neither of us expected more than... an arrangement," he stammered.

Will watched the earl as color stained his neck and face. "You're saying... your marriage to Hannah is a marriage of *convenience?*" he questioned, his brows furrowed in disbelief.

Henry took a deep breath and let it out. "It was at first," he agreed with a nod. "But... things changed. Circumstances changed. And, before I knew what was happening, I found myself feeling affection for her. At some point, her feelings changed as well, and, well..." He sighed again.

"You're hopelessly in love with her," Will said, a slight smile lighting his face.

Nodding, Henry dipped his head. "She deserved better than me. She deserved to be the first and only in a man's regard."

Confused by Henry's comment, Will leaned forward. "What are you saying?"

The earl matched Will's stance, leaning forward with his elbows on his knees. His voice pitched low, he said, "I expected to marry my childhood sweetheart. I even got a child on her thinking she would have to agree to be my wife."

Will frowned before he remembered Hannah's comment about a boy named Nathaniel in one of her letters. "She preferred to have a bastard rather than marry you?" he asked, his head shaking back in forth in disbelief.

Henry sighed. "Sarah is a farmer's daughter, and she didn't wish to be married to one. She knew I would eventually inherit an earldom and insisted I should take a wife who was the daughter of an aristocrat," he explained. "My uncle finally accepted her and my son, although he cursed her stubbornness for not marrying me until the day he died. Since he had no sons, I ended up with the earldom."

"So, that's how you ended up with my sister?" Will prodded, thinking Henry had simply gone to London for a Season and made an arrangement for Hannah to be his wife.

"No," Henry replied. "Actually, I was betrothed to marry the Wainwright girl, but she died in the same fire that killed the elder Wainwrights and their oldest son."

Hissing, Will sat back, realizing his brother-in-law spoke of the Duke and Duchess of Chichester and the Earl of Grinstead. All but Joshua Wainwright had perished in that fire at Wisborough Oaks in Sussex, a fire that left Joshua horribly burned when he attempted to rescue his sister, Jennifer. When Joshua had recovered enough to travel back to Wisborough Oaks, he took on the dukedom and a duchess in the form of Charlotte Bingham. The daughter of the Earl of Ellsworth, Charlotte had been betrothed to Joshua's older brother. With that man's death, she insisted she be allowed to do her duty and become Joshua's wife—a match far better suited to her and to Joshua. Her father hadn't shared that sentiment however.

"Jesus, I didn't know," Will said with a shake of his head. "So, you set your sights on my sister then?" he whispered.

Looking ever so embarrassed, Henry shook his head. "The property next door, Ellsworth Park, belonged to Charles Bingham—"

"The Earl of Ellsworth," Will clarified, wanting to be sure he had the right man in mind.

"Yes. Except Ellsworth Park wasn't entailed to the earldom. At one time, it had been part of the Gisborn holdings, but was lost in a game of chance more than a century ago. I wanted the back two-thirds of the property in order to extend my farm fields, and I figured I could let the house or make it the principal Gisborn residence," he explained. "So, two years ago, I went to London to buy it from Ellsworth."

Will nodded his understanding. "But Ellsworth wouldn't sell it?" he guessed.

Henry took a deep breath and shook his head. "No, he wouldn't," he admitted.

"Then how in the hell did you end up with the property?" Will asked, shaking his head quickly and then apologizing for his curse. "I fear my time at sea has my language a bit coarser than when I left."

Henry gave a shrug. "No offense taken," he replied with a smirk. "Ellsworth gave it to me."

His eyes widening, Will could almost guess why. "Gave it to you?" he repeated. No one just gave away good farmland. Not unless it was to be...

"When I made my offer, Ellsworth countered with a proposal that I accept it as a dowry. To marry his daughter, Charlotte," he said in a quiet voice as he averted his eyes. "He was of the opinion that with the death of the Earl of Grinstead, Lady Charlotte needed a husband and would end up with the Duke of Chichester—"

"But..." Will started to interrupt, knowing Charlotte *was*

married to Joshua Wainwright. "She is the Duchess of Chichester!"

"Aye," the earl replied with a nod. "Ellsworth didn't want that to happen, though—he thought the man was an abomination after having been in that awful fire—so he was happy to give me Ellsworth Park in exchange for marrying his daughter."

Will blinked. "And yet Lady Charlotte is Wainwright's duchess," he stated again, remembering the news he had received from Hannah when she first married Henry.

"She is," Henry assured him with a nod. "I accepted the title to the land, of course, but when I inquired as to the whereabouts of Lady Charlotte, I discovered she had left London in the Earl of Torrington's coach—probably at his urging—and was at Wisborough Oaks intending to marry the duke."

Will slumped into his chair, half-tempted to begin laughing at the poor earl. "You were too late."

One of Henry's hands moved to scrub his jawline. "On so many levels. Although, there was a moment when I thought Charlotte was about to accept what her father had arranged—I think if I had pressed the point with her, she would have agreed to marry me despite her feelings for Wainwright—but I knew she would resent me for taking her from the man she truly loved... probably for the rest of her life."

"So, she didn't just do her duty by marrying Wainwright?"

The earl fell silent for a moment. "No. I know she truly felt affection for her duke. And despite his insistence that she consider someone else to be her husband, Wainwright was besotted with her," he said in a quiet voice. After a moment, he added, "I intended to return the title to Ellsworth Park, but Charlotte begged me to keep it. She was of the opinion that it might end up in the hands of a greedy relative who would lose it in a game of chance."

Will nodded his understanding, remembering reading about Charlotte's cousin. The man had been convicted of attempted manslaughter after he hired a henchman to see to Charlotte's demise. Thank goodness the man's attempt to destroy Wainwright's home had failed.

"I am far better off letting her have her duke. I ended up with your sister, after all," Henry said with a quirked lip.

Leaning forward in his chair again, Will took a deep breath. "So how the hell did you end up with my *sister?*"

Henry allowed a chuckle then, his face splitting into a huge grin. "Lady Charlotte told me to marry her. Said Hannah always believed men only ever loved their mistresses and women only married to have children."

Remembering Hannah having said those words on more than one occasion, Will sobered. He knew why she felt that way. Despite their father having employed several mistresses and thinking he was keeping them a secret from his family, Will knew his mother was aware of his infidelities, knew she loved him in spite of his other life. At some point, Hannah, too, had discovered their father kept a mistress, although he never knew how. "The perfect wife for an aristocrat with a mistress on the side," he commented sadly.

Jesus. Will had left London when his mother was still alive. When Hannah hadn't yet had her come-out. Before Hannah knew she had another brother.

"Indeed. Given my situation with Sarah and my son, Hannah seemed the perfect choice for a wife," Henry finished with a shrug.

Suddenly incensed, Will straightened in his chair. "You're still with Sarah?" he accused, anger replacing his look of disappointment.

"Oh, no," Henry replied with a quick shake of his head. "God, no. She's married now. She had it all planned so she would be gone when our son went to Abdington," he explained. "Which, I admit, I was a bit angry about at first— she hadn't discussed her betrothal with me before making her plans to marry—but, in the end, it was the best possible outcome."

Will blinked. "Because?"

Henry shrugged. "Because, by then, I was hopelessly in love with your sister." He glanced over at Harold, who still appeared to be sleeping beneath the chair that held Donald. The boy's soft snores seemed to match the dog's. "The original Harold knew, of course. I was a bit... thick-headed, though, and it took this guy to rub my nose in it, until I finally figured it out," he claimed as he motioned toward the dog.

Glancing over at the Alpenmastiff, who raised his head as if he just then realized he was the topic of their conversation, Will wondered at the earl's words. The original Harold had been a smart dog. A puppy when he was brought to London from the Alps by Will's father, Harold had grown up understanding he was Hannah's pet and protector. "Where did you get this one?" Will asked. "Don't tell me you had to go to the Continent," he said, thinking the man had to be truly devoted to Hannah if he had made the trip to visit the St. Bernard monks that bred the rescue dogs.

Smiling, Henry shook his head. "From about a half-mile down the road toward Bampton, actually. A farmer named Cavanaugh has the bitch, which apparently came to these shores already pregnant. Harold is from that litter."

Perfect timing, he almost added, remembering how the first Harold had died and left Hannah in mourning for her best friend. The gift of little Harold had seemed to lift her spirits, especially during those first few months when she was expecting their son and was still too new to Gisborn Hall to have made many friends.

"I think there's still one or two left from the litter, if you're in the market for one," Henry said with an arched eyebrow. "Harold has been great with the baby," he added. He fished a chronometer out of his waistcoat pocket. "Who should be up and about any moment."

Will lifted his head. "About time I met my nephew," he said as a smile split his face.

Henry nodded. "Indeed." After a moment, he said, "You're welcome to stay as long as you'd like. Perhaps we could take the boy fishing. I expect I'll be done testing the new plow by noon tomorrow. The River Isis is just south of here."

Grinning broadly, Will dared a glance in Donald's direction and gave the earl a nod. "I think I shall take you up on that offer." After a pause, he sobered and added, "Now we just have to convince his mother."

Henry angled his head to one side. "Perhaps Hannah can help in that regard," he murmured, a plan forming in his mind's eye. "May I ask as to your plans for the next few years? Until you inherit, I mean?"

Will shook his head. "You can ask, but I'm afraid I'm at a bit of a loss. I just figured I would marry Barbara and settle us in a townhouse in Mayfair. Go about life in polite Society. Balls, soirées, *musicales*, the theatre. Occasionally play cards at the club. Do some woodworking. Have a family. But now..." He sighed and shook his head again. "I have absolutely no idea."

Ever the planner and always an inventor, Henry considered Will's response. "Hold that thought," he murmured quietly. "Sometimes 'tis better not to plan your entire future. Life has a way of hitting you upside the head just about the time you think you have it all sorted."

Frowning, Will regarded the earl for a moment before allowing a wan smile. "My sister have anything to do with that?"

Henry allowed a huge smile. "Everything, actually."

"Where's my mum?" a sleepy voice asked from behind them. Donald sat up straighter, alarm on his face at finding Barbara was no longer in the parlor.

"She's in the back gardens with Lady Gisborn," Henry answered. "Harold will take you. You'll want to ask her if you can join your father and me when we go fishing tomorrow afternoon," he added, secretly pleased when he saw the boy's look of happy surprise.

"Yes, my lord," the boy answered as he stood up and gave them a bow. "Come on, Harold. Take me to Lady Gisborn and my mum," he said as he took his leave of the parlor, Harold close on his heels.

Will watched his son leave, the oddest sensation filling his chest just then.

"You'll get used to it," Henry said quietly.

Biting his lip as he turned to regard his brother-in-law, Will shook his head. "I hope not."

CHAPTER 34

A WALK IN THE GARDEN

After checking on the napping baby in the nursery on the second floor of Gisborn Hall, Barbara and Hannah headed for the gardens. Barbara felt the tension in her shoulders slowly easing as they made their way down the hall and through a set of glass doors. At no point in Hannah's conversation or in her manner had Barbara felt *judged* by the earl's wife. Indeed, Hannah had seemed more than gracious and rather pleased to have Barbara's company.

Located on the end of the hall that looked out onto the old Ellsworth property, the garden featured a crushed granite walkway through a myriad of plants that were just beginning to bloom. From the newly-turned earth, it appeared as if most of the garden had been recently planted.

The spring air had Barbara inhaling sharply. "I wanted to say how sorry I was to hear about your mother. I didn't learn of her passing until several months after she died," Barbara remarked before allowing a sigh. "News does not arrive in a timely manner out here." The news, what little of it reached Broadwell, came by way of travelers leaving behind copies of *The Times* or *The Morning Chronicle* at *The Five Bells*.

Hannah's eyes widened a fraction. Goodness! *How long has Barbara been away from London?* "It's been four... nearly five years now," Hannah replied, realizing she no longer felt overcome at thoughts of her late mother. "But, thank you. I know it sounds awful to say, but if she hadn't died when she did, and then, a year later, if my aunt hadn't died when she did, I probably never would have met nor married Henry."

Surprised to hear Hannah refer to her husband by his given name rather than by 'Gisborn', Barbara arched an eyebrow. "It is odd how timing can be so important," she murmured. "Now it seems as if a clock and a calendar determine our fate in life."

Hannah pondered the comment, realizing Barbara had a good point. So many of her own life events had been a result of a particular event on a particular date at a particular time, those parameters always set by someone—or something—else. Fate was certainly easier to believe in than to think that what had happened since her mother's death was all a result of random events.

"Have you met my other brother?" Hannah asked as they continued their stroll through the gardens, thinking Barbara might have been in London to greet Will when her brother returned from his service in the Navy.

"I have not," Barbara replied, her brows furrowing. "Truth be told, I wasn't aware you had another."

Hannah turned her head to regard the older woman. "Half-brother, actually. Stephen Slater," she said as she angled her head. "I haven't met him yet, either, although I admit to a good deal of curiosity."

Barbara frowned and slowed her steps. "I wasn't aware your father had remarried."

Shaking her head, Hannah led them to a stone bench in the center of an ivy arch and took a seat at one end. "He has, actually. He did about the same time as I did, in fact. But I rather doubt Cherice Dubois will be adding any heirs to the family. She did not bear any for her first husband—he was a baron—and I rather doubt she plans to have a child with my father."

Frowning, Barbara considered Hannah's words. If the brother had their father's last name, then... "Who is Stephen's mother?" she asked, almost immediately chiding herself for putting voice to the query. "Forgive me—"

"It's fine," Hannah interrupted with a quick wave of her hand. "I thought Will might have told you. Stephen is the son of one of my father's mistresses."

She said the words so casually, Barbara blinked before she managed to suppress a gasp. "Oh?" she replied, not quite sure what the appropriate response could be to such news.

"My father had several mistresses before he married my mother, and then he kept his favorite for a time after that," Hannah explained, her manner so casual, Barbara realized the countess wasn't the least bit bothered by the topic.

That is, until Hannah suddenly colored up.

"I used to be of the opinion that men only ever loved their mistresses and married only to have legitimate heirs," she said quietly, her head shaking as she remembered having said the words as if they were her personal litany. But it was because of her belief in those words that had her open to the possibility of marriage to Henry Forster when he was in search of a wife.

What other daughter of an aristocrat would have been so accepting of marriage to a man who openly admitted he loved another and had fathered a son with her?

None of Hannah's friends, and certainly none of the other young women with whom she attended balls that one Season would have been.

No, they would have all been scandalized.

Barbara stilled herself, wondering if Hannah thought of her as Will's mistress. She had borne his son out of wedlock, after all. "You say that as if you have changed your opinion."

Hannah placed a hand over Barbara's, gently clasping it. "My father did love Stephen's mother. He admitted as much to me when we spoke of it after my mother died. After I found him sobbing in his study. Cursing himself because he claimed to have loved my mother, as well, and cursing God because he shouldn't have been able to love two women at the same time."

Swallowing, Barbara dared a glance at Hannah, startled to find her eyes bright with unshed tears. "Oh, Hannah," she breathed.

Hannah shook her head. "I didn't understand it at the time. I was too young, I suppose. But now... now I know exactly of what he spoke."

Barbara shook her head. "Your husband has a *mistress?*" she whispered in disbelief. But how could that be? Lord Gisborn seemed so devoted to his wife! In just the few minutes she had spent in his company in the parlor, she had caught the earl gazing at his wife as if he truly adored her.

Loved her.

Hannah shook her head. "No. Nor would I allow him to have one now. But he loved the woman who bore his son, you see. Loved her from the time they were children. She refused to marry him, even when she was about to give birth to his son, Nathaniel."

Shocked at Hannah's words, Barbara stared at the countess. Turn down an offer of marriage when you're about to bear a child? Never had she heard of such a thing! "Why ever would she turn down an earl's proposal of marriage?" she asked in surprise.

Allowing a wan smile, Hannah hoped Barbara could recognize herself in the same situation. "Henry wasn't yet an earl when Nathaniel was born, but Sarah knew Henry would one day inherit the Gisborn earldom, and she insisted he marry an aristocrat's daughter."

"But that meant her son would be a..." She stopped and moved to stand up, but Hannah tightened her hold on Barbara's hand, a bit dismayed at how bony it felt beneath her palm.

"Bastard, yes," she agreed with a nod. "But Nathan has been raised with an education. He will have all the privileges of a gentleman's son," she went on. "Just as your son will."

Barbara's eyes widened. She was about to deny Hannah's assumption that Donald was a bastard when she realized Hannah knew the truth.

But how? As far as she knew, Hannah and Will hadn't been alone to discuss Donald. Then she remembered that the gossips had no doubt spread word of her condition when she was in the process of leaving London. Her maid had known she was *enceinte*. She had probably shared her news with every other servant in Pendleton House before her dismissal. Her services wouldn't have been required after Barbara's departure. From there, the news would have spread to other households, to other servants, to other maids.

Her aunt had also known. She could have shared her news with her closest friends, ensuring Barbara would be the *on dit* in Mayfair parlors for weeks after her departure. "Who told you?" she asked, a sick feeling settling into her stomach, wondering which marchioness or countess or viscountess or baroness might have put voice to the gossip shared by a lady's maid or by her aunt. "Your maid, I suppose?" she whispered, knowing that gossip spread among neighboring servants faster than those above-stairs could manage.

Hannah shook her head, frowning at Barbara's comment. "No, actually. One has only to see a miniature of what my brother looked like at his age to know Donald is a Slater," Hannah whispered. "And it was rather thoughtful of you to give him a family name."

Barbara allowed her shoulders to slump. Here she had thought the worst, and instead Hannah had merely guessed at Donald's parentage. "Will once mentioned he had an uncle in Scotland named Donald," she whispered before a tear escaped the corner of her eye.

"Oh, Barbara, no. Do not cry," Hannah said quietly. "My brother adores you. He'll provide protection for you and for your son, I promise."

Barbara stared at Hannah, stunned by her words. Will hadn't made mention as to his intentions, other than to say he intended to take her back to London. Once she had made it clear she wasn't going back there, he hadn't said anything about their future. He had taken over the household as if he had every right to be there, though. As if he had every right to show up with dinner and remove her clothes and share her bed and clean the dishes and make repairs. She hadn't yet decided if she hated him or merely despised him for simply showing up as he had without so much as a letter to warn her he was about to upend her life.

"He showed up at the cottage where we've been living these past seven years, acting as if the intervening years hadn't even happened," Barbara said, her voice taking on the mixed notes of anger and sadness.

Hannah sighed. "Probably because he has left that other life behind and wants to resume the one he would have had with you," Hannah commented, her voice gentle. "Do you... hate him for having left London when he did? For leaving you with child? Without protection? Truth be told, I thought perhaps you two had secretly wed before he took his leave of London."

Barbara angled her head to one side. She had felt many emotions since that night she had spent with Will Slater. The night before he reported to his first assignment as a naval officer. The night she had appeared at the back door of his bachelor quarters, ready to give her virtue to him, ready to accept whatever he had to offer in the way of soft words and promises for their future.

She had loved him that night.

Allowed his kisses and soft caresses. Encouraged him to take her to his bed to make slow, passionate love to her. Held him atop her body when the last vestiges of his pleasure had subsided and he was left boneless and breathless and murmuring quiet words of affection.

Told him she loved him.

After a time, Will had held her tucked against his body as he whispered what their future would hold—a wedding, a trip to Northumberland, a house near the park, shopping, balls and soirées—a future that could never happen given his intent to leave her and London for years of service to the British Navy.

Later, as the time approached for him to take his leave of

her and head to the docks, they had engaged in a hurried, frantic coupling that seemed to generate the heat required to brand one another. "Wait for me," he had said just before his body spasmed and his seed spilled into her.

She had felt that warmth fill her insides, his caress sending shivers of pleasure dancing through her body and all over her skin.

A sensation she hadn't felt since that night.

In the intervening years, she had cursed him, cried over him, cursed herself, thanked him, hated herself, despised him, pitied herself, mourned for him, and tried to forget him.

But never had she hated him.

"I do not hate him," Barbara finally whispered with a shake of her head. "But neither do I *love* him. I don't think I can allow myself the luxury."

Hannah inhaled sharply, the quiet words far more potent than if Barbara had shouted them out loud. "Why ever not?" she asked in surprise. One look at how her brother regarded Barbara and she knew he felt affection for the woman. "I ask only because..." *Because I wish to see my brother with the mother of his son. Because I have always wanted a sister. Because I think he loves you.* "Because I did not love Henry when I married him," she finally admitted when she noticed Barbara's look of surprise. "I do now, of course. I couldn't help myself," she added with a wink and a wan smile. "And now I know husbands *can* love their wives. Henry loves me. Tells me so every day."

"Mum!"

Donald's shout had the two women turning their attention to the young boy as he ran in their direction, his steps darting around the greenery as he mostly followed the garden path. Harold bounded behind, his tail wagging as gobs of slobber followed in his wake.

"Here," Barbara called out, rising from the garden bench so the small boy could see her from his vantage point. "So much for thinking he might take a long nap," she said in a lowered voice, so only Hannah could hear her.

Hannah stood up, as well, smiling as Harold hurried to her side. He turned his body and took a seat, leaning against the stone bench as if he needed it to support his large body.

The boy paused when he caught sight of Hannah, his manner suddenly more reserved. He gave her a bow. "Pardon me, my lady," he managed to get out between gasps for air.

"Of course, Master Donald," Hannah said as she afforded him a curtsy. "What news do you bring?"

The boy beamed and seemed to blush before he turned his attention to his mother. "Lord Gisborn and Father said they would take me fishing tomorrow afternoon, if it's agreeable with you. Is it, Mum? Can I please go?"

Barbara exchanged a quick glance with Hannah, surprised not only at her son's reference to Will as 'father', but also at the implication that they would still be in residence at Gisborn Hall on the morrow. In the afternoon. "We'll see," she finally said before turning to Hannah. "We just came here on a walk, I thought. We certainly didn't intend to spend the night. I didn't bring any other clothes..." Not that she had any, she realized, remembering her only other gown was beyond repair.

"Oh, I can loan you some," Hannah interrupted with a wave of her hand. "*Give* you some, in fact," she added with a roll of her eyes. At Barbara's quick shake of her head, Hannah added, "I can no longer wear some of my gowns as they are too small." A hand went to her belly to smooth out her skirts so that her pregnancy was more evident. "I never returned to my former size after Randolph was born, you see," she explained in a voice meant only for Barbara to hear. She turned her attention to Donald and added, "I know there are plenty of short pants and a nightshirt in Master Nathan's bedchamber that Master Donald can wear."

Barbara angled her head, obviously tempted by the offer of a different gown than the threadbare one she wore. "We'll see," she said again with a sad sigh, wondering what Will had in mind.

Hannah merely nodded, deciding her brother would have to do some courting—a great deal of courting, actually—to convince Barbara to marry him, for it was apparent the woman hadn't any intention of allowing Will Slater back into her life.

But for the life of her, Hannah couldn't understand why not. Perhaps a few more hours in Barbara's company and she could discover the reason for the woman's hesitance, she considered.

A few hours without the men.

A few hours of shopping.

That would do the trick, she realized.

CHAPTER 35

A NIECE CONFIDES IN
AN AUNT

*B*ack *in London...*
Mildred Regan watched her niece as she picked at her late breakfast of coddled eggs and dry toast. For some reason, Victoria was using her left hand to hold her fork, favoring her right hand as if she had somehow injured it. "Happy birthday," she said before helping herself to a rasher of bacon. The cook had been especially busy that morning, she realized, when she noticed the number of courses available on the table. Perhaps the woman was aware of the special occasion. "Three-and-twenty now, aren't you?"

Victoria looked up from her plate and rolled her eyes. "I'd forgotten," she replied, a frown furrowing her eyebrows. Not having had a formal come-out nor spent any other years in London for a Season, she felt *old* compared to the other unmarried chits she had seen at Lord Weatherstone's ball earlier that week. Their white gowns gave them away if their immature behavior didn't.

"You needn't look so forlorn about it," Mildred replied, the sound of a scold apparent in her voice. "Did you enjoy the theatre the other night? I saw you were dropped off from a rather splendid coach."

When Victoria straightened at hearing this bit of news,

Mildred gave a shrug. "I couldn't sleep until I knew you were home safe," she said. "Whose coach brought you home?"

Victoria allowed a wan smile. "The Marquess of Devonville's. His son invited me to share their box," she added with an arched eyebrow. "So elegant. The marchioness is a very nice lady. She offered the ride."

Mildred blinked and angled her head. "However did you manage the invitation?" she asked, suspicious. Her niece had been in London less than a week but had managed to attend one of the best balls of the Season and the theatre the following evening. "I do apologize for not joining you. I just... I could not fathom the thought of being in a crowd of thousands," she said with a shake of her head.

Victoria sighed. "Someone I met at the Weatherstone ball saw me and... saved me, I suppose you could say," she murmured. She was saved from having to say more when there was a knock at the front door.

"Oh, my, it's time for callers, isn't it?" Mildred said as she excused herself from the breakfast parlor and made her way toward the small townhouse's front parlor. The housekeeper met her before she made it into the room, however.

"This came for Miss Comber," the housekeeper said, handing a bright white folded vellum to her mistress. "A *footman* delivered it," she added, one eyebrow arching up.

Mildred regarded the feminine script decorating the front of the missive, at once wondering who might have sent it. The red wax on the back was embossed with a seal she couldn't quite make out, but she was quite sure it wasn't a simple initial.

"Vicky!" she called out, hurrying back to the breakfast parlor.

"Who called?" Victoria asked when she looked up from her breakfast.

"A footman just delivered this." She held out the note to her niece and moved around the table to stand next to her, determined to read the note at the same time as Victoria.

Slipping a finger beneath the seal, Victoria unfolded the

four corners and immediately noticed the word 'Torrington' in the middle of the page. "It's an invitation to Lady Torrington's *musicale* tonight. For me and a guest," she added with a hint of awe in her voice. She gave her aunt a pointed look. "Eight o' clock. Are we going?"

Mildred Regan gave her niece a look of shock before nodding her head. "Of course we are going," she said with a nod, her heart racing with the prospect of attending the Season's most talked about *musicale*.

Before her aunt could ask her why it was Lady Torrington would extend an invitation to her, Victoria had her aunt's copy of *Debrett's Peerage and Barontage* out of the bookcase and open on the table, her left fingers causing the pages to flip until they reached the spread about the Earl of Torrington. When none of the names there seemed to make sense, she looked up the Devonville line, her brows furrowing until she saw the name 'Adele Slater Worthington' listed as a sister to the current marquess. Studying the invitation again, she realized the hostess, Adele Slater Grandby, Lady Torrington, had to be the same woman.

Stephen's aunt.

The day after the Weatherstone's ball, when she had the book out and had been trying to determine the identity of Stephen Slater, she had no idea to whose family he belonged, so she had no luck finding him in the book. Now she flipped back to the Devonville pages in an attempt to find the man listed as a son of William Slater. The only male name listed as an heir, though, was William III. Try as she might, she could find no listing for a Stephen Slater.

And yet Stephen had referred to the Marquess of Devonville as his father—even called the man 'father' when they were in the coach.

Could he be the 'William III' that was listed?

She studied the entire name, thinking perhaps 'Stephen' was one of his middle names, but she couldn't find a 'Stephen' listed anywhere in the ancestry chart.

"Who are you looking for?" Mildred asked as she picked up the invitation and read it through.

Dear Miss Comber, I write to request the honor of your and a guest's presence at my musicale this evening at eight o' clock in the evening at Worthington House in Park Lane. The favor of a reply is not expected given the short notice. I do hope you can attend as I look forward to meeting you. Sincerely yours, Adele Grandby, The Countess of Torrington.

"I don't know," Victoria whispered before shaking her head. When she noticed her aunt's expression, though, she sighed. "Stephen Slater," she finally admitted. "He's supposed to be William Slater's son, but he's not here. And I searched through the book yesterday and cannot find any other Slaters listed. Why is that?" she asked as she turned her attention back to her aunt.

Mildred sighed, realizing immediately why a son wouldn't be listed in *Debrett's*, even if he was the son of a marquess. "Because he is a bastard," she replied simply.

Victoria jerked up her head to stare at her aunt.

A bastard?

The word hit her as if it had been a punch to her middle. Her heart in her throat, Victoria slumped against the back of her chair. Fighting tears, she excused herself and took her leave of the breakfast parlor, nearly running as she made her way up the stairs to her bedchamber.

When Mildred found Victoria a few minutes later, she was in the window seat in her bedchamber, her face wet with tears, her breaths coming in staccato sobs. Mildred allowed a sigh. Taking a seat next to her niece, she gathered the girl into her arms and made a few shushing noises. "There, there," she murmured. "Did he ruin you?"

Victoria stilled herself, the words so unexpected she gasped. "No. Of course not," she replied indignantly, rather shocked her aunt could have come to that conclusion. "How could you even think such a thing?"

"But he kissed you."

It wasn't a question, but Victoria could tell from the sound of Mildred's voice that she rather hoped Victoria would deny it. She couldn't, though. She didn't want to. "Yes," she admitted. "Right after I slapped him."

Her aunt furrowed her brows in an attempt to hide the sudden humor she felt. "I would have thought the slap should have come *after* the kiss," she whispered.

Victoria merely shook her head, a handkerchief finally pressed against her cheeks in an attempt to dry to her tears. "I don't suppose it really matters," she whispered.

"Did he ever claim to be anyone other than who he said he was?" Mildred's query was spoken in a soft voice, as if she were afraid she would anger her niece.

Victoria allowed a sob before shaking her head. "No."

"How did he introduce himself?"

Sighing, Victoria remembered that moment at the ball when she had just made it into the ballroom, when she had helped herself to a glass of champagne and was suddenly face to face with the dark blond-haired, hazel-eyed man who could have been a Greek god. "Stephen Slater," she whispered, recalling how his smile came easily. How confident he seemed. She blinked, though, when she remembered more about that night. "I overheard others at the ball who claimed he was the Earl of Bellingham, though," she whispered. "The son of the Marquess of Devonville." This last was said with a firm nod, as if she'd been studying the book on the peerage.

"If he did not introduce himself as such, then you cannot find fault with him for the assumptions of others," Mildred countered carefully.

Sniffling, Victoria nodded. "True. But I was seen in his company. When we were leaving the theatre—"

"In the company of a marquess and his marchioness as well," Mildred reminded her gently.

"True," Victoria agreed, sniffling again as she allowed a nod. The marchioness had been so accommodating, affording her conversation and a front row seat for the fourth and fifth acts of the play. As the second woman to marry the marquess, she probably wasn't as offended by the presence of her husband's bastard in their company, she supposed.

Victoria and her aunt sat in companionable silence for a time before Mildred spoke. "I don't know about you, but I would dearly love to attend Lady Torrington's *musicale* this evening. Do you suppose—?"

"Oh, of course we shall attend," Victoria said with a nod, her tears having abated. "I have a gown in mind. And if I should see Mr. Slater, I shall simply act as if we are unacquainted," she added, deciding it would be safer socially if she did not know the man.

As for having kissed him, well, that was a mistake she had no intention of repeating. She wouldn't be giving Stephen Slater another moment of consideration.

The bastard!

CHAPTER 36

MUSICAL CHAIRS AT A MUSICALE

ater, in Mayfair

The short trip from Devonville House to Worthington House had Stephen wondering why his father and Cherice even bothered taking the town coach. He was quite sure they all could have walked and made it there just as quickly.

"Will there be a receiving line?" Stephen asked, nervous at the prospect of meeting his aunt and her husband for apparently the first time. If he had met his aunt at a younger age, he couldn't remember her.

From everything he had heard of Milton Grandby, he had nothing to worry about. Will's godfather was apparently a good man. But he knew nothing about Adele other than she offered the very best musicians and singers at her *musicales* and had at one time been married to a man involved in the early steamships.

And she had apparently been a rather wealthy widow when she married Milton Grandby.

"Not at all. These events are always more casual," Cherice replied with a hint of a smile. "Besides, Grandby wouldn't put up with a receiving line. And there's no need to be nervous about meeting Adele. She'll love you."

William Slater allowed a snort. "That's because she'll

think he's Will," the marquess said with a teasing grin. "One hundred pounds say she'll call him 'Bellingham' when she spots him for the first time."

"Devonville!" Cherice scolded while Stephen merely allowed a grin.

The town coach jerked to a halt just inside the curved drive in front of Worthington House. "Then perhaps I'll introduce myself as him," Stephen countered, his own grin belying his nervousness.

Although Stephen had thought the ballroom at Lord Weatherstone's mansion a bastion of elegance and light, he was nearly blinded by the glitter that decorated Worthington House. Surfaces shined, lights blazed, metallic threads gleamed and jewels reflected it all in brilliant stars and streaks of light as they made their way through the vestibule and into a parlor.

"Bellingham?"

The word had Stephen turning to regard an older gentleman he was quite sure he had never met before. *Damn*, he thought, realizing he wasn't going to get away with acting in his brother's stead at this particular event. "His brother, actually," Stephen replied as he held out his right hand. "Stephen Slater."

"Ah, the bastard!" the man said as he gripped Stephen's hand in one of the firmest handshakes Stephen had ever experienced. "Milton Grandby. I suppose I'm..." He paused a moment, his bushy eyebrows furrowing into a single caterpillar on his forehead.

"The Earl of Torrington?" Stephen suggested, wanting to ensure he had the right Grandby in mind. His father was right to bet the man would call him 'Bellingham'. *One-hundred pounds!*

Grandby gave him a quelling glance. "Well, that, too, I suppose, but more importantly I am your... *uncle*," he managed to get out as he continued to study Stephen. "By marriage, of course, and a godfather to your brother. Call me

Grandby. If you call me 'Torrington,' I'll ignore you. Where is Will, by the way?"

Stephen couldn't suppress the grin he felt at the earl's expense, realizing the man must have imbibed in a rather good brandy prior to the start of the affair. Although Grandby didn't seem drunk, he did seem rather more excited than he should have at meeting his bastard nephew-by-marriage. Stephen leaned toward the earl and said in a quiet voice, "He's gone to Oxfordshire to find his true love. And pay a call on our sister," he added with a nod.

Grandby furrowed his brows again, his manner suddenly all business. "I wasn't aware he had already decided which chit that would be. He certainly didn't waste any time."

Stephen thought to reply with "Eight years," but thought better of it. He didn't know enough about the situation to comment on it.

"Who's the gel?"

Noting the earl's sudden sobriety, Stephen blinked. "Lady Barbara Higgins," he offered. "He... offered for her hand before he left London and now is determined to make her his wife."

The earl arched an eyebrow. "I remember her. Haven't seen her in an age—"

"Apparently, no one has, my lord," Stephen said, keeping his voice low. He thought perhaps a change in subject was required. "I understand congratulations are in order. The marchioness said your countess recently gave birth to twins."

The earl grinned and waved his hand for Stephen to follow him as he turned and made his way up the grand staircase from the main hall. "They're your cousins, so it's high time you meet them. Once they start walking, there will be no catching them."

Hesitant at leaving the growing throng of guests congregating in several rooms off the parlor, Stephen followed the earl up the grand staircase to the next floor and into a well-appointed nursery. A nurse immediately stood and curtsied, although she did so with a babe sitting on her hip. The other twin was sitting on the floor, a rattle gripped in one fist and his other stuffed in his mouth. Surrounded by dozens of toys —wooden blocks, wheeled carts, and puzzle pieces—the boy appeared overwhelmed. At the sight of Milton Grandby, though, both babies began giggling and gurgling, their expressions of happiness so infectious, Stephen was forced to chuckle.

The earl took the girl from the nurse and settled her into the crook of one arm. "This is Lady Angelica," he said as he proudly displayed the pink gown-garbed cherub. He kissed his daughter's temple before he pointed toward the floor, "And that's my heir, Lord George."

Unsure of the protocol for greeting aristocratic babies, Stephen merely treated them as he would their adult counterparts. He helped himself to Angelica's hand and brushed his lips over the back of it, eliciting a giggle from the tot before she grinned and pulled her hand away. For a moment, he was struck at how tiny were her fingers, at how perfect her fingernails appeared, how her light blonde hair curled into a golden halo around her head. He imagined her as his own daughter, being held by Victoria, nursing at her breast. Smiling at him as he took her hand and kissed the back of it.

He had to give his head a shake to clear it of the odd thought.

"It's very good to make your acquaintance, Cousin Angelica," he said formally. Finally tearing his attention from the attentive babe, he turned to regard his male cousin. He bowed to George, who bobbed his head in response but reached up with both hands, as if he, too, wanted to be held. Stephen dared a glance in Grandby's direction before he dodged several toys and lifted the boy up and over his head, holding him nearly upside down as the baby squealed and screeched. Stephen was only slightly aware of the nurse's expression of shock at seeing the heir to the Torrington earldom in midair, his bare feet on display when they emerged from beneath his gown. Stephen lowered the happy tot when he realized the boy's screeches could probably be heard in the parlor below.

He didn't need the boy's mother making an appearance when she was the hostess of the event.

My aunt, he reminded himself.

CHAPTER 37

A BROTHER AND SISTER
SHARE THEIR TALES

ack in Oxfordshire
"I suppose you think the worst of me," Will said as he and Hannah made their way to the stables. He wanted to check on Thunderbolt to be sure the horse wasn't having a fit being handled by someone he didn't know. Hannah had ordered water for bathing to be taken up to Barbara's bedchamber so that she might take a bath before dinner, and Will knew his presence wouldn't be welcome whilst she bathed. He hoped to do the same thing before dinner, the odor of horse and musk becoming more apparent as the day proceeded.

"What are you implying?" Hannah asked, her brows furrowing.

Her brother took several more steps before he finally responded. "I didn't know Barbara was with child when I left London. She never mentioned anything about being with child in the few letters she sent me," he murmured in a low voice. "But if she had, I most assuredly would have made arrangements to marry her," he claimed, not quite sure how he could have done so. The *HMS Drake* was rarely near British shores the first year he was aboard, but he might have taken a leave and caught a packet back to England.

"I know," Hannah nodded, thinking her brother

intended to tell her something else. "But that's not why you wanted to talk with me. Is it?" she countered.

Will sighed, realizing he just wanted a few minutes alone with his sister. He hadn't had the opportunity to spend much time with her when he was in England for their mother's funeral. Indeed, he was only in town for two days, and back then, he hadn't yet known about Stephen. But where to start? There was so much to tell!

"Before I started my tour—a year before, in fact, when I was home from the academy for a month or so—"

"I remember," Hannah interrupted. "You might have been in London, but you certainly didn't spend the time at Devonville House," she accused with a lifted brow.

Will nodded his agreement. "True. I was... old enough to spend the nights away from home but too young to know I should have spent them in the company of my family," he murmured. "Mother was still alive back then," he added. "You had just started finishing school at Warwick's."

"And Father was spending most of his nights at home by then," Hannah interrupted, a wan smile touching her lips. "That was the best time."

"That's because his mistress had married, and her husband couldn't abide sharing her, even with a marquess," Will countered with an arched eyebrow. He stopped in his tracks, one palm slapping his forehead. "Jesus, I cannot believe I just said that in your company—"

"It's all right," Hannah claimed with a shake of her head. "I knew far more than I should have back then." At Will's look of curiosity, she added, "Mother told me all about Marie St. Clair."

Will resumed walking, almost curious enough to ask what else Hannah might have learned about their father's mistress. About their parents. About their bastard brother.

"There is a reason our brother looks so much like me," he announced.

Hannah angled her head, attempting to see her brother's face. But when he turned to look at her, she found only a passive expression. "I did not know he did," she replied with a shrug, a reminder that she hadn't yet met their bastard brother. "Do you mean in his eyes or the color of his hair or—?"

"Everything," Will responded with a nod. "He looks like he could be my identical twin." At Hannah's look of doubt, he added, "I swear. The two of us would play tricks on the crew, him giving orders as if he were me, and the men believed him to be me and followed them," he said with a wry smile. "Even you would be hard pressed to tell us apart."

Hannah arched an eyebrow. "Since I have not seen you for nearly four years, I have no reason to doubt your claim," she agreed. "Which means you could be Stephen come to play a trick on me," she reasoned, suddenly wondering if perhaps this man was Stephen Slater and her brother was still back in London. But Will knew far too much about her. About what she had been through as an unmarried chit in London. Things only he would know from her frequent letters.

Will allowed a chuckle. "You have a point. I didn't think of that."

"Why is it, then, that you believe Stephen shares your good looks?" she asked, thinking her brother must have spent some time in front of a looking glass if he thought he shared the guise of another man.

One of Will's hands went to his chest, the fingers splayed out over his topcoat as he threw back his head and laughed. "Leave it to my sister to raise my poor spirits," he said happily.

Hannah didn't respond, anxious to hear why Will and Stephen looked so much alike, but rather dismayed at hearing Will thought himself low in spirit. When she lifted her brows in query, Will sobered quickly.

"Father's mistress looked exactly like our mother."

Hannah blinked and stopped walking, her brother's words repeating themselves in her head. "How could you *know* such a thing?" she asked in alarm.

Shrugging, Will stepped in front of Hannah and regarded her for a moment. "I met her. I paid a call on the residence where she was a guest whilst I was home that one month. One of my friends from the Academy, Rufus Kincaid, had asked that I pay a call and deliver a gift to his mother, so I already had an excuse to be there."

Hannah blinked, momentarily stunned by her brother's words. "You did not!" she whispered hoarsely.

Will sighed. "I admit, it was done with poor judgement—"

"Had you already met Stephen by then?" she asked, curious as to why he would pay a call on the woman who was Stephen's mother.

"No," Will assured her. "I knew *of* him, of course, but I was merely curious as to what Father saw in this woman who had taken him away from us for too long," he explained. "I was... *angry* with her, I suppose," he added.

Hannah lowered her eyes, understanding her brother's reasons. "And?"

Will allowed a shrug. "She agreed to see me. Hosted me in the parlor at Kincaid's house. Offered me tea," he said sadly. "And the whole time, all I could think about was how much it was like having tea with Mother."

Hannah stared at Will for a very long time. "Is she... related to our mother?" she asked, her stomach threatening to cast up her accounts, and not just because she was expecting another child.

Had her Father taken the woman as a mistress because...?

"I didn't ask, but given she was born and raised in France, I rather doubt it," he replied. "I could barely form words in her company," he added. "But she was most gracious. Very refined. The perfect hostess. You would not have known of her profession—her *former* profession," he amended quickly. "—Had you spent any time in her company."

Hannah shook her head. "But if I had seen her some-where in London, would I have thought her our mother? Was she that similar in appearance?" she asked. "I only ask because, well, I haven't seen any women who bear a resemblance to Mother," she argued, wanting him to know she hadn't come across the former courtesan. "When she is in London, she must not go out in public."

"Possibly," Will said with a nod, realizing the woman probably stayed with her hostess and didn't venture out during her stay. And she wouldn't have moved in the same circles as their mother when she was still their father's mistress.

"Did you like her?"

Will gave a start, rather surprised by the simple question. "I suppose. I didn't *dislike* her, although I remember wanting to," he replied, not admitting that he could understand how his father would be attracted to such a beauty. While she shared Grace Burroughs Slater's facial features, Marie St. Clair had an air of quiet confidence about her that their mother lacked. An air of contentment that suggested she was happy with her lot in life. Will rather doubted the woman ever complained or nagged or belittled the men who employed her.

"What have you done with *Stephen*, by the way?"

Glad for the change in topic, Will took her hand back onto his arm and led them to the entrance to the stables. "I left him in London. Told him to be me and to find me a wife," he said with a hint of mischief.

Hannah's eyes widened in alarm. "You rake!" she accused, rather incensed at him. Didn't he know how difficult it already was for young ladies of the *ton* to navigate the Marriage Mart? Adding someone who had no intention of marrying to the mix merely made it worse!

But Will shook his head, a grin on his face. "I don't think he took me seriously," he replied. "But if some young lady believes him to be me and discovers how agreeable he is, he may land a wife of good breeding," he reasoned, thinking he had done the man a favor.

Hannah continued frowning. "And when she finds out he is not an earl destined to be a marquess, but merely the bastard son of one, what then?" she asked. "Oh, Will. What have you done?"

Will considered Hannah's words, thinking she was being rather dramatic. Stephen wouldn't truly seek a wife so soon after returning to England.

Would he?

"I am hoping I have made him my replacement," he whispered. "At least until I absolutely have to return to being me." At Hannah's look of confusion, he added, "If he is me, then I don't have to return to London. I don't have to find a wife..."

Hannah whirled on him, her head shaking in disbelief. "And what of Barbara? What of the woman you have *ruined*?"

Will held up a hand as if he had to defend himself, rather startled at his sister's sudden outburst. "I have every intention of marrying *her*," he claimed. "In fact, if there had been a vicar and a means to obtain a license on our trip today, I would see to it we were married in the morning."

Hannah relaxed at hearing her brother' claim, although she realized just then he was unaware of Barbara's feelings on the matter. Their earlier discussion in the garden had left Hannah believing Barbara would never consider her brother's suit, even if it made perfect sense for them to marry.

She didn't yet know what had Barbara so apprehensive —*something* had happened—but she had every intention of discovering just what it was that had Barbara so reluctant to consider marriage to her brother. "I would be honored to have her as my sister," Hannah murmured, thinking that with a bit of encouragement, Barbara would once again welcome a life more suited to how she was raised. A life that included more luxuries and less labor. More food and less hunger.

Hannah remembered the woman's claim that she didn't love Will, though. She allowed a sigh. "But do take care with her, brother. Barbara is a bit... broken."

Will furrowed his brows at Hannah's description of the

woman he had loved since before he left London for his tour in the British Navy. *Broken* was as good as any word, he supposed, to describe what had become of his lover. "If she'll allow me, I'll put all her little bits and pieces back into place and hold her so tightly she will have to mend," he whispered, his expression so intense, it had Hannah feeling alarmed.

"And what of Donald?" she asked then, one hand going to his arm to grip it. "He is your son, isn't he? You speak of your brother looking every bit like you, and yet, that boy bears every likeness to you as well."

Will nodded, glad to know he wasn't the only one who saw the family resemblance in the boy. "He is. You must believe me when I tell you that if I'd had any idea I had left Barbara with child, I would have..." He allowed the sentence to trail off.

"Married her? And then left her?" Hannah finished for him, her words rather curt.

Frowning, Will winced at her tone. "Far better she be married *before* having her babe than what did happen," he countered.

"And yet, she is free of an overbearing drunk father who gambles too much and may lose his earldom to the Crown."

The words were so unexpected, Will had to steady himself by leaning against the stable wall. "How... how do you know this?" he asked in a whisper. He knew Lord Greenley was a gambler, his assessment confirmed when he learned what had happened to force Barbara to move to Broadwell. But about to lose his earldom?

Hannah dipped her head. "Whispers in parlors is all."

"Jesus," Will whispered, wanting nothing more than to pull Barbara into his arms that very moment to comfort her. "I had some idea, of course, but not having been in London, I just don't know."

Hannah angled her head, realizing that by not being in London all those years, Will was unaware of much that had happened in the families of the *ton*. If he had no intention of returning to London any time soon, though, he wouldn't have to learn everything right away. He could take his time familiarizing himself with a new copy of *Debrett's Peerage and Barontage*, read the newspapers from London, and read Cherice's weekly letters.

Hannah noticed darkness settling over the stables. "I should be getting back. Dinner will be served soon, and I still need to change my gown," she murmured.

Will held up a hand and quickly moved into the stable, finding Thunderbolt with his nose in a bucket of oats. He had been brushed and his stall was mucked. "A favor, sister?" he asked when he determined the horse was in good hands.

Hannah gave a nod. "Of course. What is it?"

Glancing around to be sure neither of the two men working in the stables could hear him, he said, "Do not wear your best gown for dinner. Barbara has nothing but the clothes on her back."

Giving her brother a quelling glance, Hannah shook her head. "I've already given her a gown for tonight's dinner, and I have every intention of giving her more of them," she said, one eyebrow arched. "Especially since I will be unable to wear most of them in a few months. Oh, and tomorrow, whilst you go fishing, I shall take her shopping. You might want to be sure she has some money in her reticule."

Alarm had Will's eyebrows rising high before he realized what she meant. "I'll be an uncle again?" he whispered, a smile replacing his look of alarm.

"Probably just before the harvest, which is terrible timing, I know, but it cannot be helped," Hannah replied with a shake of her head.

"Does Gisborn know?"

Hannah grinned, a blush coloring her face. "Before I did, I think," she answered, leading them back toward the house and through the kitchen door. Before they parted company to dress for dinner, Hannah added, "Henry is very perceptive and very clever. Should he provide you with any advice, do give it consideration."

His brows furrowing, Will finally nodded. He supposed he could do with some advice just then.

Like what the hell I'm supposed to do now that my life's plan is in tatters, he thought as he made his way to the bedchamber he was supposed to be sharing with Barbara. When he was sure she was being seen to by a maid in the bathing chamber adjacent to their room, he pulled some coins from his purse. At least he could see to it Barbara could afford to shop on the morrow.

CHAPTER 38

A GAME OF HORSEY

$\mathcal{M}$*eanwhile, back at Worthington House*

"Have you taught him to ride a horse yet?" Stephen asked as he took a seat in the nearest rocker, George held out in front of him as he did so.

The earl frowned. "I have not. I thought perhaps I would wait until he could at least walk," he countered with a wry grin. He watched as Stephen crossed his legs and planted George onto the crook in his boot so that George's legs straddled it. With a solid grip on the baby's arms, Stephen waited until he had George's attention. "Are you ready to ride?"

George squealed in delight when Stephen began bouncing his foot up and down. "You'll have to say 'whoa' when you're ready to stop," Stephen warned, grinning as broadly as the boy, imagining what it would be like to do this to his own son. Why, his boy would be ready to ride a pony before his first birthday!

Amused by Stephen's antics, Grandby took a seat in the opposite rocker and was about to do the same with Angelica when the babe's attention was suddenly on the door. A second later, George's attention was turned there, as well.

"Mama!' the two cried out in unison.

Stephen had George scooped up and into his arms in an instant as he stood up, turned, and bowed to the stately woman who stood regarding him from the threshold of the nursery.

"Pardon me, my lady," he said, the red from his embarrassment staining his throat and cheeks. He was barely aware of Grandby doing the same, as if he'd been caught with his hand in a biscuit jar.

"Bellingham?" she said in surprise. "Oh, my. Had I known it was you who was the one causing all the ruckus up here, I would let you carry on. I sometimes think George believes he's already inherited, what with how serious he is sometimes," she said happily, moving to take Stephen into her arms. "I remember when your father used to play 'horsey' with you."

Stephen swallowed, not sure how to respond. He hadn't remembered William Slater ever bouncing him on his boot, but then he couldn't remember much from his days as a toddler. *She must mean Will*, he figured, realizing he had better admit to being the brother. "Stephen Slater, actually," he said just as she was about to embrace him, her son trying to decide if he was being transferred to her arms or if he should continue to cling to the man who had entertained him so thoroughly only a moment ago. "I am honored to make your acquaintance, my lady."

Inhaling sharply, Adele Grandby regarded her bastard nephew with a look of awe. "I haven't seen you since you were..." She held out a hand to indicate the size of a toddler. Adele continued to regard him with a look of awe. "Well, you certainly are your father's son to be sure," she murmured. She blinked, as if remembering why she had made her way to the nursery. "Now, I came up here to find my host. As usual, Milton is finding it more satisfying to entertain his daughter than to play host to the hundred or so guests who are here for a *musicale*," she complained with an arched eyebrow. She turned back to Stephen. "Escort me down, won't you. Nurse can take George. I think he's had enough fun for the evening, and it is past his bedtime."

Although George obviously didn't agree, he allowed the

nurse to take him from Stephen's arm. Meanwhile, Grandby was putting his daughter down into her bassinet. "I'll be but a moment," he said as he noticed his wife watching him.

"Give her a kiss for me, will you? I'll pay it back later." Adele shook her head as she turned her attention back to a somewhat embarrassed Stephen.

Pay it back later? The comment suggested the countess would be kissing her husband sometime later that evening!

Stephen found himself wondering if there was a rather large potted palm somewhere in the house. He smiled at the thought of his aunt kissing Grandby. The two seemed to be a rather good match, probably more affection than arrangement in their marriage. And given the number of jewels displayed on his aunt—she wore a circlet of diamonds around her neck, several bracelets sprinkled with diamonds and sapphires, earbobs of diamonds and the blue stones, and a tiara adorned in the same glittering jewels—Stephen realized the two were probably in love with one another.

Stephen offered Adele his arm, and she placed a hand on it. "Cherice tells me you've already made quite an impression on several young ladies," she ventured as they made their way to the top of the stairs.

Stephen felt the color rise in his cheeks again. "Will asked me to keep on the lookout for a potential wife in the event he was unable to locate Lady Barbara," he explained as they descended the stairs.

"And have you succeeded in finding one?" she asked, her gaze perusing the guests who still streamed in from the vestibule.

"At least one," Stephen replied with a nod as he kept his eye out for Victoria.

They had nearly reached the bottom when he caught sight of her entering the grand hall from the vestibule, an older woman by her side. He was sure she saw him, but her face didn't register an expression of recognition.

"Is she one of them perhaps?"

Stephen realized he had been caught staring. "Victoria

Comber. She's a niece of Aimsley's," he explained with a nod as they reached the main floor. "I hardly think I would make an acceptable husband, though," he added, wondering at Victoria's reaction to seeing him.

Adele regarded her nephew with a shake of her beautifully coiffed head. "You would make an exceptional husband for any of these chits in attendance this evening," she countered, her manner most serious. "Had any of them seen you bouncing my son on your boot as you were earlier, why, I rather think you would have several of them lined up to accept your proposal," she added with an arched brow.

Stephen had to stifle the laugh he nearly allowed. "I appreciate you saying so, my lady," he replied.

"Aunt Adele," she corrected him. "I don't recommend you call Grandby 'Uncle Milton', but you must refer to me as your aunt. I will accept nothing less," she claimed, an elegantly arched eyebrow emphasizing her point.

Stephen took a breath as he considered her mandate. "If you insist, my lady. Aunt Adele," he corrected himself.

"And you're welcome to come play 'horsey' with George anytime you wish, but do be warned that Angelica will probably insist you do the same with her. She's rather particular that way."

Before Stephen could reply, he found himself in the middle of a crowd of guests, their attention on his aunt. He managed to make his way out of the crush, his gaze taking in the crowd that filled the parlor and the large music room adjacent to it. Chairs had been arranged in a large semicircle around a piano forté and several music stands. Clusters of guests drank champagne and helped themselves to lobster patties and chunks of cheese displayed on large silver platters carried by footmen.

Stephen made his way into the next room, his eyes finally settling on Victoria Comber.

Dressed in a green gold silk gown with full long sleeves, she shimmered nearly as much as the metal objects displayed on the shelves. The older woman, dressed in a classic gown of deep blue watered silk, was still by her side, their heads bent in conversation. *Her aunt*, he thought, remembering her words when the coach had dropped her off at the townhouse in King Street.

Stephen nodded in Victoria's direction, sure she was watching him as he moved to make his way to her side. Before he could reach her, however, she and the older woman suddenly moved off, making their way to the other door.

Stephen stopped, wondering if Victoria didn't want to introduce him to her aunt.

Had the older woman scolded her for having ridden with him, alone, in the Devonville coach? Did she suspect they had engaged in rather passionate kissing? Or had Victoria truly not seen him as he made his way through the crowded room?

Sighing, partly because he knew so few people in attendance and partly because he had hoped to gain an introduction to the woman who was supposed to be her chaperone, Stephen made his way out the same door as he had seen Victoria use to take her leave of the library. Once again back in the grand hall, he glanced around, finally spotting her—alone—near an alcove that displayed a suit of armor and a Greek statue of Pan.

Hurrying to her side, Stephen was stunned when she suddenly moved off and made her way down the hall, passing him as she did so but not giving him any indication she recognized him.

"Did you just give me the cut direct?" Stephen whispered hoarsely, one hand having wrapped around her elbow as she passed so he could force her to face him. Her sudden inhalation of breath had her breasts mounding behind the bodice of her gown, the delicate lace edging doing little to hide the swells of her breasts nor her cleavage. The collarbones he had kissed only the night before stood out in sharp relief, accentuating her soft bare shoulders and the simple gold locket that hung at the hollow of her throat.

"Why, I do believe I did," Victoria said in a quiet voice,

her eyes not making contact with his. She was sure those hazel eyes would perform some sort of witchcraft on her, much as they had done that night at Lord Weatherstone's ball, unless she could get away from them. "Unhand me," she added, jerking her elbow away from him.

Stunned at her behavior, he frowned. "Why?" he asked in a whisper, his expression displaying his hurt.

Victoria gave him a shake of her head. "Are you truly that thick?" she countered, gathering her skirts so that she could hurry off. "*Bellingham?*" she added before rolling her eyes. "Hardly."

Stephen found his ability to breathe suddenly compromised. *What the hell had happened since the night they attended the theatre?* What could have happened to cause her to treat him like he was a...?

Stephen inhaled sharply.

Bastard.

No. Certainly she wouldn't hold that...

She would.

He had never introduced himself to her as 'Will'. Never introduced himself as 'Bellingham' despite his brother's insistence that he do so. He had introduced himself as 'Stephen Slater'. He and Victoria had spent an entire evening in his father's box at the theatre. At no point had anything been mentioned as to who his mother might be. He was sure Cherice wouldn't have said anything to her whilst they shared conversation during the intermission. Cherice seemed rather taken with Victoria—she practically had Stephen married off to the chit when they spoke in the study earlier that morning.

Stephen rolled his eyes and turned to watch Victoria's retreating back, watched her silk de Naples skirts sway with her every step, the fabric threatening to cling to her long legs.

Well, if that's what she thought of him now that she knew he was a bastard son of a marquess instead of an heir, well then, he supposed he was better off having discovered her feelings on the subject now rather than having wasted any time courting the chit.

He would miss her kisses, though, dammit.

He was almost relieved when he heard the gentle chime summoning the guests to take their seats.

CHAPTER 39

MAKING AN IMPRESSION
BEFORE DINNER

eanwhile, in Oxfordshire
Barbara regarded the guest bedchamber and allowed a sigh. It had been years since she had enjoyed such elegant accommodations, and back then, she hadn't realized how nicely appointed her bedchamber was at Pendleton House. Although the furnishings in this bedchamber were old—Hannah had mentioned that nearly everything in Gisborn Hall was old—they had been recently polished, and the velvet drapes that framed the mullioned windows appeared as if they had just been hung the day before.

She perched on the edge of the bed, giving the mattress a quick bounce. Closing her eyes, she allowed a wan smile before tears collected in the corners of her eyes. Lifting the back of her hand to her nose, she suppressed the urge to simply allow herself a good cry, but her tears would no doubt stain the deep green silk batiste gown Hannah had insisted she wear.

The gown was beautiful despite its too-long length. Barbara thought it made her appear taller, willowy, almost. Not a thought she would have had of herself during her days in London. Back then, her figure had been rather generous, made curvy with breasts and hips that didn't necessarily work well with the most fashionable gowns. Now, she was far too thin, her bones more apparent beneath her skin, her arms barely filling the elbow-length gloves Hannah had loaned her.

A quick glance in the cheval mirror gave her a start. Hannah's maid had done wonders with her hair, the blonde tresses pulled up and back in an elaborate bun while spirals graced her temples.

Donald didn't even recognize her, his mouth gaping open when she appeared at the threshold of the library door. But then, she didn't recognize her son, either. Dressed in a formal suit of black short pants and a topcoat that fit as if it had been tailored specifically for him, with his unruly hair trimmed and tamed so it was nearly plastered to his head, Donald looked every bit the aristocrat's son he was. She had to suppress a gasp when he stood up and gave her a deep bow, nearly toppling over as he did so. Curtsying, Barbara allowed a smile and was about to say something when the air in the room seemed to sizzle.

Will was at her side in an instant, offering his arm as he led her to a settee before seeing to a glass of claret for her. "You look... lovely," he whispered, his lips brushing her forehead as he gave her the crystal glass.

She stared at him, stunned at how he appeared in his uniform, the white breeches and white shirt an impressive canvas for the naval coat decorated with brass buttons and ribbons. "And you look positively... *commanding*," she breathed, keeping her voice low because she thought there might be others in the room. But a quick look around had her realizing their hosts hadn't yet joined them.

"Were that the case, do you suppose I could command you to join me for a walk in the gardens after dinner this evening?" he asked, *sotto voce*. He was well aware his son was watching his every move, the boy still not completely reconciled to his relationship to him. But then, what did he expect? Donald hadn't had any male presence in Barbara's household, such as it was. He hadn't had a father figure in his life.

Well, Will intended to change that starting the next afternoon, for he planned to join his brother-in-law on a fishing expedition on the River Isis, and he had every intention of taking Donald along.

Barbara regarded Will for a moment, figuring he probably intended to coerce her into returning to London. To steal a kiss. Or two or three. Despite the pleasant sensation that rippled down her spine just then, she gave him a shake of her head. "We'll see," she answered before urging her son to join her. "Oh, Master Donald. Let me have a look at you," she said with a huge smile, rather liking how her lean son appeared in his borrowed clothes.

"Hannah is quite insistent that he keep the clothes," Will said in a quiet voice.

Barbara gave him a quelling glance. "She has a boy who could wear these clothes in five or six years. And should her next child be a boy, too? Won't she regret having given away Master Nathan's Sunday best suit?" she countered.

Will leaned over and kissed her forehead before she could jerk away from him. He allowed a wan grin. "She's quite sure she's going to have a girl this time," he replied with a shrug, not about to add that Lord Gisborn wasn't the miser his uncle was known to be. "And I rather doubt her son will be wearing any of Master Nathan's clothes. Henry tells me Nathan's clothes were mostly worn out and are now the household rags. He was a rather active boy, playing pirates and what-not."

Barbara held her son out at arm's length and regarded him with a smile. "My, but don't you look like the perfect young gentleman?"

Donald nodded. "May I keep them? Please?" he asked, bouncing on the balls of his feet. "Aunt Hannah says I can," he added in an imploring tone.

Blinking, Barbara straightened on the settee. *Aunt*

Hannah? Had he really just referred to the Countess of Gisborn as his *aunt?*

She gave her head a shake. Well, Hannah *was* the boy's aunt, she realized. "Then I suppose you can," Barbara said in a quiet voice. She dared a glance in Will's direction, stunned to find his attention on Donald, his expression one of mild amusement and... *was that pride?*

Before she was able to ask as to the reason Will wanted to take a walk in the gardens, their hosts joined them. Followed by Harold, Lady Hannah breezed into the room, her blue silk deNaples gown draped over her figure so it was more apparent she was expecting another child. She curtsied to her brother's and nephew's bows and hurried to Donald to offer her hand as he resumed his standing position.

"You look rather handsome this evening, Master Donald," Hannah said as she took back her gloved hand. "I do hope my husband's valet was to your liking."

Donald beamed and gave a nod as he reached out to pet Harold's head. "Oh, very much so, my lady," he replied. "He never once said a cross word to me."

Barbara's eyes widened at hearing her son's claim, wondering why he might have expected a servant to scold him. She thought to ask him, but Hannah had turned her attention to her, and Barbara gave the countess a nod. "Your gown is lovely," she murmured, wondering how the fabric would feel against her skin. Wondering how she might look in the sky blue color given her blonde hair and steel gray eyes. Wondering when she might ever have an occasion to wear such a gown.

Hannah seemed to blush at the comment. "I'm glad you like it, as I expect I'll be giving it to you after this evening. I didn't realize how... how *small* it has become," she added with an arched eyebrow.

Barbara shook her head. "Oh, I couldn't accept it," she replied.

"Oh, but you must," Henry Forster said as he entered the library, giving a quick bow to the ladies as he moved to readjust the toddler he held in one arm. He grinned when he caught Donald giving him a bow in return. "My wife is quite determined to take a trip to Bampton for a new gown or two, and I suppose I'm inclined to allow her the indulgence. I would appreciate it very much if you could accompany her."

Before Barbara could counter the earl's comment, Will caught her attention and gave her a wink. Momentarily confused, she wasn't able to respond with anything other than, "Of course."

Henry led Hannah to a chair next to where Harold and Donald had settled and then announced, "And I do believe that while the ladies are in Bampton, the rest of us shall take the opportunity to go fishing." Randolph moved into his mother's arms, one fist shoved into his mouth as he regarded their visitors.

Donald grinned, knowing he wasn't allowed to say anything but wanting it known he was looking forward to the trip. As if Harold thought it was his duty to keep the boy company, the dog had settled on the floor next to where Donald sat.

"Have you ever been fishing before?" Will asked the young boy, seeing him in a whole new light now that he was clean and better dressed. Apparently one of the Gisborn Hall servants had seen to it he had a bath before the valet dressed him in Master Nathaniel's cast-offs. He could certainly make out the family resemblance more easily, see how the boy sported the same cowlick on the crown of his head has he had, the same color hair and eyes that stared back at him in a looking glass.

Donald's eyes darted to his mother, as if he thought he needed permission to answer the question—she had told him he couldn't speak—and finally replied, "I have not, sir. Will you please teach me?"

Will felt something odd in his chest just then as he regarded his son. *Pride?* No, that couldn't be it, he thought. He hadn't done anything to help raise the boy. Hadn't done anything to see to it Donald behaved as a perfect gentleman. Hadn't done anything to see to it he was prepared for life. "I look forward to it," Will finally answered with a nod, glancing at Barbara. Although her attention was on her son, Will knew she had been watching him the moment before. He had felt her gaze on him, although he didn't know if she had stared at him with contempt or longing or indifference.

"We didn't mean to be so late in joining you," Henry said as he moved to the sideboard and poured a glass of claret for Hannah. "We were up in the nursery with Randolph. He has moved from mere toddling to out and out running, I fear," he explained, his huge smile at odds with his comment.

Will moved to lift the babe from Hannah and regarded the boy as he held it at arms' length from his body. He continued to lift the babe until he was above his head. Randolph squealed in delight, especially when Will tipped him so the boy's head lowered while his bottom was still held aloft. "I don't suppose you've taught him to ride a horse yet," Will said to his sister.

Hannah's eyes widened, her amusement at his antics disappearing. "Of course not," she replied. "And do be careful. You are holding the heir to the Gisborn earldom!"

Ignoring her complaint, Will lowered his nephew until he was tucked under his arm and returned to his chair. Crossing one leg over the other, he mounted Randolph so the baby's bottom rested on the bend in his boot and his chubby legs straddled the makeshift saddle. The gown Randolph wore bunched up in the middle, exposing the baby's stockinged feet. Holding onto the baby's arms with his hands, Will gave him a huge grin. "Are you ready to ride in the Derby?"

His eyes wide, Randolph stilled himself, obviously unsure of what he was supposed to do. When Will's foot raised and lowered beneath him, though, his face split into a huge grin, a few teeth appearing. Will lifted and lowered his foot several times, making sure he had a solid hold on the baby's arms as he did so. After bouncing a few times, Randolph burst into a fit of giggles and squealed in delight. "Horsey!" he managed to get out between giggles.

Stunned her brother would even know how to do such a thing, Hannah glanced in Barbara's direction and was about to ask if she had seen him do it when she realized Barbara was smiling for the first time since she had arrived earlier that day. Smiling and watching Will as if she were seeing him for the first time. Deciding not to take her attention away from Will, Hannah instead looked to Henry. "Have you been doing that with *him*?" she asked *sotto voce*.

Henry shook his head, his attention still on his son. "No, but I believe I will be," he replied with a grin. "I may hold him in a saddle now and again, as well," he murmured thoughtfully.

Not particularly pleased to hear her husband would do such a thing so early in the boy's life, Hannah was about to put voice to her concern when Parkerhouse appeared on the threshold and bowed. "Dinner is served," he announced in his authoritative baritone.

Will lowered his leg until Randolph's feet touched the ground. "And the winner of the Derby is Randy Forster riding Black Boot," he announced in an exaggerated whisper, imitating an announcer at the race course. Extracting his foot from between the babe's legs, he made sure the boy was able to stand on his own two feet before letting go.

Still amused by his ride and his uncle's antics, Randolph turned shy and hurried off to where his mother held out her arms for him.

"Now you've got your father *and* your uncle spoiling you rotten," Hannah whispered hoarsely, giving her son a kiss before the babe's nurse appeared in the doorway.

"He's not eating with us, my lady?" Donald asked in a quiet voice, his query addressed to Hannah.

Barbara gasped. "Donald!" she admonished him.

Hannah gave a wave in Barbara's direction, an indication she didn't mind the boy's query. She angled her head and regarded Donald. "Sometimes he joins us, but not when we have guests," she said with a shake of her head.

"Oh," Donald replied, looking at once disappointed and then rather impressed. "Are we guests?"

Sighing, Barbara covered her face with a hand before Hannah could reply with a chuckle. "Yes, as a matter of fact, you are. The first guests we have had in a very long time."

Donald beamed, glancing over at his mother and then at Will, who was up and offering Barbara his arm.

"He's doing fine," Will whispered, leaning his head close to Barbara's as he clasped a hand over the one that rested on his arm. "You've done a remarkable job raising him," he added, hoping compliments might soften her stance toward him.

Staring at Will with an expression of surprise, Barbara finally lowered her eyes. "Thank you," she replied quietly, once again forced to hold her tears at bay.

CHAPTER 40

AN AUNT IS PUT TO THE TEST

eanwhile, back at Worthington House
Stephen was just about to enter the room where the chairs had been set up for the performance when he spotted the older woman Victoria had arrived with earlier that evening. He glanced around, sure Victoria was nowhere in sight. Making his way to the woman, he managed to join her at her side as she passed into the large room.

"Have we met?" he asked, turning his attention to the woman who at one time had probably been rather handsome. Her dark hair now displayed strands of gray and white in an elaborate coiffure probably better suited to balls twenty years in the past. She lifted her gaze to his and allowed a smile. "I'm quite sure I would remember meeting a man of your height," she countered with a grin.

"Stephen Slater," he said, holding out his hand in the hope she would offer her own.

She paused, her face taking on a blush appropriate for a chit fresh out of the schoolroom. "You're the son of the Marquess of Devonville," she stated, as if she remembered him from an earlier social engagement.

"I am," he agreed with a nod. "However, I am at a loss as to how I might know you," he said with a quirked brow.

"I am Mrs. Regan, wife of Dr. Anthony Regan. Perhaps

you're familiar with his older brother, Dr. William Regan, physician to the Duke of Chichester?" she replied quickly.

Stephen blinked once. Twice. He had heard the names. Anyone in need of medical care that didn't feature leeches and bloodletting had probably heard of the Regan brothers.

"It's very good to make your acquaintance, Mrs. Regan," Stephen replied. "I had the good fortune of meeting your niece, Victoria, at a ball a few nights ago. She was a guest in our box at the theatre. I do hope we didn't return her too late to your home," he added, thinking perhaps Victoria had been in trouble for her late arrival.

Mildred stared at the handsome man, wondering how her niece could decide he was unworthy of her. "She arrived exactly when I expected her," she said with a nod. "Thank you for seeing her to my home safely." She paused a moment. "I intended to join her, you see, but such large crowds are always a bit... intimidating for me," she said in a low voice. "I fear I make a poor chaperone for Vicky, but there isn't anyone else here in town for her."

Stephen gave a nod of understanding. "I fear I may have... offended her somehow," he said carefully. "I know there is a good deal of confusion because I share the same appearance as my older brother," he explained quickly, knowing they would need to take their seats at any moment.

Mildred regarded the young man who seemed a tad too earnest. "The same appearance and the same father... but not the same mother?" she ventured.

Stephen inhaled and let the breath out slowly. "I am not Bellingham, nor have I ever claimed to be," he said with a shake of his head. "But we do share the same father. A man who recognizes me as his son and has given me his name."

The older woman angled her head to one side. "And what is it you're wanting of my niece?" she asked then, her eyes twinkling with mischief. "Her virtue, perhaps?"

Stephen blinked, stunned at the woman's blunt question. He supposed she had it right, if he gave it some thought, although her question made it sound so salacious. He swallowed before he allowed a nod. "In our marriage bed, of course," he answered with a nod, realizing he meant every word he said.

Damnation!

Mildred's eyes widened in shock, but before she could say anything else, Adele Grandby, Countess of Torrington, had taken her place near the piano forté and was introducing herself and the performers she had lined up for that night's musicale.

Stephen gave Mildred a quick bow and made his way to the outer wall of the room, electing to stand for the performance along with several other gentlemen—there were simply not enough chairs for everyone in attendance.

He watched as Mildred made her way to a chair next to her niece. Although he thought the two would be in quick conversation, Mildred relaying his words to her niece, she instead appeared to give her entire attention to Lady Torrington.

Well, if he had any hope the aunt would put in a good word for him, Stephen now realized he may have placed his faith in the wrong aunt.

Would Adele speak to Victoria on his behalf?

He almost considered asking her when he remembered that Adele probably hadn't yet met Victoria. Which made him wonder how the chit ended up with an invitation to attend. *Certainly she wouldn't have crashed Aunt Adele's musicale!*

Sighing, he pretended to listen to the music, pretended to be moved by the soprano, and then pretended to be impressed by the tenor who sang in Latin, while the entire time, he found he would have preferred to be playing 'horsey' with Lord George in the nursery.

CHAPTER 41

DINNER AND A PROPOSAL

eanwhile, back in Oxfordshire
"When will you and Lady Barbara see to your nuptials?" Henry asked from where he sat at the head of an ornate dining table in the Gisborn Hall dining room. He made sure no footmen were present when he made the query, remembering his wife had the staff thinking the two were already married.

About to take a bite of food, Barbara gasped and turned her attention to the earl. Having just taken a drink from his wine glass, Will quickly swallowed and blinked, his attention turning to his sister.

Had she been the one to broach the subject with her husband?

For a moment, Will felt anger toward Hannah, that she would use her relationship with the earl to put him and Barbara on the spot.

As if he couldn't see to his own marriage proposal!

He was about to put voice to his displeasure with Hannah when he saw her expression of shock and realized she was just as surprised by her husband's query as he was. Before he could answer Henry's question, though, the earl straightened in his carver.

"I ask because I need a foreman. Someone with

command experience," Henry stated, pretending he hadn't noticed Will's initial reaction. "Someone who can act in my stead when I find myself preferring the company of my wife to spending the day in the fields."

Will blinked, as did Hannah, just before her face took on a decidedly pinkish cast. Although Henry was rather affectionate when he was behind closed doors, he had never said anything quite so inappropriate in the company of others!

Barbara merely stared at the man, her expression not giving away how she felt about the topic, but she was aware of how Donald seemed to straighten in his seat next to her. He had taken an interest in the adults' conversation.

"Are you offering me a position?" Will asked finally, his brows furrowed as his annoyance ebbed and turned to something else.

"I am," Henry replied with a nod. "You needn't give me your answer right away, but... from our discussion earlier today, I think you may find yourself in need of an avocation. At least until you inherit."

Will managed a nod, knowing the earl spoke the truth. What else could he do? Especially if Barbara refused to return to London? He couldn't leave her behind. Couldn't leave her at all. That meant he would have to remain with her, wherever they ended up living. And they certainly couldn't live in her cottage. He rather doubted the hovel would make it through the winter!

Then he remembered something the earl had said earlier that day. Something about considering a move to Ellsworth Park. To the manor house at the front of the property next door.

"May I ask when you'll be moving to the Ellsworth Park house?" Will asked, wondering why so much redecorating had taken place in Gisborn Hall if the earl intended to relocate. And if he and Hannah did move to the other house, he wondered what might become of Gisborn Hall. Would he be able to let the house from his brother-in-law?

Henry shook his head. "The Ellsworth Park house

requires a good deal of work, I'm afraid. More than I am willing to take on given the repairs would have to happen during the winter months. Although I like to tinker, I'm not much of a carpenter." He angled his head. "Besides, your sister has already seen to turning this pile into a home. I rather doubt you can tell its prior resident was an unmarried earl who prided himself on being a miser," he added with an arched brow.

Will blinked at this news, intrigued by Henry's comment. He leaned forward. "What kind of repairs does the Ellsworth Park house require?" he asked. An idea was forming. An idea that would keep him from having to return to London. An idea that might help him convince Barbara to marry him.

Frowning, Henry gave a shrug. "Mostly woodworking. Carpentry. Probably a new roof. It needs a coat of paint inside and out, and the shutters look as if they're about to fall off..." He allowed the list to trail off. "I'll take you on a tour, if you'd like," he offered, "After breakfast tomorrow morning."

Nodding his head, Will agreed. "I'd like that. Perhaps we can discuss it some more after dinner?" he suggested, realizing he had questions that weren't appropriate for dinner conversation. "I'll consider your offer of a position, certainly," Will stated with another nod, his gaze darting to Barbara.

She was staring at him, her already pale complexion suggesting she might faint at any moment. Or fall asleep. The poor woman had to be tired, although she looked resplendent in the deep green gown she wore. A maid had done her hair into a bun surrounded by tiny braids and ringlets. Emerald earbobs decorated her earlobes. Except for how thin she had become over her years in Broadwell, she looked every inch the aristocrat she was.

Henry gave a nod and turned his attention to his meal, pretending not to notice Barbara's reaction to Will's statement. Not having met her or her father, Henry wasn't yet sure he knew enough to figure out what had happened to force the aristocrat's daughter to take her leave of London, although he had a pretty good idea. He knew Hannah would tell him what she knew later that night, though.

When Hannah and Barbara took their leave of the dining room, Donald and Harold in tow, and made their way to the parlor, Will accepted Henry's offer of a port and a cheroot. "I haven't had one of these in ages," Will said before he took an experimental puff on the cheroot.

"I rarely smoke these days," Henry admitted, returning to his carver. "I think my visit to Wainwright's home must have had an effect of me. I'm always afraid of starting a fire."

Will nodded. "I couldn't allow smoking on the ship," he said. "We always had oils of one kind or another in the hold." He took another puff before he regarded Henry with a slight grin. "About the Ellsworth Park house. How much?"

Henry blinked. "How much... work, do you mean?"

"To let the house?"

Sighing, Henry gave a shrug. "As I said, it's not really in livable condition, so I've not considered how much to charge for it," he hedged. His eyes widened. "Are you really... interested?"

Will nodded. "I am if I'm going to work for you. I can probably see to most of the repairs myself—after eight years at sea, I've had to learn a thing or two about carpentry—and for those repairs I can't do myself, I can always hire someone to help," he claimed, joining Henry in a glass of port.

Henry regarded Will as the footman who served the port took his leave of the dining room. "Should you agree to take on the task, I shall not charge you to live there," he offered with a shake of his head. At Will's look of surprise, he added, "I couldn't in good conscious charge you," he explained. "And I rather doubt you could live there until the repairs are completed in at least a few of the rooms. My tenant cottages are in better shape."

"And yet, you *wanted* the property," Will reminded him.

Henry nodded. "I wanted the property for the *farmland*. Managed to get it plowed in time for last year's crops. This year's crop will be seeded later this week," he claimed proudly.

Will was curious—had the earl had given any thought to razing the house so that the entire property could be turned into farmland? He didn't put voice to the query, though, for at that moment, he was pretty sure he wanted the house. "Is anyone living in the dowager cottage right now?" he asked, remembering Henry's mention of it earlier that afternoon.

Henry shook his head. "Just you and your wife while you see to the repairs on Ellsworth Park, I suppose," he said with an arched eyebrow.

Will's eyes widened. "Truly?" he replied, a sense of relief settling over him. The last thing he wanted to do was take Barbara back to the cottage in Broadwell. Better she be able to live in a suitable dwelling and be close to his relatives.

If Barbara wasn't going to return to London, then Will knew he would have to figure out a place for them to live. What better location than a house next door to where his sister lived? And close enough to Bampton to walk or drive a gig on market day? He rather doubted his horse would appreciate having to pull a dog cart, but the Arabian might have to until Will could find a bay or draft horse to do the job.

And there was the opportunity to work. To earn his keep.

"We'll walk over to Ellsworth Park after breakfast in the morning. You can have a look and decide then," Henry offered, stifling a yawn.

Will felt his own yawn coming on. "I look forward to it. In the meantime, I've been up since before the sun. I need to get some sleep," he said as he stood up. "Thank you. For hosting us. For dinner. Will you excuse me?"

Henry nodded his head. "I'm right behind you," he said with a grin.

The two took their leave of the dining room and headed to the parlor, intending to say their 'good nights' to the women. But the room was empty.

"The rest of the household is abed," Parkerhouse said from down the hall.

Exchanging glances, Will and Henry each gave a shrug and headed up the stairs to their respective bedchambers.

Although Henry didn't intend to spend the night in his bedchamber but rather in his wife's, Will rather hoped he would have a place to sleep, for he had no idea if Barbara would even allow him into their bedchamber.

CHAPTER 42

A BASTARD MAKES HIS CASE
DURING THE INTERMISSION

*M*eanwhile, back at Worthington House

Stephen barely heard the duet featuring a soprano and a tenor, although he certainly heard the applause that followed. Then a young woman took a seat at the piano-forté and proceeded to play a series of selections by Brahms and Mozart. When she finished, Lady Torrington announced it was time for an intermission and more refreshments.

Feeling rather sorry for himself—he had made a cake of it with Victoria and yet he knew he wasn't at fault—Stephen was staring at the carpet beneath his feet when he became aware of someone standing next to him.

Victoria!

He turned and angled his head in surprise. "My lady," he said as he bowed and took her hand. She allowed it, although Stephen could tell she did so to appear polite.

"My aunt insisted I come speak with you," she stated, her gaze elsewhere.

Stephen wondered if the woman intended for Victoria to speak with him or slap him. He probably deserved another slap across the face, although he could still feel the faint sting of the one she had already bestowed on him. "I never meant for you to think I was anyone other than who I am," he said in a quiet voice.

"And yet you would have everyone think you are Bellingham," she countered with a hint of impatience.

Stephen frowned. "Have you ever met Bellingham?" he whispered, rather glad there was a steady background of murmuring to fill the music room. A trio of musicians moved to take their places and tune their instruments.

"Apparently not," Victoria replied with a roll of her eyes, her attention flitting about as if she pretended to look for someone. "I don't suppose he's here?" she added, her voice dripping with sarcasm.

Stephen felt relief at learning he wasn't the subject on which her silver-gray eyes had rested just then. He could imagine little beams of fire bursting forth, burning his skin and whatever else happened to be in her line of sight. "No, but you wouldn't know it if he were," Stephen replied in a whisper, rather liking that he had to lean over and direct his comments toward her ear. Had they been anywhere else, he would have used the tip of his tongue to trace the whorl of it before using his tongue and teeth to pull her plump earlobe —earbob and all—past his lips.

Victoria stiffened as she felt his breath on her ear, on her neck. Was it really appropriate for him to be whispering as he was, his voice sounding ever so secretive? So seductive? Another inch closer, and he could have his tongue in her ear, her earlobe in his mouth. The mere thought had her nipples hardening into buds behind her corset, her breasts swelling so the tops appeared rounded above the neckline of the green gold silk. "And why might that be?" she managed to get out without her voice sounding too breathy.

Stephen dared another glance in her direction, aware of her perfect posture, of how the tops of her breasts strained against the neckline of her gown. Of how her skin had taken on a glow as ethereal as the golden light that shimmered throughout the entire room. "He looks *exactly* like me."

He heard her slight inhalation of breath and had to bite his inner cheek in an attempt to keep his manhood from reacting. He was quite sure if she inhaled again, there wouldn't be enough room for her breasts in her corset and they would simply escape their confines. He would be forced to remove his coat and cover her, but at the moment, he found himself wishing she would inhale just one more time.

He wouldn't mind it one bit if he had to once again divest himself of his topcoat for a damsel in distress.

How would she look out of the gown? Entirely out of it and anything else she wore beneath it? Stripped bare and lying on her back in his bed, lit only by the golden glow from the fireplace? Her pale blonde hair spread out like a halo around her face, her mouth left slightly open and ready for his tongue and lips?

A strangled groan escaped his throat, bringing him out of his reverie.

He bit the inside of his other cheek, rather wishing he could take off his coat if only to cover himself. The damned cutaway coat was cutaway in precisely the wrong place!

"Does he now? I suppose that makes it rather convenient for you."

Convenient? Stephen furrowed his brows. *How is this convenient?* Having taken on the task of imagining how good it would feel to be buried in the naked woman who lay spread out on his bed—the woman who was standing right next to him—his cock was hardening at an alarming rate.

"Convenient?" he managed to get out, the word sounding almost garbled.

Victoria blinked as she turned to regard him, wondering why he sounded as if he were struggling to breathe. She dropped her gaze, afraid he might make eye contact, and found it rather hard to ignore how tented his breeches appeared at the base of his cutaway coat. Inhaling sharply, she lifted her gaze so she was staring at the violinist, a rather inopportune time to be doing so for the man's attention was entirely on her.

As was Stephen's, she realized. Daring a surreptitious glance down, she realized her breasts had nearly escaped the confines of her corset.

Damnation! The modiste had warned her this might happen with this particular gown!

Rounding her shoulders slightly, she was able to maneuver herself back into the corset, much to the dismay of the violinist. Stephen's attention turned to the painted cherubs on the ceiling. A moment later, Victoria's attention lifted. That is, until she turned her face in his direction, her upturned chin just reaching his shoulder. He lowered his shoulder, realizing she wanted to say something intended only for his ears. "Convenient in that he can be you, and you can be him whenever it should strike your fancy," Victoria whispered, imagining what it might be like to reach out with her tongue to trace the whorl of his ear, to put her lips together and blow gently into it, to use her tongue and teeth to pull his earlobe past her lips and nibble on it.

A rather garbled, mewling sound emerged from her throat.

Stephen jerked his head around to stare down at her upturned face, his own face mere inches from hers. Was she struggling to catch her breath? Or was she choking on her words? "More convenient for him, actually," he replied. "He is my commander. I do as he tells me to."

This had Victoria's eyebrows arched up in surprise. "You said you were retired from the Navy," she countered in a low voice.

"He is my older brother. If I know what is good for me, I shall always do what he tells me to," he said with a shake of head.

"Including answering to 'Bellingham'?" she argued, her manner becoming more agitated until she felt his hand wrap around her gloved one, his thumb rubbing into her palm. The contact was so unexpected, she nearly let out a squeak, but she also realized she had to calm herself. The violinist kept glancing in her direction, no doubt hoping she would pop out of her bodice.

"I cannot help that I look like him," Stephen said in a

quiet voice. "And I cannot prevent others from using his name when they see me."

"Would you if they did, though?" Victoria asked, her silver-gray eyes searching his. "Correct them, I mean," she added, her gaze suddenly aimed at the Aubusson carpet beneath their feet. She didn't dare try to hold his gaze. Despite her obvious displeasure with him, he was behaving with grace and quiet dignity, answering her every complaint with logical replies. His thumb was still doing its magic, his touch surreptitious in that he kept their hands hidden in the folds of her gown.

She found herself studying the carpet, rather amazed at how new it looked despite the hundred or so people who had trampled on it during the reception. She also hadn't noticed the repeating pattern of birds in the weave of the fibers. *Doves*, she thought in passing. *Peace.*

Stephen regarded her for a moment, his lips pressed together for fear the words he spoke would be the wrong ones. "Would you have me make it known I was eavesdropping on their conversation? I think not," he finally replied. He could tell by how her shoulders lowered—her beautiful, bare shoulders—that she accepted his reasoning just then.

He had a passing thought of what it had been like to hold those shoulders as he kissed her, to slide his palms over the smooth, soft skin as his tongue plundered her mouth, as his lips took purchase on her lips, her earlobe, her throat. Just thinking about it had his hands quivering, his lips tingling.

"I did not mean for you to assume I was anyone other than Stephen Slater," he continued quietly. "Which begs the question—how did you discover I wasn't who you thought I was? I did introduce myself as Stephen Slater, as I recall."

Victoria lifted her eyes, this time so she was staring into his. *Dammit.* Why did he have to have such fetching eyes?

Their browns and greens flecked with gold—they matched her gown to perfection and threatened to hold her hostage. "I couldn't find you listed in *Debrett's*," she whispered, feeling rather foolish. Why was it so damned important that he be who she thought he was? Did it matter if he was an heir to a marquessate or merely a gentleman of bastard birth? Despite how beautiful Cherice appeared wearing her coronet, Victoria knew she didn't care a whit if she ever had one.

She would have bolted but for the room full of people who surely would have noticed her departure from where she had been standing for the intermission. And for Stephen's grip on her hand, his thumb still rubbing circles into her palm.

"That's because they don't list illegitimate children," he said quietly. "I found *you* in there, by the way," Stephen added, wondering how she would react to having been looked up in a book of the peerage.

Victoria gave a start as she lifted her eyes to meet his, knowing she would be lost in them but not caring just then. "So, you know I am almost on the shelf," she replied, immediately regretting the comment, especially the tone that made her sound disgusted.

"Happy birthday," he said as he lifted the hand he held to his lips. His other joined it so one was beneath her hand while the other rested atop it. Then he kissed her knuckles, aware of how her eyes tracked his every move.

"Thank you." For some reason, the words had her rather glad it was an auspicious day. She wasn't really *that* old, after all.

"You have the most beautiful eyes," Stephen whispered, "Angel's eyes."

A pink blush colored Victoria's face just then, but she couldn't look away from him. He had her under his hazel-eyed spell. "Oh?" she managed to respond.

"Aye. I think I should like to see those eyes every morning when I awake, and every night before I close my own," he murmured, once again lowering his lips to her knuckles.

"I would like that, too," she replied on a breath, not quite realizing what his words meant. That is, until she realized everyone in the music room was staring at them, champagne glasses held at the ready as if the guests were expecting some grand announcement.

Victoria's eyes widened as she glanced around the room before settling them back on Stephen's, rather stunned to find he seemed entirely unaware of anyone but her just then.

"Marry me, Victoria. Marry me, because I dearly want to get a child on you, and I don't want him to be a bastard," he said with a hint of amusement.

Her mouth nearly as wide as her eyes, Victoria finally nodded. "Yes," she whispered, her free hand moving up to grasp his lapel to pull him down for a kiss.

Stephen made it quick, if only because the applause in the room had him thinking his aunt was about to announce the next performer. Instead, he realized he and Victoria had that honor, for the earl and countess stood regarding them with broad smiles and raised champagne glasses.

"You might have given me fair warning my *musicale* was to be the setting for your proposal," Adele scolded as she joined them.

Giving her a shake of his head, Stephen could only sigh.

"Another goddaughter about to be married off," Grandby said as he touched the edge of his glass to his wife's.

"Goddaughter?" Stephen repeated, his attention darting between Victoria and Grandby. "Her?"

"Oh, aye," Grandby replied proudly. "Her father and I were in school together. She wasn't my first goddaughter, of course, but..." He allowed the comment to trail off as several well-wishers stepped forward to shake Stephen's hand and wish Victoria a happy marriage.

When the second half of Adele Slater Worthington Grandby's *musicale* finally got underway, it did so much later than planned. Although Adele didn't seem to mind, and neither did her guests, one particular violinist certainly did.

"He's only been back a week and already Bellingham has ruined my evening," he said to one of his fellow musicians.

Although Stephen overheard the remark, he decided not to correct the man.

CHAPTER 43

ONE MORE DAY

The following day in Oxfordshire

"Are you quite sure you can look after Donald whilst you're fishing this afternoon?" Barbara asked, her hand moving to touch Will's arm as they were about to leave Gisborn Hall for Ellsworth Park.

Stunned at her touch, as if a jolt of something had struck him, Will stopped in his tracks and turned to stare at Barbara. "I will not let him *drown*, if that's what you're worried about," he said with a shake of his head. But after a moment, when he realized how truly frightened she seemed at the thought of her son spending the afternoon fishing, Will furrowed a brow. Barbara's worry was palpable, her hand nearly quaking where it rested on his arm. Didn't she realize he would see to his own son's safety? That he would ensure nothing dire would happen to Donald?

And then he realized something.

"Is this the first time you will be separated from him?" he asked in a quiet voice. "For more than a few minutes?" he amended, remembering that at least the two didn't share the same bedchamber, if the tiny rooms in their cottage could be called such.

Barbara stared up at Will, wondering how to respond. Would her son seem a weakling to Will if she admitted he had guessed correctly? That Donald hadn't been parted from her since his birth? Will seemed so shocked by the possibility, she inhaled sharply and shook her head. "Of course not," she lied. "It's just... he doesn't know how to swim," she blurted out, thinking that was reason enough to be concerned.

Will placed his other hand atop hers and slowly pulled the hand to his lips. "Then I shall see to it he doesn't end up in the river," he said before kissing the back of her hand. Where his lips touched her skin, he could feel her erratic pulse. "And if he does, I shall fish him out," he added in a playful voice.

Barbara's eyes widened in horror as she attempted to pull her hand from his grasp. "Bellingham!" she admonished him. But Will held onto her hand and pulled her hard against the front of his body, his lips coming down onto hers.

He was reminded of the night before, when he had entered the bedchamber to which they had been taken by the servant that thought they were married. His sister had been wise to introduce them as a married couple, he thought, although he knew Barbara wasn't happy with the ruse. They couldn't be seen as unmarried travelers, though, especially with a young boy in tow and no sign of a chaperone for Barbara.

Perhaps the after-dinner port had him feeling happier than he should have been, or perhaps it was merely the thought of sharing a large bed with Barbara—platonic or not —that had Will pulling Barbara into his arms and settling his lips onto hers, had him using his tongue to separate her lips so that he might share the taste of port and tangle his tongue with hers.

Whatever the reason he had decided Barbara would accept his overtures was soon proved wrong, however. She had struggled in his embrace, used her hands to push his shoulders away from her body, and threatened to scream should he come near her. Stunned and more than a bit hurt, Will had stepped back and stared at her.

Could she really be denying she had feelings for him?

Denying his claim to her? He had ruined her, after all. She had lain with him—at her insistence—and made a vow of undying love and affection. And he had countered it with his own vow, assuring her he would return after his service to King and Country, and they would be together.

She had borne his child.

Well, he was back now. He had kept up his end of the bargain and was ready to resume their lives, only to discover she seemed to despise him.

Just because his letters hadn't reached her was no fault of his. She seemed to realize her father or someone else had intercepted them—either destroyed them or hadn't sent them on to Broadwell. When she discovered she was carrying his child and was about to be put out of Pendleton House, she might have gone to his mother for assistance, or perhaps a relative who could have seen to suitable housing and financial support.

Instead, she had fled to a remote village and taken up residence in a ramshackle cottage with no hope for a future. Ceased sending him letters to let him know what had happened to her. Cut herself off from everyone she knew in London and insisted she could never return for fear of... well, he didn't know what she was afraid of in London, but she had certainly made it clear she would never go back.

At least Lord Gisborn had promised he would have seen to it she had decent housing. The dowager cottage was close to Gisborn Hall and seemed in good repair. And Henry had mentioned she would be under his protection.

But what sort of future could she expect to have without a husband? Without her son's father?

She's stubborn, Will decided. Proud, perhaps. Hurt. Confused.

Try as he might, Will realized she might never accept him back into her life. But, dammit, he wasn't ready to simply give up on her. She was the mother of his son! He had been in love with her—was still in love with her—and he wasn't about to give up his claim to her. To his son.

How long, though, could he pursue her before she might change her mind? Before she realized he was sincere and that she still loved him?

One more day, he decided. He would spend the time it took for them to tour Ellsworth Park in her company, and then he would take Donald fishing whilst she and Hannah shopped in Bampton. They would see each other again at dinner and then... well, hopefully she would accept his vow of love and devotion and agree to be his wife when he proposed following dinner. If not, he would simply see to it she was relocated into the dowager cottage and either pursue the position Henry had offered and live apart from her or make his way back to London knowing his sister and brother-in-law would look after Barbara. Try as he might, he couldn't think of another option.

One more day.

Barbara stared up at Will, realizing almost at once that he was teasing her when he said he would simply save their son from drowning should the boy fall into the river. But didn't he realize just how frightened she was for her son? She had never been parted from him for more than a few minutes his entire life! Now she would be leaving with Hannah for the afternoon whilst Donald and his father and uncle took him fishing. Before she could put voice to her concerns, Will had her hand in his, kissing the back of it and pulling her hard against the front of his body.

Surprised, Barbara didn't have an opportunity to close her mouth before his lips had captured hers, before his tongue invaded her mouth and tangled with hers, reminding her of what he had done to her the night before—before he took her protests seriously and realized she didn't want him sharing her bed. He had removed himself from the embrace, although not from the bedchamber—she supposed he had no where else to go—merely settling himself into the only upholstered chair near the fire. "I'm not leaving you alone," he had whispered when she glared at him from the other side of the bed, her fierce expression suggesting he had better remove himself from the bedchamber entirely or she would make her displeasure with him known to the rest of the household.

Realizing his determination exceeded her energy to protest—she had been bone-tired and on the verge of tears for several hours—she had settled into the comfortable mattress and quietly wept.

She knew not when he had joined her in the bed. Perhaps she had awakened and beckoned him to do so, or perhaps he had decided he'd had enough of the chair and wanted the comfort of the bed, or perhaps he felt the need to wrap her in his arms and sooth her sobs. Whatever the reason, Barbara awoke this morning with an overwhelming sense of contentment. She hadn't even realized one of his arms was draped over her waist, that his hand was cupped over one of her breasts and that her head was tucked beneath his chin. In fact, if she hadn't been aware of his soft breaths and his heartbeat against her spine, she might have thought she was simply wrapped in a warm, comfortable quilt.

"I love you," he had whispered.

Pretending to be asleep, she hadn't responded. After a time, she inhaled sharply and realized she was alone in the bed, all evidence of Will's presence erased as if he had never been there. All except for the scent of him left on the pillow when she turned over to look for him.

She remembered his whispered words and wondered if she could ever again feel for him what he claimed to feel for her.

At the thought of how bereft she felt at finding him gone from the room, though, she realized she must feel something for him. How could she not? He had come to rescue her from her hardscrabble life. Accepted her son as his almost without question. Vowed to make her his wife and pick up where they had left off as if the last eight years had never happened.

If she denied him one more time, she was quite sure he would leave her and Donald to live their lives in quiet desperation. At least they would do so in better quarters than the cottage in Broadwell. And they would be under the protection of the Earl of Gisborn.

But would she ever feel that contentment she had felt when she first awoke that morning? Ever feel that sense of knowing she was loved? Even if she wasn't sure she could ever return it?

One more day, she decided. She would give herself one more day to determine if she could abide a life with Will Slater. If she could feel for him what she had felt all those years ago as a young, naive chit in London. If she could foresee a future that might include an occasional trip back to London, to where she was no doubt vilified in every Mayfair parlor and the subject of gossip mongers. If she could once again allow herself to love another when she was quite sure she didn't deserve it return.

One more day.

CHAPTER 44

A HOUSE TOUR

The earls strolled through the garden, following the crushed granite path until they came upon Hannah and Barbara. The two women were sitting on a stone bench, their heads bent in quiet conversation. At the sound of the men's approach, they looked up in unison, surprise crossing their faces. Neither man wore a coat or a hat, but then the two women weren't wearing bonnets, either. They both stood to curtsy to the men's bows.

Hannah offered her hand to her husband, who took it and quickly kissed the back of it. After an awkward pause, Barbara offered her hand to Will, and he took it to his lips. He paused over it longer than he should have, bestowing a complete kiss on the suntanned skin.

"We're off to Ellsworth Park. Your brother wants to see the place," Henry said after he let go of his wife's hand. "Would you care to come along?"

Hannah's smile appeared to wipe away the worried expression she had been displaying when the men first approached. "I should like that. I've never been inside the house before," she commented, turning to Barbara.

"I'll come along, of course," the older woman agreed. "But I suppose I should see to Donald—"

"Mum, I finished with my numbers and letters. May I

play with Harold?" the young boy's voice came from the backyard. Barbara turned to find her son holding a rubber ball, the Alpenmastiff bouncing around him, his tail wagging in anticipation.

"He can come with us," Henry said, waving his hand to beckon the boy and Harold.

Will caught Barbara's look of concern and leaned in to whisper. "He'll be fine," he murmured, allowing his lips to graze her temple.

Shivering at his intimate touch, Barbara suppressed the urge to gasp and scold him. "All right," she finally agreed, wondering how far they would be traveling. Her legs already felt rubbery from their walk the day before. Having had a decent breakfast and a dose of sunlight whilst in the garden, she was feeling rather drowsy.

The four headed out the back garden gate toward the property to the west, the manor house mostly obscured by trees and shrubs. Donald and Harold bounded behind them, occasionally pausing to play.

"Who lives there?" Barbara asked as they made their way through the stand of trees.

"No one," Hannah replied, one of her arms hooked into Henry's. Although Will had offered Barbara his arm, she had declined and simply walked with her arms at her sides. "The Binghams only used it in the summers when they owned it," she added, remembering how lonely she would be in London when Charlotte Bingham was at Ellsworth Park and Elizabeth Carlington was in Brighton with her folks.

"Seems rather a shame it's been empty all this time," Will said, remembering it appeared rather regal when they passed it the day before on their way to Gisborn Hall. Unaware it was owned by Henry, Will had simply assumed it belonged to a member of the landed gentry. Now that he was closer to the manor house, he realized what Henry meant when he said it was in need of repairs.

"If anyone had been in need of housing last winter, I would have opened it to them," Henry replied as they approached. "But I fear they would have had an uncomfortable stay given its condition." He pulled a key from his pocket and unlocked the front door while Will regarded the windows on the first story of the house.

"Nothing appears impossible to fix," he said as he joined the others on the stoop. Henry had the front door opened and was allowing the women to enter when he gave a nod to Will.

"Let's hope that's your general consensus for the rest of the house," he whispered hoarsely.

When a mouse scurried across the vestibule, Hannah let out a startled gasp while Barbara merely ignored the creature. Harold was quick to follow the intruder, however, proudly dangling the mouse by its tail once he had captured it. "Take it outside, Harold," Hannah ordered with a hint of disgust in her voice, pointing back toward the open door. Harold complied, returning to join Donald when he had dispatched the mouse.

Holland cloths covered all the furnishings, leaving the visitors to guess what might lie beneath given their ghostly silhouettes. Barbara lifted one to reveal a beautifully upholstered settee, while Hannah uncovered the low table in front of it. "Rather nice," she murmured as Barbara moved on to uncover a chair.

"It's all very elegant," Barbara said in a whisper, as if she were afraid to disturb the quiet house. "'Tis a shame no one has lived here to take care of it."

Will and Henry had moved to study the mullioned windows and their frames, not finding any evidence of water damage, but Will was paying more attention to Barbara's words. Did he detect a hint of wonder in her voice? As if she might be able to see herself as the mistress of this house? Or was she merely commenting on it because she thought the house was a lost cause?

Given she was living in a cottage in far worse condition than this, Will hoped for the former. Perhaps now that she had spent a couple of days away from that cottage and a life of destitution, he could convince her a life with him would be far better. Perhaps he could convince her to marry him if he promised they wouldn't have to live in London.

Henry had moved to study the stone fireplace, but he gave Will a telling glance. "Having second thoughts?" he murmured, ducking down to take a look up the fire box.

"Not like you're thinking," Will replied as he surveyed the mortar in the seams between the rocks. Everything seemed intact, although he was sure the chimney would require a good sweeping before it could be used again. "I am thinking I will accept your offer, but there will be a contingency."

Henry stood up and regarded Will with a frown. "And what might that be?"

Will gave a nod toward where the women were studying the rows of shelves mounted on the long wall. "I have to convince her."

Nodding, Henry raised an eyebrow. "Or perhaps you could let her think it's her idea," he suggested in a whisper.

Giving a start, Will regarded his brother-in-law with a look of confusion. *Her idea?* She seemed so dead set against marrying him, he rather doubted she would see the house as an opportunity to erase the past and begin a life with him.

The four adults moved to the next room, apparently a library that now contained only a few shelves of books. A wide table flanked by wooden chairs seemed in good condition, though, as did the fireplace and the series of windows along the front of the house.

And so it went as they surveyed each room, Will making mental notes about repairs and the women commenting on the furnishings and draperies until they completed a tour of the first floor.

Harold preceded them up the stairs, his nose busy sniffing everything as he made his way with Donald in tow.

"Could you see yourself in a house like this?" Hannah asked Barbara as they returned to the library. She had thought to borrow a book or two and was perusing the shelves.

"I used to live in a house much like this," Barbara murmured, her gaze taking in the coffered ceiling and dark paneled walls. "Another time. A different life," she added wistfully.

Hannah paused in pulling out a book and regarded Barbara, her brows furrowed. "And if you could again?"

Sighing, Barbara shook her head. "It's a lot to manage. Too much for me, certainly."

Angling her head to one side, Hannah replied, "But if you had servants, you could manage quite well, I should think."

Barbara allowed a grin. "I suppose," she agreed, although her tone was non-committal.

A crashing sound above them had both women gasping. "Donald!" Barbara breathed, quickly making her way out of the library and to the stairwell. She climbed the steps, her breaths coming in short gasps as she tried to call for her son, sure he had done something to upend a piece of furniture or knock a vase onto the floor. Once she reached the top of the stairs, she nearly collided with Will.

He caught her easily, his hands going to her waist to steady her. "Whoa," he said with a grin. When he saw her look of fear, though, he sobered. "Our son is fine," he whispered. "Harold's tail knocked over a plant stand is all."

Barbara took a steadying breath before she realized she had both hands gripped on Will's forearms so tight, her fingernails were leaving crescents in his skin. "Are you sure Donald had nothing to do with it?" she whispered just as Hannah appeared at the top of the stairs.

"Harold Forster Paddlepaws!" Hannah called out, her voice sounding more stern than Will had ever heard it.

The Alpenmastiff, his body close to the ground as he nearly crawled to reach his mistress, whined a few times before licking one of her slippers. Donald appeared in the doorway to the room from which Harold had come. "It was an accident, my lady. He has a very strong tail."

Having a hard time keeping a strict expression on her face, Hannah rolled her eyes and finally looked down at Harold. "Downstairs," she ordered, her finger pointing to the stairwell. Slowly, Harold made his way down the marble stairs, his body still low to the ground as Donald watched him from the top of the stairs. "That tail tends to leave a trail of destruction wherever he goes," Hannah said to the boy, one brow arcing up in amusement. "Especially when he's excited. It will be safer for all of us if he's downstairs."

Will had used his hold on Barbara to pull her closer to him, although she had given up her tight hold on him when Hannah called for the dog. "You can let go of me now," she said, struggling to keep from sounding like a shrew as she said the words.

"Do I have to?" Will countered, one brow arching up as he quirked his lips.

Barbara inhaled sharply and blinked once before color suffused her face. "You're incorrigible," she whispered firmly.

"Only with you, my lady," he replied, his grin widening. He caught sight of Henry perusing the room where the plant stand had been upended and realized he should be doing the same. "Pardon me while I see to your future home." He stepped from in front of her and disappeared into a bedchamber, leaving Barbara open-mouthed and staring at his retreating back.

"He can be so vexing," Hannah said with a shake of her head, her gaze following her brother. "But he is a good man. Come. Let's see if we can't find the master bedchamber."

About to put voice to a reply, Barbara instead closed her mouth and followed Hannah into a large bedchamber. Blue Aubusson carpet covered the floor, and blue velvet drapes hung on either side of the windows, although they appeared sun-bleached. The papered walls had the appearance of watered silk. Although Holland cloths covered most of the furnishings, the tall chest of drawers was uncovered, its inlaid maple and polished brass hardware dusty. Drawn to the open door on the short wall of the room, Barbara made her way into the dressing room. Void of clothes and without any windows of its own, it was almost too dark to see. A sliver of light shown beneath a door in the opposite wall, though, and Barbara made her way to it.

Trying the handle, she found it turned easily. Once she had it opened, she stepped through into a brightly lit bedchamber of greens and golds, the gold shimmering from gilt that decorated the drawer fronts, the bedposts and even the walls. The sea foam green carpet beneath her feet had her closing her eyes as her slippered feet sunk into it. She inhaled deeply, recognizing the scents of lavender and rosemary.

"You look like a goddess."

Barbara gave a start and whirled to find Will leaning against the bedchamber's door jamb, his arms crossed over his chest. "You look like a bounder," she countered, not about to admit he had startled her with his words. Startled and flattered her with his simple statement.

"In that case, I do believe I will join you." Will pushed himself away from the jamb and made his way into the room, his gaze taking in the condition of the wood moldings and windows. "Of course your bedchamber would be in perfect condition," he murmured, noting there wasn't any evidence of water damage on the ceiling nor down the walls.

Barbara inhaled sharply at his words. "*My* bedchamber?" she repeated.

Will nodded. "Unless you prefer the blue one, but I think this color suits you so much better."

"The gilt is a bit much, though, don't you think?" she replied, watching him carefully. *What is he doing?* Why was he talking about the bedchamber as if it was hers?

"All the gold in the world wouldn't be enough to honor you," he whispered, his slow steps bringing him closer to her as he continued studying the room.

"You make me sound like a..." She struggled to find a word that suited his comment.

"Goddess."

Barbara felt the blush even before her face colored up.

"Bounder," she countered.

"Only if I'm allowed to worship you," he whispered, now close enough that he could reach out and touch her.

"I hardly think I'm worthy of worship," she replied, her voice nearly breaking when she realized he was so close he could almost kiss her.

"Oh, I disagree," Will replied with a shake of his head. He straightened. "As does our son," he added, turning on one heel to find Donald watching them from the doorway. "Your mother is a goddess, isn't she Donald?"

The boy's look of consternation slowly changed to one of humor. "She is," he replied. "Not Athena, though," he added, his head shaking.

Will chuckled as an eyebrow went up. *The kid already knew his mythology!* He sighed when he realized his opportunity to kiss Barbara had passed, though. "Aphrodite," he stated then, wondering at how her expression changed when he realized they were being watched.

Henry and Hannah appeared behind Donald, holding hands as they studied the room from the doorway. "Have you seen enough?" Henry asked. "'Bout time we take the ladies back to Gisborn Hall so they can go shopping, and we can go fishing."

Will nodded. "Indeed." He turned to Barbara. "My lady?" he added as he offered his arm.

Barbara regarded it for a moment and finally placed hers on it, her fingers lightly resting on the lawn of his shirt as Donald took her other hand. The five made their way back to Gisborn Hall, their conversations about repairs and fishing.

Harold followed slowly behind them, tail between his legs, still convinced his mistress was upset with him.

CHAPTER 45

A HOUSE TO CALL
THEIR OWN

*M*eanwhile, *back in Mayfair*

Victoria stood next to her betrothed and stared up at the white stone townhouse with the dark blue door. "You can afford this?" she murmured, rather stunned they were standing in Curzon Street admiring a townhouse Stephen had just claimed was theirs.

"I can," he said with a nod. Of course, he couldn't afford it on the salary he was making at the Foreign Office, but his allowance was rather more generous than his father had suggested it would be that one day in his study. Just a week ago. "Do you like it?"

Barely able to suppress her excitement, Victoria bounced on the balls of her slippered feet. "Oh, I think I do. May we go inside?"

Stephen grinned as he held up the key. "There are some furnishings, of course, but not a lot in the way of *things*," he warned. "And the ballroom is rather small." He had looked at two other nearby townhouses, finding they were beautiful and perfectly outfitted, but both lacked ballrooms. Given how he had met the woman who had agreed to be his wife, he decided his townhouse would have a ballroom.

"A ballroom?" Victoria repeated, her expression of delighted surprise making Stephen want to kiss her right then and there. They would be seen by someone, he was sure, though, and given their neighbors included a marquess, two earls and several relations to aristocrats, the last thing he wanted to do was offend anyone by displaying his affection for his soon-to-be wife where anyone could see them.

Her hand on his arm, Victoria watched as Stephen inserted the key into the lock and pushed down on the door handle. "The staff is on holiday, but usually there is a butler, a maid, a cook and a scullery maid. You'll need a lady's maid, of course, but perhaps yours will join you from Middlesex," he suggested as he pushed the door open to reveal the vestibule.

"Since I was sharing a maid with my mother, I rather doubt I would be allowed to bring her to London," Victoria countered, her gaze moving from him to what appeared through the open door.

"Then we'll see to one for you," Stephen assured her, rather happy to see her stunned expression. "What do you think?" he asked, watching her reaction as she took in the sight of the vestibule.

With its marble floor inlaid with the pattern of the mariner's compass, its northern point oriented to true north, and the walls papered in a pale gold, the room was light and welcoming. Beyond was the central hall, its staircase to the second floor swooping up in a curve from the left side while the hall wrapped around to the right. "It's so elegant," Victoria whispered.

Stephen allowed a chuckle. "You don't have to whisper," he said, although when he heard his voice echo, he lowered it to add, "But you can if you want."

The ceiling of the hall went all the way to the roof of the house, so as Victoria's gaze swept up, she took in the balustrade railing wrapping around the second story mezzanine. "It's so modern," she breathed.

"Aye," Stephen agreed as he pointed to their left. "This will be one of your rooms, I should think."

Victoria regarded him for a moment. *Your rooms.* The

words had her feeling humble. She was more than glad she had agreed to accept Stephen's offer of marriage. To think, his status as a bastard had nearly prevented her from considering him. *I would have been a fool to turn him down.*

The only door to the left before the staircase revealed a tastefully decorated parlor, its furnishings upholstered in rose and deep green fabrics. Victoria could imagine hosting callers in the cozy room, the tea set taking up most of the low table in front of the settee, a fire crackling in the brick fireplace. She would have to make the acquaintance of other young matrons before doing so, though. She only knew her aunt and the people to whom Stephen had introduced her at the theatre and at his aunt's *musicale*.

Across the hall, Victoria boggled at the sky blue powder room, stunned to learn the house was piped for gas lighting and outfitted with indoor plumbing and toilets.

Stephen stood just inside the small study, imagining himself behind the walnut desk while reading invitations to Society events and perhaps performing some work for the Foreign Office there.

A library, the shelves bare but otherwise furnished with comfortable chairs and lamps on the side tables, would need some work, but Victoria was sure she could manage the task. There were several bookstores in London, after all. Depending on how much pin money Stephen thought to bestow on her, she was fairly sure she would have the basic necessities on the shelves before the year was out.

Although not nearly as large as the one in Devonville House, the dining room could seat twelve comfortably if the table and chairs currently on display were any indication. "Unfortunately, there's not a breakfast parlor," Stephen said as he watched Victoria take a walk about the entire room, her gloved hands touching the backs of every chair as she went.

"Oh, I wouldn't have expected one," she replied with a shake of her head. "But I do hope I'll be allowed to sit closer to you than the other end of the table," she said as she pointed to the end of the long room.

Stephen gave her a nod. "Of course," he replied. "We needn't stand on ceremony, unless we're hosting guests, I suppose," he added.

"Who might they be, do you suppose?" she asked as she opened a sideboard to discover a collection of bone china plates and bowls. She pulled one out to study the delicate floral pattern around the rim. *Royal Worcester.*

Stephen considered the question. "I was hoping to host my father and his wife when you were ready for guests," he replied. "And your parents, of course, should they make a trip to London." They wouldn't be at the wedding since Victoria insisted on a quiet affair with only her aunt and uncle as her witnesses. Anthony Regan would be returning from Sussex later that day specifically to attend. Stephen had sent a note via courier to his mother, asking if she might make the trip from Kent to be a witness. Her reply had arrived earlier that day. *See you at nine o' clock in the morning. Do let your father know. I shouldn't want to embarrass him. Mother.*

By noon tomorrow, he and Victoria would be wed.

Stephen still wasn't quite sure what had happened to have him marrying so soon after returning to London. Perhaps it had been the letter from his brother, the bright white missive displaying the seal of the Earl of Gisborn in the dark red wax.

Dear bastard brother, I hope this letter finds you enjoying the benefits of being an earl. A note from Lady Devonville included in father's letter informed me you have done well in my name when it comes to potential wives. Please note that you no longer need to court ladies on my behalf. In the event father hasn't informed you, I found my Barbara in Broadwell. I found something else, as well. Someone, rather. His name is Donald, and he is my son. As a bastard, the boy will have a life much like yours, I expect, although it will probably be far from London. Barbara does not wish to live in the capital, and I do not wish to live anywhere where she is not. At seven years of age, Donald is the spitting image of me at that age (and probably you, as well), or so Hannah claims as she has seen the painting of me in my mother's room. She was too young to remember me at that age. She has embraced my Barbara as her own sister. Now, if I can convince Barbara to marry me, I have the earl's assurances I shall have a position as a foreman and Ellsworth's old summer house in which to reside. Here's hoping you have chosen a woman to court from among those Lady Devonville mentioned in her note. My money is on the one who crashed the ball. Sincerely, your legitimate brother.

Bastard! Stephen couldn't help but thinking when he read the note. But he knew his brother had a point. As the daughter of a man who had eschewed his position in the aristocracy, Victoria was much like him—on the outside, looking in, the heels of their hands pressed against the glass on either side of their faces so they could better see everything.

He had a feeling she would be referred to as the one who had crashed the ball for the rest of her life, though.

Or perhaps he had decided to marry Victoria because his physical reaction to her was so profound. When he paid a call on her aunt's house in order so that he could bring Victoria to the Curzon Street townhouse, his cock had responded even before she appeared at the door. Dressed in a deep blue carriage gown and pelisse, her silver-gray eyes appeared more intense than usual. He had kissed her, not intending to do so, but *dammit*—what else could he do?

He was attracted to her.

She had already agreed to be his wife. He had a special license tucked into his pocket and a bishop lined up to perform the ceremony at Devonville House—Cherice insisted it take place in her parlor—so what was the harm in a quick peck on the lips?

"A penny for your thoughts," Victoria whispered from where she stood at his side, her gaze still admiring the dining room.

"I fear you would be shortchanged, my sweeting," Stephen replied. "Shall we?" he asked as he led them back into the hall.

The last set of double doors at the end of the hall opened onto the ballroom. As Stephen had warned, the space was not large, but Victoria still had to grin when her gaze lifted to the ceiling and she realized it was a miniature version of Lord Weatherstone's grand ballroom. Even the ceiling was painted with a similar motif, cherubs and all. Columns flanked a single pair of French doors that lead to the back-yard garden.

"Oh, Stephen," she breathed as she moved into the room, spinning about much like she had done at Lord Weatherstone's ball, the expression on her face pure bliss. "It's simply divine."

Stephen didn't bother to suppress his smile as he pulled her into his arms and kissed her. "You can see yourself as mistress of this abode then?" he queried.

"Oh, aye," she answered, rather liking how he still held her, how he swayed their bodies from side to side as if they were dancing a rather slow, scandalous dance. "When I came to London, I didn't have an expectation of this," she said in a quiet voice.

Stephen angled his head to one side, noting how her joy seemed to have changed to reflection in a heartbeat. "Didn't you come to make your debut?" he asked. "To find a husband—?"

"Yes, yes, of course," she interrupted, although the shake of her head was at odds with her words. "What I said to you at Lady Torrington's *musicale*. I'm so sorry. I was mean because I thought you had deliberately misrepresented your-self, but it was I who thought you were Bellingham. I jumped to a conclusion I shouldn't have."

Stephen allowed a nod, rather glad she didn't think he had passed himself off as his brother in an attempt to steal a kiss in the gardens. "I forgive you," Stephen whispered before he planted a kiss on her forehead.

"Thank you," she murmured. She allowed a sigh. "Anyway, I meant that I didn't come to London expecting to marry a future marquess, or any aristocrat for that matter."

Stephen allowed a shrug. "Well, I suppose that's a good thing since I'll never inherit a title," he replied, worried by the sudden change in her manner.

"You see, having grown up with a father who never embraced *this*..." She held out her hands and glanced about the elegant ballroom, still feeling a bit of disbelief that she would soon be living in Curzon Street. "Well, it meant that I didn't have the expectation. I lived in a modest home—a nice one, please don't misunderstand—but certainly nothing like this."

"But that doesn't mean you didn't *want* to live in something like this," Stephen continued for her, hoping he guessed her line of thinking.

"Exactly. And now, here you are, a... a—"

"Bastard," Stephen interrupted, finding the word not as insulting as he usually did.

"And yet, you're offering me a life... and a house—"

"A home," Stephen interrupted again, wondering if she had changed her mind about marrying him.

"Even after the awful things I said to you," she finished, tears collecting in her eyes.

Stephen regarded her for a moment before pulling her into his arms. "It did hurt a bit," he finally admitted. "But then you kissed me and made it all..."

This time, it was Victoria who interrupted when her lips were suddenly on his, kissing him with a fervor she hadn't shown before. "I love you," she whispered when she ended the kiss.

Happy wife, happy life, Stephen remembered.

Stephen recaptured her lips to resume the kiss—until he realized how the rest of this body was responding. "If we do this much longer, I may not be able to wait until tomorrow to take you to my bed," Stephen whispered, his lips sliding along her jawline.

Victoria blushed, a giggle erupting. "Is there a bed?" she asked. "You haven't even shown me any bedchambers yet," she whispered.

"Oh, aye," he replied. "And don't be thinking I'll be allowing you to sleep in your own bed any time soon," he warned with an arched brow.

Own bed?

"I'll have my own?" Victoria asked in surprise.

Stephen allowed a wan smile. "Your own bedchamber, of course," he allowed. "As to your own bed, I suppose that will depend on if I'm invited into it or not."

Victoria grinned. "Do you snore?"

Stephen stopped swaying as he pulled his body away from hers. "What do you know of *snoring?*" he asked in alarm. He had certainly heard his fill of it as he slept in his hammock aboard ship. As to whether or not he snored, he really had no idea.

Her eyes widening with his question, Victoria shook her head. "My father's snoring causes the entire house to vibrate," she replied.

"Oh."

When he didn't elaborate, Victoria angled her head to one side. "Shall we go upstairs and find out?" she asked with an arched eyebrow.

Stephen blinked. And blinked again when he realized what she might be suggesting. "After you, my lady," he replied as he waved a hand toward the hall. "After you."

CHAPTER 46

A TRIP TO BAMPTON

eanwhile, back in Oxfordshire
Will assisted first his sister and then Barbara into the ancient carriage, impressed with the clothes Hannah had loaned Barbara to wear on their shopping excursion. The deep blue pelisse over a lighter blue carriage gown made her gray eyes even more arresting than usual. A matching bonnet, its deep blue feathers and fabric flowers rather restrained compared to the riot of color decorating Hannah's hat, topped the ensemble. A pair of black half-boots appeared when Barbara stepped up into the equipage.

"You two look rather lovely," he said. He had a thought that some young buck might think they were unchaperoned and take advantage, but then he dared a glance at the driver and decided they would be safe enough. He remembered the groom's name, Bill, from when he had checked on Thunderbolt the night before. The young man seemed all business as he finished checking the tack of the matched pair he had hitched up a few minutes ago.

Fishing his purse from a pocket, Will dumped a number of coins into his hand. "Hand me your reticules," he said to the women.

Her brow arching in surprise, Barbara regarded him a moment before lifting the borrowed reticule from her lap.

"I've nothing to put into it, so it's merely acting as decoration," she said with a hint of humor.

Will grinned, rather happy Barbara seemed in such a good mood since their tour of the house. Being able to sleep in a real bed with a comfortable mattress had probably helped in that regard. He transferred the coins into the reticule and pulled the drawstring so the fabric gathered and closed.

"What did you do?" Barbara asked, pulling the reticule from his grasp.

"Buy what you need, sweeting," he murmured, helping himself to one of her gloved hands so he could kiss the back of it. "And then buy something for our son, and then buy something you *want.*"

Her eyes wide at the use of the endearment, Barbara blushed. "Bellingham!" she admonished him, pulling her hand from his grasp.

Hannah watched the two with a grin. "And what am I to buy?" she asked as she held out her reticule to him.

"The earl said to remind you that his birthday is next week," Will replied with an arched brow. He held out several pound notes.

Hannah stared at the money, blinking several times before she reached for the bills. "I don't suppose he mentioned what he might *like* for his birthday?" she replied as she stuffed the bills into her reticule. She already had something on order. With any luck, it had been delivered the day before and would be waiting for her at the hardware store.

Will gave her a grin and shook his head. "I'm sure whatever you pick out will suit him," he said, his manner full of mischief. "See you at dinner," he added, ignoring the stunned looks of the women as he made his way to the driver. "Keep an eye on them," he said to Bill, tossing a coin to the driver.

"Aye, sir," Bill said as he caught the coin. A crack of his whip and the carriage jerked into motion, heading down the lane toward Bampton. Before it disappeared from view,

Donald came racing from the house, calling out for Will. Just as he reached his father, Will grabbed the boy beneath his arms, lifting him high into the air and spinning him around before lowering him back to the road.

Donald screeched in delight, a bit unsteady on his feet when he landed. "Uncle Henry says he's ready to go fishing," he managed to get out before Will set to tickling him around his ribs. Escaping Will's hold, Donald raced on ahead, Harold bouncing about and barking.

Barbara turned around from having heard her son's call and watched Will launch the boy into the air to spin him around. Her heart gave a leap at seeing the spectacle, although she was torn between being fearful of the boy landing in a heap on the ground and glad Will was so accepting of her son. He never once doubted her claim that Donald was his son, never once questioned the possibility that he could be someone else's bastard child.

Was it wise to allow this to continue? Some part of her still believed Will would change his mind and return to London.

"He'll make an excellent father," Hannah said after having watched a little of what her brother had just done. Even now, Will and Donald were making their way back toward the house, apparently engaged in easy conversation.

"I suppose," Barbara allowed, although not with a lot of conviction. She returned her attention to the road ahead, deciding she rather liked this part of Oxfordshire better than the one in which her cottage of the past seven years was located. Tenant cottages dotted the landscape on either side, their occupants busy in the fields or working in gardens or tending to animals in pens. An occasional manor house broke up the fields, the Portland stone exteriors hung with ivy.

"What is it that has you so vexed when it comes to my brother?" Hannah asked, hoping she wasn't offending Barbara with the question.

"Vexed?" Barbara repeated, realizing it was as good a

word as any to describe how torn she had felt since Will had shown up in Broadwell. She sighed. "I had given up ever seeing him again," she said. "I thought I was quite done with him. And now... now I am torn between allowing myself to love him again and hoping he'll go away."

Hannah frowned. "He loves you very much. And your son, as well. Why ever would you send him away?"

Barbara shook her head. "He'll insist we return to London. I cannot go back there."

Turning on the carriage seat so she could better see Barbara, Hannah gave her a quizzical stare. "What are you so afraid of?" she asked, realizing she was close to discovering whatever had Barbara staying away from her home.

Barbara stared ahead, wondering if she should admit what she hadn't been able to tell Will. Hannah would no doubt tell her brother when she had the chance, but then at least he would know. "I went to your brother's apartment the night before he was to leave London," she said in a quiet voice, hoping she couldn't be overheard by their driver. "I... gave myself to him, you see. I suppose I thought he might change his mind and stay in London, but instead, he vowed to return when he had finished his duty to King and Country." She said the words with derision, her bitterness apparent. "He said he would marry me then, and promised me we would have a townhouse and a life in London."

Her brows furrowing, Hannah shook her head. "And now that he's done with his duty and has come for you—"

"I cannot show my face in London. I cannot bear what the gossip mongers will say behind my back. Everywhere I go, they know..." She stopped.

"Know what?" Hannah interrupted. "That you had to leave London because your father's gambling was bankrupting the earldom?" The words were out of her mouth before she had a chance to soften them, to censor them. Hannah swallowed. "Everyone knows he gambles. Everyone knows he might end up in debtor's prison," she went on. "So, of course you had to leave. There's no shame in that."

Barbara frowned, stunned by Hannah's words. "But the reason I left is because he banished me..." She paused, swallowing hard before lowering her voice to a whisper. "I was with child. My maid knew. My aunt knew—"

"But no one else seems to have known," Hannah interrupted. "Barbara, I was in London until two years ago, and there hasn't been a word of gossip about you."

Staring at Hannah in disbelief, Barbara began shaking her head. "How is that possible?" she asked. She had always assumed her maid would have spread the gossip among the other servants, especially when she realized she would be losing her position when Barbara left the household. Her aunt? Well, the woman could spread gossip like the very best gossip monger, but apparently she hadn't said a word about her niece. Perhaps she realized the family couldn't abide anymore gossip given her father's reputation as a gambler.

Hannah sighed, one hand gripping Barbara's hand. "In fact, those that remember you wonder where you've been living. Your father has apparently gambled away all the unentailed properties of the Greenley earldom. He owes money to every gaming hell. It's possible he's already in debtor's prison. Your brothers have had to take positions to earn their livings, at least until the oldest inherits, in the event the earldom hasn't already reverted to the Crown."

Biting her lower lip, Barbara nodded, remembering what her father's solicitor had last written to her. Hannah's words merely confirmed his news. "How often do you suppose your brother will wish to return to London?" she asked in a small voice.

Remembering what Will had said about leaving his brother behind as a stand-in for him, Hannah allowed a grin. "As long as Stephen is willing to act in his stead, Will won't have to return to London. At least, not until he inherits the Devonville marquessate," she replied with a shrug. "Until that happens, he has a position as a foreman to help my husband with the farming. A position and a place to live," she added, hoping Barbara would agree to stay. She rather liked the woman, and the thought of having her nephew nearby when she would soon have another baby merely meant more children in the household.

Barbara considered Hannah's words, her thoughts of Will and his behavior over the past two days changing. "Thank you," she murmured. "You have given me much to think about."

The carriage pulled up to the raised boardwalk along the line of shops in Bampton and came to a halt. "Well, don't be thinking of all that right now," Hannah admonished her. "We have some shopping to do."

Barbara smiled, the sounds of coins in the bottom of her reticule a reminder that she needed to buy a few things. *Wanted* to buy a few things.

CHAPTER 47

FISHING FOR ADVICE

eanwhile, on the banks of the River Isis
As Will, Henry and Donald took up positions on the riverbank near where the gates for the irrigation ditches were installed, Will dared a glance at Henry while he helped Donald impale a worm with a hook. Harold was off exploring farther down the riverbank, occasionally stopping for a drink of water.

"I suppose Hannah told you about Barbara and me," Will said as he knelt down.

Henry regarded Will for a moment before giving a shake of his head. "Just said you two had been apart for the entire time you were at sea," he replied. "Eight years?"

"Aye." Pulling a length of line from the rod, Will handed it to Donald. "Now, toss the hook into the water, and whatever you do, don't get it caught in your breeches," he instructed. He stood back and watched as Donald did as he was told, rather proud when the hook plopped into the water. "Be sure to keep a firm grip on the handle like this," he demonstrated first before giving the rod back to the boy. "And when you feel a tug on the line, then start reeling it in."

Donald nodded his understanding and gripped the cork-covered handle.

"I didn't have a chance to actually marry her before I left London," Will said, his comment directed to Henry.

The earl finished baiting his hook and used a flick of his wrist to launch his hook and line into the water, his reel spinning as he did so. "But you're going to in the next few days," he replied finally.

The comment wasn't a question, and Will realized he had to agree. "That's the plan. Know any vicars?"

"Aye." Henry reeled in his line and recast. "Hannah will be speaking with him right about now," he added.

Will nearly did a double-take. "I would have seen to that." *Once Barbara actually agreed to marry me.*

"She said she would see to it, and you know your sister," Henry countered with a smirk.

Swallowing, Will realized he didn't know his sister if she was off lining up a vicar without telling him. "I thought I did," he finally said, *sotto voce.*

"Well, she's a countess, and she takes it very seriously. Won't be the first time she sees to it a couple gets married," Henry added with an arched brow, remembering how his stableboy and Hannah's maid ended up married before Hannah had even been at Gisborn Hall more than a week or two. He recast his line, directing it to a different part of the river. He could feel Donald's eyes on him as he cast the line and gave the boy a nod. "Is this really your first time fishing?" he asked just as Harold rejoined them and settled himself on the bank.

Donald nodded. "Aye. I don't think my mother likes worms."

Will had to suppress a grin as he cast his line. "It's rather handy you have so many fishing poles," he commented, his voice kept low so as not to scare away the fish.

"Indeed. My uncle wasn't much of a farmer, but he sure liked to fish," Henry replied. After a few moments, he added, "I rather think Hannah will want to host your wedding breakfast."

Suppressing a grin at the change in subject, Will allowed

a nod. "I will be sure to formally ask her to do so," he replied.

"Don't suppose you have any wedding clothes with you," Henry said, slowly reeling in his line.

"As a matter of fact, I do," Will replied, reeling in his own line, watching his son's line as he did so. When he was aware of Henry giving him a look of surprise, he allowed a shrug. "I'm an optimist."

At that moment, Donald's line suddenly tightened, the reel spinning. "Hold on!" Will said, moving laterally along the bank so he could help the boy if needed. "Grab the handle, and reel in the line as fast as you can."

But Donald had already started cranking the handle, occasionally struggling and then reeling as fast as he could. Before long, a small trout bounced out of the water, and Henry held out a net to capture it. By that time, Will had his own line reeled in and the rod set aside so he could help.

"Now for the hard part," he said as he took hold of the trout and worked to get the hook out of its mouth.

Donald watched intently, his eyes wide as Will pulled out the hook and tossed the fish into the basket. "Your turn to put a worm on," Will said. He watched as Donald dug into the box of worm-filled mud they had brought along. "Careful you don't poke your finger." Soon, a squirming worm was secured on the hook and Donald was throwing out his line.

Three hours, four pints of ale and three sandwiches later, nearly twenty trout filled the basket. "I do believe we have enough for tonight's dinner," Henry announced with a good deal of satisfaction. Although they had nearly lost the net—Will's second fish had proved especially hard to land—they still had all the gear.

He turned to find Donald napping against a rock. Grinning, he finished securing his rod's line and regarded Will. "Shall we wake him?"

Will shook his head. "I'll carry him if you can manage the fish," he replied, lifting Donald so he was standing atop the rock. "Climb on," he said to the drowsy boy, "And wrap your arms around my neck."

Doing as he was told, Donald was soon riding on Will's back, his legs wrapped around his father's middle. "How many fish did you catch?" he asked sleepily.

"Eight, I think," Will said. "But you got the largest and the smallest." He felt the boy's laughter as it burbled forth. "I'll let you be the one to tell your mother."

The three made their way back to Gisborn Hall by way of the irrigation ditch that ran along the edge of the farm fields, Harold following when he wasn't stopping to dig up something.

"Does it work?" Stephen asked as he indicated the new plow sitting at the edge of the field.

Henry pointed to the adjacent field to the west, newly plowed and ready for seeding. "It does, indeed. Finished the entire Ellsworth field earlier today," he said proudly.

Will allowed a grin. "You really need to give that place a new name," he said.

The earl nodded. "Perhaps I'll leave that to you," he countered. "Since you're the one who will be living there."

Wide awake but rather enjoying the ride on his father's back, Donald piped up. "We should call it Bellingham Park."

The two gentleman laughed at first but then traded amused glances. "Bellingham Park it is," Henry announced.

"Mum is back," Donald said as he pointed toward the road from Bampton, his vantage as good as his father's. "The carriage looks full."

Will glanced in the direction Donald indicated to see the carriage with its two occupants and boxes and parcels filling the remaining space. "That's far more than a birthday present," he murmured, remembering his comment to Hannah earlier that day. He matched Henry's faster pace so they could intercept the carriage as it made its way up the drive to the back of Gisborn Hall.

"Hallo!" Hannah called out, her face beaming from beneath her parasol as the men walked up. "Were you successful in catching our dinner?" she asked as the driver halted the carriage.

Henry held up the closed basket of fish. "Indeed. It appears you were successful on your shopping trip, as well," he ventured, rather stunned at the varied assortment of parcels filling the carriage. "Is there anything left in the shops in Bampton?"

Barbara and Hannah both giggled, the sound almost musical to Will's hears. "Of course," Barbara replied. "Although I did have to pull your wife out of one store. I do believe she would have emptied all the shelves if she could have," she claimed.

"Shh, it's a surprise," Hannah said, her smile broadening.

Henry reached over and gave his wife a peck on the cheek. "I'm off to the kitchens with our catch," he said.

"And then a bath, I hope," she suggested, one eyebrow arching up.

"And then a bath," Henry agreed, giving a nod to Will. "I'll have hot water taken up to your bedchamber, too," he said before he headed off to the door leading into the kitchens.

Will assisted Hannah from the carriage and then turned to help Barbara. "Our son caught both the largest and the smallest trout," he said as he offered his arm. He grimaced when he remembered he had said Donald could give his mother the news.

"He's the one that needs the bath," she said with a grin, giving Donald a kiss on his cheek as Will lowered him to the ground.

"Father let me ride him all the way from the river," the boy said happily.

"Did he now?" Barbara replied as she turned her attention back to the carriage. "Well, now he's going to have to carry some packages. And you will, as well," she said as she indicated which ones they should take.

"What's in the big box?" Will asked as he passed a couple of smaller parcels to Donald.

"Lord Gisborn's birthday present," she replied with an arched eyebrow. She lowered her voice to a whisper. "A welding device, your sister called it. She said it produces an arc between two..." She paused and gave a slight shrug.

"Electrodes?" Will guessed.

Barbara's eyes widened. "Yes! For metals," she said. "How is it you know that?" she asked as she pointed to another parcel.

Will grinned as he climbed up into the carriage, finding it amusing his sister would have the wherewithal to order an arc welder for her husband. "We had one aboard ship, of course," he replied. He gathered the parcels she indicated, his curiosity finally getting the better of him. "Did you buy something for me?"

Her head angled to one side, Barbara regarded him for a moment. "Yes, but it's a surprise."

Blinking, Will allowed an, "Oh," before he gathered the rest of the smaller hat boxes into a stack. "Are these all yours?" he asked. "Or my sister's."

"Donald's," she replied with a nod. "He needs clothes desperately," she whispered as she handed several to her son and sent him off. "Take these to your room, but don't open them until after you've had a bath," she ordered.

"Yes, mum," he replied as he hurried off.

"I do hope you bought some for yourself as well."

Barbara nodded. "I did. Thank you for the money. You didn't have to do that."

Will jumped down from the carriage to regard her for a moment. "I did, actually. He's my son. And there's more where that came from. I didn't spend much while I was away, so I have most of eight years of my naval pay in my bank account," he explained. "I expect I'll be using some of it do the repairs to Bellingham Park, but there's plenty to cover our other expenses. My father gives me an allowance, as well."

Had they been in London, he never would have spoken of money with anyone but his banker, but out here, far away from the *ton* and with a woman who'd had to manage her funds, he thought it acceptable to tell her of his plans.

Barbara stiffened at his words. "Bellingham Park?"

Will chuckled as he picked up the boxes and led her to the front door of Gisborn Hall. "Ellsworth Park has a new name. It was Donald's idea, and since he'll be the one inheriting it, it seemed appropriate," he explained.

Her eyes widening at his words, Barbara stopped in her tracks. "Inheriting?" she repeated. "But, he cannot."

"It's unentailed property. When I buy it from Henry, it will be mine to do with as I please. Since Donald won't be able to inherit any of the Devonville properties, I wanted to be sure there would be something for him," he explained. "He'll be next door to his cousins," he added.

Barbara blinked back tears, stunned by his words. "You've given this a lot of thought, haven't you?" she whispered.

Will allowed a sigh before he leaned down to kiss one of her eyelids. "A bit," he admitted. "I have a bastard brother. He had all the privileges most don't. He still does."

Like father, like son, he realized. *Jesus.*

"Anyway, it's only fair," he added and then realized tears were dripping down her cheeks. "Oh, please don't cry."

Barbara sniffled before allowing a nod. "All right. But I'll not be giving you your package until after you've had a bath. You smell like a fishmonger," she accused with a wry grin.

Behaving as if he'd been mortally wounded, Will led her up the steps to the front doors of Gisborn Hall. "Will you wash my back?" he teased just as the butler appeared.

Her gasp of shock had Will suppressing a grin as he gave Parkerhouse a wink.

The ancient butler merely rolled his eyes as he closed the doors.

CHAPTER 48

A BEDCHAMBER TO CALL HIS OWN

eanwhile, back in Mayfair

Victoria regarded the mistress suite for nearly a full minute before she turned her attention to Stephen. "This is my room?" she asked, stunned to find a large mahogany four-poster bed, two large chest-of-drawers, a dressing table topped by an oval mirror, and a cheval mirror tucked into a corner.

"It is, my lady," Stephen answered, his own attention entirely on the bed.

"May I see yours?"

Stephen swallowed. Hard. "If you'd like," he replied, leading her to the connecting dressing room door. They passed through the long room, its emptiness at odds with the rest of the house. "I don't believe I would ever own enough clothes to fill this," Victoria said as she regarded the row of hooks on one wall and the row of shelving along the other.

"Good, because we have to share," Stephen said with a wink. He opened the door into the master bedchamber and stepped aside to allow Victoria to pass. She did so, pausing to spin around slowly as she took in the deep blue fabrics trimmed with gold, the masculine furnishings, the giant stone fireplace, and the thick carpet beneath her feet.

"Are you sure you wish to share this with me?" Victoria

asked as her gloved hands slid over the mahogany dresser top. She moved to the window, where velvet drapes were pulled back to reveal sheers and the windows of other townhouses. Below, a mews housed carriages and horses.

"Just the bed," Stephen replied, once again fighting his reaction to her suggestive comment. "I wasn't necessarily referring to the whole room..."

Victoria removed the tiebacks from the drapes and the room dimmed to near darkness. She was suddenly in front of him, pulling her bonnet from her head. "I've never been with a man before," she said, her words sounding rather breathless.

Stephen blinked. "I rather hope not," he replied, his brows furrowing as he wondered why she would close the drapes.

"About tomorrow... I don't wish to spend my wedding day being nervous about what it is that happens in a marriage bed," she whispered as she unbuttoned her pelisse and removed it. She draped it over the back of a chair and then removed her gloves, pulling on the fingers one by one until they were completely free of her hands.

Stephen could only watch, mesmerized by her slow movements, his heart racing in anticipation. He cleared his throat. "Oh?" was all he could manage.

"If we do this now, then I will at least know what to expect tomorrow night," she continued, as if she were talking herself into allowing him to bed her.

"Now?" Stephen gulped, hardly believing his ears. *Good God! I'm marrying a wanton!*

"Do you need help with your buttons?" Victoria asked as she stepped in front of him, her fingers deftly undoing the fastenings of his topcoat and then his waistcoat.

"No," Stephen replied, although his own fingers seemed to refuse to assist hers in undressing him. He was still finding it hard to believe she was suggesting he bed her before it was his right to do so.

"I've never been undressed in front a man before," Victoria stated as she turned around, hoping Stephen would undo the buttons down the back of her gown without being told to do so.

"I should hope not," he replied, managing to gulp without making a sound. After a pause, he realized what he was supposed to do. Unfortunately, his fingers were all thumbs, and he struggled to open her gown. When he did, though, a different part of his brain seemed to take over, the part of his brain that knew exactly what to do and how to do it.

The flat of first one hand and then the other settled onto her exposed back, just above her corset. They slid over her bare skin as he pushed the edges of her gown aside, guiding the fabric over her shoulders and down to her elbows. She did the rest to remove her arms from the sleeves, and the gown fell into a puddle at her feet. Stephen had the tapes of her petticoats undone next, and they followed the gown down to her ankles. Pantaloons soon fell, and wordless, Victoria stepped out of them.

"May I remove your corset?" Stephen whispered just before his lips took purchase on a shoulder blade and kissed it.

Victoria inhaled sharply and allowed a nod, not trusting her voice just then. She had felt so confident only a moment ago, and then, as her clothing fell from her body, she suddenly felt exposed, vulnerable. Was he expecting her to be fleshy? Slender? Buxom? Flat? She was none of those!

He had to have seen naked women before. Everyone who had ever seen paintings by the masters had, she supposed. But she also figured he had to have bedded other women. He had been in the Navy. He had probably been with a different woman in every port!

She felt the tug on her corset ties, felt them give way and the bindings loosen from around her torso.

Tamping down her nervousness, Victoria turned around then, her hands making quick work of removing his topcoat and waistcoat. She draped them over the chair and returned to stand before him, her gaze darting about in an attempt to learn what to remove next.

"Cravat," Stephen suggested, his breaths becoming shorter and the suddenly tight neckcloth not helping the situation.

Victoria carefully removed the onyx-tipped pin from his snowy white cravat and set it onto the nearby dresser. Her fingers pulled the ends of the cravat from their anchors, and she slowly unwound the silk from around his neck until it was one long strip of fabric.

"What do I do next?"

Stephen swallowed and considered how to respond. "Nothing," he finally said, his hands moving to lower the corset down over her hips and to the floor. He felt Victoria place a hand on his shoulder for support as she stepped out of the garment. Although he was about to stand up, he realized he could undo the ribbon garters of her stockings from where he was.

Placing a hand behind her thigh—he could feel Victoria's startled reaction and hear her gasp as his hand made contact —he used the other hand to untie the blue satin ribbon. With both hands, he carefully unrolled the stocking, his hands shaking nearly as much as Victoria's legs seemed to shiver beneath his touch.

She stepped out of her slipper as the stocking came off her foot completely, unaware of Stephen moving to kiss her thigh before he started on the other garter.

The sensation of his lips on the tender skin had Victoria inhaling sharply and leaning harder on his shoulder, the tips of her fingernails digging into his skin through the fabric of his shirt to leave half-moon indentations in his skin. She stepped out of her other slipper and stocking, acutely aware that the only garment still on her body was a translucent chemise.

"Jesus," Stephen breathed when he stood up, his hardening cock tenting his already tight breeches.

Victoria's eyebrows shot up as she moved to cover her

breasts with her arms, not even realizing the dark curls at the tops of her thighs were visible through the chemise. "Are they—?"

"Gorgeous," Stephen managed to croak. "Every bit of you," he added, not bothering to hide his perusal of her near nakedness.

Victoria seemed to relax, and she stepped forward to undo the closure at the top of his shirt. She had it untied in an instant before her hands began pulling the fine lawn from where it was tucked into his breeches. She soon had it pulled up and over his head, not bothering to drape it over the chair back but rather tossing it in the general direction of the chair. His bare chest had her swallowing hard, one hand coming out to touch it so only the pads of her fingers made contact. She quickly pulled it away, blinking as she did so.

Stephen captured the hand with one of his own, bringing it up to his lips so that he could bestow a kiss on her knuckles. "Please, don't change your mind now," he whispered, his voice barely able say the words.

Her eyebrows arching up, Victoria merely shook her head. "I might say the same to you," she replied, aware of how heavy her breasts felt, of the moisture that had developed between her thighs, of how something there seemed to throb in anticipation. Even though the bedchamber was comfortably warm, her entire body was quivering.

Realizing Stephen was just as nervous as she was, her eyes darted to the bed and then back to him. "I don't want you to be... disappointed," she whispered.

Stephen's arms were around her in an instant, pulling her hard against the front of his body as his lips sought hers. The kiss, urgent and quick, was nothing like the other kisses they had shared before. "I won't be. I promise," he whispered, his eyes closed as his forehead pressed against hers.

She nodded and seemed to relax against him, the fingers of one hand smoothing through the light dusting of hair on his chest, the pads barely touching his skin. She felt his body shiver and pulled her hand away as if she had burned her fingers. Feeling more than hearing his light chuckle, Victoria slid her hand down his torso. "What do I do next?" she asked in a whisper, her hands reaching for the fastenings of his breeches.

Realizing he would need to remove his boots before he could remove anything else, Stephen dared a glance toward the bed, hoping there were bed linens beneath the velvet counterpane. "Why don't you... get into bed?" he replied, thinking if she wasn't standing before him nearly naked, his brain might figure out how to remove his boots and breeches.

He watched as she moved to the bed, watched as the chemise shifted so one shoulder was left bare, watched as she bent over the mattress to pull down the counterpane, watched as the short chemise did nothing to cover the globes of her bare bottom, and finally allowed a sigh of relief when she slipped beneath the bed linens.

When she pulled the chemise from her body and tossed it to the end of the bed, her bare breasts on display above the counterpane as she sat regarding him, he nearly fainted.

"Jesus," he murmured again.

Working one of his boot heels loose with his other foot, he was able to pull off one boot and then the other. Once he had his boots off, the stockings followed. Turning around, he undid the fastening on the placket of his breeches. He moved to pull down his breeches and smalls all at once, realizing too late his bare buttocks were aimed in the direction of the bed. And Victoria.

"Are you eyes closed, perchance?" he asked over his shoulder as he slowly straightened.

"Not a chance," Victoria replied, a hint of humor in her voice.

Stephen turned around to make his way to the bed, doing nothing to hide his bobbing erection. He didn't notice Victoria's look of shock until he was climbing onto the bed. "What's wrong?"

Victoria blinked. And blinked again. "I... I didn't expect it to look quite like that," she stammered.

Stephen considered her response. "On what did you base your expectation?" he asked, rather glad they were having a conversation that helped to tamp down his erection. If he wasn't careful, he would take his release far too early, the very last thing he wanted to do just then.

"Statues," she replied, her knees rising beneath the covers. "Paintings." She wrapped her arms around them in an effort to hide her nakedness.

Stephen nodded his understanding. At least she hadn't seen a naked man in person before. "Statues rarely show a man in the company of a beautiful woman who is naked in his bed," he said carefully.

Victoria considered the explanation. "So, it's not always like that?" she questioned, her face and throat displaying a rather pink blush.

Sighing, Stephen shook his head. "Only when I think of you, or see you, or... *now*," he said, his voice breathless. "It's no different than your nipples," he whispered as he leaned over, his hand reaching out to gently push one of her knees down. He drew a finger over her hardened nipple and had to suppress a grin at her sudden gasp as she jerked away.

Realizing she rather liked what he had been doing, Victoria took his hand in hers and brought it back to her breast. Recognizing the invitation, Stephen leaned over and kissed the nipple, hearing and feeling her inhalation of breath.

Her fingers were suddenly in his hair, her fingernails scraping his scalp as his tongue and teeth replaced his lips. She continued to hold his head as he moved his lips to her other breast, forcing her to straighten her other leg. Before he was finished with that nipple, he had managed to push her down into the pillows so she was lying nearly flat.

Her breaths became shorter as Stephen moved his lips down to her belly, his hands to her thighs to gently spread them apart.

"Tell me what to do," she whispered, lifting her head so she could better see what he was doing.

"Lie back and allow me to pleasure you. I want you in ecstasy when I enter you," he whispered. "I don't want you to feel any pain."

Victoria did as she was told, her gaze on the canopy above the bed. She had to close her eyes, though, when she felt Stephen's body move between her legs. They were open in an instant when his hands slid beneath her bottom and lifted, forcing her thighs apart. She let out a yelp of surprise when she realized it was his tongue and not his manhood that had suddenly invaded her most private place. She was about to put voice to a protest when his tongue flicked something that sent a jolt of pure pleasure shooting through her belly. He did it again, and before the sharp darts of pleasure had passed, he did it again and again.

Jerking reflexively, Victoria cried out with each wave of pleasure, her chest rising from the bed as her hands struggled to take purchase on anything to keep her anchored.

Just when she thought he was done, she felt his lips take purchase on her swollen womanhood and suckle until the pleasure was so profound, she thought she might faint. She barely noticed as Stephen rose up from between her legs and moved his manhood to where his lips had just been.

Although he could have impaled her with just one thrust, Stephen prolonged his own agony another moment, entering her slowly, groaning as her wet haven barely opened for him. He thought to ask if she had changed her mind, but he knew it was too late. He wouldn't be able to stop, not now that he was half-buried within her.

He used first one hand and then the other to guide her thighs up to his hips. "Are you all right?"

Lightheaded—she had been practically panting when his tongue and lips were seeing to her pleasure—Victoria allowed a wan smile and nodded. "Tell me what to do."

Stephen lowered his lips to hers and kissed her. "You'll just know," he murmured. "Jesus, you feel so good." He pushed into her farther, his groan of satisfaction audible.

Victoria felt the fullness of his manhood inside her.

Although her body still vibrated beneath his, her uncertainty and nervousness dissipated with his words. When she felt him pull out of her, she relaxed, and when he thrust into her, she pushed against him, thrilling at his sighs of "yes". Her hands let go of the bedding and moved to his sides, her palms sliding down to feel his ribs, his hips, his muscular thighs and back up to hold onto his solid buttocks. When he moved to pull out too far, she panicked and pulled hard just as he began another thrust into her. The move had her chest lifting from the mattress, her head angled back as another flutter of pleasure filled her lower body.

She knew immediately something had happened, for Stephen stilled his movements, a groan emanating from deep within his throat, his upturned face contorting into an expression of what looked like pain, the cords of his throat showing in stark relief. He held the pose for several seconds before he drew breath and slowly lowered his body down onto hers.

Victoria felt a wash of warmth fill her lower body as she wrapped her arms around his shoulders and helped to guide him down. His head ended up in the pillow next to her face, his arms on either side of her body.

"Are you all right?" she whispered in alarm, barely able to catch her own breath even as another flutter passed through her body.

Stephen murmured something unintelligible followed by words that suggested he was not. Then he sighed. "I do believe I am in love, my beautiful Victoria," he whispered before kissing her earlobe.

Victoria turned her head to find his eyes closed and felt his body relax atop hers.

She couldn't help but smile when she heard his snores only moments later.

CHAPTER 49

A HEART TO HEART TO MEND
A BROKEN HEART

ater that evening in Oxfordshire
"How can you want to marry me?" Barbara asked, her head shaking with her query. "You must think the worst of me."

Will shook his head, his hair still damp from his bath. He found he was stunned by her statement. "No, of course not. If anything, I'm rather... humbled by you," he replied, continuing to hold her hand. He was sure if he let go, she would run away from him. Run away and never let him get this close again. Here in the gardens behind Gisborn Hall, he could at least keep her close.

"Humbled?" she repeated in surprise. "Don't you mean 'disappointed' or 'embarrassed' or... I will not have you thinking you must marry me because I bore your child," she managed to get out.

Will pulled on her hand, hard, so she was suddenly falling against the front of his body. He wrapped an arm around her waist and held her there. "No, I don't think any of those things," he answered, his head still shaking. "How can you even think that?"

Barbara held her body ramrod straight, afraid if she allowed herself to rest against Will, she would lose all her resolve. Allow the scents of amber and sandalwood to

348

scramble her senses. Give in to his soft words and promises of a better life and end up back where it all started. Back where she was considered a wanton woman. Bad *ton*. A whore. Daughter of an earl who was headed for debtor's prison if he wasn't there already. To suffer the cut direct whenever she walked down Bond Street or was forced to attend a *ton* event because Will was obligated by rank to do so.

Shame was all she could feel. All she *would* feel if she should go back to London.

But she couldn't allow Will to ruin his life—to give up his life in London—because of something she had done all those years ago. Behaved like a wanton. Shown up at his apartment and offered herself to him, afraid if she didn't, he would leave and forget her. Leave her to the life she would have had to endure with a father who gambled too much. Perhaps end up married to a man she did not love and simply endure her lot in life while her father ended up in prison for his gambling debts.

But she had given herself to Will. And Will still left London, just as he warned her he would, although he had made her a promise.

I will return. I will make you my wife. I promise.

The few letters from him had reinforced his promise, each one claiming that he loved her, that he would return to her when his duty to King and Country was complete.

Once she found herself pregnant, with no one to turn to and the gossips of the *ton* about to sink their teeth into her, she had done the only thing she could do. She had left London. Escaped with only a trunk filled with some clothes, a gold ring, and enough money to last at least a year in a forgotten cottage. Pretended to be a war widow, for how else could she explain her condition? Her situation?

At least she'd had the help and sympathy of her father's solicitor, but even Mr. Barton couldn't perform a miracle once her father's funds had dried up, especially after he had been fired from his position. He couldn't see to forwarding her correspondence since her father was probably burning it out of spite or rage. And not having received word from Will for several years, she had simply accepted that he no longer cared for her. That he had met someone else on his travels overseas or transferred his affections to some other young chit in London.

Perhaps he, too, had heard the gossip and decided he couldn't abide a woman who acted as she had done that last night. Couldn't abide the gossip that would follow them everywhere they went in polite Society.

"I was... I behaved like a wanton—"

"You behaved like a woman who wanted her future husband to know she would be there for him when he returned," he interrupted. "You gave me hope, Barbara. You gave me the gift of you. And then you gave me the greatest gift you could give me by having my child," he continued, his other arm wrapping around her shoulders and pulling her hard against him so she was forced to allow her slight body to mold to the front of his. "I love you," he whispered harshly. "I wanted you then, and I want you now, only this time, I will have you as my wife."

Barbara stared up at him, stunned by the ferocity of his words. "You won't make me go back there?" she whispered, a spark of hope the only thing she could hang on to just then, although being held in Will's arms was rather comforting as well.

"You never have to go back there again," he said with a shake of his head. "But I think you should know that *you* are not a subject of gossip mongers. Whoever knew about your condition—"

"My maid," Barbara whispered.

"She was dismissed from Pendleton House. She left London shortly after you did," he remarked, remembering the butler's comment.

Barbara frowned. "She didn't say anything about me?"

Will shook his head, deciding he could provide a white lie. "The butler was quite clear—no one thought there was any scandal regarding you. Only surprise at your sudden departure, although I rather imagine some believed you needed to get away from your father. That you probably feared for your reputation because of his gambling. You simply left London to live in the country."

"My aunt," Barbara murmured. "She knew."

"Then she took the secret with her to her grave," Will countered, wincing when he realizing she probably hadn't learned of her relative's death.

"Oh," Barbara breathed as she relaxed some more and gave in completely to Will's hold on her. She could hear his heartbeats beneath her face, smell the scents of lemon soap and musk in his linen shirt, feel his warmth permeate her body as if he were a comforting blanket.

Remembering the letter he had received earlier that day from Stephen, just before he had gone fishing, Will swallowed. "You should know your father doesn't always gamble with the earldom's funds."

Barbara stiffened. "What do you mean?"

Will led her to the stone bench she had shared with Hannah earlier that morning. "My brother wrote to say that he has taken a position with the Foreign Office. He's helping with an investigation into missing currency, something that happens often. Apparently, English money is rather popular for use by those wishing to purchase weapons and pay their spies," he explained. "Guineas are made of gold, and bank notes are honored. Anyway, when necessary, your father gambles with the Crown's money so that the men he loses to can be tracked down and arrested if they turn out to be foreign operatives."

Staring at Will for several moments, Barbara frowned. "How long...?"

"Since before you left London," Will interrupted. "He does tend to gamble with his own funds as well, when he's not working for the Crown, of course, but he's not on the verge of debtor's prison as so many are led to believe," he continued quietly. "Looking back, it seems as though he made a deal with the devil."

Barbara swallowed as she remembered asking her father about his gambling. *I am not allowed to tell*, he would say. *But rest assured, all is well.*

A deal with the devil, indeed.

"There's something else," Will added, sighing before he told her the rest. "Last year, he had to fire his solicitor because he was afraid the man was about to discover his arrangement with the Foreign Office. It was never his intention for your funds to be cut off. Apparently he knew Barton was sending you money and always made sure there was some in the account the man oversaw. I suppose he thought you would return to London when you ran out of money."

Barbara shook her head. "I would have starved first," she whispered.

Will resisted the urge to hiss, realizing she spoke the truth. It would be a few weeks of decent meals before her body was back to the one he remembered holding his last night in London all those years ago.

"Rather stubborn, aren't you?" he murmured, his hand lifting hers to his lips.

"I am," she agreed as she considered his news about her father. "But... but he was the one who banished me," she whispered. "I had to leave."

"He's quite sick about having lost you, but he knows it's all his fault," Will said quietly. "And mine, too, of course." He wondered if her life would have been any better had he never met her. "Do you regret what happened between us? You must—"

"I don't," she replied, shaking her head. "I have my son because of you," she said, closing her eyes and leaning her head against his shoulder. "I've been a fool, haven't I?" she whispered finally.

"Only because you loved me," Will countered, his lip quirked. His brows furrowed. "You *do* still love me, don't you?" he asked gently. "I wondered back then, you must know. You seemed rather indifferent with me at first, back when we were courting, and then, just before I left, I was sure you loved me."

Barbara took a deep breath, not quite ready to admit her feelings for him. "How is it you knew how to give little Randolph a ride on your boot like you did?"

Surprised by the change in subject, Will lessened his hold on her and allowed a shrug. "My father used to do it with me when I was a toddler," he replied. "Why do you ask?"

"Hmm," Barbara replied, not surprised by the response. Of course, he would play with a child the same way he had played as a child. "While I watched you do it, I noticed our son seemed almost jealous of the babe. Like he realized he missed out on something." A tear suddenly collected in the corner of her eye.

Our son.

Barbara had never said the words to Will, and hearing them now only gave him more hope. He shook his head and kissed her forehead. "He won't ever feel like that again. I promise," he vowed. At Barbara's look of confusion, he added, "I'll simply teach him how to ride a real horse."

Barbara blinked a couple of times, as if she wasn't quite sure that was the answer she wanted to hear. "Do you... do you think that's wise?" she whispered.

"Well, I can't exactly let him ride my boot," Will countered with a grin. "He's too tall. Although I suppose I could get down on all fours, and he could climb on my back..."

His words were interrupted by Barbara's lips, their soft pillows touching his so that she could kiss him. She reached up to place one of her hands behind his neck, pulling his head down so that she could kiss him harder.

Stunned but ever so relieved by her simple gesture, Will kissed her back, his arms hugging her even harder to him, pulling her onto his lap. He reveled in the feel of her body pressed against his, thrilled at the sensation of her heartbeat through the fabric of her new gown and his shirt, delighted at the faint moan that came from her throat as he moved his lips over hers and then to her jawline and her neck.

By the time his tongue reached the hollow of her throat and he felt her body shiver at the light touch, he was delirious.

Despite the passing of eight years since they had engaged in such intimate contact, Will remembered their last night together as if it had been just the night before. He used what he had learned then to incite every bit of pleasure he could as he continued to kiss and nip at Barbara's throat, as he moved his lips and tongue along her collarbones and then kissed the tops of her breasts.

When he stopped, his breaths coming in labored gasps, he moved his forehead up to press against hers. "What did you buy me?"

Barbara shook her head. "It's nothing, really—"

"Tell me."

She rolled her eyes. "You'll think me ridiculous—"

"Tell me."

Angling her head to one side, she sighed. "A hammer and nails, a saw, a chisel, a plane—"

"Marry me, Barbara," he whispered urgently. "Please, be my wife."

A slight grin appearing on her bee-stung lips, Barbara nodded against his forehead. "Of course. Yes," she managed to get out before her lips once again took his.

Neither were aware of their son happily watching them from behind a cluster of daisies. That is, they weren't until Harold came bounding through the garden to chase Donald into their arms.

CHAPTER 50

AN EARL AND COUNTESS
CONTEMPLATE THE FUTURE

From the vantage of his bedchamber window, Randolph sound asleep on his bare shoulder, Henry Forster watched Will and Barbara as they kissed on the garden bench below. He chuckled when Harold appeared, and he smiled broadly when Donald was suddenly up and out of his hiding place and in their arms. He could practically hear their laughter from where he stood.

Hannah, a bed linen wrapped around her body, joined him at the window, her tousled hair and high color a testament to what they had been doing only moments ago. "What are you...?" She followed his line of sight and stared at the scene in the waning light below before breathing a long sigh. "Finally," she whispered, one of her arms wrapping around her husband's waist as she leaned against him.

"Indeed," Henry murmured. "You do know what this means?" he whispered, not wanting to wake up his napping son just yet. He had every intention of giving him a horsey ride when he did, though. The sound of Randolph's giggles had become the highlight of his day. Well, the *other* highlight, anyway. He rather looked forward to making love to his wife even more.

Hannah grinned. "You're going to have a new foreman," she murmured.

"Aye," he agreed. "The cousins will grow up together."

"We're going to have neighbors," Hannah said with a bit more excitement.

"You'll be helping to arrange a wedding, I expect."

Hannah's excitement seemed to mount. "Aye."

"And you're going to have the sister you've always wanted."

Hannah smiled. "As it turns out, I'll have two! If all goes as planned, Stephen will get married tomorrow morning," she said, rather glad her brother had shared the letter he had received earlier that day. "He would dearly love to bring his bride here for their wedding trip."

Henry arched an eyebrow. "They are more than welcome," he murmured, rather glad he'd have the opportunity to meet another Slater. They were having a rather positive effect on his life. "Perhaps he'll like to fish, too."

"Do you suppose Barbara will have another baby?" Hannah asked.

"She'll have to," Henry whispered. "He'll need an heir."

Hannah's hand rested against her belly, her smile broadening. "I do hope she has one soon."

Henry had to suppress the urge to laugh. "At the rate they're going, I expect a babe in nine months," he murmured. "In fact, I'd be willing to put money on it."

Hannah gave him a quelling glance. "You always make the easy bets," she accused.

"I'm not much of a gambler," he countered before he planted a kiss on her forehead.

"And yet you win every time," Hannah replied with a grin as she took their son from him and rested him on her shoulder.

Henry sighed before allowing a grin of his own. "I do, don't I?" He paused a moment. "What's for dinner tonight?"

Hannah rolled her eyes, wondering how he could already have forgotten, but then a late afternoon tumble did seem to leave him discombobulated sometimes. "Whatever you caught when you went fishing this afternoon," she whispered.

He grinned. "Trout! My favorite," he claimed, his usual response when told what they were having for dinner. "And what did you get me for my birthday? I spotted a rather large box in the carriage. Was it for me?"

Hannah rolled her eyes. "It is, but it's supposed to be a surprise," she replied with a pout.

"But it's a tool?" he half-questioned.

Sighing, Hannah nodded. "Of course, it's a tool," she replied. "Aren't they all?" One thing about being married to an inventor meant it was easy to find gifts he appreciated.

Henry kissed her thoroughly before taking the now wide awake Randolph from her arms. "We're off to play horsey," he said as he headed for the door.

Hannah thought about reminding him he wore no clothes and certainly no boots, but when she saw that their house guests were still in the gardens below, she decided she would let him discover it on his own.

The nurse discovered it before Henry, however.

It took every bit of control she had not to burst into a fit of giggles when she heard the nurse screeching.

EXCERPT

July 1818

Harry studied the nautilus shell he had brought up with him from the sea bottom, wondering at the curve of the spiral that seemed to form its backbone. What little of the interior he could see appeared a pearly pink, the color fading as it reached the edge. The exterior, rough with years of other sea creatures having attached themselves to its surface, looked as if it might have at one time been a light brown sprinkled with lighter dots. Remembering a comment from Lord Brougham about being able to hear the ocean should he put the shell up near his ear, he did so. "Beautiful," he murmured, wondering what phenomena could explain how anything could be heard from inside a chambered shell.

When the sound suddenly changed—a whooshing followed by a loud splash and an inhalation of breath, Harry jerked the shell away from his ear. Only a few feet in front of him, a young lady—or perhaps she was a mermaid—stood regarding him as she pulled her long, drenched hair to one side and squeezed the water from it with long, slender fingers. Since she was still knee-deep in the water, it was impossible to tell if she stood on a pair of feet or on a flipper tail. The part of her body that appeared above the water's edge was mostly naked, her sun-kissed flesh turning to goose bumps as seawater sluiced from her body. The scrap of fabric that covered her breasts, and as Harry slowly realized, the rest of the torso of her body, clung to her curves and allowed the silhouette of her erect nipples to show in relief.

Harry blinked, thinking she was merely an apparition at first. It had been some time since he had eaten anything, after all. He was simply famished and seeing things. But he had felt water droplets on his skin from when she emerged from the water, she appeared quite solid in form and, well, he rather doubted an apparition could cause the arousal he was feeling in his breeches.

"Do you always gawk like that?"

The voice was definitely feminine. Definitely alluring. And quite possibly that of a siren.

Having read Homer's epic poems, *The Iliad* and *The Odyssey,* Harry was well aware of what a siren was capable of doing. Luring a man to her and then to his death beneath the ocean's waves.

He realized he might actually be willing to drown should she send him into the water.

Harry shook his head. Sirens were merely mythological characters, he reasoned. She couldn't be a siren. And that fact that she was standing implied she had two feet—he rather doubted a flipper tail could support her, which meant she had to be a human woman.

Angling her head to one side, the woman took a step toward him, her knees showing above the water as she did so, which meant she most definitely had feet. Harry was about to tear his eyes from hers and look down into the water to be sure when she spoke again.

"You really shouldn't stare like that," she admonished him, although she did nothing to cover herself. Obviously not modest, or perhaps having determined it was too late to cover herself—Harry had seen everything and was still seeing everything—she didn't even raise an arm to cover her breasts. Instead, she bent down. Her hand disappeared beneath the water only to reappear holding a piece of pottery. Although it had several pieces missing, it was easy to tell what its original shape had been. Covered with a layer of barnacles, though, it was impossible to tell what its original color and finish might have been.

Harry blinked again, unable to come up with a suitable response. He had never been so tongue-tied in his entire life!

The woman's eyes widened. "Oh!" she said as her free hand went to her bosom, which only caused his cock to harden. Given the way he was crouched on the sandy beach, he found himself rather uncomfortable but not about to stand up and make his situation more apparent. "You must not understand English," she said with a sigh.

Frowning, Harry shook his head. "It's actually my native language," he replied, finally finding his voice. He had to clear his throat, though, when he realized it sounded higher than normal. "I am British, in fact," he added, his voice thankfully sounding more like his own.

The hand that had been on the woman's chest moved to her hip and she regarded him with a roll of her eyes. "I should think a Brit would know better than to stare at a woman. You'd think you were seeing a ghost or—"

"Venus, actually," Harry interrupted. "Although, I rather doubt she was as beautiful as you."

It was the woman's turn to blink. And then to blush when she comprehended his words. "Why, thank you, Mister—?"

"Tennison," he replied, not about to mention his title. *Faith!* The woman probably thought him a thick imbecile for staring at her as he was still doing. But, damn! He had never seen a nearly naked woman in the light of day before. His favorite courtesan at Norwick's high-end brothel had usually been half-wrapped in a snake while illuminated by the light from a candle lamp. The challenge for any man wishing to bed her was to first remove the snake from her body, a task which Harry accomplished on many occasions. Not wanting another man to have her so easily after he took his leave of her bed, he would simply return the snake to its favorite place along her body.

He felt a stab of disappointment when he remembered it had been several years since the two of them had engaged in sexual intercourse. Once Lord Norwick had inherited the earldom and was forced to divest himself of *The Elegant Courtesan* and his gaming hell, most of the girls who had worked for him had married or become exclusive mistresses. Harry never discovered the fate of Debra. Or her boa constrictor.

Now, the beauty who stood before him didn't look a bit British. Her skin wasn't the pale porcelain of most English misses. Her entire body was tanned from the sun, her auburn hair streaked with sun-bleached strands and her nose sporting a sprinkle of freckles. Harry found the combination so enticing, he was curious as to what he might have to do to bed her. "You're welcome, Miss...?"

The woman's attention was suddenly on something else, her treasure from the sea forgotten as she lifted a hand to her shield her eyes from the sun's glare.

Without another word, she disappeared into the water, leaving Lord Everly wondering if perhaps he'd had too much sun.

ABOUT THE AUTHOR

A self-described nerd and lover of science, Linda Rae spent many years as a published technical writer specializing in 3D graphics workstations, software and 3D animation (her movie credits include SHREK and SHREK 2). An interest in genealogy led to years of research on the Regency era and a desire to write fiction based in that time.

A fan of action-adventure movies, she can frequently be found at the local cinema. Although she no longer has any tropical fish, she does follow the San Jose Sharks. She makes her home in Cody, Wyoming.

For more information:
www.lindaraesande.com